Up until the moment when the screen had come alive with the image, the pregnancy had been an abstract thing to Jake.

But there on the screen had appeared a baby. Only about six centimetres at this stage, the radiographer had explained, but a totally recognisable baby. With hands and feet and a *face*. To the palpable relief of everyone in the room, a strong and steady amplified heartbeat had been clearly audible.

Jake had felt as if his own heart had stopped beating, and his lungs gone into arrest as, mesmerised, he'd watched that image. He was a man who never cried, but he'd felt tears of awe and amazement threatening to betray him. He hadn't been able to look at Eliza—the sheer joy shining from her face would have tipped him over. Without seeming to be aware that she was doing it, she had reached for his hand and gripped it hard. All he'd been able to do was squeeze it back.

This was a real baby. A child. A *person*. Against all odds, he and Eliza had created a new life.

What he had to do became very clear.

THE BRIDESMAID'S BABY BUMP

BY
KANDY SHEPHERD

First Published in Great Britain 2016
By Mills & Boon, an imprint of HarperCollins*Publishers*
1 London Bridge Street, London, SE1 9GF

© 2016 Kandy Shepherd

ISBN: 978-0-263-92000-0

23-0716

Our policy is to use papers that are natural, renewable and recyclable products and made from wood grown in sustainable forests. The logging and manufacturing processes conform to the legal environmental regulations of the country of origin.

Printed and bound in Spain
by CPI, Barcelona

Kandy Shepherd swapped a career as a magazine editor for a life writing romance. She lives on a small farm in the Blue Mountains near Sydney, Australia, with her husband, daughter and lots of pets. She believes in love at first sight and real-life romance—they worked for her! Kandy loves to hear from her readers. Visit her at www.kandyshepherd.com.

To my wonderful editor, Laura McCallen,
whose insight and encouragement help me make
my books the best they can be. Thank you, Laura!

CHAPTER ONE

ELIZA DUNNE FELT she had fallen into a fairytale as Jake Marlowe waltzed her around the vast, glittering ballroom of a medieval European castle. Hundreds of other guests whirled around them to the elegant strains of a chamber orchestra. The chatter rising and falling over the music was in a mix of languages from all around the world. Light from massive crystal chandeliers picked up the gleam of a king's ransom in jewellery and the sheen of silk in every colour of the rainbow.

Eliza didn't own any expensive jewellery. But she felt she held her own in a glamorous midnight-blue retro-style gown with a beaded bodice, nipped-in waist and full skirt, her dark hair twisted up with diamante combs, sparkling stilettos on her feet. Jake was in a tuxedo that spoke of the finest Italian tailoring.

The excitement that bubbled through her like the bubbles from expensive champagne was not from her fairytale surroundings but from her proximity to Jake. Tall, imposing, and even more handsome than the Prince whose wedding they had just witnessed, he was a man who had intrigued her from the moment she'd first met him.

Their dance was as intimate as a kiss. Eliza was intensely aware of where her body touched Jake's—his arm around her waist held her close, her hand rested on his broad shoulder, his cheek felt pleasantly rough against the smoothness of her own. She felt his warmth, breathed in his scent—spicy and fresh and utterly male—with her eyes closed, the better to savour the intoxicating effect it had on her senses. Other couples danced around them but she was scarcely aware of their presence—too lost in the rhythm of her private dance with him.

She'd first met Jake nearly two years ago, at the surprise wedding of her friend and business partner Andie Newman to *his* friend and business partner Dominic Hunt. They'd been best man and bridesmaid and had made an instant connection in an easy, friends of friends way.

She'd only seen him once since, at a business function, and they'd chatted for half the night. Eliza had relived every moment many times, unable to forget him. He'd been so unsettlingly *different*. Now they were once more best man and bridesmaid at the wedding of mutual friends.

Her other business partner, Gemma Harper, had just married Tristan, Crown Prince of Montovia. That afternoon she and Jake, as members of the bridal party, had walked slowly down the aisle of a centuries-old cathedral and watched their friends make their vows in a ceremony of almost unimaginable splendour. Now they were celebrating at a lavish reception.

She'd danced a duty dance with Tristan, then with Dominic. Jake had made his impatience obvious, then had immediately claimed her as his dance partner. The room was full of royalty and aristocrats, and Gemma had breathlessly informed her which of the men was single, but Eliza only wanted to dance with Jake. This was the first chance she'd had to spend any real time with the man who had made such a lasting impression on her.

She sighed a happy sigh, scarcely realising she'd done so.

Jake pulled away slightly and looked down at her. Her breath caught in her throat at the slow-to-ignite smile that lit his green eyes as he looked into hers. With his rumpled blond hair, strong jaw and marvellous white teeth he was as handsome as any actor or model—yet he seemed unaware of the scrutiny he got from every woman who danced by them.

'Having fun?' he asked.

Even his voice, deep and assured, sent shivers of awareness through her.

'I don't know that *fun* is quite the right word for something so spectacular. I want to rub my eyes to make sure I'm not dreaming.' She had to raise her voice over the music to be heard.

'It's extraordinary, isn't it? The over-the-top opulence of a royal wedding… It isn't something an everyday Australian guy usually gets to experience.'

Not quite an everyday guy. Eliza had to bite down on the words. At thirty-two, Jake headed his own technology solutions company and had become a billionaire while he was still in his twenties. He could probably fund an event like this with barely a blip in his bank balance. But on the two previous occasions when she'd met him, for all his wealth and brilliance and striking good looks, he had presented as notably unpretentious.

'I grew up on a sheep ranch, way out in the west

of New South Wales,' she said. 'Weddings were more often than not celebrated with a barn dance. This is the stuff of fairytales for a country girl. I've only ever seen rooms like this in a museum.'

'You seem like a sophisticated city girl to me. Boss of the best party-planning business in Sydney.' Jake's green eyes narrowed as he searched her face. 'The loveliest of the Party Queens.' His voice deepened in tone.

'Thank you,' she said, preening a little at his praise, fighting a blush because he'd called her lovely. 'I'm not the boss, though. Andie, Gemma and I are equal partners in Party Queens.'

Eliza was Business Director, Andie looked after design and Gemma the food.

'The other two are savvy, but you're the business brains,' he said. 'There can be no doubt about that.'

'I guess I am,' she said.

She was not being boastful in believing that the success of Party Queens owed a lot to her sound financial management. The business was everything to her and she'd given her life to it since it had launched three years ago.

'Tristan told me Gemma organised the wedding herself,' Jake said. 'With some long-distance help from you and Andie.'

'True,' said Eliza.

Jake—the 'everyday Aussie guy'—was good friends with the Prince. They'd met, he'd told her, on the Montovian ski-fields years ago.

'Apparently the courtiers were aghast at her audacity in breaking with tradition.'

'Yet look how brilliantly it turned out—another success for Party Queens. My friend the Crown Princess.'

Eliza shook her head in proud wonderment. 'One day she'll be a real queen. But for Gemma it isn't about the royal trappings, you know. It's all about being with Tristan—she's so happy, so in love.'

Eliza couldn't help the wistful note that crept into her voice. That kind of happiness wasn't for her. Of course she'd started out wanting the happy-ever-after love her friends had found. But it had proved elusive. So heartbreakingly elusive that, at twenty-nine, she had given up on hoping it would ever happen. She had a broken marriage behind her, and nothing but dating disasters since her divorce. No way would she get married again. She would not risk being trapped with a domineering male like her ex-husband, like her father. Being single was a state that suited her, even if she did get lonely sometimes.

'Tristan is happy too,' said Jake. 'He credits me for introducing him to his bride.'

Jake had recommended Party Queens to his friend the Crown Prince when Tristan had had to organise an official function in Sydney. Tristan had been incognito when Gemma had met him and they'd fallen in love. The resulting publicity had been off the charts for Party Queens, and Eliza would always be grateful to Jake for putting the job their way.

Jake looked down into her face. 'But you're worried about what Gemma's new status means for your business, aren't you?'

'How did you know that?' she asked, a frown pleating her forehead.

'One business person gets to read the signs in another,' he said. 'It was the way you frowned when I mentioned Gemma's name.'

'I didn't think I was so transparent,' she said, and realised she'd frowned again. 'Yes, I admit I *am* concerned. Gemma wants to stay involved with the business, but I don't know how that can work with her fifteen thousand kilometres away from our headquarters.' She looked around her. 'She's moved into a different world and has a whole set of new royal duties to master.'

Eliza knew it would be up to her to solve the problem. Andie and Gemma were the creatives; she was the worrier, the plotter, the planner. The other two teased her that she was a control freak, let her know when she got too bossy, but the three Party Queens complemented each other perfectly.

Jake's arm tightened around her waist. 'Don't let your concern ruin the evening for you. I certainly don't want to let it ruin mine.'

His voice was deep and strong and sent a thrill of awareness coursing through her.

'You're right. I just want to enjoy every moment of this,' she said.

Every moment with him. She closed her eyes in bliss when he tightened his arms around her as they danced. He was the type of man she had never dreamed existed.

The Strauss waltz came to an end. 'More champagne?' Jake asked. 'We could drink it out on the terrace.'

'Excellent idea,' she said, her heart pounding a little harder at the prospect of being alone with him.

The enclosed terrace ran the length of the ballroom, with vast arched windows looking out on the view across the lit-up castle gardens to the lake, where a huge pale moon rode high in the sky. Beyond the lake were snow-capped mountains, only a ghostly hint of their peaks to be seen under the dim light from the moon.

There was a distinct October chill to the Montovian air. It seemed quite natural for Jake to put his arm around her as Eliza gazed out at the view. She welcomed his warmth, still hyper-aware of his touch as she leaned close to his hard strength. There must be a lot of honed muscle beneath that tuxedo.

'This place hardly seems real,' she said, keeping her voice low in a kind of reverence.

'Awesome in the true sense of the word,' he said.

Eliza sipped slowly from the flute of champagne. Wine was somewhat of a hobby for her, and she knew this particular vintage was the most expensive on the planet, its cost per bubble astronomical. She had consulted with Gemma on the wedding wine list. But she was too entranced with Jake to be really aware of what she was drinking. It might have been lemon soda for all the attention she paid it.

He took the glass from her hand and placed it on an antique table nearby. Then he slid her around so she faced him. He was tall—six foot four, she guessed—and she was glad she was wearing stratospheric heels. She didn't like to feel at a disadvantage with a man—even this man.

'I've waited all day for us to be alone,' he said.

'Me too,' she said, forcing the tremor out of her voice.

How alone? She had a luxurious guest apartment in the castle all to herself, where they could truly be by themselves. No doubt Jake had one the same.

He looked into her face for a long moment, so close

she could feel his breath stir her hair. His eyes seemed
to go a deeper shade of green. *He was going to kiss
her.* She found her lips parting in anticipation of his
touch as she swayed towards him. There was nothing
she wanted more at this moment than to be kissed by
Jake Marlowe.

Yet she hesitated. Whether she called it the elephant
in the room, or the poisoned apple waiting to be offered
as in the fairytale, there was something they had not
talked about all day in the rare moments when they had
been alone. Something that had to be said.

With a huge effort of will she stepped back, folded
her arms in front of her chest, took a deep breath. 'Jake,
has anything changed since we last spoke at Tristan's
party in Sydney? Is your divorce through?'

He didn't immediately reply, and her heart sank to
the level of her sparkling shoes. 'Yes, to your first
question. Divorce proceedings are well under way. But
to answer your second question: it's not final yet. I'm
still waiting on the decree nisi, let alone the decree
absolute.'

'Oh.' It was all she could manage as disappointment
speared through her. 'I thought—'

'You thought I'd be free by now?' he said gruffly.

She chewed her lip and nodded. There was so much
neither of them dared say. Undercurrents pulled them
in the direction of possibilities best left unspoken. Such
as what might happen between them if he wasn't still
legally married…

It was his turn to frown. 'So did I. But it didn't
work out like that. The legalities… The property set-
tlements…'

'Of course,' she said.

So when will *you be free?* She swallowed the words before she could give impatient voice to them.

He set his jaw. 'I'm frustrated about it, but it's complex.'

Millions of dollars and a life together to be dismantled. Eliza knew all about the legal logistics of that, but on a much smaller scale. There were joint assets to be divided. Then there were emotions, all twisted and tangled throughout a marriage of any duration, that had to be untangled—and sometimes torn. Wounds. Scars. All intensely personal. She didn't feel she could ask him any more.

During their first meeting Jake had told her his wife of seven years wanted a divorce but he didn't. At their second meeting he'd said the divorce was underway. Eliza had sensed he was ambivalent about it, so had declined his suggestion that they keep in touch. Her attraction to him was too strong for her ever to pretend she could be 'just friends' with him. She'd want every chance to act on that attraction.

But she would not date a married man. She wouldn't kiss a married man. Even when he was nearly divorced. Even when he was Jake Marlowe. No way did she want to be caught up in any media speculation about being 'the other woman' in his divorce. And then there was the fact that her ex had cheated on her towards the end of their marriage. She didn't know Jake's wife. But she wouldn't want to cause her the same kind of pain.

Suffocating with disappointment, Eliza stepped back from him. She didn't have expectations of any kind of relationship with him—just wanted a chance to explore the surprising connection between them. Starting with a kiss. Then…? Who knew?

She cleared her throat. 'I wish—' she started to say.

But then an alarm started beeping, shrill and intrusive. Startled, she jumped.

Jake glanced down at his watch, swore under his breath. 'Midnight,' he said. 'I usually call Australia now, for a business catch-up.' He switched off the alarm. 'But not tonight.'

It seemed suddenly very quiet on the terrace, with only faint strains of music coming from the ballroom, distant laughter from a couple at the other end of the terrace. Eliza was aware of her own breathing and the frantic pounding of her heart.

'No. Make your call. It's late. I have to go.'

She doubted he'd guessed the intensity of her disappointment, how much she'd had pinned on this meeting—and she didn't want him to see it on her face. She turned, picked up her long, full skirts and prepared to run.

Then Jake took hold of her arm and pulled her back to face him. 'Don't go, Eliza. Please.'

Jake watched as Eliza struggled to contain her disappointment. She seemed to pride herself on having a poker face. But her feelings were only too apparent to him. And her disappointment had nothing on his.

'But I have to go,' she said as she tried to pull away from him. 'You're still married. We can't—'

'Act on the attraction that's been there since the get go?'

Mutely, she nodded.

Their first meeting had been electric—an instant *something* between them. For him it had been a revelation. A possibility of something new and exciting beyond the dead marriage he had been struggling to revive. Eliza had been so beautiful, so smart, so interesting—yet so unattainable. The second time they'd met he'd realised the attraction was mutual. And tonight he'd sensed in her the same longing for more that he felt.

But it was still not their time to explore it. She'd made it very clear the last time they'd met that she could not be friends with a married man—and certainly not more than friends. He'd respected her stance. As a wealthy man he'd met more than a few women with dollar signs flashing in their eyes who had held no regard for a man's wedding vows—or indeed their own.

When Tristan had asked him to be best man at his wedding he'd said yes straight away. The bonus had been a chance to see Eliza again. In her modest lavender dress she'd been the loveliest of the bridesmaids, eclipsing—at least in his admittedly biased eyes—even the bride. Tonight, in a formal gown that showed off her tiny waist and feminine curves, she rivalled any of the royalty in the ballroom.

'This is not what I'd hoped for this evening,' he said.

'Me neither.' Her voice was barely louder than a whisper as she looked up to him.

He caught his breath at how beautiful she was. Her eyes were a brilliant blue that had him struggling to describe them—like sapphires was the closest he could come. They were framed by brows and lashes as black as her hair, in striking contrast to her creamy skin. Irish colouring, he suspected. He knew nothing about her heritage, very little about her.

Jake thirsted to know more.

He—a man who had thought he could never be interested in another woman. Who had truly thought he had married for life. He'd been so set on hanging on to his marriage to a woman who didn't want to be married any more—who had long outgrown him and he her—that he hadn't let himself think of any other. Until he'd met Eliza. And seen hope for the future.

He cursed the fact that the divorce process was taking so long. At first he'd delayed it because he'd hoped he could work things out with his soon-to-be ex-wife. Even though she'd had become virtually a stranger to him. Then he'd discovered how she'd betrayed him. Now he was impatient to have it settled, all ties severed.

'A few months and I'll be free. It's so close, Eliza. In fact it's debatable that I'm not single again already. It's just a matter of a document. Couldn't we—?'

He could see her internal debate, the emotions flitting across her face. Was pleased to see that anticipation was one of them. But he was not surprised when she shook her head.

'No,' she said, in a voice that wasn't quite steady. 'Not until you're legally free. Not until we can see each other with total honesty.'

How could he fault her argument? He admired her integrity. Although he groaned his frustration. Not with her, but with the situation.

He pulled her close in a hug. It was difficult not to turn it into something more, not to tilt her face up to his and kiss her. A campaign of sensual kisses and subtle caresses might change her mind—he suspected she wanted him as much as he wanted her. But she was right. He wasn't ready—in more ways than one.

'As soon as the divorce is through I'll get in touch,

come see you in Sydney.' He lived in Brisbane, the capital city of Queensland, about an hour's flight north.

Scarcely realising he was doing so, he stroked the smooth skin of her bare shoulders, her exposed back. It was a gesture more of reassurance than anything overtly sexual. He couldn't let himself think about Eliza and sex. Not now. Not yet. Or he'd go crazy.

Her head was nestled against his shoulder and he felt her nod. 'I'd like that,' she said, her voice muffled.

He held her close for a long, silent moment. Filled his senses with her sweet floral scent, her warmth. Wished he didn't have to let her go. Then she pulled away. Looked up at him. Her cheeks were flushed pink, which intensified the blue of her eyes.

'I've been in Montovia for a week. I fly out to Sydney tomorrow morning. I won't see you again,' she said.

'I have meetings in Zurich,' he said. 'I'll be gone very early.'

'So…so this is goodbye,' she said.

He put his fingers to the soft lushness of her mouth. 'Until next time,' he said.

For a long moment she looked up at him, searching his face with those remarkable eyes. Then she nodded. 'Until next time.'

Without another word Eliza turned away from him and walked away down the long enclosed terrace that ran along the outside of the ballroom. She did not turn back.

Jake watched her. Her back was held erect, the full skirts of her deep blue dress with its elaborately beaded bodice nipped into her tiny waist swishing around her at each step. He watched her until she turned to the right through an archway. Still she didn't look back, although he had his hand ready to wave farewell to her. Then she disappeared out of sight.

She left behind her just the lingering trace of her scent. He breathed it in to capture its essence. Took a step to go after her, then halted himself. He had no right to call her back a second time. He groaned and slammed his hand against the ancient stone wall.

For a long time he looked out through the window to the still lake beyond. Then he looked back to the ball-room. Without Eliza to dance with there was no point in returning. Besides, he felt like an impostor among the glittering throng. His role as best man, as friend to the Prince, gave him an entrée to their world. His multi-million-dollar houses and string of prestige European cars made him look the part.

Would they welcome him so readily into their elite company if they knew the truth about his past? Would Eliza find him so appealing if she knew his secrets?

He took out his phone and made his business call, in desperate need of distraction.

CHAPTER TWO

Six months later

ELIZA NOTICED JAKE MARLOWE the instant he strode into the business class lounge at Sydney's Kingsford Smith Airport. Tall, broad-shouldered, with a surfer's blond hair and tan, his good looks alone would attract attention. The fact that he was a billionaire whose handsome face was often in the media guaranteed it. Heads turned discreetly as he made his way with his easy, athletic stride towards the coffee station.

He was half a room away from her, but awareness tingled down Eliza's spine. A flush of humiliation warmed her cheeks. She hadn't seen him or heard from him since the wedding in Montovia, despite his promise to get in touch when his divorce was through. And here he was—on his way out of Sydney.

Jake had been in her hometown for heaven knew how long and hadn't cared to get in touch. She thought of a few choice names for him but wouldn't let herself mutter them, even under her breath. Losing her dignity over him was not worth it.

Over the last months she'd gone past disappointed, through angry, to just plain embarrassed that she'd be-

lieved him. That she'd allowed herself to spin hopes
and dreams around seeing him again—finally being
able to act on that flare of attraction between them. An
attraction that, despite her best efforts to talk herself
out of it, had flamed right back to life at the sight of
him. She'd failed dismally in her efforts to extinguish
it. He looked just as good in faded jeans and black
T-shirt as he looked in a tuxedo. Better, perhaps. Every
hot hunk sensor in her body alerted her to that.

But good looks weren't everything. She'd kidded
herself that Jake was something he wasn't. Sure, they'd
shared some interesting conversations, come close to
a kiss. But when it boiled down to it, it appeared he
was a slick tycoon who'd known how to spin the words
he'd thought would please her. And she'd been sucker
enough to fall for it. Had there been *anything* genuine about him?

Jake had put her through agony by not getting in
touch when he'd said he would. She never wanted that
kind of emotional turmoil in her life again. Especially
not now, when Party Queens was in possible peril. She
needed all her wits about her to ensure the future of
the company that had become her life.

Perhaps back then she'd been convenient for Jake—
the bridesmaid paired with the best man. An instant
temporary couple. Now he was single and oh-so-
eligible he must have women flinging themselves at
him from all sides. Even now, as she sneaked surrepti-
tious glances at him, a well-dressed woman edged up
close to him, smiling up into his face.

Jake laughed at something she said. Eliza's senses
jolted into hyper mode. *He looked so handsome when*

he laughed. Heck, he looked so handsome whatever he did.

Darn her pesky libido. Her brain could analyse exactly what she didn't want in a man, but then her body argued an opposing message. She'd let her libido take over at Gemma's wedding, when she'd danced with Jake and let herself indulge in a fantasy that there could be something between them one day. But she prided herself on her self-control. Eliza allowed herself a moment to let her eyes feast on him, in the same way she would a mouthwatering treat she craved but was forbidden to have. Then she ducked her head and hid behind the pale pink pages of her favourite financial newspaper.

Perhaps she hadn't ducked fast enough—perhaps she hadn't masked the hunger in her gaze as successfully as she'd thought. Or perhaps Jake had noticed her when he came in as readily as she had noticed him.

Just moments later she was aware of him standing in front of her, legs braced in a way that suggested he wasn't going anywhere. Her heart started to thud at a million miles an hour. As she lowered the newspaper and looked up at him she feigned surprise. But the expression in his green eyes told her she hadn't fooled him one little bit.

She gathered all her resolve to school her face into a mask of polite indifference. He could not know how much he'd hurt her. Not *hurt*. That gave him too much power. *Offended.* His divorce had been splashed all over the media for the last three months. Yet there'd been no phone call from him. What a fool she'd been to have expected one. She'd obviously read way too much into that memorable 'next time' farewell.

Eliza went to get up but he sat down in the vacant seat next to her and angled his body towards her. In doing so he brushed his knee against her thigh, and she tried desperately not to gasp at his touch. Her famed self-control seemed to wobble every which way when she found herself within touching distance of Jake Marlowe.

He rested his hands on his thighs, which brought them too close for comfort. She refused to let herself think about how good they'd felt on her body in that close embrace of their dance. She could not let herself be blinded by physical attraction to the reality of this man.

'Eliza,' he said.

'Jake,' she said coolly, with a nod of acknowledgment.

She crossed her legs to break contact with his. Made a show of folding her newspaper, its rustle satisfyingly loud in the silence between them.

There was a long, awkward pause. She had no intention of helping him out by being the first one to dive into conversation. Not when he'd treated her with such indifference. Surely the thread of friendship they'd established had entitled her to better.

She could see he was looking for the right words, and at any other time she might have felt sorry for this intelligent, successful man who appeared to be struggling to make conversation. Would have fed him words to make it easier for him. But she knew how articulate Jake could be. How he had charmed her. This sudden shyness must be all part of his game. It seemed he felt stymied at seeing her by accident when he'd so obviously not wanted to see her by intent.

She really should hold her tongue and let him stumble through whatever he had to say. But she knew there wasn't much time before her flight would be called. And this might be her only chance to call him on the way he had broken his promise.

Of course it hadn't been a *promise* as such. But, spellbound by the magic of that royal wedding in Montovia, she had believed every word about there being a 'next time', when he was free. She'd never believed in fairytales—but she'd believed in *him*.

Even though the lounge chairs were spaced for privacy in the business class lounge—not crammed on top of each other like at the airport gate, where she was accustomed to waiting for a flight—she was aware that she and Jake were being observed and might possibly be overheard. She would have to be discreet.

She leaned closer to him and spoke in an undertone. 'So whatever happened to getting in touch? I see from the media that your divorce is well and truly done and delivered. You're now considered to be the most eligible bachelor in the country. You must be enjoying that.'

Jake shifted in his seat. Which brought his thigh back in touch with her knee. She pointedly crossed her legs again to break the contact. It was way too distracting.

'You couldn't be more wrong.' He cleared his throat. 'I want to explain.'

Eliza didn't want to hear his half-hearted apologies. She glanced at her watch. 'I don't think so. My flight is about to be called.'

'So is mine. Where are you headed?'

It would be childish to spit, *None of your business*, so she refrained. 'Port Douglas.'

She'd been counting the days until she could get

up to the resort in far north-east tropical Queensland. From Sydney she was flying to Cairns, the nearest airport. She needed to relax—to get away from everyday distractions so she could get her head around what she needed to do to ensure Party Queens' ongoing success.

Jake's expression, which had bordered on glum, brightened perceptibly. 'Are you on Flight 321 to Cairns? So am I.'

Eliza felt the colour drain from her face. It couldn't be. It just *couldn't* be. Australia was an enormous country. Yet she happened to be flying to the same destination as Jake Marlowe. What kind of cruel coincidence was that?

'Yes,' she said through gritted teeth.

Port Douglas was a reasonably sized town. The resort she was booked into was pretty much self-contained. She would make darn sure she didn't bump into him.

Just then they called the flight. She went to rise from her seat. Jake put his hand on her arm to detain her. She flinched.

He spoke in a fierce undertone. 'Please, Eliza. I know it was wrong of me not to have got in touch as I said I would. But I had good reason.'

She stared at him, uncertain whether or not to give him the benefit of the doubt. He seemed so sincere. But then he'd seemed so sincere at the wedding. Out there on the terrace, in a place and at a time that hardly seemed real any more. As if it *had* been a fairytale. How could she believe a word he said?

'A phone call to explain would have sufficed. Even a text.'

'That wouldn't have worked. I want you to hear me out.'

There was something about his request that was difficult to resist. She wanted to hear what he had to say. Out of curiosity, if nothing else. Huh! Who was she kidding? How could she *not* want to hear what he had to say? After six months of wondering why the deafening silence?

She relented. 'Perhaps we could meet for a coffee in Port Douglas.' At a café. Not her room. Or his. For just enough time to hear his explanation. Then she could put Jake Marlowe behind her.

'How are you getting to Port Douglas from Cairns?' he asked.

'I booked a shuttle bus from the airport to the resort.'

His eyebrows rose in such disbelief it forced from her a reluctant smile.

'Yes, a shuttle bus. It's quite comfortable—and so much cheaper than a taxi for an hour-long trip. That's how we non-billionaires travel. I'm flying economy class, too.'

When she'd first started studying in Sydney, cut off from any family support because she'd refused to toe her father's line, she'd had to budget for every cent. It was a habit she'd kept. Why waste money on a business class seat for a flight of less than three hours?

'Then why…?' He gestured around him at the exclusive waiting area.

'I met a friend going through Security. She invited me in here on her guest pass. She went out on an earlier flight.'

'Lucky for me—otherwise I might have missed you.'

She made a *humph* kind of sound at that, which drew a half-smile from him.

'Contrary to what you might think, I'm very glad to see you,' he said, in that deep, strong voice she found so very appealing.

'That's good to hear,' she said, somewhat mollified. Of course she was glad to see him too—in spite of her better judgement. How could she deny even to herself that her every sense was zinging with awareness of him? She would have to be very careful not to be taken in by him again.

'Are you going to Port Douglas on business or pleasure?'

'Pleasure,' she said, without thinking. Then regretted her response as a flush reddened on her cheeks.

She had fantasised over pleasure with *him*. When it came to Jake Marlowe it wasn't so easy to switch off the attraction that had been ignited at their very first meeting. She would have to fight very hard against it.

It had taken some time to get her life to a steady state after her divorce, and she didn't want it tipping over again. When she'd seen the media reports of Jake's divorce, but hadn't heard from him, she'd been flung back to a kind of angst she didn't welcome. She cringed when she thought about how often she'd checked her phone for a call that had never come. It wasn't a situation where she might have called *him*. And she hated not being in control—of her life, her emotions. Never did she want to give a man that kind of power over her.

'I mean relaxation,' she added hastily. 'Yes, relaxation.'

'Party Queens keeping you busy?'

'Party Queens always keeps me busy. Too busy right

now. That's why I'm grabbing the chance for a break. I desperately need some time away from the office.'

'Have you solved the Gemma problem?'

'No. I need to give it more thought. Gemma will always be a director of Party Queens, for as long as the company exists. It's just that—'

'Can passengers Dunne and Marlowe please make their way to Gate Eleven, where their flight is ready for departure?'

The voice boomed over the intercom.

Eliza sat up abruptly, her newspaper falling in a flurry of pages to the floor. Hissed a swearword under her breath. 'We've got to get going. I don't want to miss that plane.'

'How about I meet you at the other end and drive you to Port Douglas?'

Eliza hated being late. For anything. Flustered, she hardly heard him. 'Uh…okay,' she said, not fully aware of what she might be letting herself in for. 'Let's go!'

She grabbed her wheel-on cabin bag—her only luggage—and half-walked, half-ran towards the exit of the lounge.

Jake quickly caught up and led the way to the gate. Eliza had to make a real effort to keep up with his long stride. They made the flight with only seconds to spare. There was no time to say anything else as she breathlessly boarded the plane through the cattle class entrance while Jake headed to the pointy end up front.

Jake had a suspicion that Eliza might try to avoid him at Cairns airport. As soon as the flight landed he called through to the garage where he kept his car to have it brought round. Having had the advantage of being the first to disembark, he was there at the gate to head Eliza off.

She soon appeared, head down, intent, so didn't see him as he waited for her. The last time he'd seen her she'd been resplendent in a ballgown. Now she looked just as good, in cut-off skinny pants that showed off her pert rear end and slim legs, topped with a form-fitting jacket. Deep blue again. She must like that colour. Her dark hair was pulled back in a high ponytail. She might travel Economy but she would look right at home in First Class.

For a moment he regretted the decision he'd made to keep her out of his life. Three months wasted in an Eliza-free zone. But the aftermath of his divorce had made him unfit for female company. Unfit for *any* company, if truth be told.

He'd been thrown so badly by the first big failure of his life that he'd gone completely out of kilter. Drunk too much. Made bad business decisions that had had serious repercussions to his bottom line. Mistakes he'd had to do everything in his power to fix. He had wealth, but it would never be enough to blot out the poverty of his childhood, to assuage the hunger for more that had got him into such trouble. He had buried himself in his work, determined to reverse the wrong turns he'd made. But he hadn't been able to forget Eliza.

'Eliza!' he called now.

She started, looked up, was unable to mask a quick flash of guilt.

'Jake. Hi.'

Her voice was higher than usual. Just as sweet, but strained. She was not a good liar. He stored that information up for later, as he did in his assessments of clients. He'd learned young that knowledge of people's weaknesses was a useful tool. Back then it had been for survival. Now it was to give him a competitive advantage and keep him at the top. He could not let himself slide again.

'I suspected you might try and avoid me, so I decided to head you off at the pass,' he said.

Eliza frowned unconvincingly. 'Why would you do that?'

'Because you obviously think I'm a jerk for not calling you after the divorce. I'm determined to change your mind.' He didn't want to leave things the way they were. Not when thoughts of her had intruded, despite his best efforts to forget her.

'Oh,' she said, after a long pause. 'You could do that over coffee. Not during an hour's drive to Port Douglas.'

So she'd been mulling over the enforced intimacy of a journey in his car. So had he. But to different effect.

'How do you know I won't need an hour with you?'

She shrugged slender shoulders. 'I guess I don't. But I've booked the shuttle bus. The driver is expecting me.'

'Call them and cancel.' He didn't want to appear too high-handed. But no way was she going to get on that shuttle bus. 'Come on, Eliza. It will be much more comfortable in my car.'

'Your rental car?'

'I have a house in Port Douglas. And a car.'

'I thought you lived in Brisbane?'

'I do. The house in Port Douglas is an escape house.'

He took hold of her wheeled bag. 'Do you need to pick up more luggage?'

She shook her head. 'This is all I have. A few bikinis and sundresses is all I need for four days.'

Jake forced himself not to think how Eliza would look in a bikini. She was wearing flat shoes and he realised how petite she was. Petite, slim, but with curves in all the right places. She would look sensational in a bikini.

'My car is out front. Let's go.'

Still she hesitated. 'So you'll drop me at my resort hotel?'

Did she think he was about to abduct her? It wasn't such a bad idea, if that was what it took to get her to listen to him. 'Your private driver—at your service,' he said with a mock bow.

She smiled that curving smile he found so delightful. The combination of astute businesswoman and quick-to-laughter Party Queen was part of her appeal.

'Okay, I accept the offer,' she said.

The warm midday air hit him as they left the air-conditioning of the terminal. Eliza shrugged off her jacket to reveal a simple white top that emphasised the curves of her breasts. She stretched out her slim, toned arms in a movement he found incredibly sensual, as if she were welcoming the sun to her in an embrace.

'Nice and hot,' she said with a sigh of pleasure. 'Just what I want. Four days of relaxing and swimming and eating great food.'

'April is a good time of year here,' he said. 'Less chance of cyclone and perfect conditions for diving on the Great Barrier Reef.'

The garage attendant had brought Jake's new-model four-by-four to the front of the airport. It was a luxury to keep a car for infrequent use. Just as it was to keep a house up here that was rarely used. But he liked being able to come and go whenever he wanted. It had been his bolthole through the unhappiest times of his marriage.

'Nice car,' Eliza said.

Jake remembered they'd talked about cars at their first meeting. He'd been impressed by how knowledgeable she was. Face it—he'd been impressed by *her*. Period. No wonder she'd been such a difficult woman to forget.

He put her bag into the back, went to help her up into the passenger's seat, but she had already swung herself effortlessly up. He noticed the sleek muscles in her arms and legs. Exercise was a non-negotiable part of her day, he suspected. Everything about her spoke of discipline and control. He wondered how it would be to see her come to pieces with pleasure in his arms.

Jake settled himself into the driver's seat. 'Have you been to Port Douglas before?' he asked.

'Yes, but not for some time,' she said. 'I loved it and always wanted to come back. But there's been no time for vacations. As you know, Party Queens took off quickly. It's an intense, people-driven business. I can't be away from it for long. But I need to free my head to think about how we can make it work with Gemma not on the ground.'

Can't or *didn't want to* be away from her job? Jake had recognised a fellow workaholic when he'd first met her.

'So you're familiar with the drive from Cairns to Port Douglas?'

With rainforest on one side and the sea on the other,

it was considered one of the most scenic drives in Australia.

'I planned the timing of my flight to make sure I saw it in daylight.'

'I get the feeling very little is left to chance with you, Eliza.'

'You've got it,' she said with a click of her fingers. 'I plan, schedule, timetable and organise my life to the minute.'

She was the total opposite of his ex-wife. In looks, in personality, in attitude. The two women could not be more different.

'You don't like surprises?' he asked.

'Surprises have a habit of derailing one's life.'

She stilled, almost imperceptibly, and there was a slight hitch to her voice that made him wonder about the kind of surprises that had hit her.

'I like things to be on track. For me to be at the wheel.'

'So by hijacking you I've ruined your plans for today?'

His unwilling passenger shrugged slender shoulders.

'Just a deviation. I'm still heading for my resort. It will take the same amount of time. Just a different mode of transportation.' She turned her head to face him. 'Besides. I'm on vacation. From schedules and routine as much as from anything else.'

Eliza reached back and undid the tie from her ponytail, shook out her hair so it fell in a silky mass to her shoulders. With her hair down she looked even lovelier. Younger than her twenty-nine years. More relaxed. He'd like to run his hands through that hair, bunch it back from her face to kiss her. Instead he tightened his hands on the steering wheel as she settled back in her seat.

'When you're ready to tell me why I had to read about your divorce in the gossip columns rather than hear it from you,' she said, 'I'm all ears.'

CHAPTER THREE

JAKE WAS VERY good at speaking the language of computers and coding. At talking the talk when it came to commercial success. While still at university he had come up with a concept for ground-breaking software tools to streamline the digital workflow of large businesses. His friend Dominic Hunt had backed him. The resulting success had made a great deal of money for both young men. And Jake had continued on a winning streak that had made him a billionaire.

But for all his formidable skills Jake wasn't great at talking about emotions. At admitting that he had fears and doubts. Or conceding to any kind of failure. It was one of the reasons he'd got into such trouble when he was younger. Why he'd fallen apart after the divorce. No matter how much he worked on it, he still considered it a character flaw.

He hoped he'd be able to make a good fist of explaining to Eliza why he hadn't got in touch until now.

He put the four-by-four into gear and headed for the Captain Cook Highway to Port Douglas. Why they called it a highway, he'd never know—it was a narrow two-lane road in most places. To the left was dense vegetation, right back to the distant hills. To the right was the vastness of the Pacific Ocean, its turquoise sea bounded by narrow, deserted beaches, broken by small islands. In places the road ran almost next to the sand. He'd driven along this road many times, but never failed to be impressed by the grandeur of the view.

He didn't look at Eliza but kept his eyes on the road. 'I'll cut straight to it,' he said. 'I want to apologise for not getting in touch when I said I would. I owe you an explanation.'

'Fire away,' Eliza said.

Her voice was cool. The implication? *This had better be good.*

He swallowed hard. 'The divorce eventually came through three months ago.'

'I heard. Congratulations.'

He couldn't keep the cynical note from his voice. 'You *congratulate* me. Lots of people congratulated me. A divorce party was even suggested. To celebrate my freedom from the ball and chain.'

'Party Queens has organised a few divorce parties. They're quite a thing these days.'

'Not *my* thing,' he said vehemently. 'I didn't want congratulations. Or parties to celebrate what I saw as a failure. The end of something that didn't work.'

'Was that because you were still…still in love with your wife?'

A quick glance showed Eliza had a tight grip on the red handbag she held on her lap. He hated talking about stuff like this. Even after all he'd worked on in the last months.

'No. There hadn't been any love there for a long

time. It ended with no anger or animosity. Just indifference. Which was almost worse.'

He'd met his ex when they were both teenagers. They'd dated on and off over the early years. Marriage had felt inevitable. He'd changed a lot; she hadn't wanted change. Then she'd betrayed him. He'd loved her. It had hurt.

'That must have been traumatic in its own way.' Eliza's reply sounded studiously neutral.

'More traumatic than I could have imagined. The process dragged on for too long.'

'It must have been a relief when it was all settled.'

Again he read the subtext to her sentence: *All settled, but you didn't call me.* It hinted at a hurt she couldn't mask. Hurt caused by *him.* He had to make amends.

'I didn't feel relief. I felt like I'd been turned upside down and wasn't sure where I'd landed. Couldn't find my feet. My ex and I had been together off and on for years, married for seven. Then I was on my own. It wasn't just her I'd lost. It was a way of life.'

'I understand that,' she said.

The shadow that passed across her face hinted at unspoken pain. She'd gone through divorce too. Though she hadn't talked much about it on the previous occasions when they had met.

He dragged in a deep breath. *Spit it out. Get this over and done with.* 'It took a few wipe-out weeks at work for me to realise going out and drinking wasn't the way to deal with it.'

'It usually isn't,' she said.

He was a guy. A tough, successful guy. To him, being

unable to cope with loss was a sign of weakness. Weakness he wasn't genetically programmed to admit to. But the way he'd fallen to pieces had lost him money. That couldn't be allowed to happen again.

'Surely you had counselling?' she said. 'I did after my divorce. It helped.'

'Guys like me don't do counselling.'

'You bottle it all up inside you instead?'

'Something like that.'

'That's not healthy—it festers,' she said. 'Not that it's any of my business.'

The definitive turning point in his life had not been his divorce. That had come much earlier, when he'd been aged fifteen, angry and rebellious. He'd been forced to face up to the way his life was going, the choices he would have to make. To take one path or another.

Jake didn't know how much Eliza knew about Dominic's charity—The Underground Help Centre in Brisbane for homeless young people—or Jake's involvement in it. A social worker with whom both Dominic and Jake had crossed paths headed the charity. Jim Hill had helped Jake at a time when he'd most needed it. He had become a friend. Without poking or prying, he had noticed Jake's unexpected devastation after his marriage break-up, and pointed him in the right direction for confidential help.

'Someone told me about a support group for divorced guys,' Jake said, with a quick, sideways glance to Eliza and in a tone that did not invite further questions.

'That's good,' she said with an affirmative nod.

He appreciated that she didn't push it. He still choked at the thought he'd had to seek help.

The support group had been exclusive, secret, limited to a small number of elite men rich enough to pay the stratospheric fees. Men who wanted to protect their wealth in the event of remarriage, who needed strategies to avoid the pitfalls of dating after divorce. Jake had wanted to know how to barricade his heart as well as his bank balance.

The men and the counsellors had gone into lockdown for a weekend at a luxury retreat deep in the rainforest. It had been on a first-name-only basis, but Jake had immediately recognised some of the high-profile men. No doubt they had recognised him too. But they had proved to be discreet.

'Men don't seem to seek help as readily as women,' Eliza said.

'It was about dealing with change more than anything,' he said.

'Was that why you didn't get in touch?' she said, with an edge to her voice. 'You changed your mind?'

Jake looked straight ahead at the road. 'I wasn't ready for another relationship. I needed to learn to live alone. That meant no dating. In particular not dating *you*.'

Her gasp told him how much he'd shocked her.

'*Me?* Why?'

'From the first time we met you sparked something that told me there could be life after divorce. I could see myself getting serious about you. I don't want serious. But I couldn't get you out of my head. I had to see you again.'

To be sure she was real and not some fantasy that had built up in his mind.

* * *

Eliza didn't even notice the awesome view of the ocean that stretched as far as the eye could see. Or the sign indicating the turn-off to a crocodile farm that would normally make her shudder. All she was aware of was Jake. She stared at him.

'*Serious?* But we hardly knew each other. Did you think I had my life on hold until you were free so I could bolt straight into a full-on relationship?'

Jake took his eyes off the road for a second to glance at her. 'Come on, Eliza. There was something there between us. Something more than a surface attraction. Something we both wanted to act on.'

'Maybe,' she said.

Of course there had been something there. But she wasn't sure she wanted to admit to it. Not when she'd spent all that time trying to suppress it. Not when it had the potential to hurt her. Those three months of seeing his divorce splashed over the media, of speculation on who might hook up with the billionaire bachelor had hurt. He had said he'd get in touch. Then he hadn't. How could she trust his word again? She couldn't afford to be distracted from Party Queens by heartbreak at such a crucial time in the growth of her business.

The set of his jaw made him seem very serious. 'I didn't want to waste your time when I had nothing to offer you. But ultimately I had to see you.'

'Six months later? Maybe you should have let *me* be the one to decide whether I wanted to waste my time or not?' She willed any hint of a wobble from her voice.

'I needed that time on my own. Possibly it was a mistake not to communicate that with you. I was married a long time. Now I'm single again at thirty-two. I haven't had a lot of practice at this.'

Eliza stared in disbelief at the gorgeous man beside her in the driver's seat. At his handsome profile with the slightly crooked nose and strong jaw. His shoulders so broad they took up more than his share of the car. His tanned arms, strong and muscular, dusted with hair that glinted gold in the sunlight coming through the window of the car. His hands— Best she did not think about those hands and how they'd felt on her bare skin back in magical Montovia.

'I find that difficult to buy,' she said. 'You're a really good-looking guy. There must be women stampeding to date you.'

He shrugged dismissively. 'All that eligible billionaire stuff the media likes to bang on about brings a certain level of attention. Even before the divorce was through I had women hounding me with dollar signs blazing in their eyes.'

'I guess that kind of attention comes with the territory. But surely not *everyone* would be a gold-digger. You must have dated *some* genuine women.'

She hated the thought of him with another woman. Not his ex-wife. That had been long before she'd met him. But Eliza had no claim on him—no right to be jealous. For all his fine talk about how he hadn't been able to forget her, the fact remained she was only here with him by accident.

Jake slowly shook his head. 'I haven't dated anyone since the divorce.' He paused for a long moment, the silence only broken by the swish of the tyres on the road, the air blowing from the air-conditioning unit.

Jake gave her another quick, sideward glance. 'Don't you get it, Eliza? There's only one woman who interests me. And she's sitting here, right beside me.'

Eliza suddenly understood the old expression about having all the wind blown out of her sails. A stunned, 'Oh…' was all she could manage through her suddenly accelerated breath.

Jake looked straight ahead as he spoke, as if he was finding the words difficult to get out. 'The support group covered dating after divorce. It suggested six months before starting to date. Three months was long enough. The urge to see you again became overwhelming. I didn't get where I am in the world by following the rules. All that dating-after-divorce advice flew out the window.'

Eliza frowned. 'How can you *say* that? You left our seeing each other again purely to chance. If we hadn't met at the airport—'

'I didn't leave anything to chance. After six months of radio silence I doubted you'd welcome a call from me. Any communication needed to be face to face. I flew down to Sydney to see you. Then met with Dominic to suss out how the land lay.'

'You *what*? Andie didn't say anything to me.'

'Because I asked Dominic not to tell her. He found out you were flying to Port Douglas this morning. I couldn't believe you were heading for a town where I had a house. Straight away I booked onto the same flight.'

Eliza took a few moments to absorb this revelation. 'That was very cloak and dagger. What would have happened if you hadn't found me at the airport?'

He shrugged those broad shoulders. 'I would have abducted you.' At her gasp he added, 'Just kidding. But I *would* have found a way for us to reconnect in Port Douglas. Even if I'd had to call every resort and hotel I would have tracked you down. I just had to see you, Eliza. To see if that attraction I'd felt was real.'

'I… I don't know what to say. Except I'm flattered.'

There was a long beat before he spoke. 'And pleased?'

The tinge of uncertainty to his voice surprised her. 'Very pleased.'

In fact her heart was doing cartwheels of exultation. She was so dizzy that the warning from her brain was having trouble getting through. Jake tracking her down sounded very romantic. So did his talk of abduction. But she'd learned to be wary of the type of man who would ride roughshod over her wishes and needs. Like her domineering father. Like her controlling ex. She didn't know Jake very well. It must take a certain kind of ruthlessness to become a billionaire. She couldn't let her guard down.

'So, about that coffee we talked about…?' he said. 'Do you want to make it lunch?'

'Are you asking me on a *date*, Jake?' Her tone was deliberately flirtatious.

His reply was very serious. 'I realise I've surprised you with this. But be assured I've released the baggage of my marriage. I've accepted my authentic self. And if you—'

She couldn't help a smile. 'You sound like you've swallowed the "dating after divorce" handbook.'

His brows rose. 'I told you I was out of practice. What else should I say?'

Eliza started to laugh. 'This is getting a little crazy.

Pull over, will you, please?' she said. She indicated a layby ahead with a wave of her hand.

Jake did so with a sudden swerve and squealing of tyres that had her clutching onto the dashboard of the car. He skidded to a halt under the shade of some palm trees.

Still laughing, Eliza unbuckled her seatbelt and turned to face him. 'Can I give you a dating after divorce tip? Don't worry so much about whether it's going to lead to something serious before you've even gone on a first date.'

'Was that what I did?'

She found his frown endearing. How could a guy who was one of the most successful entrepreneurs in the country be having this kind of trouble?

'You're over-thinking all this,' she said. 'So am I. We're making it so much harder than it should be. In truth, it's simple. There's an attraction here. You're divorced. I'm divorced. We don't answer to anyone except ourselves. There's nothing to stop us enjoying each other's company in any way we want to.'

He grinned in that lazy way she found so attractive. 'Nothing at all.'

'Shall we agree not to worry about tomorrow when we haven't even had a today yet?'

Eliza had been going to add *not even a morning*. But that conjured up an image of waking up next to Jake, in a twist of tangled sheets. Better not think about mornings. Or nights.

Jake's grin widened. 'You've got four days of vacation. I've got nothing to do except decide whether or not to offload my house in Port Douglas.'

'No expectations. No promises. No apologies.'

'Agreed,' he said. He held out his hand to shake and seal the deal.

She edged closer to him. 'Forget the handshake. Why don't we start with a kiss?'

CHAPTER FOUR

JAKE KNEW THERE was a dating after divorce guideline regarding the first physical encounter, but he'd be damned if he could think about that right now. Any thoughts other than of Eliza had been blown away in a blaze of anticipation and excitement at the invitation in her eyes—a heady mix of sensuality, impatience and mischief.

It seemed she had forgiven him for his broken promise. He had a second chance with her. It was so much more than he could have hoped for—or probably deserved after his neglect.

He hadn't told her the whole truth about why he hadn't been in touch. It was true he hadn't been able to forget her, had felt compelled to see her again. He was a man who liked to be in the company of one special woman and he'd hungered for her. But not necessarily to commit to anything serious. Not now. Maybe not ever again. Not with her. Not with any woman. However it seemed she wasn't looking for anything serious either. Four days without strings? That sounded like a great idea.

She slid a little closer to him from her side of the car. Reached down and unbuckled his seat belt with a low, sweet laugh that sent his awareness levels soaring. When her fingers inadvertently trailed over his thigh he shuddered and pulled her kissing distance close.

He focused with intense anticipation on her sweet mouth. Her lips were beautifully defined, yet lush and soft and welcoming. She tilted her face to him, making her impatience obvious. Jake needed no urging. He pressed his mouth against hers in a tender kiss, claiming her at last. She tasted of salt—peanuts on the plane, perhaps?—and something sweet. Chocolate? Sweet and sharp at the same time. Like Eliza herself—an intriguing combination.

She was beautiful, but his attraction had never been just to her looks. He liked her independence, her intelligence, her laughter.

The kiss felt both familiar and very different. Within seconds it was as if *her* kiss was all he'd ever known. Her lips parted under his as she gave a soft sigh of contentment.

'At last,' she murmured against his mouth.

Kissing Eliza for the first time in the front seat of a four-by-four was hardly ideal. Jake had forgotten how awkward it was to make out in a car. But having Eliza in his arms was way too exciting to be worrying about the discomfort of bumping into the steering wheel or handbrake. She held his face between her hands as she returned his kiss, her tongue sliding between his lips to meet his, teasing and exploring. He was oblivious to the car, their surroundings, the fact that they were parked in a public layby. He just wanted to keep kissing Eliza.

Was it seconds or minutes before Eliza broke away from him? That kind of excitement wasn't easily measured. Her cheeks were flushed, her eyes shades brighter, her lips swollen and pouting. She was panting, so it took her some effort to control her voice. 'Kissing you was all I could think about that night in the castle.'

'Me too,' he said.

Only his thoughts had marched much further than kissing. That last night he hadn't been able to sleep, taunted by the knowledge she was in the apartment next to his at the castle, overwhelmed by how much he wanted her. Back then his married state had been an obstacle. Now there was nothing stopping them from acting on the attraction between them.

He claimed her mouth again, deeper, more demanding. There'd been enough talking. He was seized with a sense of urgency to be with her while he could. He wasn't going to 'over-think' about where this might lead. Six months of pent-up longing for this woman erupted into passion, fierce and hungry.

As their kiss escalated in urgency Jake pulled her onto his lap, one hand around her waist, the other resting against the side of the car to support her. He bunched her hair in his hand and tugged to tilt her face upward, so he could deepen the kiss, hungry for her, aching for more. The little murmurs of pleasure she made deep in her throat drove him crazy with want.

His hands slid down her bare arms, brushed the side curves of her breasts, the silkiness of her top. She gasped, placed both hands on his chest and pushed away. She started to laugh—that delightful, chiming laughter he found so enchanting.

'We're steaming up the windows here like a coupled of hormone-crazed adolescents,' she said, her voice broken with laughter.

'What's wrong with being hormone-crazed *adults*,' he said, his own voice hoarse and unsteady.

'Making out in a car is seriously sexy. I don't want to stop,' she said, moaning when he nuzzled against the delicious softness of her throat, kissing and tasting.

The confined area of the car was filled with her scent, heady and intoxicating. 'Me neither,' he said.

Eliza was so relaxed and responsive she took away any thought of awkwardness. He glanced over to the back seat. There was more room there. It was wider and roomier.

'The back seat would be more comfortable,' he said.

He kissed her again, manoeuvring her towards the door. They would have to get out and transfer to the back, though it might be a laugh to try and clamber through the gap between the front seats. Why not?

Just then another car pulled into the layby and parked parallel to the four-by-four. Eliza froze in his arms. Their mouths were still pressed together. Her eyes communicated her alarm.

'That puts paid to the back seat plan,' he said, pulling away from her with a groan of regret.

'Just as well, really,' Eliza said breathlessly.

She smoothed her hair back from her face with her fingers and tucked it behind her ears. Even her ears were lovely—small and shell-like.

'The media would love to catch their most eligible bachelor being indiscreet in public.'

He scowled. 'I hate the way they call me a *bachelor*. Surely that's a term for someone who has never been married?'

'*Most eligible divorcé* doesn't quite have the same headline potential, does it?' she said.

'I'd rather not feature in *any* headlines,' he growled.

'You might just have to hit yourself with the ugly stick, then,' she said. 'Handsome and rich makes you a magnet for headlines. You're almost too good to be true.' She laughed. 'Though if you scowl like that they might forget about calling you the most eligible guy in the country.'

Jake exaggerated the scowl. He liked making her laugh. 'Too good to be true, huh?'

'Now you look cute,' she said.

'*Cute?* I do *not* want to be called cute,' he protested.

'Handsome, good-looking, hot, smokin', babelicious—'

'Stop right there,' he said, unable to suppress a grin. 'You don't call a guy *babelicious*. That's a girl word. Let me try it on you.'

'No need,' she protested. 'I'm not the babelicious type.'

'I think you are—if I understand it to mean sexy and desirable and—' Her mock glare made him stop. 'How about lovely, beautiful, sweet, elegant—?'

'That's more than enough,' she said. 'I'll take elegant. Audrey Hepburn's style is my icon. Not that I'm really tall enough to own *elegant*. But I try.'

'You succeed, let me assure you,' he said.

'Thank you. I like *smokin'* for you,' she said, her eyes narrowing as she looked him over.

Her flattering descriptive words left him with a warm feeling. No matter how he'd tried to put a brave face on it, the continued rejection by his ex had hurt. She'd found someone else, of course. He should have realised earlier, before he'd let his ego get so bruised.

The admiration in Eliza's eyes was like balm to those bruises. He intended to take everything she offered.

'I'd rather kiss than talk, wouldn't you?' he said.

He'd rather do so much more than kiss.

'If you say so,' she said with a seductive smile.

They kissed for a long time, until just kissing was not enough. It was getting steamy in the car—and not in an exciting way. It was too hot without the air-conditioning, but they couldn't sit there with the engine on.

The windows really were getting fogged up now. Visibility was practically zero. Eliza swiped her finger across the windscreen. Then spelled out the word KISSING. 'It's very obvious what's going on in here.'

He found her wicked giggle enchanting.

'More so now you've done that,' he said.

Spontaneity wasn't something he'd expected from cool and controlled Eliza. He ached to discover what other surprises she had in store for him.

'We really should go,' she said breathlessly. 'How long will it take to get to Port Douglas?'

'Thirty minutes to my place,' he said.

She wiggled in her seat in a show of impatience. 'Then put your foot to the floor and get us there ASAP, will you?'

Jake couldn't get his foot on the accelerator fast enough.

Eliza had a sense she was leaving everything that was everyday behind her as the four-by-four effortlessly climbed the steep driveway which led from the street in Port Douglas to Jake's getaway house. His retreat, he'd called it. As she slid out of the high-set car she gaped at the magnificence of the architectural award-winning house nestled among palm trees and vivid tropical gardens. Large glossy leaves in every shade of green contrasted with riotous blooms in orange, red and yellow. She breathed in air tinged with salt, ginger and the honey-scented white flowers that grew around the pathway.

This was his second house. No, his third. He'd told her he had a penthouse apartment in one of the most fashionable waterfront developments in Sydney, where his neighbours were celebrities and millionaires. His riverfront mansion in Brisbane was his home base. There were probably other houses too, but she'd realised early on that Jake wasn't the kind of billionaire to boast about his wealth.

Then Jake was kissing her again, and she didn't think about houses or bank balances or anything other than him and the way he was making her feel. He didn't break the kiss as he used his fingerprints on a sensor to get into the house—nothing so mundane as a key—and pushed open the door. They stumbled into the house, still kissing, laughing at their awkward progress but refusing to let go of each other.

Once inside, Eliza registered open-plan luxury and an awesome view. Usually she was a sucker for a water view. But nothing could distract her from Jake. She'd never wanted a man more than she wanted him. Many times since the wedding in Montovia she'd wondered if she had been foolish in holding off from him. There would be no regrets this time—no 'if only'. She didn't want him to stop…didn't want second thoughts to sneak into her consciousness.

In the privacy of the house their kisses got deeper, more demanding. Caresses—she of him and he of her—got progressively more intimate. Desire, warm and urgent, thrilled through her body.

She remembered when she'd first met Jake. He'd flown down to Sydney to be best man for Dominic at the surprise wedding Dominic had organised for Andie. Eliza had been expecting a geek. The athletic, handsome best man had been the furthest from her image of a geek as he could possibly have been. She'd been instantly smitten—then plunged into intense disappointment to find he was married.

Now she had the green light to touch him, kiss him, undress him. *No holds barred.*

'Bedroom?' he murmured.

He didn't really have to ask. There had been no need for words for her to come to her decision of where to take this mutually explosive passion. Their kisses, their caresses, their sighs had communicated everything he needed to know.

She had always enjoyed those scenes in movies where a kissing couple left a trail of discarded clothing behind them as they staggered together towards the bedroom. To be taking part in such a scene with Jake was like a fantasy fulfilled. A fantasy that had commenced in the ballroom of a fairytale castle in Europe and culminated in an ultra-modern house overlooking a tropical beach in far north Australia.

They reached his bedroom, the bed set in front of a panoramic view that stretched out over the pool to the sea. Then she was on the bed with Jake, rejoicing in the intimacy, the closeness, the confidence—the wonderful new entity that was *them*.

Eliza and Jake.

CHAPTER FIVE

ELIZA DIDN'T KNOW where she was when she woke up some time later. In a super-sized bed and not alone. She blinked against the late-afternoon sunlight streaming through floor-to-ceiling windows with a view of palm trees, impossibly blue sky, the turquoise sea beyond.

Jake's bedroom.

She smiled to herself with satisfaction. Remembered the trail of discarded clothes that had led to this bed. The passion. The fun. The ultimate pleasure. Again and again.

He lay beside her on his back, long muscular limbs sprawled across the bed and taking up much of the space. The sheets were tangled around his thighs. He seemed to be in a deep sleep, his broad chest rhythmically rising and falling.

She gazed at him for a long moment and caught her breath when she remembered what a skilled, passionate lover he'd proved to be. Her body ached in a thoroughly satisfied way.

Beautiful wasn't a word she would normally choose to describe a man. But he *was* beautiful—in an intensely masculine way. The tawny hair, green eyes—shut tight at the moment—the sculpted face, smooth tanned skin, slightly crooked nose. His beard had started to shadow his jaw, dark in contrast to the tawny blond of his hair.

There were some things in life she would never, ever forget or regret. Making love with Jake was one of them. Heaven knew where they went from here, but even if this was all she ever had of him she would cherish the memory for the rest of her days. In her experience it was rare to want someone so intensely and then not be disappointed. Nothing about making love with Jake disappointed her.

Eliza breathed in the spicy warm scent of him; her own classic French scent that was her personal indulgence mingled with it so that it became the scent of *them*. Unique, memorable, intensely personal.

She tentatively stretched out a leg. It was starting to cramp under his much larger, heavier leg. Rolling cautiously away, so her back faced him, she wondered where the bathroom was, realised it was en suite and so not far.

She started to edge cautiously away. Then felt a kiss on her shoulder. She went still, her head thrown back in pleasure as Jake planted a series of kisses along her shoulder to land a final one in her most sensitive spot at the top of her jaw, below her ear. She gasped. They had so quickly learned what pleased each other.

Then a strong arm was around her, restraining her. 'You're not going anywhere,' he said as he pulled her to him.

She turned around to find Jake lying on his side. His body was so perfect she gasped her admiration. The sculptured pecs, the flat belly and defined six-pack, the muscular arms and legs… He was without a doubt the hottest billionaire on the planet.

Eliza trailed her hand over the smooth skin of his chest. *'Smokin','* she murmured.

He propped himself up on his other elbow. Smiled that slow smile. 'Okay?' he asked.

'Very okay,' she said, returning his smile and stretching like one of her cats with remembered pleasure. 'It was very sudden. Unexpected. So soon, I mean. But it was good we just let it happen. We didn't get a chance to over-think things. Over-analyse how we felt, what it would mean.'

'Something so spontaneous wasn't in my dating after divorce guidebook,' he said with that endearing grin.

His face was handsome, but strong-jawed and tough. That smile lightened it, took away the edge of ruthlessness she sensed was not far from the surface. He couldn't have got where he had by being Mr Nice Guy. That edge excited her.

'Lucky you threw it out the window, then,' she said. 'I seriously wonder about the advice in that thing.'

'Best thing I ever did was ignore it,' he said.

He kissed her lightly on the shoulder, the growth of his beard pleasantly rough. She felt a rush of intense triumph that she was here with him—finally. With her finger she traced around his face, exploring its contours, the feel of his skin, smooth in parts, rough with bristle in others. Yes, she could call this man *beautiful.*

He picked up a strand of her hair and idly twisted it between his fingers. 'What did you do to get over *your* divorce?'

The question surprised her. It wasn't something she

really wanted to remember. 'Became a hermit for a while. Like you, I felt an incredible sense of failure. I'm not used to failing at things. There was relief though, too. We got married when I was twenty-four. I'd only known him six months when he marched me down the aisle. Not actually an aisle. He'd been married before so we got hitched in the registry office.'

'Why the hurry?'

'He was seven years older than me. He wanted to start a family. I should have known better than to be rushed into it. Big mistake. Turned out I didn't know him at all. He showed himself to be quite the bully.'

She had ended up both fearing and hating him.

'Sounds like you had a lucky escape.'

'I did. But it wasn't pleasant at the time. No break-up ever is, is it? No matter the circumstances.'

Jake nodded assent. 'Mine dragged on too long.'

'I know. I was waiting, remember.'

'It got so delayed at the end because her new guy inserted himself into the picture. He introduced an element of ugliness and greed.'

Ugliness. Eliza didn't want to admit to Jake how scary *her* marriage had become. There hadn't been physical abuse, but she had endured some serious mental abuse. When she'd found herself getting used to it, even making excuses for Craig because she'd hated to admit she'd made a mistake in marrying him, she'd known it was time to get out. The experience had wounded her and toughened her. She'd vowed never again to risk getting tied up in something as difficult to extricate herself from as marriage.

'It took me a while to date again,' she said. 'I'd lost faith in my judgement of men. Man, did I date a few duds. And I turned off a few guys who were probably quite decent because of my interrogation technique. I found myself trying to discover anything potentially wrong about them before I even agreed to go out for a drink.'

Jake used her hair to tug her gently towards him for a quick kiss on her nose before he released her. 'You didn't interrogate me,' he said.

'I didn't need to. You weren't a potential date. When we first met at Andie and Dominic's wedding you were married. I could chat to you without expectation or agenda. You were an attractive, interesting man but off-limits.'

He picked up her hand, began idly stroking first her palm and then her fingers. Tingles of pleasure shot through her body right down to her toes. Nothing was off-limits now.

'You were so lovely, so smart—and so accepting of me,' he said. 'It was a revelation. You actually seemed interested in what I had to say.'

As his ex hadn't been? Eliza began to see how unhappy Jake had been. Trapped in a past-its-use-by-date marriage. Bound by what seemed to have been misplaced duty and honour.

'Are you kidding me?' she said. 'You're such a success story and only a few years older than me. I found you fascinating. And a surprise. All three Party Queens had been expecting a stereotype geek—not a guy who looked like an athlete. You weren't arrogant either, which was another surprise.'

'That was a social situation. I can be arrogant when it comes to my work and impatient with people who don't get it.'

His expression hardened and she saw again that underlying toughness. She imagined he would be a demanding boss.

'I guess you have to be tough to have got where you are—a self-made man. Your fortune wasn't handed to you.'

'I see you've done your research?'

'Of course.' She'd spent hours on the internet, looking him up—not that'd she'd admit to the extent of her 'research'. 'There's a lot to be found on Jake Marlowe. The media loves a rags-to-riches story.'

'There were never rags. Clothes from charity shops, yes, but not rags.' The tense lines of his mouth belied his attempt at a joke. 'My mother did her best to make life as good for me as she could. But it wasn't easy. Struggle Street is not where I ever wanted to stay. Or go back to. My ex never really got that.'

'You married young. Why?' There hadn't been a lot in the online information about his early years.

He replied without hesitation. 'Fern was pregnant. It was the right thing to do.'

'I thought you didn't have kids?'

'I don't. She lost the baby quite early.'

'That's sad…' Her voice trailed away. *Very* sad. She would not—could not—reveal how very sad the thought made her. How her heart shrank a little every time she thought about having kids.

'The pregnancy was an accident.'

'Not a ploy to force your hand in marriage?' She had always found the 'oldest trick in the book' to be despicable.

'No. We'd been together off and on since my last year of high school. Marriage was the next step. The

pregnancy just hurried things along. Looking back on
it, though, I can see if she hadn't got pregnant we might
not have ended up married. It was right on the cusp,
when everything was changing. Things were starting
to take off in a big way for the company Dominic and
I had started.'

'You didn't try for a baby again?'

'Fern didn't want kids. Felt the planet was already
over-populated. That it was irresponsible to have children.'

'And you?' She held her breath for his answer.

During her infrequent forays into dating she'd found
the children issue became urgent for thirty-somethings.
For women there was the very real fact of declining
fertility. And men like her ex thought they had biological clocks too. Craig had worried about being an old
dad. He'd been obsessed with being able to play active sports with his kids. Boys, of course, in particular. Having come from a farming family, where boys
had been valued more than girls, that had always ran-
kled with her.

Jake's jaw had set and she could see the hard-headed
businessman under the charming exterior.

'I've never wanted to have children. My ex and I
were in agreement about not wanting kids.'

'What about in the future?'

He shook his head. 'I won't change my mind. I don't
want to be a father. *Ever.*'

'I see,' she said, absorbing what he meant. What it
meant to her. It was something she didn't want to share
with him at this stage. She might be out of here this
afternoon and never see him again.

'My support group devoted a lot of time to warnings

about women who might try and trap a wealthy, newly single guy into marriage by getting pregnant,' he said.

'Doesn't it take two to get a woman pregnant?'

'The odds can be unfairly stacked when one half of the equation lies about using contraception.'

Eliza pulled a face. 'Those poor old gold-diggers again. I don't know *any* woman I could label as a gold-digger, and we do parties through all echelons of Sydney society. Are there really legions of women ready to trap men into marriage by getting pregnant?'

'I don't know about legions, but they definitely exist. The other guys in that group were proof of that. It can be a real problem for rich men. A baby means lifetime child support—that's a guaranteed income for a certain type of woman.'

'But surely—'

Jake put up a hand at her protest. 'Hear me out. Some of those men were targeted when they were most vulnerable. It's good to be forewarned. I certainly wouldn't want to find myself caught in a trap like that.'

'Well, you don't have to worry about me,' she said. In light of this conversation, she *had* to tell him. 'I can't—'

He put a finger over her mouth. She took it between her teeth and gently nipped it.

'Be assured I don't think of you like that,' he said. 'Your fierce independence is one of the things I like about you.'

'Seriously, Jake. Listen to me. I wouldn't be able to hold you to ransom with a pregnancy because…because…' How she hated admitting to her failure to be able to fulfil a woman's deepest biological purpose. 'I… I can't have children.'

He stilled. 'Eliza, I'm sorry. I didn't know.'

'Of course you didn't know. It's not something I blurt out too often.' She hated to be defined by her infertility. Hated to be pitied. *Poor Eliza—you know she can't have kids?*

'How? Why?'

'I had a ruptured appendix when I was twelve years old. No one took it too seriously at first. They put my tummy pains down to something I ate. Or puberty. But the pain got worse. By the time they got me to hospital—remember we lived a long way from the nearest town—the appendix had burst and septicaemia had set in.'

Jake took her hand, gripped it tight. 'Eliza, I'm so sorry. Couldn't the doctors have done something?'

'I don't know. I was twelve and very ill. Turned out I was lucky to be alive. Unfortunately no one told me, or my parents, what damage it had done to my reproductive system—the potential for scar tissue on the fallopian tubes. I wasn't aware of the problem until I tried to have a baby and couldn't fall pregnant. Only then was I told that infertility is a not uncommon side effect of a burst appendix.'

He frowned. 'I really don't know what to say.'

'What *can* you say? Don't try. You can see why I don't like to talk about it.'

'You said your ex wanted to start a family? Is that why you split?'

'In part, yes. He was already over thirty and he really wanted to have kids. His *own* kids. Adoption wasn't an option for him. I wanted children too, though probably later rather than sooner. I never thought I wouldn't be able to have a baby. I always believed I would be a mother. And one day a grandmother. Even a great-grandmother. I'll miss out on all of that.'

'I'm sorry, Eliza,' he said again.

She couldn't admit to him—to anyone—her deep, underlying sense of failure as a woman. How she grieved the loss of her dream of being a mother, which had died when the truth of her infertility had been forced into her face with the results of scans and X-rays.

'They don't test you until after a year of unsuccessfully trying to get pregnant,' she said. 'Then the tests take a while. My ex couldn't deal with it. By that stage he thought he'd invested enough time in me.'

Jake spat out a number of choice names for her ex. Eliza didn't contradict him.

'By that stage he'd proved what a dreadful, controlling man he was and I was glad to be rid of him. Still, my sense of failure was multiplied by his reaction. He actually used the word "barren" at one stage. How old-fashioned was that?'

'I'd call it worse than that. I'd call it cruel.'

'I guess it was.' One of a long list of casual cruelties he'd inflicted on her.

Eliza hadn't wanted to introduce such a heavy subject into her time with Jake, those memories were best left buried.

'Where did you meet this jerk—your ex, I mean—and not know what he was really like? Online?'

'At work. I told you when I first met you how I started my working life as an accountant at a magazine publishing company. I loved the industry, and jumped at the chance to move into the sales side when it came up. My success there and my finance background gave me a good shot at a publisher's role with another company. He was my boss at the new company.'

'You married the boss?'

'The classic cliché,' she said. 'But what made him a good publisher made him a terrible husband. Now, I don't want to waste another second talking about him. He's in my past and staying there. I moved to a different publishing company—and a promotion—and never looked back. Then when the next magazine I worked on folded—as happens in publishing—Andie, Gemma and I started Party Queens.'

'And became the most in-demand party-planners in Sydney,' he said.

Sometimes it seemed to Eliza as if her brief marriage had never happened. But the wounds Craig had left behind him were still there. She'd been devastated at the doctor's prognosis of infertility caused by damaged fallopian tubes. Craig had only thought about what it meant to *him*. Eliza had realised she couldn't live with his mental abuse. But she still struggled with doubt and distrust when it came to men.

Thank heaven she'd had the sense to insist they signed a pre-nup. He'd had no claim on her pre-marriage apartment, and she'd emerged from the marriage financially unscathed.

'I suppose your "dating after divorce" advice included getting a watertight pre-nup before any future nuptials?' she said. 'I'm here to suggest it's a good idea. To add to all his faults, my ex proved to be an appalling money-manager.'

'Absolutely,' he said. 'That was all tied up with the gold-digger advice.'

Eliza laughed, but she was aware of a bitter edge to

her laughter. 'I interrogated all my potential dates to try and gauge if they were controlling bullies like my ex. You're on the lookout for gold-diggers. Are we too wounded by our past experiences just to accept people for what they appear to be?'

Jake's laugh added some welcome levity to the conversation. 'You mean the way you and I have done?' he said.

Eliza thought about that for a long moment. Of course. That was exactly what they'd done. They'd met with no expectation or anticipation.

'Good point,' she conceded with an answering smile. 'We just discovered we liked each other, didn't we? In the old-fashioned boy-meets-girl way. The best man and the bridesmaid.'

'But then had to wait it out until we could pursue the attraction,' he said.

She reached out and placed her hand on his cheek, reassuring herself that he really was there and not one of the dreams she'd had of him after she'd got home from Montovia. 'And here we are.'

When it came to a man, Eliza had never shut down her good sense to this extent. She wasn't looking any further ahead than right here, right now. She'd put caution on the back burner and let her libido rule and she intended to enjoy the unexpected gift of time with this man she'd wanted since she'd first met him.

Jake went to pull her closer. Mmm, they could start all over again... Just then her stomach gave a loud, embarrassing rumble. Eliza wished she could crawl under the sheets and disappear.

But Jake smiled. 'I hear you. My stomach's crying out the same way. It's long past lunchtime.'

As he got up from the bed the sheet fell from him. Naked, he walked around the room with a complete lack of inhibition. He was magnificent. Broad shoulders tapered down to a muscled back and the most perfect male butt, his skin there a few shades lighter than his tan elsewhere. He was just gorgeous. The prototype specimen of the human male. She felt a moment's regret for humanity that his genes weren't going to be passed on to a new generation. That combination of awesome body and amazing brain wouldn't happen too often.

She had nothing to be ashamed of about her own body—she worked out and kept fit. But she suddenly felt self-conscious about being naked and tugged the sheets up over her chest. It was only this morning that she'd encountered him at the airport lounge. She wasn't a one-night stand kind of person. Or hadn't been up until now. *Until Jake.*

He slung on a pale linen robe. 'I'll go check what food there is in the kitchen while you get dressed.'

Eliza remembered their frantic dash into the bedroom a few hours before. 'My bag with my stuff in it—it's still in the car.'

'It's in the dressing room,' said Jake, pointing in the direction of the enormous walk-in closet. 'I went out to the car after you fell asleep. Out like a light and snoring within seconds.'

Eliza gasped. 'I do *not* snore!' *Did* she? It was so long since she'd shared a bed with someone she wouldn't know.

'Heavy breathing, then,' Jake teased. 'Anyway, I brought your bag in and put it in there.'

'Thank you,' said Eliza.

The bathroom was as luxurious as the rest of the house. All natural marble and bold, simple fittings like in an upscale hotel. She quickly showered. Then changed into a vintage-inspired white sundress with a full skirt and wedge-heeled white sandals she'd bought just for the vacation.

Standing in front of the mirror, she ran a brush through the tangles of her hair. Then scrutinised her face to wipe the smeared mascara from under her eyes. Thank heavens for waterproof—it hadn't developed into panda eyes. She slicked on a glossy pink lipstick.

Until now she hadn't planned on wearing make-up at all this vacation. But hooking up with Jake had changed all that. Suddenly she felt the need to look her most feminine best. She wanted more than a one-night stand. Four days stretched out ahead of her in Port Douglas and she hoped she'd spend all of them with Jake. After that—who knew?

CHAPTER SIX

JAKE WAITED IMPATIENTLY for Eliza to get dressed and join him in the living area. He couldn't believe she was here in his house with him. It was more than he could have hoped for when he'd intercepted her at the airport.

He welcomed the everyday sounds of running taps, closing doors, footsteps tapping on the polished concrete floors. Already Eliza's laughter and her sweet scent had transformed the atmosphere. He'd like to leave that sexy trail of clothing down the hallway in place as a permanent installation.

This house was a prize in a property portfolio that was filled with magnificent houses. But it seemed he had always been alone and unhappy here. There had been many opportunities for infidelity during the waning months of his marriage but he'd never taken them up. He'd always thought of himself as a one-woman man.

That mindset had made him miserable while he'd refused to accept the demise of his marriage. But meeting Eliza, a woman as utterly different from his ex as it was possible to be, had shown him a different possible path. However he hadn't been ready to set foot on that path. Not so soon after the tumult and turmoil that had driven him off the rails to such detriment to his business.

Extricating himself from a marriage gone bad had made him very wary about risking serious involvement again. He'd stayed away from Eliza for that very reason—she did not appear to be a pick-her-up-and-put-her-down kind of woman, and he didn't want to hurt her. Or have his own heart broken. Ultimately, however, he'd been *compelled* to see her again—despite the advice from his divorce support group and his own hard-headed sense of self-preservation.

She'd told him he'd been over-thinking the situation. Too concerned about what *might* happen before they'd even started anything. Then she'd gifted him with this no-strings interlude. *No expectations or promises, no apologies if it didn't work out.* What more could a man ask for?

Eliza had surprised and enthralled him with her warm sensuality and lack of inhibition. He intended to make the most of her four days in Port Douglas. Starting by ensuring that she spent the entire time of her vacation with him.

He sensed Eliza's tentative entry into the room from the kitchen before he even heard her footsteps. He looked up and his breath caught at the sight of her in a white dress that was tight at the waist and then flared to show off her slim figure and shapely legs.

He gave a wolf whistle of appreciation. 'You're looking very babelicious.'

Her eyes narrowed in sensual appraisal as she slowly looked him up and down. 'You don't look too smokin' bad yourself,' she said.

He'd quickly gone into one of the other bathrooms, showered and changed into shorts and a T-shirt.

'Comfortable is my motto,' he said. He dragged at his neck as if at an imaginary necktie. 'I hate getting trussed up in a suit and tie.'

'I don't blame you. I feel sorry for guys in suits, sweltering in the heat of an Australian summer.'

'It's a suit-free zone at *my* company headquarters.' A tech company didn't need to keep corporate dress rules.

'I enjoy fashion,' she said. 'After a childhood spent in jeans and riding boots—mostly hand-me-downs from my brothers—I can't get enough girly clothes.'

'Your dress looks like something from my grandma's wardrobe,' he said. Then slammed his hand against his forehead 'That didn't come out quite as I meant it to. I meant from when my grandma was young.'

'You mean it has a nice vintage vibe?' she said. 'I take that as a compliment. I love retro-inspired fashion.'

'It suits you,' he said. He thought about saying that he preferred her in nothing at all. Decided it was too soon.

She looked around her. 'So this is your vacation house? It's amazing.'

'Not bad, is it?'

The large open-plan rooms, with soaring ceilings, contemporary designer furniture, bold artworks by local artists, were all designed to showcase the view and keep the house cool in the tropical heat of far north Queensland. As well as to withstand the cyclones that lashed at this area of the coast with frequent violence.

'He says, with the modest understatement of a billionaire…' she said.

Jake liked her attitude towards his wealth. He got irritated by people who treated him with awe because of it. Very few people knew the truth about his past. How closely he'd courted disaster. But a mythology had built up around him and Dominic—two boys from nowhere who had burst unheralded into the business world.

He had worked hard, but he acknowledged there had been a certain element of luck to his meteoric success. People referred to him as a genius, but there were other people as smart as he—smarter, even—who could have identified the same need for ground-breaking software. He'd been in the right place at the right time and had been savvy enough to recognise it and act on it—to his and Dominic's advantage. Then he'd had the smarts to employ skilled programmers to get it right. Come to think of it, maybe there *was* a certain genius to that. Especially as he had replicated his early success over and over again.

'I found some gourmet pizzas in the freezer,' he said. 'I shoved a couple of them in the oven. There's salad too.'

'I wondered what smelled so good,' she said. 'Breakfast seems a long time ago.'

'We can eat out for dinner. There are some excellent restaurants in Port Douglas—as you no doubt know.'

'Yes…' she said. Her brow pleated into a frown. 'But I need to check in at my resort. I haven't even called them. They might give my room to someone else.'

'Wouldn't you rather stay here?' he asked.

Her eyes narrowed. 'Is that a trick question?'

'No tricks,' he said. 'It's taken us a long time—

years—to get the chance to spend time together. Why waste more time to-ing and fro-ing from a resort to here? This is more private. This is—'

'This is fabulous. Better than any resort. Of course I'd like to stay here. But is it too soon to be—?'

'Over-thinking this?'

'You're throwing my own words right back at me,' she said, with her delightful curving smile.

Her eyes seemed to reflect the colour of the sea in the vista visible through the floor-to-ceiling windows that looked out over the beach to the far reaches of the Pacific Ocean. He didn't think he'd ever met anyone with eyes of such an extraordinary blue. Eyes that showed what she was feeling. Right now he saw wariness and uncertainty.

'I would very much like to have you here with me,' he said. 'But of course it's entirely your choice. If you'd rather be at your resort I can drive you there whenever you want.'

'No! I... I want to be with you.'

'Good,' he said, trying to keep his cool and not show how gratified he was that he would have her all to himself. 'Then stay.'

'There's just one thing,' she said hesitantly. 'I feel a little...uncomfortable about staying here in a house you shared with your ex-wife. I notice there aren't any feminine touches in the bathroom and dressing room. But I—'

'She's never visited here,' he said. 'I bought this house as my escape when things started to get untenable in my marriage. That was not long before I met you at Dominic's wedding.'

'Oh,' she said.

'Does that make you feel better?' he asked.

She nodded. 'Lots better.'

He stepped closer, placed his hands on her shoulders, looked into her eyes. 'You're the only woman who has stayed here. Apart from my mother, who doesn't count as a woman.'

'I'm sure she'd be delighted to know that,' Eliza said, strangling a laugh.

'You know what I mean.' Jake felt more at home with numbers and concepts than words. Especially words evoking emotion and tension.

'Yes. I do. And I'm honoured to be the first.'

He took her in his arms for a long, sweet kiss.

The oven alarm went off with a raucous screech. They jumped apart. Laughed at how nervous they'd seemed.

'Lunch is ready,' he said. He was hungry, but he was tempted to ignore the food and keep on kissing Eliza. Different hungers required prioritising.

But Eliza had taken a step back from him. 'After we eat I need to cancel my resort booking,' she said. 'I'll have to pay for today, of course, but hopefully it will be okay for the other days. Not that I care, really. After all I—'

'I'll pay for any expense the cancellation incurs.'

He knew straight away from her change of expression that he'd made a mistake.

'You will *not* pay anything,' she said. 'That's my responsibility.'

Jake backed down straight away, put up his hands as if fending off attack. That was one argument he had no intention of pursuing. He would make it up to her in other ways—make sure she didn't need to spend another cent during her stay. He would organise everything.

'Right. I understand. My credit cards will remain firmly in my wallet unless you give me permission to wield them.'

She pulled a rueful face. 'Sorry if I overreacted. My independence is very important to me. I get a bit prickly when it's threatened. I run my own business and my own life. That's how I like it. And I don't want to ever have to answer to anyone again—for money or anything else.'

'Because of your ex-husband? You described him as controlling.'

'To be honest, he's turned me off the entire concept of marriage. And before him I had a domineering father who thought he had the right to rule my life even after I grew up.'

Jake placed his hand on her arm. 'Hold it right there. Don't take offence—I want to hear more. But right now I need food.' His snack on the plane seemed a long time ago.

She laughed. 'I grew up with three brothers. I know the rules. Number one being never to stand between a hungry man and his lunch.'

Jake grinned his relief at her reply. 'You're right. The pizza will burn, and I'm too hungry to wait to heat up more.'

'There are *more*?'

'The housekeeper has stocked the freezer with my favourite foods. She doesn't live in. I like my privacy too much for that. But she shops for me as well as keeps the house in order.'

'Unlimited pizza? Sounds good to me.'

From the look of her slim body, her toned muscles, he doubted Eliza indulged in pizza too often. But at his height and activity level he needed to eat a lot. There had been times when he was a kid he'd been hungry. Usually the day before his mother's payday, when she'd stretched their food as far as it would go. That would never happen again.

He headed for the oven. 'Over lunch I want to hear about that country upbringing of yours,' he said. 'I grew up here in Queensland, down on the Gold Coast. Inland Australia has always interested me.'

'Trust me, it was *not* idyllic. Farming is tough, hard work. A business like any other. Only with more variables out of the farmer's control.'

She followed him through the kitchen to the dining area, again with a view of the sea. 'I was about to offer to set the table,' she said. 'But I see you've beaten me to it.'

'I'm domesticated. My mother made sure of that. A single mum working long hours to keep a roof over our heads couldn't afford to have me pulling less than my weight,' he said.

That was when he'd chosen to *be* at home, of course. For a moment Jake wondered what Eliza would think of him if he revealed the whole story of his youth. She seemed so moralistic, he wondered if she could handle the truth about him. Not that he had any intention of telling her. There was nothing he'd told her already that couldn't be dug up on an online search—and she'd already admitted to such a search. The single mum. The hard times. His rise to riches in spite of a tough start. The untold story was in a sealed file never to be opened.

'It must have been tough for her. Your mother, I mean.'

'It was,' he said shortly. 'One of the good things about having money is that I can make sure she never has to worry again.' As a teenager he'd been the cause of most of her worries. As an adult he tried to make it up to her.

'So your mother lets you take care of her?'

'I don't give her much of a choice. I owe her so much and I will do everything I can to repay her. I convinced her to let me buy her a house and a business.'

'What kind of business did you buy for her?'

Of course Eliza would be interested in that. She was a hard-headed businesswoman herself.

'She worked as a waitress for years. Always wanted her own restaurant—thought she could do it better. Her café in one of the most fashionable parts of Brisbane is doing very well.' Again, this was nothing an online search wouldn't be able to find.

'There's obviously a family instinct for business,' she said.

He noted she didn't ask about his father, and he didn't volunteer the information.

'There could be something in that,' he said. 'She's on vacation in Tuscany at the moment—doing a residential Italian cooking course and having a ball.'

Eliza smiled. 'Not just a vacation. Sounds like it's work as well.'

'Isn't that the best type of work? Where the line between work and interest isn't drawn too rigidly?'

'Absolutely,' she said. 'I always enjoyed my jobs in publishing. But Party Queens is my passion. I couldn't imagine doing anything else now.'

'From what I hear Party Queens is so successful you never will.'

'Fingers crossed,' she said. 'I never take anything for granted, and I have to be constantly vigilant that we don't slip down from our success.'

She seated herself at the table, facing the view. He swooped the pizza onto the table with an exaggerated flourish, like he'd seen one of his mother's waiters do. 'Lunch is served, *signorina*,' he said.

Eliza laughed. 'You're quite the professional.'

'A professional heater-upper of pizza?'

'It isn't burned, and the cheese is all bubbly and perfect. You can take credit for *that*.'

Jake sat down opposite her. He wolfed down three large slices of pizza in the time it took Eliza to eat one. 'Now, tell me about life on the sheep ranch,' he said. And was surprised when her face stilled and all laughter fled from her expression.

Eliza sighed as she looked across the table at Jake. Her appetite for pizza had suddenly deserted her. 'Are you sure you want to hear about that?'

Did she want to relive it all for a man who might turn out to be just a fling? He'd told her something of the childhood that must have shaped the fascinating man he had become. But it was nothing she didn't already know. She really didn't like revisiting *her* childhood and adolescence. Not that it had been abusive, or anything near it. But she had been desperately unhappy and had escaped from home as soon as she could.

'Yes,' he said. 'I want to know more about you, Eliza.'

His gaze was intense on her face. She didn't know

him well enough to know what was genuine interest and what was part of a cultivated image of charm.

'Can I give you the short, sharp, abbreviated version?' she said.

'Go ahead,' he said, obviously bemused.

She took a deep, steadying breath. 'How about city girl at heart is trapped in a rural backwater where boys are valued more than girls?'

'It's a start.'

'You want more?'

He nodded.

'Okay…smart girl with ambition has hopes ridiculed.'

'Getting there,' he said. 'What's next?'

'Smart girl escapes to city and family never forgives her.'

'Why was that?' He frowned.

She knew there was danger now—of her voice getting wobbly. 'No easy answer. How about massive years-long drought ruins everything?' She took in another deep breath. 'It's actually difficult to make light of such disaster.'

'I can see that,' he said.

She wished he'd say there was no need to go on, but he didn't.

'Have you ever seen those images of previously lush green pastures baked brown and hard and cracked? Where farmers have to shoot their stock because there's no water, no feed? Shoot sheep that have not only been bred on your land so you care about their welfare, but also represent income and investment and your family's daily existence?'

'Yes. I've seen the pictures. Read the stories. It's terrible.'

'That was my family's story. Thankfully my father didn't lose his land or his life, like others did, before the rains eventually came. But he changed. Became harsher. Less forgiving. Impossible to live with. He took it out on my mother. And nothing *I* could do was right.'

Jake's head was tilted in what seemed like real interest. 'In what way?'

'Even at the best of times life in the country tends to be more traditional. Men are outdoors, doing the hard yakka—do you have that expression for hard work in Queensland?'

'Of course,' he said.

'Men are outside and women inside, doing the household chores to support the men. In physical terms it makes a lot of sense. And a lot of country folk like it just the way it's always been.'

'But you didn't?'

'No. School was where I excelled—maths and legal studies were my forte. My domestic skills weren't highly developed. I just wasn't that interested. And I wasn't great at farm work either, though I tried.' She flexed her right arm so her bicep showed, defined and firm. 'I'm strong, but not anywhere near as strong as my brothers. In my father's eyes I was useless. He wouldn't even let me help with the accounts; that was not my business. In a time of drought I was another mouth to feed and I didn't pull my weight.'

She could see she'd shocked Jake.

'Surely your father wouldn't really have thought that?' he said.

She remembered he'd grown up without a father.

'I wanted to be a lawyer. My father thought lawyers were a waste of space. My education was a drain on the farm. Looking back, I can see now how desperate he must have been. If he'd tried to communicate with me I might have understood. But he just walked all over me—as usual.'

'Seems like I've got you to open a can of worms. I'm sorry.'

She shrugged. 'You might as well hear the end of it. I was at boarding school. One day when I was seventeen I was called to the principal's office to find my father there to take me home so I could help my mother. For good. It was my final year of high school. I wasn't to be allowed to sit my end-of-school exams.'

Jake frowned. 'You're right—your dad must have been desperate. If there was no money to feed stock, school fees would have been out of the question.'

'For *me*. Not for my younger brother. My father found the fees for *him*.' She couldn't keep the bitterness from her voice. 'A boy who was never happier than when he was goofing off.'

'So the country girl went home? Is that how the story ended?'

She shook her head. 'Thankfully, no. I was a straight-A student—the school captain.'

'Why does that not surprise me?' said Jake wryly.

'The school got behind me. There was a scholarship fund. My family were able to plead hardship. I got to sit my final exams.'

'And blitzed them, no doubt?'

'Top of the state in three out of five subjects.'

'Your father must have been proud of you then.'

'If he was, he never said so. I'd humiliated him with the scholarship, and by refusing to go home with him.'

'Hardly a humiliation. Half of the eastern states were in one of the most severe droughts in Australia's history. Even *I* knew that at the time.'

'Try telling *him* that. He'd call it pride. I'd call it pig-headed stubbornness. The only thing that brought me and my father together was horses. We both loved them. I was on my first horse before I was two years old. The day our horses had to go was pretty well the end of any real communication between me and my father.'

There was real sympathy in his green eyes. 'You didn't have to shoot—?'

'We were lucky. A wonderful horse rescue charity took them to a different part of the state that wasn't suffering as much. The loss hit my father really hard.'

'And you too?'

She bowed her head. 'Yes.'

Jake was quiet for a long moment before he spoke again. 'You don't have to talk about this any more if you don't want to. I didn't realise how painful it would be for you.'

'S'okay,' she said. 'I might as well gallop to the finish.' She picked up her fork, put it down again, twisted a paper serviette between her fingers. 'Country girl wins scholarship to university in Sydney to study business degree. Leaves home, abandoning mother to her menfolk and a miserable marriage. No one happy about it but country girl…' Her voice trailed away.

Jake got up from the table and came to her side. He leaned down from behind her and wrapped big, strong muscular arms around her. 'Country girl makes good in the big city. That's a happy ending to the story.'

'I guess it is,' she said, leaning back against him, enjoying his strength and warmth, appreciating the way he was comforting her. 'My life now is just the way I want it.'

Except she couldn't have a baby. Underpinning it all was the one area of her life she'd been unable to control, where the body she kept so healthy and strong had let her down so badly.

She twisted around to look up at him. 'And Day One of my vacation is going perfectly.'

'So how about Days Two, Three and Four?' he said. 'If you were by yourself at your resort what would you be doing?'

'Relaxing. Lying by the pool.'

'We can do that here.'

'Swimming?'

'The pool awaits,' he said, gesturing to the amazing wet-edge pool outside the window, its aquamarine water glistening in the afternoon sunlight.

'That water is calling to me,' she said, twisting herself up and out of the chair so she stood in the circle of his arms, looking up at him. She splayed her hands against his chest, still revelling in the fact she could touch him.

For these few days he was hers.

His eyes narrowed. 'I'm just getting to know you, Eliza. But I suspect there's a list you want to check off before you fly home—you might even have scheduled some activities in to your days.'

'List? Schedules?' she said, pretending to look

around her. 'Have you been talking to Andie? She always teases me about the way I order my day.'

'I'm not admitting to anything,' he said. 'So there *is* a list?'

'We-e-ell…' She drew out the word. 'There *are* a few things I'd like to do. But only if you want to do them as well.'

'Fire away,' he said.

'One: go snorkelling on the Great Barrier Reef. Two: play golf on one of the fabulous courses up here. Then—'

Jake put up one large, well-shaped hand in a halt sign. 'Just wait there. Did I hear you say "play golf"?'

'Uh, yes. But you don't have to, of course. I enjoy golf. When I was in magazine advertising sales it was a very useful game to play. I signed a number of lucrative deals after a round with senior decision-makers.'

He lifted her up and swooped her around the room. 'Golf! The girl plays *golf*. One of my favourite sports.'

'You being a senior decision-maker and all,' she said with a smile.

'Me being a guy who likes to swing a club and slam a little white ball,' he said.

'In my case a neon pink ball. I can see it better on the fairway,' she said.

'She plays with a pink ball? Of *course* she does. Are you the perfect woman, Eliza Dunne?' He sounded more amused than mocking. 'I like snorkelling and diving too. Port Douglas is the right place to come for that. All can be arranged. Do you want to start checking off your list with a swim?'

'You bet.'

He looked deep into her face. Eliza thrilled to the message in his green eyes.

'The pool is very private. Swimsuits are optional.'

Eliza smiled—a long, slow smile of anticipation. 'Sounds very good to me.'

CHAPTER SEVEN

ELIZA SOON REALISED that a vacation in the company of a billionaire was very different from the vacation she had planned to spend on her own. Her own schedule of playing tourist and enjoying some quiet treatments in her resort spa had completely gone by the board.

That was okay, but she hadn't had any time to plan her strategy to keep the company thriving without the hands-on involvement of Gemma, Crown Princess of Montovia—and that worried her. Of course Princess Gemma's name on the Party Queens masthead brought kudos by the bucketload—and big-spending clients they might otherwise have struggled to attract. However, Gemma's incredible skills with food were sorely missed. Party Queens was all Eliza had in terms of income and interest. She needed to give the problem her full attention.

But Jake was proving the most enthralling of distractions.

She had stopped insisting on paying for her share of the activities he had scheduled for her. Much as she valued her independence, she simply couldn't afford a vacation Jake-style. Her wish to go snorkelling on the Great Barrier Reef had been granted—just her and

Jake on a privately chartered glass-bottom boat. Their games of golf had been eighteen holes on an exclusive private course with a waiting list for membership. Dinner was at secluded tables in booked-out restaurants.

Not that she was complaining at her sudden elevation in lifestyle, but there was a nagging feeling that she had again allowed herself to be taken over by a man. A charming man, yes, but controlling in his own quietly determined way.

When she'd protested Jake had said he was treating her, and wanted to make her vacation memorable. It would have seemed churlish to disagree. Just being with him was memorable enough—there was no doubt he was fabulous company. But she felt he was only letting her see the Jake he wanted her to see—which was frustrating. It was almost as if there were two different people: pre-divorce Jake and after-divorce Jake. After she'd spilled about her childhood, about her fears for the business, she'd expected some reciprocal confidences. There had been none but the most superficial.

On the afternoon of Day Four, after a long walk along the beach followed by a climb up the steep drive back home, Eliza was glad to dive into Jake's wet-edge pool. He did the same.

After swimming a few laps she rested back against him in the water, his arms around her as they both kicked occasionally to keep afloat. The water was the perfect temperature, and the last sunlight of the day filtered through the palm trees. Tropical birds flew around the trees, squawking among themselves as they settled for the evening. In the distance was the muted sound of the waves breaking on the beach below.

'This is utter bliss,' she said. 'My definition of heaven.'

The joy in her surroundings, in *him*, was bittersweet as it was about to end—but she couldn't share that thought with Jake. *This was just a four-day fling.*

'In that case you must be an angel who's flown down to keep me company,' he said.

'That's very poetic of you,' she said, twisting her head to see his face.

He grinned. 'I have my creative moments,' he replied as he dropped a kiss on her forehead.

It was a casual kiss she knew didn't mean anything other than to signify their ease with the very satisfying physical side of this vacation interlude.

'I could see *you* with a magnificent set of angel man wings, sprouting from your shoulder blades,' she said. 'White, tipped with gold.' *And no clothes at all.*

'All the better to fly you away with me,' he said. 'You must have wings too.'

'Blue and silver, I think,' she mused.

She enjoyed their light-hearted banter. After three days with him she didn't expect anything deeper or more meaningful. He was charming, fun, and she enjoyed being with him.

But he wasn't the Jake Marlowe who had so intrigued her with hints of hidden depths when she'd first met him. That Jake Marlowe had been as elusive as the last fleeting strains of the Strauss waltz lilting through the corridor as she had fled that ballroom in Montovia. She wondered if he had really existed outside her imagination. Had she been so smitten with his fallen angel looks that she'd thought there was more there for her than physical attraction?

'We did an angel-themed party a few months ago,' she said. 'That's what made me think about the wings.'

'You feasted on angel food cake, no doubt?'

'A magnificent celestial-themed supper was served,' she said. 'Star-shaped cookies, rainbow cupcakes, cloud-shaped meringues. Gemma planned it all from Montovia and Andie made sure it happened.'

The angel party had worked brilliantly. The next party, when Gemma had been too caught up with her royal duties to participate fully in the planning, hadn't had quite the same edge. Four days of vacation on, and Eliza was still no closer to finding a solution to the lack of Gemma's hands-on presence in the day-to-day running of the company. Party Queens was heading to crisis point.

'Clever Gemma,' said Jake. 'Tristan told me she's shaken up all the stodgy traditional menus served at the castle.'

'I believe she has,' Eliza said. 'She's instigated cooking programmes in schools, too. They're calling her the people's princess, she told me. Gemma's delighted.'

'No more than Tristan is delighted with Gemma.'

Gemma and Tristan had found true love. Whereas *she* had found just a diverting interlude with Jake. After the royal wedding both Gemma and Andie had expressed high hopes for romance between the best man and the bridesmaid. Eliza had denied any interest. But deep in Eliza's most secret heart she'd entertained the thought too. She couldn't help a sense of regret that it so obviously wasn't going to happen.

Idly, Eliza swished her toes around in the water. 'They call these wet-edge pools infinity pools, don't they? Because they stretch out without seeming to end?'

'That's right,' he said.

'In some way these four days of my vacation seemed to have gone on for ever. In another they've flown. Only this evening left.'

'Can you extend your break? By another day, perhaps?'

She shook her head. 'There's still the Gemma problem to solve. And there are some big winter parties lined up for the months ahead. I have back-to-back appointments for the day after I get back. Some of which took me weeks to line up.'

'That's what happens when you run a successful business,' he said.

'As you know only too well,' she said. Party Queens was insignificant on the corporate scale compared to *his* company.

'I'd have trouble squeezing in another day here, too,' Jake said. 'I'm out of the country a lot these days. Next week I fly to Minnesota in the United States, to meet with Walter Burton on a joint venture between him and Dominic in which I'm involved. My clients are all around the world. I'll be in Bangalore in India the following week. Singapore the week after that.'

'Are you ever home?' Her voice rose.

'Not often, these days. My absences were a bone of contention with my ex. She was probably right when she said that I didn't give her enough time.'

Eliza paused. 'It doesn't sound like you have any more time now.'

Jake took a beat to answer. 'Are you any different? Seems to me you're as career-orientated as I am. How much room does Party Queens leave for a man in your life?'

'Not much,' she admitted. She felt bad that she had

fielded so many phone calls while she'd been with him. But being a party planner wasn't a nine-to-five week-day-only enterprise. 'The business comes first, last and in between.'

It could be different! she screamed silently. *For the right man.* But was she being honest with herself? Could Jake be the right man?

'Seems to me we're both wedded to our careers,' he said slowly. 'To the detriment of anything else.'

'That's not true,' she said immediately. Then thought about it. 'Maybe. If neither of us can spare another day to spend here together when it's been so perfect.'

'That tells *me* something,' he said, his voice guarded.

Eliza swallowed hard against the truth of his words. The loss of *what might have been* hurt.

'It could be for the best,' she said, trying to sound matter of fact, but inwardly weeping over a lost op-portunity.

She didn't know him any better than on Day One. His body, yes. His heart and soul—no. Disappointment stabbed deep that Jake hadn't turned out to be the man she'd expected him to be when he'd been whirling her around that fairytale ballroom.

Why had she ever hoped for more? When she thought about it, the whole thing with Jake hadn't seemed quite real. From the moonlit terrace in Mon-tovia to the way he'd intercepted her at the airport and whisked her away to this awesome house perched high above the beach, it had all had an element of fantasy.

Jake held her for a long moment without replying. She could feel the thudding of his heart against her back. The water almost stilled around them, with only the occasional slap against the tiled walls of the pool. She had a heart-stopping feeling he was saying goodbye.

Finally he released her, then swam around her so he faced her, with her back to the edge of the pool. His hair was dark with water and slick to his head. Drops of water glistened on the smooth olive of his skin. Her heart contracted painfully at how handsome he looked. At how much she wanted him.

But although they got on so well, both in bed and out of it, it was all on the surface. Sex and fun. Nothing deeper had developed. She needed something more profound. She also needed a man who cared enough to make time to see her—and she him.

'Do you really think so?' he asked.

'Sometimes things are only meant to be for a certain length of time,' she said slowly. 'You can ruin them by wanting more.'

Jake's heart pounded as he looked down into Eliza's face. She'd pushed her wet hair back from her face, showing the perfect structure of her cheekbones, the full impact of her eyes. Water from the pool had dripped down over her shoulders to settle in drops on the swell of her breasts. The reality of Eliza in a bikini had way exceeded his early fantasies.

Eliza was everything he'd hoped she'd be and more. She was an extraordinary woman. They were compatible both in bed and out. They even enjoyed the same sports. But she'd been more damaged by her divorce than he had imagined. Not to mention by the tragedy of her inability to have a baby.

The entire time he'd felt he had to tread carefully around her, keeping the conversation on neutral topics, never digging too deep. For all her warmth and laughter and seeming openness, he sensed a prickly barrier around her. And then there was her insistence on answering her phone at all but their most intimate of moments. Eliza seemed so determined to keep her independence—there appeared little room for compromise. And if there was one lesson he'd learned from his marriage it was that compromise was required when two strong personalities came together as a couple.

She was no more ready for a serious relationship than he was.

Day Four was practically done and dusted—and so, it seemed, was his nascent relationship with Eliza.

And yet… He couldn't tolerate the thought of this being a final goodbye. There was still something about her that made him want to know more.

'We could catch up again some time, when we find ourselves in each other's cities,' he said.

'Absolutely.'

She said it with an obviously forced enthusiasm that speared through him.

'I'd like that.'

She placed her hand on his cheek, cool from the water, looked into his eyes. It felt ominously like a farewell.

'Jake, I'm so glad we did this.'

He had to clear his throat to speak. 'Me too,' he managed to choke out. There was a long pause during which the air seemed heavy with words unsaid before he spoke again. 'We have mutual friends. One day we might get the chance to take up where we left off.'

'Yes,' she said. 'That would be nice.'

Nice? Had all that passion and promise dwindled to *nice?*

Maybe that was what happened in this brave new world of newly single dating. Jake couldn't help a nagging sense of doubt that it should end like this. Had they missed a step somewhere?

'Jake, about our mutual friends…?' she said.

'Yes?' he said.

'I didn't tell them I'd met you here. Can Dominic be discreet?'

'He doesn't know we caught up with each other either.'

'Shall we keep it secret from them?' she asked. 'It would be easier.'

'As far as they're concerned we went our separate ways in Port Douglas,' he said.

He doubted Dominic would be surprised to hear it had turned out that way. He had warned Jake that, fond as he was of Eliza, she could be 'a tough little cookie'. Jake had thought there was so much more to her than that. Perhaps Dominic had been right.

'That's settled, then,' she said. There was an air of finality to her words.

Eliza swam to the wide, shallow steps of the pool, waded halfway up them, then turned back. Her petite body packed a powerfully sexy punch in her black bikini. High, firm breasts, a flat tummy and narrow waist flaring into rounded hips and a perfectly curved behind. Perhaps he'd read too much into this episode. *It was just physical—nothing more.* A fantasy fulfilled.

'I need to finish packing,' she said. 'Then I can enjoy our final dinner without worrying.'

That was it? 'Eliza, don't go just yet. I want to tell you—'

She paused, turned back to face him. Their gazes met for a long moment in the dying light of the day. Time seemed to stand still.

'I've booked a very good restaurant,' he said.

'I'll… I'll look forward to it,' she said. She took the final step out of the pool. 'Don't forget I have an early start in the morning.'

'I'll be ready to drive you to Cairns,' he said.

He dreaded taking that journey in reverse with her, when the journey here from the airport had been so full of promise and simmering sensuality. Tomorrow's journey would no doubt be followed by a stilted farewell at the airport.

'That's so good of you to offer,' she said with excess politeness. 'But I didn't cancel my return shuttle bus trip. It would be easier all round if we said goodbye here tomorrow morning.'

'You're sure, Eliza?' He made a token protest.

'Absolutely sure,' she said, heading towards the house without a backward glance.

Jake watched her, his hands fisted by his sides. He fancied blue angel wings unfurling as she prepared to fly right out of his life.

It was stupid of him ever to have thought things with Eliza could end any other way.

CHAPTER EIGHT

TEN WEEKS LATER Eliza sat alone in her car, parked on a street in an inner western suburb of Sydney, too shaken even to think about driving away from an appointment that had rocked her world. She clutched her keys in her hand, too unsteady to get the key into the ignition.

Eliza hated surprises. She liked to keep her life under control, with schedules and timetables and plans. Surprises had derailed her life on more than one occasion. Most notably the revelation that her burst appendix had left her infertile. But in this case the derailment was one that had charged her with sheer bubbling joy in one way and deep, churning anxiety in the other.

She was pregnant.

'It would take a miracle for you to get pregnant.'

Those had been her doctor's words when Eliza had told her of her list of symptoms. Words that had petered out into shock at the sight of a positive pregnancy test.

That miracle had happened in Port Douglas, with Jake—most likely the one time there had been a slip with their protection. Eliza hadn't worried. After all, she couldn't get pregnant.

Seemed she could.

And she had.

She laid her hand on her tummy, still flat and firm. But there was a tiny new life growing in there. *A baby.* She could hardly believe it was true, still marvelled at the miracle. But she had seen it.

Not *it*.

Him or her.

The doctor had wanted an ultrasound examination to make absolutely sure there wasn't an ectopic pregnancy in the damaged tube.

Active—like me, had been Eliza's first joyous thought when she'd seen the image of her tiny baby, turning cartwheels safe and sound inside her womb. Her second thought had been of loneliness and regret that there was no one there to share the miraculous moment with her. But she wanted this more than she had ever wanted anything in her life.

Her baby.

Eliza realised her cheeks were wet with tears. Fiercely, she scrubbed at her eyes.

Her third thought after the initial disbelief and shock had been to call Jake and tell him. There was absolutely no doubt he was the father.

His baby.

But how could she? He'd made it very clear he didn't *ever* want to be a father.

Dear heaven, she couldn't tell him.

He would think she was one of the dollar signs flashing gold-diggers he so despised. What had he said?

'A baby means lifetime child support—that's a guaranteed income for a certain type of woman.'

She dreaded the scorn in his eyes if she told him.

You know I told you I couldn't have a baby? Turns out I'm pregnant. You're going to be a daddy.

And what if he wanted her not to go forward with the pregnancy? No way—ever—would that be an option for her.

How on earth had this happened?

'Nature can be very persistent,' her doctor had explained. 'The tube we thought was blocked must not have been completely blocked. Or it unblocked itself.'

It really was a miracle—and one she hugged to herself.

She was not daunted by the thought of bringing the baby up by herself. Not that she believed it would be easy. But she owned her own home—a small terraced house in Alexandria, not far from the converted warehouse that housed the Party Queens headquarters. And Party Queens was still doing well financially, thanks to her sound management and the talent and drive of her business partners. And a creative new head chef was working out well. The nature of the business meant her hours could be flexible. Andie had often brought baby Hugo in when he was tiny, and did so even now, when he was a toddler. Eliza could afford childcare when needed—perhaps a nanny. Though she was determined to raise her child herself, with minimal help from nannies and childminders.

Her impossible dream had come true. *She was going to be a mother.* But the situation with her baby's father was more of a nightmare.

Eliza rested her head on her folded arms on top of the steering wheel, slumped with despair. *Pregnant from a four-night stand.* By a man she hadn't heard from since he'd walked her down the steep driveway that led away from his tropical hideaway and waved her goodbye.

Now he'd think she'd tried to trap him.

'I certainly wouldn't want to find myself caught in a trap like that,' he'd said, with a look of horror on his handsome face.

Eliza raised her head up off her folded arms. Took a few deep, steadying breaths. She wouldn't tell Jake. Nor would she tell her best friends about her pregnancy. Not yet. Not when both their husbands were friends with Jake.

If her tummy was this flat now, hopefully she wouldn't show for some time yet. Maybe she could fudge the dates. Or say the baby had been conceived by donor and IVF. The fact that Jake lived in Brisbane would become an advantage once she couldn't hide her pregnancy any longer. He wouldn't have to see her and her burgeoning bump.

But what if the baby looked like Jake? People close to Jake, like Andie and Dominic, would surely twig to the truth. *What if...what if...what if?* She covered her ears with her hands, as if to silence the questions roiling in her brain. But to no effect.

Was it fair *not* to tell him he was going to be a father? If she didn't make any demands on him surely he wouldn't believe she was a gold-digger? Maybe he would want to play some role in the baby's life. She wouldn't fight him if he did. It would be better for the baby. The baby who would become a child, a teenager, a person. A person with the right to know about his or her father.

It was all too much for her to deal with. She put her hand to her forehead, then over her mouth, suddenly feeling clammy and nauseous again.

The sickness had been relentless—so had the bone-deep exhaustion. She hadn't recognised them as symptoms of pregnancy. Why would she when she'd believed herself to be infertile?

Instead she had been worried she might have some terrible disease. Even when her breasts had started to become sensitive she had blamed it on a possible hormonal disturbance. She'd believed she couldn't conceive right up until the doctor's astonished words: *'You're pregnant.'*

But why would Jake—primed by both his own experience with women with flashing dollar signs in their eyes and the warnings of what sounded like a rabid divorce support group—believe her?

She was definitely in this on her own.

Eliza knew she would feel better if she could start making plans for her future as a single mother. Then she would feel more in control. But right now she had to track down the nearest bathroom. No wonder she had actually lost weight rather than put it on, with this morning, noon and night sickness that was plaguing her.

Party Queens was organising a party to be held in two weeks' time—the official launch of a new business venture of Dominic's in which Jake held a stake. No doubt she would see him there. But she would be officially on duty and could make their contact minimal. Though it would be difficult to deal with. And not just because of her pregnancy. She still sometimes woke in the night, realising she had been dreaming about Jake and full of regrets that it hadn't worked out between them.

CHAPTER NINE

THE NEARER JAKE got to Dominic's house in Sydney for the launch party, the drier his mouth and the more clammy his hands on the wheel of the European sports car he kept garaged there. Twelve weeks since he'd seen Eliza and he found himself feeling as edgy as an adolescent. Counting down the minutes until he saw her again.

The traffic lights stayed on red for too long and he drummed his fingers impatiently on the steering wheel.

For most of the time since their four-day fling in Port Douglas he'd been out of the country. *But she'd rarely been out of his mind.* Jake didn't like admitting to failure—but he'd failed dismally at forgetting her. From the get-go he'd had trouble accepting the finality of their fling.

The driveway up to his house in Port Douglas had never seemed so steep as that morning when he had trudged back up it after waving Eliza off on the shuttle bus. He'd pushed open his door to quiet and emptiness and a sudden, piercing regret. Her laughter had seemed to dance still on the air of the house.

No matter how much he'd told himself he was cool about the way his time had gone with her, he hadn't been able to help but think that by protecting himself he had talked himself out of something that might have been special. Cheated himself of the chance to be with a woman who might only come along once in a lifetime.

He'd had no contact with her at all since that morning, even though Party Queens were organising this evening's launch party. Dominic had done all the liaising with the party planners. Of course he had—he was married to the Design Director.

By the time he reached Dominic's house, Jake was decidedly on edge. He sensed Eliza's presence as soon as he was ushered through the door of Dominic's impressive mansion in the waterfront suburb of Vaucluse. Was it her scent? Or was it that his instincts were so attuned to Eliza they homed in on her even within a crowd? He heard the soft chime of her laughter even before he saw her. Excitement and anticipation stirred. Just seeing Eliza from a distance was enough to set his heart racing.

He stood at a distance after he'd found her, deep in conversation with a female journalist he recognised. This particular journalist had been the one to label Dominic—one of the most generous men Jake had ever known—with the title of 'Millionaire Miser'.

Andie and Party Queens had organised a party on Christmas Day two years ago that had dispelled *that* reputation. Planning that party was how Andie had met Dominic. And a week after Christmas Dominic had arranged a surprise wedding for Andie. Jake had flown down from Brisbane to be best man, and that wedding was where he'd met Eliza for the first time.

Jake looked through the wall of French doors that

opened out from the ballroom of Dominic's grand Art Deco house to the lit-up garden and swimming pool beyond. He remembered his first sight of Eliza, exquisite in a flowing pale blue bridesmaid's dress, white flowers twisted through her dark hair. She had laughed up at him as they'd shared in the conspiracy of it all: the bride had had no idea of her own upcoming nuptials.

Jake had been mesmerised by Eliza's extraordinary blue eyes, captivated by her personality. They had chatted the whole way through the reception. He'd been separated from Fern at that stage, but still trying to revive something that had been long dead. Not wanting to admit defeat. Eliza had helped him see how pointless that was—helped him to see hope for a new future just by being Eliza.

Now she wasn't aware that he was there, and he watched her as she chatted to the journalist, her face animated, her smile at the ready. She was so lovely—and not just in looks. He couldn't think of another person whose company he enjoyed more than Eliza's. *Why had he let her go?*

He couldn't bear it if he didn't get some kind of second chance with her. He'd tried to rid himself of the notion that he was a one-woman man. After all, a billionaire bachelor was spoiled for choice. He didn't have to hunt around to find available woman—they found *him*. Theoretically, he could date a string of them—live up to his media reputation. Since Port Douglas he'd gone out with a few women, both in Australia and on his business travels. Not one had captured his interest. None had come anywhere near Eliza.

Tonight she looked every inch the professional, but with a quirky touch to the way she was dressed that was perfectly appropriate to her career as a party planner. She wore a full-skirted black dress, with long, tight, sheer sleeves, and high-heeled black stilettos. Her hair was twisted up behind her head and finished with a flat black velvet bow. What had she called her style? Retro-inspired? He would call the way she dressed 'ladylike'. But she was as smart and as business-savvy as any guy in a suit and necktie.

Did she feel the intensity of his gaze on her? She turned around, caught his eye. Jake smiled and nodded a greeting, not wanting to interrupt her conversation. He was shocked by her reaction. Initially a flash of delight lightened her face, only to be quickly replaced by wariness and then a conscious schooling of her features into polite indifference.

Jake felt as if he had been kicked in the gut. *Why?* They'd parted on good terms. He'd even thought he'd seen a hint of tears glistening in her eyes as she'd boarded the shuttle bus in Port Douglas. They'd both been aware that having mutual friends would mean they'd bump into each other at some stage. She must have known he would be here tonight—he was part of the proceedings.

He strode towards her, determined to find out what was going on. Dismissing him, she turned back to face the journalist. Jake paused mid-stride, astounded at her abruptness. Then it twigged. Eliza didn't want this particular newshound sniffing around for an exclusive featuring the billionaire bachelor and the party planner.

Jake changed direction to head over to the bar.

He kept a subtle eye on Eliza. As soon as she was free he headed towards her, wanting to get her attention before anyone else beat him to it.

'Hello,' he said, for all the world as if they weren't anything other than acquaintances with mutual friends. He dropped a kiss on her cool, politely offered cheek.

'Jake,' Eliza said.

This was Eliza the Business Director of Party Queens speaking. Not Eliza the lover, who had been so wonderfully responsive in his arms. Not Eliza his golfing buddy from Port Douglas, nor Eliza his bikini-clad companion frolicking in the pool.

'So good that you could make it down from Brisbane,' the Business Director said. 'This is a momentous occasion.'

'Indeed,' he said.

Momentous because it was the first time they'd seen each other after their four-day fling? More likely she meant it was momentous because it was to mark the occasion not only of the first major deal of Dominic's joint venture with the American billionaire philanthropist Walter Burton, but also the setting up the Sydney branch of Dominic's charity, The Underground Help Centre, for homeless young people.

'Walter Burton is here from Minnesota,' Eliza said. 'I believe you visited with him recently.'

'He flew in this morning,' he said.

Jake had every right to be talking to Eliza. He was one of the principals of the deal they were celebrating tonight. Party Queens was actually in *his* employ.

However, when that pushy journalist's eyes narrowed with interest and her steps slowed as she walked by him and Eliza, Jake remembered she'd been in Montovia to report on the royal wedding. As best man and bridesmaid, he and Eliza had featured in a number of photo shoots and articles. If it was rumoured they'd had an affair—and that was all it had been—it would be big tabloid news.

He gritted his teeth. There was something odd here. Something else. Eliza's reticence could not be put down just to the journalist's presence.

Jake leaned down to murmur in her ear, breathed in her now familiar scent, sweet and intoxicating. 'It's good to see you. I'd like to catch up while I'm in Sydney.'

Eliza took a step back from him. 'Sorry—not possible,' she said. She gave an ineffectual wave to indicate the room, now starting to fill up with people. The action seemed extraordinarily lacking in Eliza's usual energy. 'This party is one of several that are taking up all my time.'

So what had changed? Work had always seemed to come first with Eliza. Whereas *he* was beginning to see it shouldn't. That there should be a better balance to life.

'I understand,' he said. But he didn't. 'What about after the party? Catch up for coffee at my apartment at the wharf?' He owned a penthouse apartment in a prestigious warehouse conversion right on the harbour in inner eastern Sydney.

Eliza's lashes fluttered and she couldn't meet his eyes. 'I'm sorry,' she said again. 'I… I'm not in the mood for company.'

Jake was too flabbergasted to say anything. He eventually found the words. 'You mean not in the mood for *me*?'

She lifted her chin, looked up at him. For once he couldn't read the expression in those incredible blue eyes. Defiance? Regret? *Fear?* It both puzzled and worried him.

'Jake, we agreed to four days only.'

The sentence sounded disconcertingly well-rehearsed. A shard of pain stabbed him at her tone.

'We left open an option to meet again, did we not?' He asked the question, but he thought he could predict the answer.

She put her hand on her heart and then indicated him in an open-palmed gesture that would normally have indicated togetherness. 'Me. You. We tried it. It…it didn't work.'

The slight stumble on her words alerted him to a shadow of what looked like despair flitting across her face. *What was going on?*

'I don't get it.' Jake was noted for his perseverance. He wouldn't give up on Eliza easily.

A spark of the feisty Eliza he knew—or thought he knew—flashed through.

'Do I have to analyse it? Isn't it enough that I just don't want to be with you again?'

He didn't believe her. Not when he remembered her unguarded expression when she'd first noticed him this evening.

There was something not right here.

Or was he being arrogant in his disbelief that Eliza simply didn't want him in her life? That the four days had proved he wasn't what she wanted? Was he falling back into his old ways? Unable to accept that a woman he wanted no longer wanted *him*? That wanting to persevere with Eliza was the same kind of blind stubbornness that had made him hang on to a marriage in its death throes—to the ultimate misery of both him and his ex-wife? Not to mention the plummeting profit margins of his company—thankfully now restored.

'Is there someone else?' he asked.

A quick flash of something in her eyes made him pay close attention to her answer.

'Someone else? No. Not really.'

'What do you mean "not really"?'

'Bad choice of words. There's no other man.'

He scrutinised her face. Noticed how pale she looked, with dark shadows under her eyes and a new gauntness to her cheekbones. Her lipstick was a red slash against her pallor. More colour seemed to leach from her face as she spoke.

'Jake. There's no point in going over this. It's over between us. Thank you for understanding.' She suddenly snatched her hand to her mouth. 'I'm afraid I have to go.'

Without another word she rushed away, heading out of the ballroom and towards the double arching stairway that was a feature of the house.

Jake was left staring after her. Dumbfounded. Stricken with a sudden aching sense of loss.

He knew he had to pull himself together as he saw Walter Burton heading for him. He pasted a smile on his face. Extended his hand in greeting.

The older man, with his silver hair and perceptive pale eyes, pumped his hand vigorously. 'Good to see you, Jake. I'm having fun here, listening to people complain that it's cold for June. Winter in Sydney is a joke. I'm telling them they don't know what winter is until they visit Minnesota in February.'

'Of course,' Jake said.

He was trying to give Walter his full attention,

but half his mind was on Eliza as he looked over the heads of the people who now surrounded him, nodded vaguely at guests he recognised. *Where had she gone?*

Walter's eyes narrowed. 'Lady trouble?' he observed.

'Not really,' Jake said. He didn't try to deny that Eliza was his lady. Dominic and Andie had had to stage a fake engagement because of this older man's moral stance. He found himself wishing Eliza really was his lady, with an intensity that hurt so much he nearly doubled over.

'Don't worry, son, it'll pass over,' Walter said. 'They get that way in the first months. You know…a bit erratic. It gets better.'

Jake stared at him. 'What do you mean?'

'When a woman's expecting she—'

Jake put up his hand. 'Whoa. I don't know where you're going with this, Walter. Expecting? Not Eliza. She…she can't have children.' And Eliza certainly didn't *look* pregnant in that gorgeous black dress.

'Consider me wrong, then. But I've had six kids and twice as many grandkids.' Walter patted his rather large nose with his index finger. 'I've got an instinct for when a woman's expecting. Sometimes I've known before she was even aware herself. I'd put money on it that your little lady is in the family way. I'm sorry for jumping the gun if she hasn't told you yet.'

Reeling, Jake managed to change the subject. But Walter's words kept dripping through his mind like the most corrosive of acids.

Had she tricked him? His fists clenched by his sides. Eliza? A scheming gold-digger? Trying to trap him with the oldest trick in the book? She had sounded so convincing when she'd told him about the burst appendix and her subsequent infertility. Was it all a lie? If so, what else had she lied about?

He felt as if everything he'd believed in was falling away from him.

Then he was hit by another, equally distressing thought. If she wasn't pregnant, was she ill?

One thing was for sure—she was hiding something from him. And he wouldn't be flying back to Brisbane until he found out what it was.

CHAPTER TEN

JAKE USUALLY NEVER had trouble sleeping. But late on the night of the launch party, back in his waterfront apartment, he tossed and turned. The place was luxurious, but lonely. He'd had high hopes of bringing Eliza back here this evening. To talk, to try and come to some arrangement so he could see more of her. If they'd ended up in bed that would have been good too. He hadn't been with anyone else since her. Had recoiled from kissing the women he'd dated.

Thoughts of his disastrous encounter with her kept him awake for what seemed like most of the night. And then there was Walter's observation to nag at him. Finally, at dawn, he gave up on sleep and went for a run. Vigorous physical activity helped his thought processes, he'd always found.

In the chill of early morning he ran up past the imposing Victorian buildings of the New South Wales Art Gallery and through the public green space of The Domain.

He paused to do some stretches at the end of the peninsula at Mrs Macquarie's Chair—a bench cut into a sandstone slab where it was reputed a homesick early governor's wife had used to sit and watch for sailing ships coming from Great Britain. The peaceful spot gave a panoramic view of Sydney Harbour: the 'coat hanger' bridge and the white sails of the Opera House. Stray clouds drifting around the buildings were tinted pink from the rising sun.

Jake liked Sydney and thought he could happily live in this city. Brisbane seemed all about the past. In fact he was thinking about moving his company's headquarters here. He had wanted to talk to Eliza about that, to put forward the idea that such a move would mean he'd be able to see more of her if they started things up between them again. Not much point now.

The pragmatic businessman side of Jake told him to wipe his hands of her and walk away. Eliza had made it very clear she didn't want him around. A man who had graduated from a dating after divorce workshop would know to take it on the chin, cut his losses and move on. After all, they'd only been together for four days, three months ago.

But the more creative, intuitive side of him, which had guided him through decisions that had made him multiple millions, wouldn't let him off that easily. Even if she'd lied to him, tricked him, deceived him—and that was only a suspicion at this stage—he had a strong feeling that she needed him. And he needed to find out what was going on.

He'd never got a chance to chat with her again at the party—she had evaded him and he'd had official duties to perform. But he'd cancelled his flight back to Brisbane, determined to confront her today.

Jake ran back home, showered, changed, ate breakfast. Predictably, Eliza didn't reply to his text and her phone went to voicemail. He called the Party Queens headquarters to be told Eliza was working at home today. Okay, so he would visit her at home—and soon.

He hadn't been to Eliza's house before, but he knew where it was. Investment-wise, she'd been canny. She'd bought a worker's terraced cottage in an industrial area of the inner city just before a major push to its gentrification. The little house, attached on both sides, looked immaculately restored and maintained. Exactly what he'd expect from Eliza.

It sat on one level, with a dormer window in the roof, indicating that she had probably converted the attic. External walls were painted the colour of natural sandstone, with windows and woodwork picked out in white and shades of grey. The tiny front garden was closed off from the sidewalk by a black wrought-iron fence and a low, perfectly clipped hedge.

Jake pushed open the shiny black gate and followed the black-and-white-tiled path. He smiled at the sight of the front door, painted a bold glossy red to match the large red planter containing a spiky-leaved plant. Using the quaint pewter knocker shaped like a dragonfly, he rapped on the door.

He heard footsteps he recognised as Eliza's approaching the door. They paused while, he assumed, she checked out her visitor through the peephole. Good. He was glad she was cautious about opening her door to strangers.

The pause went on for rather too long. Was she going to ignore him? He would stay here all day if he had to. He went to rap again but, with his hand still on its knocker, the door opened and she was there.

Jake didn't often find himself disconcerted to the

point of speechlessness. But he was too shocked to
greet her.

This was an Eliza he hadn't seen before: hair di-
shevelled, face pale and strained with smudges of last
night's make-up under her eyes. But what shocked him
most was her body. Dark grey yoga pants and a snug
pale grey top did nothing to disguise the small but definite baby bump. Her belly was swollen and rounded.

Eliza's shoulders slumped, and when she looked up
at him her eyes seemed weary and dulled by defeat. In
colour more denim than sapphire.

She took a deep breath and the rising of her chest
showed him that her breasts were larger too. The dress
she'd worn the previous night had hidden everything.

'Yes, I'm pregnant. Yes, it's yours. No, I won't be
making any claims on you.'

Jake didn't mean to blurt out his doubt so baldly, but
out it came. 'I thought you couldn't conceive.'

'So did I. That I'm expecting a baby came as a total
surprise.' She gestured for him to follow her. 'Come
in. Please. This isn't the kind of conversation I want
to have in the street.'

The cottage had been gutted and redesigned into an
open usable space, all polished floors and white walls.
It opened out through a living area, delineated by carefully placed furniture, to a kitchen and eating area. Two
black cats lay curled asleep on a bean bag, oblivious to
the fact that Eliza had company. At the back, through
a wall of folding glass doors, he saw a small courtyard
with paving and greenery. A staircase—more sculpture than steps—led up to another floor. The house was
furnished in a simple contemporary style, with care-

fully placed paintings and ornaments that at another time Jake might have paused to examine.

'I need to sit down,' Eliza said, lowering herself onto the modular sofa, pushing a cushion behind her back, sighing her relief.

'Are you okay?' Jake asked, unable to keep the concern from his voice. A sudden urge to protect her pulsed through him. But it was as if there was an invisible barrier flashing *Don't Touch* around her. The dynamic between them was so different it was as if they were strangers again. He hated the feeling. Somehow he'd lost any connection he'd had with her, without realising how or why.

She gave that same ineffectual wave she'd made the night before. It was as if she were operating at half-speed—like an appliance running low on battery. 'Sit down. Please. You towering over me is making me feel dizzy.'

She placed her hand on her bump in a protective gesture he found both alien and strangely moving.

He sat down on the sofa opposite her. 'Morning sickness?' he asked warily. He wasn't sure how much detail he'd get in reply. And he was squeamish about illness and female things—very squeamish.

'I wish,' she said. 'It's non-stop nausea like I couldn't have imagined. All day. All night.' She closed her eyes for a moment and shook her head before opening them again. 'I feel utterly drained.'

Jake frowned. 'That doesn't sound right. Have you seen your doctor?'

'She says some women suffer more than others and nausea is a normal part of pregnancy. Though it's got much worse since I last saw the doctor.' She grimaced.

'But it's worth it. Anything is worth it. I never thought I could have a baby.'

'So what happened? I mean, how—?'

She linked her hands together on her lap. 'I can see doubt in your eyes, Jake. I didn't lie to you. I genuinely believed I was infertile. Sterile. Barren. All those things my ex called me, as if it was my fault. But I'm not going to pretend I'm anything but thrilled to be having this baby. I… I don't expect you to be.'

Jake had believed in Eliza's honesty and integrity. She had sounded so convincing when she'd told him about her ruptured appendix and the damage it had caused. Her personal tragedy. And yet suddenly she was pregnant. Could a man be blamed for wanting an explanation?

'So what happened to allow—?' He couldn't find a word that didn't sound either clinical or uncomfortably personal.

'My doctor described it as a miracle. Said that a microscopic-sized channel clear in a sea of scar tissue must have enabled it to happen. I can hardly believe it myself.' A hint of a wan smile tilted the corners of her mouth. 'Though the nausea never allows me to forget.'

'Are you sure—?'

She leaned forward. 'Sure I'm pregnant? Absolutely. Up until my tummy popped out it was hard to believe.' She stilled. Pressed her lips together so hard they became colourless. 'You didn't mean that, did you? You meant am I sure the baby is yours.'

Her eyes clouded with hurt. Jake knew he had said inextricably the wrong thing. Though it seemed reasonable for him to want to be sure. He *still* thought it was reasonable to ask. They'd had a four-day fling and he hadn't heard a word from her since.

'I didn't mean—'

Her face crumpled. 'Yes, you did. For the record, I'll tell you there was no one else. There had been no one else for a long time and has been no one since. But feel free to ask for a DNA test if you want proof.'

He moved towards her. 'Eliza, I—'

Abruptly she got up from the sofa. Backed away from him. 'Don't come near me. Don't touch me. Don't quote your dating after divorce handbook that no doubt instructs you about the first question to ask of a scheming gold-digger trying to trap you.'

'Eliza, I'm sorry. I—'

She shrugged with a nonchalance he knew was an absolute sham.

'You didn't know me well at Port Douglas,' she said. 'I could have bedded a hundred guys over the crucial time for conception for all you knew. It's probably a question many men would feel justified in asking under the circumstances. But not *you* of *me*. Not after I'd been straightforward with you. Not when we have close friends in common. A relationship might not have worked for us. But I thought there was mutual respect.'

'There was. There is. Of course you're upset. Let me—'

'I'm not *upset*. I'm *disappointed*, if anything. Disappointed in *you*. Again, for the record, I will not ask anything of you. Not money. Not support. Certainly not your name on the birth certificate. I am quite capable of doing this on my own. *Happy* to do this on my own. I have it all planned and completely under control. You can just walk out that door and forget you ever knew me.'

Jake had no intention of leaving. If indeed this baby was his—and he had no real reason to doubt her—he would not evade his responsibilities. But before he had a chance to say anything further Eliza groaned.

'Oh, no. Not again.'

She slapped her hand over her mouth, pushed past him and ran towards the end of the house and, he assumed, the bathroom.

He waited for what seemed like a long time for her to do what she so obviously had to do. Until it began to seem too long. Worried, he strode through the living room to find her. That nagging sense that she needed him grew until it consumed him.

'Eliza! Answer me!' he called, his voice raw with urgency.

'I... I'm okay.' Her voice, half its usual volume, half its usual clarity, came from behind a door to his left.

The door slowly opened. Eliza put one foot in front of the other in an exaggerated way to walk unsteadily out. She clutched the doorframe for support.

Jake sucked in a breath of shock at how ashen and weak she looked. Beads of perspiration stood out on her forehead. He might not be a doctor, but every instinct told him this was not right. 'Eliza. Let me help you.'

'You...you're still here?' she said. 'I told you to leave.'

'I'm not going anywhere.'

'There...there's blood.' Her voice caught. 'There shouldn't be blood. I... I don't know what to do. Can you call Andie for me, please?'

Jake felt gutted that he was right there and yet not the first person she'd sought to help her.

She wanted him gone.

No way was he leaving her.

He took her elbow to steady her. She leaned into him and he was stunned at how thin she'd become since he'd last held her in his arms. Pregnant women were meant to put *on* weight, not lose it. *Something was very wrong*.

Fear grabbed his gut. He mustn't let her sense it. Panic would make it worse. She felt so fragile, as if she might break if he held her too hard. Gently he lifted her and carried her to a nearby chair. She moaned as he settled her into it.

She cradled her head in her hands. 'Headache. Now I've got a headache.' Her voice broke into a sob.

Jake realised she was as terrified as he was. He pulled out his phone.

'Call Andie…' Her voice trailed away as she slumped into the chair.

He supported her with his body as he started to punch out a number with fingers that shook. 'I'm not calling Andie. I'm calling an ambulance,' he said, his voice rough with fear.

CHAPTER ELEVEN

WHEN ELIZA WOKE up in a hospital bed later that day, the first thing she saw was Jake sprawled in a chair near her bed. He was way too tall for the small chair and his long, blue-jeans-clad legs were flung out in front of him. His head was tilted back, his eyes closed. His hair looked as if he'd combed it through with his hands and his black T-shirt was crumpled.

She gazed at him for a long moment. Had a man ever looked so good? Her heart seemed to skip a beat. Last time she had seen him asleep he had been beside her in his bed at Port Douglas on Day Three. She had awoken him with a trail of hungry little kisses that had delighted him. Now here he was in a visitor's chair in a hospital room. She was pregnant and he had doubts that the baby was his. How had it come to this?

Eliza had only vague memories of the ambulance trip to the hospital. She'd been drifting in and out of consciousness. What she did remember was Jake by her side. Holding her hand the entire time. Murmuring a constant litany of reassurance. *Being there for her.*

She shifted in the bed. A tube had been inserted in the back of her left hand and she was attached to a drip. Automatically her hand went to her tummy. She was still getting used to the new curve where it had always been flat.

Jake opened his eyes, sat forward in his chair. 'You're awake.' His voice was underscored with relief.

'So are you. I thought you were asleep.' Her voice felt croaky, her throat a little sore.

He got up and stood by her bed, looked down to where her hand remained on her tummy. The concern on his face seemed very real.

'I don't know what you remember about this morning,' he said. 'But the baby is okay. *You're* okay.'

'I remember the doctor telling me. Thank heaven. And seeing the ultrasound. I couldn't have borne it if—'

'You'd ruptured a blood vessel. The baby was never at risk.'

She closed her eyes, opened them again. 'I felt so dreadful. I thought I must be dying. And I was so worried for the baby.'

'Severe dehydration was the problem,' he said.

She felt at a disadvantage, with him towering so tall above her. 'I can see how that happened. I hadn't even been able to keep water down. The nausea was so overwhelming. It's still there, but nothing like as bad.'

'Not your everyday morning sickness, according to your doctor here. An extreme form known as *Hyperemesis gravidarum.* Same thing that put the Duchess of Cambridge in hospital with her pregnancies, so a nurse told me.'

He sounded both knowledgeable and concerned. Jake here with her? The billionaire bachelor acting nurse? How had this happened?

'A lot of the day is a blur,' she said. 'But I remember the doctor telling me that. No wonder I felt so bad.'

'You picked up once the doctors got you on intravenous fluids.'

She raised her left wrist and looked up at the clear plastic bag hooked over a stand above. 'I'm still on them, by the looks of it.'

'You have to stay on the drip for twenty-four hours. They said you need vitamins and nutrients as well as fluids.'

Eliza reeled at the thought of Jake conversing with the doctors, discussing her care. It seemed surreal that he should be here, like this. 'How do you know all this? In fact, how come you're in my room?' Eliza didn't want to sound ungrateful. But she had asked him to leave her house. Though it was just as well he hadn't, as it had turned out.

'I admitted you to the hospital. They asked about my relationship to you. I told them I was your partner and the father of the baby. On those terms, it's quite okay for me to be in your room.'

'Oh,' she said. She slumped back on the pillows. Their conversation of this morning came flooding back. How devastated she'd felt when he'd asked if she sure he was the father. 'Even though you don't actually think the baby is yours?' she said dully.

He set his jaw. 'I never said that. I believed you couldn't get pregnant. You brushed me off at the party. Didn't tell me anything—refused to see me. Then I discovered you were pregnant. It's reasonable I would have been confused as to the truth. Would want to be sure.'

'Perhaps,' she conceded.

It hurt that his first reaction had been distrust. But she had no right to feel a sense of betrayal—they'd had a no-strings fling. They'd been lovers with no commitment whatsoever. And he was a man who had made it very clear he never wanted children.

'I believe you when you say the baby is mine, Eliza. It's unexpected. A shock. But I have no reason to doubt you.'

Eliza was so relieved at his words she didn't know what to say and had to think about her response. 'I swear you *are* the father. I would never deceive you about something so important.'

'Even about the hundred other men?' he said, with a hint of a smile for the first time.

She managed a tentative smile in return. 'There was only ever you.'

'I believe you,' he said.

'You don't want DNA testing to be certain? Because I—'

'No,' he said. 'Your word is enough.'

Eliza nodded, too overcome to say anything. She knew how he felt about mercenary gold-diggers. But the sincerity in his eyes assured her that he no longer put her in that category. If, indeed, he ever had. Perhaps she had been over-sensitive. But that didn't change the fact that he didn't want to be a father.

'I don't want to be a father—ever.'

How different this could have been in a different universe—where they were a couple, had planned the child, met the result of her pregnancy test with mutual joy. But that was as much a fantasy as those frozen in time moments of him whirling her around in a waltz, when the future had still been full of possibilities for Eliza and Jake.

Now here he was by her bedside, acting the concerned friend. She shouldn't read anything else into his care of her. Jake had only done for her what he would have done for any other woman he'd found ill and alone.

Eliza felt a physical ache at how much she still wanted him. She wondered—not for the first time—if she would *ever* be able to turn off her attraction to him. But physical attraction wasn't enough—no matter how good the sex. A domineering workaholic, hardly ever in the same country as her, was scarcely the man she would have chosen as the father of her child. Though his genes were good.

'Thank you for calling the ambulance and checking me in to the hospital,' she said. 'And thank you for staying with me. But can I ask you one more thing, please?' *Before we say goodbye.*

'Of course,' he said.

'Can you ask the hospital staff to fix their mistake with my room?' She looked around her. The room was more like a luxurious hotel suite than a hospital room. 'I'm not insured for a private room. They'll need to move me to a shared ward.'

'There's been no mistake,' he said. 'I've taken responsibility for paying your account.'

Eliza stared at him. '*What?* You can't do that,' she said.

'As far as the hospital is concerned I am the baby's father. I pay the bills.'

Eliza gasped. This wasn't right. She needed to keep control over her pregnancy and everything involved with it. 'That was a nice gesture, but I can't possibly accept your offer,' she said.

'You don't have a choice,' he said. 'It's already done.'

Eliza had never felt more helpless, lying in a hospital bed tied up to a drip and monitors. It wasn't a feeling she was used to. 'Jake, please don't make me argue over this.' She was feeling less nauseous, but she'd been told she had to avoid stress and worry as well as keep up fluids and nourishment. 'What happened to you keeping your credit cards in your wallet when it comes to me?'

'You can't have it both ways, Eliza. You want me to acknowledge paternity? That means I take financial responsibility for your care. It's not negotiable.'

This was the controlling side of Jake that had made her wary of him for more than a no-strings fling. 'You don't make decisions for me, Jake. I will not—'

At that moment a nurse came into the room to check on Eliza's drip and to take her temperature and blood pressure. Jake stepped back from the bed and leaned against the wall to let the nurse get on with what she needed to do.

'She's looking so much better now than when you brought her in,' the nurse said.

'Thankfully,' said Jake. 'I was very worried about her.'

Eliza fumed. The nurse was addressing Jake and talking about her as if she was some inanimate object. 'Yes, I *am* feeling much better,' she said pointedly to the nurse. But Jake's smile let her know he knew exactly what was going on—and found it amusing. Which only made Eliza fume more.

'That's what we want to hear,' said the nurse with

a cheerful smile, seemingly oblivious to the under-currents.

She was no doubt well meaning, but Eliza felt she had to assert herself. It was *her* health. *Her* baby. Under *her* control. 'When can I go home?' Eliza asked.

The nurse checked her chart. 'You have to be on the intravenous drip for a total of twenty-four hours.'

'So I can go home tomorrow morning?'

'If the doctor assesses you as fit to be discharged. Of course you can't leave by yourself, and there has to be someone at home to care for you.'

'That's okay,' said Jake, before Eliza could say anything. 'I'll be taking her home and looking after her.'

The nurse smiled. 'That's settled, then.'

'No, it's not. I—' Eliza protested.

'Thank you,' said Jake to the nurse.

Eliza waited until the nurse had left the room. 'What was that about?' she hissed.

Jake moved back beside her bed. 'I'll be picking you up when you're discharged from hospital tomorrow. We can talk about whether you'd like me to stay with you for a few days or whether I organise a nurse.'

She had to tilt her head back to confront him. 'Or how about I look after myself?' she said.

'That's not an option,' said Jake. 'Unless you want to stay longer in hospital. *Hyperemesis gravidarum* is serious. You have to keep the nausea under control and get enough nourishment for both your health and your baby's sake. You know all this. The doctor has told you that you're still weak.'

'That doesn't mean *you* have to take over, Jake.'

Eliza felt she was losing control of the situation and

she didn't like it one bit. At the same time she didn't want to do anything to risk harming the baby.

'You have another choice,' he said. 'You could move in with Andie. She's offered to have you to stay with her and Dominic.'

'You've spoken to Andie? But she doesn't know—'

'That you're pregnant? She does now. You asked me to call her this morning. So I did while you were asleep.'

'What did she say?' Andie would not appreciate being left out of the loop.

'She was shocked to find out you and I had had an affair and you'd kept it from her. And more than a little hurt that you didn't take her into your confidence about your pregnancy.'

'I would have, but I didn't want her telling...'

'Telling me?'

'That's right.'

'If I'd flown back to Brisbane this morning instead of coming to see you would you have *ever* told me?' His mouth was set in a grim line.

'I wasn't thinking that far ahead. I just didn't want you to think I was trying to trap you into something you didn't want. You were so vehement about gold-diggers. I... I couldn't bear the thought of seeing disgust in your eyes when you looked at me.'

'You will *never* see disgust in my eyes when it comes to you, Eliza,' he said. 'Disbelief that you would try to hide this from me, but not disgust. We have mutual friends. I would have heard sooner or later.'

'I would rather it had been later. I didn't want you trying to talk me out of it.'

The look of shock on his face told her she might have said the wrong thing.

'I would never have done that,' he said.

She realised how out-of-the-blue her situation had been for him. And how well he was handling it.

'I wasn't to know,' she said. 'After all, we hardly know each other.'

For a long moment Jake looked into her face—searching for what she didn't know.

Finally he spoke. 'That's true. But there should be no antagonism between us. Here isn't the time or the place to discuss how we'll deal with the situation on an ongoing basis.' He glanced down at his watch. 'Andie will be here to visit you soon. I'm going to go. I'll see you in the morning.'

Eliza's feelings were all over the place. She didn't know whether she could blame hormones for the tumult of her emotions. No way did she want Jake—or any other man—controlling her, telling her what to do with her life. But she had felt so safe and comforted with him by her side today. Because while her pregnancy had changed the focus of everything, it didn't change the attraction she'd felt for Jake from the get-go. He had been wonderful to her today. She wished she could beg him to stay.

'Before you leave, let me thank you again for your help today, Jake. I can't tell you how much I appreciate you being with me.'

'You're welcome,' he said. 'I'm just glad you're okay. And so glad I called by to your house this morning.'

She sat up straighter in an attempt to bring him closer. Put out her hand and placed it on his arm. 'I'm sorry,' she said. 'Not sorry about the baby—my miracle baby. But sorry our carefree fling had such consequences and that we've been flung back together again in such an awkward situation.'

'No need to apologise for that,' he said gruffly.

Jake kept up the brave front until he was out of the hospital and on the pavement. He felt totally strung out from the events of the last day. Everything had happened so quickly. He needed time to think it through and process it.

Thank heaven he hadn't encountered Andie on the way out. He'd liked Andie from the moment Dominic had first introduced him to her, on the day of their surprise wedding. Each time he met his friend's wife he liked her more. Not in a romantic way—although she was undoubtedly gorgeous. He liked the way Andie made his best friend so happy after the rotten hand life had dealt Dominic when it came to love. If Jake had had a sister, he would have wanted her to be just like Andie.

But Andie told it how it was. And Eliza was her dearest friend, whom she would defend with every weapon at hand. Jake wouldn't have appreciated a face-to-face confrontation with her on the steps of the hospital. Not when he was feeling so on edge. Not after the conversation he'd already had with her on the phone.

When he'd called to tell her Eliza was in hospital Andie been shocked to hear the reason. Shocked and yet thrilled for Eliza, as she knew how much her friend had wanted to have children but had thought she couldn't conceive.

'This is a miracle for her!' Andie had exclaimed, and had promptly started to sob on the phone. Which had been further proof—not that he'd needed it—that Eliza had not been lying. Then, in true sisterly fashion, Andie had hit Jake with some advice. Advice he hadn't thought he'd needed but he'd shut up and listened.

'Don't you hurt her, Jake,' she'd said, her voice still thick with tears. 'I had no idea you two had had a…a thing. Eliza is Party Queens family. *You're* family. She thinks she's so strong and independent, but this pregnancy will make her vulnerable. She's not some casual hook-up girl. You can't just write a cheque and walk away.'

'It's not like that—' he'd started to protest. But the harsh truth of it, put into words, had hit him like blows to the gut.

Eliza was connected to his life through his best friends, Dominic and Tristan, and their wives. He could argue all he liked that their fling had been a mutually convenient scratching of the itch of their attraction. But that sounded so disrespectful to Eliza. In his heart he knew he'd wanted much more time with her. Which was why he had been considering a move to Sydney. But Eliza's pregnancy had put everything on a very different footing.

Andie had continued. 'Oh, what the heck? This is none of my business. You're a big boy. *You* figure out what Eliza needs. And give it to her in spades.'

Jake was beginning to see what Eliza needed. And also what *he* needed. He'd never been so scared than when she'd passed out on the chair while they were waiting for the ambulance to arrive. In a moment of stricken terror he'd thought he was going to lose her. And it had hit him with the power of a sledgehammer hurtling towards his head how much she had come to mean to him—as a friend as well as a lover. Suddenly a life without Eliza in it in some way had become untenable.

But the phone call with Andie wasn't what had him still staggering, as if that sledgehammer really had connected. It was the baby.

First he'd been hit with the reality of absorbing the fact that Eliza was expecting a baby—and the realisation that it had irrevocably changed things between them. Then he'd been stricken by seeing Eliza so frighteningly ill. But all that had been eclipsed by the events at the hospital.

Once the medical team had stabilised Eliza with fluids—she'd been conscious enough to refuse any antinausea medication—they'd wheeled her down, with him in attendance, to have an ultrasound to check that all was well with her developing foetus.

The technician had covered Eliza's bump with a jelly—cold, and it had made her squeal—and then pressed an electronic wand over her bump. The device had emitted high-frequency soundwaves that had formed an image when they'd come into contact with the embryo.

Up until the moment when the screen had come alive with the image, the pregnancy had been an abstract thing to Jake. Even—if he were to be really honest with himself—an *inconvenient* thing. But there on the screen had appeared a *baby*. Only about six centimetres at this stage, the radiographer had explained, but a totally recognisable baby. With hands and feet and a *face*.

To the palpable relief of everyone in the room, a strong and steady amplified heartbeat had been clearly audible. The baby had been moving around and showing no signs of being affected by Eliza's inability to keep down so very little food over the last weeks. It had looked as if it was having a ball, floating in the amniotic fluid, secure in Eliza's womb.

Jake had felt as if his heart had stopped beating, and his lungs had gone into arrest as, mesmerised, he'd watched that image. He was a man who never cried but he'd felt tears of awe and amazement threatening to betray him. He hadn't been able to look at Eliza—the sheer joy shining from her face would have tipped him over. Without seeming to be aware she was doing it, she had reached for his hand and gripped it hard. All he'd been able to do was squeeze it back.

This was a real baby. A child. A *person*. Against all odds he and Eliza had created a new life.

What he had to do had become very clear.

CHAPTER TWELVE

THE NEXT DAY Eliza was surprised at how weak she still felt as Jake helped her up the narrow, steep stairs to her bedroom in the converted attic of her house. She usually bounded up them.

'Just lean on me,' he said.

'I don't want to lean on anyone,' she said, more crossly than she had intended.

Forcing herself to keep her distance from this gorgeous man was stressful. Even feeling weak and fatigued, she still fancied him like crazy. But way back in Port Douglas she'd already decided that wasn't enough. Just because she was pregnant it didn't change things.

'Sometimes you have to, Eliza.'

She knew he wasn't only referring to her taking the physical support his broad shoulders offered.

'You can't get through this on your own.'

There was an edge of impatience to his voice she hadn't heard before. Looking after her the way he'd done yesterday, and now today, wasn't part of their four-day fling agreement. That had been about uncomplicated fun and uninhibited sex. Now he must feel he was stuck with her when she was unwell. He couldn't be more wrong. She didn't need his help.

'I appreciate your concern, truly I do,' she said. 'You've been so good to me. But I'm not on my own. I have friends. My GP is only a block away. I spoke to her yesterday after you left the hospital. Both she and the practice nurse can make home visits if required.'

'You need to be looked after,' he said stubbornly.

Eliza's heart sank as she foresaw them clashing over this. She had been perturbed at how Jake had taken over her vacation—how much more perturbing was the thought that he might take over her life?

Eliza reached the top of the stairs. Took the few steps required to take her to her bed and sat down on the edge with a sigh of relief.

'I'd prefer to look after myself,' she said. 'I'm quite capable of it, you know.'

'It didn't look that way to me yesterday.' He swore under his breath. 'Eliza, what might have happened if I hadn't got here when I did? What if you'd passed out on the bathroom floor? Hit your head on the way down?'

She paused for a long moment. 'It's a very scary thought. I will never be able to thank you enough for being there for me, Jake. Why *did* you come to my house when you did?'

'The obvious. I didn't get why you blanked me at the party and I wanted an explanation.'

Her chin lifted. 'Why did you feel you were owed an explanation? We had a fling. I didn't want to pick up from where we left off. Enough said.'

'Now you're pregnant. That makes it very different. From where I stand, it doesn't seem like you're doing a very good job of looking after yourself.'

Her hackles rose. 'This is all very new to me. It's a steep learning curve.' Eliza took a deep, calming breath. She couldn't let herself get too defensive. Not when Jake had pretty much had to pick her up from the floor.

'There's a lot at stake if you don't learn more quickly,' he said.

She gritted her teeth. 'Don't you think I *know* that? While I was lying there in that hospital bed I kept wondering how I had let myself get into that state.'

'I suspect you thought the sickness was a natural part of pregnancy. That you had to put up with the nausea. Perhaps if you'd told your friends you were pregnant they might have seen what you were going through wasn't normal and that you were headed into a danger zone.'

Eliza wasn't sure whether he was being sympathetic or delivering a reprimand. 'When did you get to know so much?' she said, deciding to err on the side of offered sympathy. The direction of where this conversation was beginning to go scared her. It almost sounded as though it might lead into an accusation that she was an incompetent mother—before she'd even give birth.

'Since yesterday, when the hospital doctor explained it,' he said with a shrug of his broad shoulders. 'I learned more than I ever thought I'd need to know about that particular complication.'

How many men would have just dropped her at the hospital and run? She was grateful to Jake—but she did *not* want him to take over.

'I've learned a lot too,' she said. 'If I keep on top of the nausea, and don't let myself get dehydrated, that shouldn't happen again. I admit this has given me a real shock. I had no reason to think I wouldn't fly through pregnancy with my usual good health. But the doctors have given me strategies to deal with it. Including more time in the hospital on a drip if required. I'll be okay.'

He shook his head. 'I wish I could believe that. But I suspect you'll be back at Party Queens, dragging a drip on its stand along behind you, before you know it.'

That forced a reluctant smile from her. But he wasn't smiling and her smile quickly faded. He was spot-on in his assessment of her workaholic tendencies. Though she didn't appreciate his lack of faith in her ability to look after herself.

'Jake, trust me—I won't over-extend myself. Miracles don't come along too often in a person's life.' She placed her hand protectively on her bump. 'Truth is, this is almost certainly my only chance to have a baby. I won't jeopardise anything by being foolish. Believe me—if I need help, I'll ask for it.'

Asking for help didn't come easily to her. Because with accepting help came loss of control. One of her biggest issues in management training had been learning to delegate. Now it looked as if she might have to learn to give over a degree of control in her private life too. To doctors, nurses, other health professionals. Because she had to consider her baby as well as herself. But she would not give control over to a man.

For a converted attic in a small house, the bedroom was spacious, with an en suite shower room and a study nook as well as sleeping quarters. But Jake was so tall, so broad-shouldered, he made the space seem suddenly cramped.

How she wished things could be different. Despite all that had happened desire shimmered through her when she feasted her eyes on him, impossibly handsome in black jeans and a black T-shirt. Jake, here in her bedroom, was looking totally smokin'.

Then there was her—with lank hair, yesterday's clothes, a big wad of sterile gauze taped to the back of her hand where the drip had been, and a plastic hospital ID band still around her wrist. Oh, and pregnant.

Jake paced the length of the room and back several times, to the point when Eliza started to get nervous without really knowing why. He stood in front of the window for a long moment with his back to her. Then pivoted on his heel to turn back to face her.

'We have to get married,' he said, without preamble.

Eliza's mouth went dry and her heart started to thud. She was so shocked all she could do was stare up at him. *'What?'* she finally managed to choke out. 'Where did *that* come from?' She pulled herself up from the bed to face him, though her shaky knees told her she really should stay seated.

'You're pregnant. It's the right thing to do.'

He looked over her head rather than directly at her. There was no light in his eyes, no anticipation—nothing of the expression she might expect from a man proposing marriage.

'Get married because I'm pregnant?'

She knew she was just repeating his statement but she needed time to think.

'We have to get married,' he'd commanded. There had been no joy, no feeling, certainly no talk of love— and that hurt more than it should have. Not that *love* had ever come into their relationship. Worse, there had been no consultation with her. She'd rank it more as a demand than a proposal. And demands didn't sit well with her.

What would she have done if he had actually proposed? With words of affection and hope? She couldn't think about that. That had never been part of their agreement.

'You being pregnant is reason enough,' he said.

'No, it isn't. You know I don't want to marry again. Even if I did, we don't know each other well enough to consider such a big step.'

The irony of it didn't escape her. They knew each other well enough to make a baby. Not well enough to spend their lives together.

She shook her head. 'I can't do it, Jake.'

The first time she'd married for love—or what she'd thought was love—and it had been a disaster. Why would marrying for less than love be any better? Marrying someone she'd known for such a short time? An even shorter time than she'd known her ex.

'Your pregnancy changes everything,' Jake said. His face was set in severe lines.

'It does. But not in that way.'

'You're having a baby. *My* baby. I want to marry you.'

'Why? For my reputation? Because of the media?'

There was a long pause before he spoke. 'To give the baby a father,' he said. 'The baby deserves to have two parents.'

That was the last reason she would have anticipated from him and it took her aback for a moment. She put her hand to her heart to try and slow its sudden racing. 'Jake, that's honourable of you. But it's not necessary for you to marry me. If you want to be involved with the baby I'm happy—'

'I want the baby to have my name,' he said. 'And a good life.'

'*I* can give him or her a good life. You don't have to do this. We knew marriage wasn't an option for us.'

'It's important to me, Eliza.'

She noticed his fists, clenched by his sides. The tension in his voice. There was something more here—something that belied the straightforwardness of his words.

'You married your ex-wife because she was pregnant,' she said. 'I don't expect that. Really I don't. Please stop pacing the room like a caged lion.'

Her knees felt suddenly too weak to support her. She wanted to collapse back onto the bed. Instead she sat down slowly, controlled, suddenly fearing to show any weakness. Jake was a man used to getting what he wanted. Now it seemed he wanted *her*. Correction. He wanted her for the baby she was carrying. *His baby.*

'Why, Jake? You said you never wanted to be a father. Why this sudden interest?'

Jake sat down on the bed beside her, as far away from her as he could without colliding with the bedhead. He braced both hands on his knees. Overlying Eliza's nervousness was a pang of mingled longing and regret. Back in Port Douglas they wouldn't have been sitting side by side on a bed, being careful not to touch. They would have been making love by now, lost in a breathtaking world of intimacy and mutual pleasure. *Lovemaking that had created a miracle baby.*

'Seeing the baby on the ultrasound affected me yesterday,' he said now. 'The pregnancy which, up until then had been an abstract thing, became very real for me.'

Eliza noticed how weary he looked, with shadows

under his eyes, lines she hadn't noticed before etched by his mouth. She wondered how much sleep he'd had last night. Had he been awake half the night, wrangling with the dilemma she had presented him with by unexpectedly bearing his baby?

'It affected me too.'

She remembered she had been so overcome that she had gripped his hand—so tightly it must have hurt him. Then she had intercepted a smiling glance from the nurse. She and Jake must have looked quite the proud parents-to-be. If only that sweet nurse had known the less than romantic truth.

'You didn't see a scan when your ex—Fern—was pregnant?' she asked Jake.

'She didn't believe in medical intervention of any kind.'

'But an ultrasound isn't like an X-ray. It's safe and—'

'I know that. But that's beside the point. The point is I saw a little person yesterday. A tiny baby who is going to grow up to be a boy, like I was, or a girl like you were. We didn't plan it. We didn't want—'

She put up a hand in a halt sign, noticed her hand wasn't quite steady. 'Stop right there. You mightn't want it—I mean him or her… I hate calling my baby "it"—but I *do* want him or her. Very much.'

'I'm aware of how much you want the baby. Of the tragedy it was for you to discover you couldn't conceive. But the fact is I didn't want children. I would never have chosen to embark on a pregnancy with you. You know that.'

His words stung. Not just because of his rejection of her but because of her baby, unwanted by its father. No

way would she have chosen a man she scarcely knew—
a man who didn't want kids—as the father of her baby.

'I know we had a deal for four days of no-strings
fun,' she said. 'Mother Nature had other ideas. Trust
me—I wouldn't have *chosen* to have a child this way
either.'

He indicated her bump. 'This is no longer just about
me or about you; it's about another person at the start
of life. And it's *my* responsibility. This child deserves
a better life than you can give it on your own.'

If that wasn't an insult from an arrogant billionaire,
she didn't know what was.

She forced herself to sound calm and reasonable.
'Jake, I might not be as wealthy as you, but I can give
my child a more than decent life, thank you very much.
I'm hardly a pauper.'

'Don't delude yourself, Eliza. You can't give it anything *like* what I have the resources to provide.'

Perspiration beaded on her forehead and she had to
clasp her hands to stop them from trembling. It wasn't
just that she was still feeling weak. She had a sudden,
horrible premonition that she was preparing to do battle for her own child.

So quickly this had turned adversarial. From a proposal to a stand-off. She couldn't help but think how
different this would be if she and Jake were together on
this. As together and in tune as they had been in bed.
Instead they were sitting here, apart on the bed, glar-
ing at each other—she the mother, he the inadvertent
sperm donor who wanted to take things further than
he had any right to do.

'I can—and will—give this child a good life on

my own,' she said. 'He or she will have everything they need.'

Jake was so wealthy. He could buy anything he wanted. What was he capable of doing if he wanted to take her child from her?

'Except its father's name,' he said.

Eliza was taken aback. She'd expected him to talk about private schooling, a mansion, travel, the best of everything as far as material goods went. Not the one intangible thing she could not provide.

'Is *that* what this is about?' she said. 'Some patriarchal thing?'

'What is that meant to mean?' He stared at her as if she'd suddenly sprouted horns. 'This is about making my child legitimate. Giving it its rightful place in the world.'

My child. How quickly he had claimed her baby as his own.

'Legitimate? What does *that* mean these days?' she asked.

He gave a short, sharp bark of laughter she'd never heard from him before. 'I went through hell as a kid because I was illegitimate. Life for a boy with no father was no fun at all.' His mouth set in a grim line.

'That was thirty years ago, Jake,' she said, trying not to sound combative about an issue that was obviously sensitive for him. 'Attitudes have changed now.'

'Have they really? I wonder… I walked the walk. Not just the bullying from the kids, but the sneering from the adults towards my mother, the insensitivity of the schoolteachers. Father's Day at school was the worst day of the year. The kids all making cards and gifts for their dads… Me with no one. I don't want to risk putting my child through what I went through.'

He traced the slight crookedness of his nose with his index finger. The imperfection only made him more handsome, Eliza had always thought.

'Surely it wasn't such a stigma then?' she asked.

He scowled. 'You have no idea, do you?' he said. 'Born into a family with a father who provided for you. Who gave you his name. His protection.'

Eliza felt this was spiralling away from her. Into something so much deeper than she'd realised. 'No, I don't. Have any idea, I mean.'

One of her first memories was of her father lifting her for the first time up onto a horse's back, with big, gentle hands. How proud he'd been of her fearlessness. No matter what had come afterwards, she had that. Other scenes of her father and her with their beloved horses jostled against the edges of her memory.

Jake's face was set into such grim lines he almost looked ugly. 'Every time I got called the B-word I had to answer the insult with my fists. My mother cried the first time I came home with a broken nose. She soon ran out of tears. Until the day I got big enough to deliver some broken noses of my own.'

Eliza shuddered at the aggression in his voice, but at the same time her heart went out to that little boy. 'I didn't realise how bad it was not to have a dad at home.'

'It's a huge, aching gap.'

His green eyes were clouded with a sadness that tore at her.

'Not one I want my own child to fall into.'

'Why wasn't your father around?'

'Because he was a selfish pig of a man who denied my existence. Is that a good enough answer?'

The bitterness in his voice shocked Eliza. She imagined a dear little boy, with a shock of blond hair and green eyes, suffering a pain more intense than that of any broken nose. She yearned to comfort him but didn't know what she could say about such a deep-seated hurt. At the same time she had to hold back on her feelings of sympathy when it came to Jake. She had to be on top of her game if Jake was going to get tough.

He sighed. Possibly he didn't realise the depth of anguish in that sigh.

She couldn't stop herself from placing her hand over his. 'I'm sorry, Jake. It was his loss.'

He nodded a silent acknowledgment.

Back in Port Douglas she had yearned for Jake to share his deeper side with her. Now she'd been tossed into its dark depths and she felt she was drowning in a sea of hurts and secrets, pulled every which way by conflicting currents. On top of her nausea, and her worries about handling life as a single mother, she wasn't sure she had the emotional fortitude to deal with this.

'Do you know anything about your father?'

About the man who was, she realised with a shock, her unborn child's grandfather. Jake's mother would be his or her grandmother. Through their son or daughter she and Jake would be connected for the rest of their lives—whether they wanted to be or not.

'It's a short, ugly story,' he said, his mouth a grim line. 'My mother was a trainee nurse at a big Brisbane training hospital. She was very pretty and very naïve. He was a brilliant, handsome doctor and she fell for him. She didn't know he was engaged to a girl from a wealthy family. He seduced her. She fell pregnant. He didn't want to know about it. She got booted out of her job in disgrace and slunk home to her parents at the Gold Coast.'

The father handsome, the mother pretty... Both obviously intelligent... For the first time a thought flashed through Eliza's head. Would the baby look like her or like Jake? Be as smart? It wasn't speculation she felt she could share with him.

'That's the end of it?' she said. 'What about child support?'

'Not a cent. He was tricky. My mother's family couldn't afford lawyers. She wanted nothing to do with him. Just to get on with her life. My grandparents helped raise me, though they didn't have much. It was a struggle.'

Poor little Jake. Imagine growing up with *that* as his heritage. Before the drought her parents had loved to tell the story of how they had met at an agricultural show—her dad competing in the Western riding, her mum winning ribbons for her scones and fruitcake. She wondered if they remembered it now. Would her child want to know how she and his or her dad had met? How would she explain why they weren't together?

'You never met him?' she asked.

'As a child, no.' Jake's mouth curled with contempt. 'But when media reports started appearing on the "young genius" who'd become a billionaire, he came sniffing around, looking for his long-lost son.'

'What did you do?'

'Kicked him to the kerb—like he'd sent my mother packing.'

Eliza shuddered at the strength of vengeful satisfaction in his voice. Jake would make a formidable enemy if crossed.

Jake got up from the bed. It was hard to think straight, sitting so close to Eliza She looked so wan and frail, somehow even more beautiful. Her usual sweet, floral scent had a sharp overtone of hospital from the bandage on her hand, which reminded him of what she had been through. He would never forget that terrifying moment when he'd thought she had stopped breathing.

He fought a powerful impulse to fold her in his arms and hold her close. She needed him, and yet he couldn't seem to make her see that. He wanted to look after her. Make sure she and the baby had everything they needed. If his own father had looked after his mother the way he wanted to look after Eliza, how different his life might have been. Yet he sensed a battle on his hands even to get access to his child.

He hadn't intended to confide in her about his father. Next thing he'd be spilling the details of his criminal record. Of his darkest day of despair when he'd thought he couldn't endure another minute of his crappy life. But he'd hoped telling her something of his past might make her more amenable to the idea of getting married to give their child a name.

'I'm asking you again to marry me, Eliza. Before the baby is born. So it—'

'Can you please not call the baby *it*? Try *he* or *she*. This is a little person we're talking about here. I thought you got that?'

He felt safer calling the baby *it*. Calling it *he* or *she* made it seem too real. And the more real it seemed, the more he would get attached. And he couldn't let himself get too attached if Eliza was going to keep the baby from him.

He didn't know a lot about custody arrangements for a child with single parents—though he suspected he was soon to know a whole lot more. But he doubted the courts were much inclined to give custody of a newborn to anyone other than its mother. No matter how much money he threw at the best possible legal representation. Once it got a little older that would be a different matter. His child would not grow up without a father the way he had.

'I want you to marry me before the baby is born so *he* or *she* is legitimate,' he said.

She glared at him. 'Jake, I've told you I don't want to get married. To you or to anyone else. And if I did it would be because I was in love with my husband-to-be.'

Jake gritted his teeth. He had married before for love and look where it had got him. 'That sounds very idealistic, Eliza. But there can be pragmatic reasons to marry, too. There have been throughout history. To secure alliances or fortunes. Or to gain property or close a business deal. Or to legitimise a child.'

Slowly she shook her head. A lock of her hair fell across her eyes. She needed a haircut. She'd obviously been neglecting herself. Why couldn't she see that she needed someone to look after her? *Vulnerable*. That was what Andie had called her. Yet Eliza just didn't seem to see it.

Her eyes narrowed. 'I wish you could hear how you sound, Jake. Cold. Ruthless. This isn't a business deal we're brokering. It's our lives. You. Me. A loveless marriage.'

'A way to ensure our child is legitimate.'

'What about a way to have a woman squirming under a man's thumb? That was *my* experience of marriage. And I have no desire to experience it again.'

'Really?' he said. 'I wouldn't want to see you squirming. Or under my thumb.' Jake held up his fingers in a fist, his thumb to the side. 'See? It's not nearly large enough to hold you down.'

It was a feeble attempt at levity and he knew it. But this was the most difficult conversation he had ever had. The stakes were so much higher than in even the most lucrative of potential business deals.

'I don't know whether to take that as an insult or not. I'm not *that* big.'

'No, you're not. In fact you're not big enough. You've lost weight, Eliza. You need to gain it. I can look after you as well as the baby.'

Her chin lifted in the stubborn way he was beginning to recognise.

'I don't *want* to be looked after. I can look after both myself and my baby on my own. You can see him or her, play a role in their life. But I most certainly don't want to *marry* you.'

'You're making a mistake, Eliza. Are you sure you don't want to reconsider?'

'You can't force me to marry you, Jake.'

'But I can make life so much easier for you if you do,' he said.

'Love is the only reason to marry. But love hasn't entered the equation for us. For that reason alone, I can't marry you.'

'That's your final word?'

She nodded.

He got up. 'Then you'll be hearing from my lawyer.'

Eliza's already pale face drained of every remaining scrap of colour. *'What?'*

She leapt up from the bed, had to steady herself as she seemed to rock on her feet as if she were dizzy. But she pushed aside his steadying hand and glared at him.

'You heard me,' he said. 'I intend to seek custody.'

'You can't have custody over an unborn child.' Her voice was high and strained.

'You're about to see what I can do,' he said.

He turned on his heel, strode to the top of the stairs. Flimsy stairs. Too dangerous. She couldn't bring up a child in this house. He ignored the inner voice that told him this house was a hundred times safer and nicer than the welfare housing apartment he'd grown up in. *Nothing but the best for his child.*

She put up her hand in a feeble attempt to stop him. 'Jake. You can't go.'

'I'm gone, Eliza. I suggest you get back to bed and rest. An agency nurse will be arriving in an hour. I've employed her to look after you for the next three days, as per doctor's orders. I suggest you let her in and allow her to care for you. Otherwise you might end up back in hospital.'

He swung himself on to the top step.

'I'll see you in court.'

CHAPTER THIRTEEN

So it had come to this. Eliza placed her hand protectively on her bump as she rode the elevator up to the twenty-third floor of the prestigious building in the heart of the central business district of Sydney, where the best law firms had their offices. She hadn't heard from Jake for three weeks. All communication had been through their lawyers. Except for one challenging email.

Now she was headed to a meeting with Jake and his lawyers to finalise a legal document that spelled out in detail a custody and support agreement for the unborn Baby Dunne.

She must have paled at the thought of the confrontation to come, because her lawyer gave her arm a squeeze of support. Jake had, of course, engaged the most expensive and well-known family law attorney in Sydney to be on his side of the battle lines.

He'd sent her an email.

Are you sure you can afford not to marry me, Eliza? Just your lawyer's fees alone will stop you in your tracks.

What he didn't realise, high up there in his billionaire world, where the almighty dollar ruled, was that not everybody could be bought. She had an older cousin who was a brilliant family lawyer. And Cousin Maree was so outraged at what Jake was doing that she was representing Eliza *pro bono*. Well, not quite for free. Eliza had agreed that Party Queens would organise the most spectacular twenty-first birthday party possible for Maree's daughter.

Now, Maree squeezed her arm reassuringly. 'Chin up. Just let me do the talking, okay?'

Eliza nodded, rather too numbed at the thought of what she was about to face to do anything else *but* keep quiet.

She saw Jake the moment she entered the large, traditionally furnished meeting room. Her heart gave such a jolt she had to hold on for support to the back of one of the chairs that were ranged around the boardroom table. He was standing tall, in front of floor-to-ceiling windows that looked out on a magnificent mid-morning view of Sydney Harbour. The Bridge loomed so closely she felt she could reach out and touch it.

Jake was wearing a deep charcoal-grey business suit, immaculately tailored to his broad shoulders and tapered to his waist. His hair—darker now, less sun-streaked—crept over his collar. No angel wings in sight—rather the forked tail and dark horns of the demon who had tormented her for the last three weeks with his demands.

At the sound of her entering the room Jake turned. For a split second his gaze met hers. There was a flash of recognition—and something else that was gone so soon she scarcely registered it. But it could have been regret. Then the shutters came down to blank his expression.

'Eliza,' he said curtly, acknowledging her presence with a brief nod in her direction.

'Jake,' she said coolly, despite her inner turmoil.

Her brain, so firmly in charge up until now, had been once more vanquished by her libido—she refused to entertain for even one second the thought that it might be her heart—which flamed into life at the sight of the beautiful man who had been her lover for those four, glorious days. So treacherous her libido, still to clamour for this man. Her lover who had become her enemy—the hero of her personal fairytale transformed into the villain.

Eliza let Jake's lawyer's assistant pull out the chair for her. Before she sat she straightened her shoulders and stood proud. Her tailored navy dress with its large white collar was tucked and pleated to accommodate and show off her growing bump. She hoped her silent message was loud and clear—*she* was in possession of the prize.

But at the same time as she displayed the ace in her hand she felt swept by a wave of inexplicable longing for Jake to be sharing the milestones of her pregnancy with her. She hadn't counted on the loneliness factor of single motherhood. There was a vague bubbling sensation that meant the baby was starting to kick, she thought. At fifteen weeks it was too soon for her to be feeling vigorous activity; she knew that from the 'what to expect' pregnancy books and websites she read obsessively. But she had a sudden vision of Jake, resting his hand on her tummy, a look of expectant joy on his face as he waited to feel the kicking of their baby's tiny feet.

That could only happen in a parallel universe. Jake had no interest in her other than as an incubator.

She wondered, too, if he had really thought ahead to his interaction with their son or daughter? His motivation seemed purely to be making up for the childhood he felt he'd lost because of his own despicable father. To try to right a family wrong and force a certain lifestyle on her whether she liked it or not.

What if their child—who might be equally as smart and stubborn as his or her parents—had other ideas about how he or she wanted to live? He or she might be as fiercely independent as both her, Eliza, and the paternal grandmother—Jake's mother.

Would she ever get to meet his mother? Unlikely. Unless she was there when Eliza handed over their child for Jake's court-prescribed visits.

That was not how it was meant to be. She ached at the utter *wrongness* of this whole arrangement.

Jake settled in to a chair directly opposite her, his lawyer to his right. That was *his* silent statement, she supposed. Confrontation, with the battlefield between them. *Bring it on,* she thought.

It was fortunate that the highly polished dark wooden table was wide enough so there was no chance of his knees nudging hers, her foot brushing against his when she shifted in her seat. Because, despite all the hostility, her darn libido still longed for his touch. It was insane—and must surely be blamed on the up-and-down hormone fluctuations of pregnancy.

Maree cleared her throat. 'Shall we start the proceedings? This is very straightforward.'

Maree had explained all this to her before, but Eliza listened intently as her cousin spoke, at the same time keeping her gaze firmly fixed on Jake's face. He gave nothing away—not the merest flicker of reaction. He ran his finger along his collar and tugged at his tie—obviously uncomfortable at being 'trussed up'. But she guessed he'd wanted to look like an intimidating billionaire businessman in front of the lawyers.

Maree explained how legally there could not be any formal custody proceedings over an unborn child. However, the parties had agreed to prepare a document outlining joint custody to present to a judge after the event of a live birth.

Eliza had known that particular phrase would be coming and bit her lip hard. She caught Jake's eye, and his slight nod indicated his understanding of how difficult it was for her to hear it. Because its implication was that something could go wrong in the meantime. Her greatest fear was that she would lose this miracle baby—although her doctor had assured her the pregnancy was progressing very well.

Jake's hands were gripped so tightly together that his knuckles showed white—perhaps he feared it too. He had been so brilliant that day he'd taken her to hospital.

Eliza was looking for crumbs to indicate that Jake wasn't the enemy, that this was all a big misunderstanding. That brief show of empathy from him might be it. Then she remembered why she was here in the first place. To be coerced into signing an agreement she didn't want to sign.

She was being held to a threat—hinted at rather than spoken out in the open—that if she didn't cooperate Jake would use his influence to steer wealthy clients away from Party Queens. Right at a time when her ongoing intermittent nausea and time away from work, plus the departure of their new head chef to a rival firm, meant her beloved company—and her livelihood—was tipping towards a precipice. What choice did she have?

Maree continued in measured tones, saying that both parties acknowledged Jake Marlowe's paternity, so there would be no need for a court-ordered genetic test once the baby was born. She listed the terms of the proposed custody agreement, starting with limited visits by the father while the child was an infant, progressing to full-on division of weekends and vacations. The baby's legal name would be Baby Dunne-Marlowe—once the sex was known a first name satisfactory to both parents would be agreed upon.

Then Jake's lawyer took over, listing the generous support package to be provided by Mr Marlowe—all medical expenses paid, a house to be gifted in the child's name and held in trust by Mr Marlowe, a trust fund to be set up for—

Eliza half got up from her chair. She couldn't endure this sham a second longer. 'That's enough. I know what's in the document. Just give it to me and I'll sign.'

She subsided in her chair. Bent her head to take Maree's counsel.

'Are you sure?' her cousin asked in a low voice. 'You don't want further clarification of the trust fund provisions? Or the—?'

'No. I just want this to be over.'

The irony of it struck her. Jake had been worried about gold-diggers. Now he was insisting she receive money she didn't want, binding her with ties that were choking all the joyful anticipation of her pregnancy. She tried to focus on the baby. That precious little person growing safe and happy inside her. Her unborn child was all that mattered.

She avoided looking at Jake as she signed everywhere the multiple-paged document indicated her signature was required, stabbing the pen so hard the paper tore.

Jake followed Eliza as she departed the conference room, apparently so eager to get away from him that she'd broken into a half-run. She was almost to the bank of elevators, her low-heeled shoes tapping on the marble floor, before he caught up with her.

'Eliza,' he called.

She didn't turn around, but he was close enough to hear her every word.

'I have nothing to say to you, Jake. You've got what you wanted, so just go away.'

Only she didn't say *go away*. She used far pithier language.

She reached the elevator and jabbed the elevator button. Once, twice, then kept on jabbing it.

'That won't get it here any faster,' he said, and immediately regretted the words. *Why had he said something so condescending?* He cursed his inability to find the right words in moments of high tension and emotion.

She turned on him, blue eyes flashing the brightest he'd seen them. Bright with threatening tears, he realised. Tears of anger—directed at *him*.

'Of course it won't. But I live in hope. Because the sooner I can get away from you, the better. Even a second or two would help.' She went back to jabbing the button.

Her baby bump had grown considerably since he'd last seen her. She looked the picture of an elegant, perfectly groomed businesswoman. The smart, feisty Eliza he had come to— Come to what? Respect? Admire? Something more than that. Something, despite all they'd gone through, he couldn't put a name to.

'You look well,' he said. *She looked more beautiful than ever.*

With a sigh of frustration she dropped her finger from the elevator button. Aimed a light kick at the elevator door. She turned to face him, her eyes narrowed with hostility.

'Don't try and engage me in polite chit-chat. Just because you've forced me to sign a proposed custody agreement it doesn't mean you own me—like you're trying to own my baby.'

You didn't own children—and you couldn't force a woman to marry you. Belatedly he'd come to that realisation.

Jake didn't often admit to feeling ashamed. But shame was what had overwhelmed him during the meeting, as he'd watched the emotions flickering over Eliza's face, so easy to read.

He'd been a teenage troublemaker—the leader of a group of other angry, alienated kids like himself. Taller and more powerful than the others, he'd used his off-the-charts IQ and well-developed street-smarts to control and intimidate the gang—even those older than him.

He'd thought he'd put all that long behind him. Then in that room, sitting opposite Eliza—proud, brave Eliza—it had struck him in the gut like a physical blow. He'd behaved as badly towards her as he had in his worst days as a teenage gang leader. Jim Hill would be ashamed of him—but not as ashamed as he was of himself.

'I'm sorry, Eliza. I didn't mean it to go this far.'

She blinked away the threatening tears. 'You played dirty, Jake. I wouldn't marry you, so you brought in the big guns. I would have played fair with you. Visitation rights. Even the Dunne-Marlowe name. For the sake of our baby. I was *glad* you wanted to play a role in our child's life. But I wasn't in a space for making life-changing decisions right then. I'd just got out of hospital.'

How had he let this get so far? 'I was wrong. I should have—'

'Now the document is signed you think you can placate me? Forget it. Don't you see? You're so concerned about giving this child your name, you're bequeathing to him or her something much worse. A mother who resents her baby's father. Who hates him for the way she's had to fight against him imposing his will on her, riding roughshod over her feelings.'

Now he was on the ground, being kicked from all sides. And the blows were much harder than those Eliza had given the elevator door.

'*Hate?* That's a strong word.'

'Not strong enough for how I feel about you,' she said, tight-lipped. 'I reckon you've let the desire to win overcome all your common sense and feelings of decency.'

Of course. He'd been guilty of *over-thinking* on a grand scale. 'I just want to do the right thing by our child,' he said. 'To look after it and to look after you too, Eliza. You need me.'

She shook her head. 'I don't need you. At one stage I wanted you. And…and I… I could have cared for you. When you danced me around that ballroom in Montovia I thought I was on the brink of something momentous in my life.'

'So did I,' he said slowly.

'Then there was Port Douglas. Leaving you seemed so *wrong*. We had something *real*. Only we were so darn intent on protecting ourselves from hurt we didn't recognise it and we walked away from it. The baby gave us a second chance. To be friends. Maybe more than friends. But we blew that too.'

'There must be such a thing as a third chance,' he said.

She shook her head so vehemently it dislodged the clip that was holding her hair off her face and she had to push it back into place with hands that trembled.

'No more chances. Not after what happened in that room today. You won't break me. I will never forgive you. For the baby's sake, I'll be civil. It would be wrong to pump our child's mind with poison against his or her father. Even if I happen to think he's a…a bullying thug.' Her cheeks were flushed scarlet, her eyes glittered.

Now he'd been kicked to a pulp—bruised black and blue all over. Hadn't the judge used a similar expression when sentencing him to juvenile detention? The words *bully* and *thug* seemed to be familiar. But that had been so long ago. He'd been fifteen years of age. Why had those tendencies he'd thought left well and truly behind him in adolescence surfaced again?

Then it hit him—the one final blow he hadn't seen coming. It came swinging again like that sledgehammer from nowhere to slam him in the head. This wasn't about Eliza needing him—it was about *him* needing *her*. Needing her so desperately he'd gone to crazy lengths to try to secure her.

Just then the elevator arrived.

'At last,' Eliza said as she stepped towards it. She had to wait until a girl clutching a bunch of legal folders to her chest stepped out.

'Eliza.'

Jake went to catch her arm, to stop her leaving. There was so much he had to say to her, to explain. But she shrugged off his hand.

'Please, Jake, no more. I can't take it. I'll let you know when the baby is born. As per our contract.'

She stood facing him as the elevator doors started to slide slowly inward. The last thing he saw of her was a slice of her face, with just one fat, glistening tear sliding down her cheek.

Jake stood for a long time, watching the indicator marking the elevator's progress down the twenty-three floors. He felt frozen to that marble floor, unable to step backwards or forwards.

When the elevator reached the ground floor he turned on his heel and strode back to his meeting. He needed to rethink his strategy. Jake Marlowe was not a man who gave up easily.

CHAPTER FOURTEEN

THE LAST PLACE Eliza expected to be a week after the lawyers' meeting with Jake was on an executive jet flying to Europe. Despite the gravity of the reason for her flight, it was a welcome distraction.

Gemma had called an emergency meeting of the three Party Queens directors. Eliza's unexpected pregnancy had tipped the problem of an absentee director into crisis point. And because Gemma was Crown Princess, as well as their Food Director, she had sent the Montovian royal family's private jet to transport Eliza and Andie from Sydney to Montovia for the meeting.

Just because Gemma *could*, Eliza had mused with a smile when she'd got the summons, along with the instructions for when a limousine would pick her up to take her to the airport where she would meet Andie.

Dominic had decided to come along for the flight, too. He and Andie's little boy Hugo was being looked after by his doting grandma and grandpa—Andie's parents.

Eliza was very fond of Andie's husband. But despite the luxury of the flight—the lounge chair comfort of leather upholstery, the crystal etched with the Montovian royal coat of arms, the restaurant-quality food, the hotel-style bathrooms—she hadn't been able to relax because of the vaguely hostile emanations coming her way from Dominic.

Jake was Dominic's best male friend. The bonds between them went deep. According to the legend of the two young billionaires they went way back, to when they'd been in their first year at university. Together, they had built fortunes. Created a charitable foundation for homeless kids. And cemented that young friendship into something adult and enduring.

In the air, somewhere over Indonesia, Dominic told Eliza in no uncertain terms that Jake was unhappy and miserable. He couldn't understand why Eliza wouldn't just marry Jake and put them *all* out of their misery.

Dominic got a sharp poke in the ribs from his wife's elbow for *that* particular opinion. He was referring to the fact that sympathies had been split down the middle among the other two Party Queens and their respective spouses.

Andie and Gemma were on her side—though they'd been at pains to state that they weren't actually *taking* sides. Neither of her friends saw why Eliza should marry a man she didn't love just to give her baby Jake's name when he or she was born. Nor did they approve of the domineering way Jake had tried to force the issue.

Dominic and Tristan, however, thought differently.

Dominic had an abusive childhood behind him—tough times living on the streets. He'd told Eliza she was both crazy and unwise not to jump straight into the safety net Jake was offering.

Tristan, a hereditary Crown Prince, also couldn't

see the big deal. There was only one way forward. The baby carried Jake's blood. As far as Tristan was concerned, Gemma had told Eliza, Jake was doing the correct and honourable thing in offering Eliza marriage. Eliza must do the right thing and accept. That from a man who had changed the laws of his country regarding marriage so he could marry for love and make Gemma his wife.

Both men had let Eliza know that they saw her stance as stubborn in the extreme, and contributing to an unnecessary rift between very close friends. They stood one hundred per cent by their generous and maligned buddy Jake. The women could not believe how blindly loyal their husbands were to the *bullying thug* that was Jake.

Of course Eliza was well aware that neither Andie nor Gemma had ever called Jake that in front of Dominic or Tristan. They were each way too wise to let problems with their mutual friends interfere with their own blissfully happy marriages to the men they adored. Besides, as Andie told Eliza, they actually still liked Jake a lot. They just didn't like the way he'd treated her.

'Although Jake *is* very generous,' Andie reminded her.

'Of course he is—exceedingly generous,' said Eliza evenly.

Inside she was screaming: *And sexy and kind and even funny when he wants to be.* As if she needed to be reminded of his good points when they were all she seemed to think about these days.

She kept remembering that time in the ambulance, as she'd drifted in and out of consciousness and the man who had never let go of her hand had murmured reassurance and encouragement all the way to the hospital. The man who'd chartered a private boat for her because she'd said she wanted to dive on the Great Barrier Reef. The man who hadn't needed angel wings to send her soaring to heaven when they'd made love.

Eliza wished, not for the first time, that she hadn't actually called Jake a bullying thug—or told Andie she'd called him that. That day she'd got all the way to the bottom of the building on the elevator and seriously considered going all the way back up to apologise. Then realised, as she had just told him she hated him, that it might not be the best of ideas.

'Do you ever regret not marrying him?' Andie asked. 'You would never have to worry about money again.'

'No,' Eliza replied firmly. 'Because I don't think financial security is a good enough reason to marry—not for me, anyway. Not when I'm confident I'll always be able to earn a good living.'

What she couldn't admit—not even to her dearest friend Andie, and certainly not to Dominic—was that these weeks away from Jake had made her realise how much she had grown to care for him. That along with all the other valid reasons for her not to marry Jake there was one overwhelming reason—she couldn't put herself through the torture of a pragmatic arrangement with a man she'd begun to realise she was half in love with but who didn't love her.

By the end of the long-haul flight to Montovia—Australia to Europe being a flight of some twenty-two hours—Eliza was avoiding Dominic as much as she could within the confines of the private jet. Andie was okay. Eliza didn't think she had a clue about how much Eliza was beginning to regret the way she had handled her relationship with Jake. But she didn't want to share those thoughts with anyone.

She hoped she and Dominic would more easily be able to steer clear of each other in the vast expanses of the royal castle. Avoiding Tristan might not be so easy.

The day after she'd landed in Montovia, Eliza sat in Gemma's exquisitely decorated office in the Crown Prince's private apartment at the castle. A 'small' room, it contained Gemma's desk and a French antique table and chairs, around which the three Party Queens were now grouped. Under the window, which looked out onto the palace gardens, there was a beautiful chaise longue that Eliza recognised from her internet video conversations with Gemma.

What a place for three ordinary Aussie girls to have ended up for a meeting, Eliza couldn't help thinking.

The three Party Queens were more subdued than usual, with the future of the company they had started more as a lark than any seriously considered business decision now under threat. It was still considered the best party planning business in Sydney, but it was at a crossroads—Eliza had been pointing that out with increasing urgency over the last months.

'I thought it would be too intimidating for us to meet in the castle boardroom,' auburn-haired Gemma explained once they were all settled. 'Even after we were married it took me a while before I could overcome my nerves enough to make a contribution there.'

Andie laughed. 'This room is so easy on the eye I might find it difficult to concentrate from being too busy admiring all the treasures.'

'Not to mention the distraction of the view out to those beautiful roses,' Eliza said.

It felt surreal to be one day in the late winter of Australia, the next day in the late summer of Europe.

'Okay, down to business,' said Gemma. 'We all know Party Queens is facing some challenges. Not least is the fact that I now live here, while the business is based in Sydney.'

'Which makes it problematical when your awesome skills with food are one of the contributing factors to our success,' said Eliza.

'True,' said Andie. 'Even as Creative Director, there are limitations to what I can do in terms of clever food ideas. Those ideas need to be validated by a food expert to tell me if they can be practical.'

Gemma nodded. 'I can still devise menus from here. And I can still test recipes myself, as I like to do.' The fact that Gemma had been testing a recipe for a white chocolate and citrus mud cake when she had first met Tristan, incognito in Sydney, had been fuel for a flurry of women's magazine articles. More so when the recipe had become the royal wedding cake. 'But the truth is both the time difference between Montovia and Sydney and my royal duties make a hands-on presence from me increasingly difficult.'

Eliza swallowed hard against a dry throat. 'Does that mean you want to resign from the partnership, Gemma?'

'Heavens, no,' said Gemma. 'But maybe I need to look at my role in a different way.'

'And then there's your future as a sole parent to consider, Eliza,' said Andie.

'Don't think I haven't thought of the challenges that will present,' Eliza said.

'Think about those challenges and multiply them a hundred times,' said Andie, and put up her hand to stop the protest Eliza was already formulating. 'Being a parent is tough, Eliza. Even tougher without a pair of loving hands from the other parent to help you out.'

Eliza gritted her teeth. She was sure Andie had meant 'the other parent' in abstract terms. But of course she could only think of Jake in that context.

'I understand that, Andie,' she said. 'And my bouts of extreme nausea showed me that even with the best workaholic will in the world there are times when the baby will have to come before the business.'

Andie raised her hand for attention. 'May I throw into the mix the fact that Dominic and I would like another baby? With two children, perhaps more, I might have to scale down my practical involvement as well.'

'It's good to have everything on the table,' said Eliza. 'No doubt a royal heir might factor into *your* future, Gemma.'

'I hope so,' said Gemma with a smile. 'We're waiting until a year after the wedding to think about that. I need to learn how to be a princess before I tackle motherhood.'

'Now we've heard the problems, I'm sure you've come armed with a plan to solve them, Eliza,' said Andie.

This kind of dilemma was something Eliza was more familiar with than the complications of her relationship with Jake. She felt very confident on this turf.

'Of course,' she said. 'The business is still very healthy, so option one is to sell Party Queens.'

She was gratified at the wails of protest from Gemma and Andie.

'It *is* a viable option,' she continued. 'There are two possible buyers—'

'No,' said Andie.

'No,' echoed Gemma.

'How could the business be the same without us?' said Andie, with an arrogant flick of her blonde-streaked hair. 'We *are* the Party Queens.'

'Good,' said Eliza. 'I feel the same way. The other proposal is to bring in another level of management in Sydney. Gemma would become a non-executive director, acting as ongoing adviser to a newly appointed food manager.'

Gemma nodded. 'Good idea. I have someone in mind. I've worked with her as a consultant and she would be ideal.'

Eliza continued. 'And Andie would train a creative person to bring on board so she can eventually work part-time. I'm thinking Jeremy.'

Freelance stylist Jeremy had been working with them since the beginning—long forgiven for his role in the disastrous Christmas tree incident that had rocked Andie and Dominic's early relationship.

Andie frowned. 'Jeremy is so talented… He's awesome. And he's really organised. But he's not a Party Queen.' She paused. 'Actually, he's a queen of a different stripe. I think he'd love to come on board.'

'Which brings us to *you*, Eliza,' said Gemma.

Eliza heaved a great sigh, reluctant to be letting go.

'I'm thinking I need to appoint a business manager to deal with the day-to-day finances and accounting.'

'Good idea.' Andie reached out a hand to take Eliza's. 'But you, out of all of us, might have a difficult time relinquishing absolute control over the business we started,' she said gently.

'I… I get that,' Eliza said.

Gemma smiled her friendship and understanding. 'Will you be able to give a manager the freedom to make decisions independent of you? Not hover over them and micro-manage them? Like watching a cake rise in the oven?'

Eliza bowed her head. 'I really am a control freak, aren't I?'

Andie squeezed her hand. 'You said it, not me.'

'I reckon your control freak tendencies are a big part of Party Queens's success,' said Gemma. 'You've really kept us on track.'

'But they could also lead to its downfall if I don't loosen the reins,' said Eliza thoughtfully.

'It's a matter of believing someone can do the job as well as you—even if they do it differently,' said Andie.

'Of accepting help because you need it,' said Gemma.

Her friends were talking about Party Queens. But, seen through the filter of her relationship with Jake, Eliza saw how she might have done things very differently. She'd fought so hard not to relinquish control over her life, over her baby—over her heart—she hadn't seen what Jake could bring to her. Not just as a father but as a life partner. Maybe she had driven him to excessive control on his side because she hadn't given an inch on hers.

In hindsight, she realised she might have thought

more about compromise than control. When it came to giving third chances, maybe it should have been *her* begging *him* for a chance to make it right.

CHAPTER FIFTEEN

DINNER AT THE royal castle of Montovia was a very formal affair. Luckily Eliza had been warned by Gemma to pack appropriate clothes. From her experiences of dinners at the castle before the wedding she knew that meant a dress that would be appropriate for a ball in Sydney. Thank heaven she still fitted into her favourite vintage ballgown in an empire style in shimmering blue that was very flattering to her pregnant shape.

Still, when she went down to dinner in the private section of the palace that was never opened to the public, she was astounded to see the level of formality of the other guests. She blinked at the dazzle of jewellery glinting in the lights from the chandeliers. It took her a moment to realise they were all members of Tristan and Gemma's bridal party. Tristan's sister Princess Natalia, his cousin with his doctor fiancée, she and Andie, other close friends of Tristan's. Natalia waved when she caught her eye.

'It's a wedding reunion,' Andie said when Eliza was seated beside her at the ornate antique banqueting table.

'So I see. Did you know about it?' Eliza asked.

'No. Gemma didn't either. Apparently when Tristan knew we were coming to visit he arranged it as a surprise. He invited everyone, and these are the ones who could make it. Obviously we're the only Australians.'

'What a lovely thing for him to do,' Eliza said.

Gemma was glowing with happiness.

'Very romantic,' said Andie. 'Gemma really struck husband gold with Tristan, in more ways than one.'

It was romantic in a very heart-wrenching way for Eliza. Because the most important member of the wedding party was not here—the best man, Jake.

Bittersweet memories of her last visit to the castle came flooding back in a painful rush. During the entire wedding she'd been on the edge of excitement, longing for a moment alone with him. How dismally it had all turned out. Except for the baby. Her miracle baby. Why couldn't it be enough to have the baby she'd yearned for? Why did she ache to have the father too?

What with being in a different time zone, Eliza was being affected by more than a touch of jet-lag. She also had to be careful about what she ate. The worst, most debilitating attacks of nausea seemed to have passed, but she still had to take care. She just picked at course after course of the magnificent feast—in truth she had no appetite. As soon as it was polite to do so she would make her excuses and go back up to her guest suite—the same luxurious set of rooms she'd been given on her last visit.

After dessert had been cleared Tristan asked his guests to move into the adjoining reception room, where coffee was to be served. There were gasps of surprise as the guests trooped in, at the sight of a large screen on one wall, with images of the wedding projected onto it. The guests burst into spontaneous applause.

Eliza stared at the screen. There was Gemma, getting ready with her bridesmaids. And Eliza herself, smiling as she patted a stray lock of Gemma's auburn hair back into place. The images flashed by. Andie. Natalia. The Queen placing a diamond tiara on Gemma's head.

Then there were pictures at the cathedral. The cluster of tiny flower girls. The groomsmen. The best man—Jake—standing at the altar with Tristan. Jake was smiling straight at the first bridesmaid coming up the aisle. *Her.* She was smiling back at him. It must have been so obvious to everyone what was going on between them. And here she was—without him. But pregnant with his baby.

Her hand went to her heart when she saw a close-up of Jake saying something to Tristan. The image was so large he seemed life-size. Jake looked so handsome her mouth went dry and her heart started to thud so hard she had to take deep breaths to try and control it.

She couldn't endure this. It was cruel. No one would realise if she slipped away. They were all too engrossed with the photographs.

She turned, picked up her long skirts.

And came face to face with Jake.

It was as if the image of him that had so engrossed her on the screen had come to life. Was she hallucinating? With a cautious hand, she reached out and connected with warm, solid Jake. He was real all right. She felt the colour drain from her face. He was wearing a similar tuxedo as he was in the photo, but his smile was more reticent. *He was unsure of his welcome from her.*

'Jake...' she breathed, unable to say another thing.

She felt light-headed and swayed a little. *Please. Not now.* She couldn't pass out on him again.

'You need some fresh air,' he said, and took her arm.

She let him look after her. *Liked* that he wanted to look after her. Without protest she let him lead her out of the room and then found her voice—though not any coherent words to say with it.

'What…? How…?'

'I was in London when Tristan called me about the wedding party reunion. I got here as soon as I could when I heard you were in Montovia.'

Eliza realised he was leading her onto the same terrace where they'd parted the last time they'd been in Montovia. Not quite the same view—it must be further down from that grand ballroom—and not a full moon over the lake either. But a new moon—a crescent moon that gave her a surge of hope for a new start.

She took another deep, steadying breath. Looked up at him and hoped he saw in her eyes what she was feeling but was unable to express.

'Jake, I'm asking for a third chance. Will you give it to me?'

Jake prided himself on being able to read Eliza's expressions. But he couldn't put a label on what he saw shining from her eyes. He must be reading into it what he longed to see, not what was really there. But he took hope from even that glimmering of emotion.

'Of course I give you a third chance,' he said hoarsely. He'd give her a million chances if they brought her back to him. 'But only if you'll give *me* a third chance.'

'Third chance granted,' she said, a tremulous edge to her voice.

He pulled her into his arms and held her close, breathed in her sweet scent. She slid her arms around his back and pressed closer with a little sigh. He smiled at the feel of her slender body, with the distinct curve of his baby resting under her heart. *His baby. His woman.* Now he had to convince her—not coerce her—into letting him be her man.

He looked over her head to the dark night sky, illuminated only by a sliver of silver moon, and thanked whatever power it was that had given him this chance to make good the wrongs he'd done her.

'I've missed you,' he said, not sure how to embellish his words any further.

'I've missed you too. Terribly.'

He'd flown back to Brisbane after she'd left him at the lawyer's office. His house had seemed empty—his life empty. He'd longed to be back with Eliza in her little house, with the red front door and the dragonfly doorknocker. Instead he'd tied her down to a contract to ensure his child's presence in his life and in doing so had driven her away from him.

Over and over he'd relived his time with her in Port Douglas. The passion and wonder of making love with her. Thought of the real reason he wanted to spend millions to relocate his company to Sydney. The overwhelming urge to protect her he'd felt as he'd held her hand in the ambulance and soothed her fears she might lose the baby she'd longed for. *His baby.* The incredible gift he'd been able to give her. The baby was a bonus. Eliza was the prize. But he still had to win her.

Eliza pulled away from his arms but stayed very close.

'Jake, I don't hate you—really, I don't.' The words tumbled out of her as if she had been saving them up. 'And I don't think you're a bullying thug. I… I'm really sorry I called you that.'

He'd always known he'd have to tell her the truth about his past some time—sooner rather than later. Her words seemed to be a segue into it. There was a risk that she would despise him and walk away. But he had to take that risk. If only because she was the mother of his child.

He cleared his throat. 'You're not the first person to call me a bully and a thug,' he said.

She frowned. 'What do you mean?'

'When I was fifteen years old I came up in front of the children's court and was charged with a criminal offence. The magistrate used just those words.'

'Jake!'

To his relief, there was disbelief in her voice, in the widening of her eyes, but not disgust.

'I was the leader of a gang of other young thugs. We'd stolen a car late one night and crashed it into a shopfront. I wasn't driving, but I took responsibility. The police thought it was a ram-raid—that we'd driven into the shop on purpose. In fact it was an accident. None of us could drive properly. We didn't have a driver's licence between us—we were too young. With the pumped-up pride of an adolescent male, I thought it was cooler to be charged with a ram-raid than admit to being an idiot. It was my second time before the court so I got sentenced to a spell in juvenile detention.'

Eliza kept close, didn't back away from him in horror. 'You? In a gang? I can't believe it. Why?'

'Things weren't great at home. My grandfather,

who was the only father I'd ever known, had died. My mother had a boyfriend I couldn't stand. I was angry. I was hurting. The gang was a family of sorts, and I was the kingpin.'

'Juvenile detention—that's jail, isn't it?'

'A medium security prison for kids aged from eleven to sixteen.'

She shuddered. 'I still can't believe I'm hearing this. How awful for you.'

He gritted his teeth. 'I won't lie. It *was* awful. There were some really tough kids in there.'

'Thank heaven you survived.' Her voice was warm with compassion.

She placed her hand on his cheek. He covered it with his own.

'My luck turned with the care officer assigned to me. Jim Hill. He saw I was bored witless at school and looking for diversion.'

'The school hadn't realised you were a genius?'

'They saw me as a troublemaker. Jim really helped me with anger management, with confidence-building. He showed me I had choices.' Jake smiled at the memory. 'He knew I hungered for what I didn't have, after growing up poor. Jim told me I had the brains to become a criminal mastermind or to make myself a fortune in the commercial world. The choice was mine. When my detention was over he worked with my mother to get me moved to a different school in a different area, further down the coast. The new school put me into advanced classes that challenged me. I chose to take the second path. You know the rest.'

Eliza's eyes narrowed. 'Jim Hill? The name sounds familiar.'

'He heads up The Underground Help Centre. You must have met him at the launch party.'

'So you introduced him to Dominic?'

'Jim introduced *me* to Dominic. Dominic was under his care too. But that's Dominic's story to tell. Thanks to Jim, Dominic and I already knew each other by the time we started uni. We both credit Jim for getting our lives on track. That's why we got him on board to help other young people in trouble like we were.'

'How have you managed to keep this under wraps?'

'Juvenile records are sealed when a young offender turns eighteen. I was given a fresh start and I took it. Now you know the worst about me, Eliza.'

Jake was such a tall, powerfully built man. And yet at that moment he seemed to Eliza as vulnerable as his fifteen-year-old self must have been, standing before a magistrate, waiting to hear his sentence.

She leaned up and kissed him on his cheek. It wasn't time yet for any other kind of kiss. Not until they knew where this evening might take them. Since they'd last stood on this terrace together they'd accumulated so much more baggage. Not to mention a baby bump.

'That's a story of courage and determination,' she said. 'Can you imagine if someone ever made a movie of your life story?'

'Never going to happen,' he growled.

'Well, it will make a marvellous story to tell your child one day.'

'Heavily censored,' he said, with a hint of the grin she had got so fond of.

She slowly shook her head. 'I wish you'd told me before. It helps me understand you. And I've been struggling to understand you, Jake.'

To think she had thought him superficial. He'd just been good at hiding his wounds.

He took both her hands in his and drew her closer. 'Would it have made a difference if I'd told you?'

'To help me see why you're so determined to give your child a name? Yes. To make me understand why you're so driven? Yes. To make me love you even more, knowing what you went through? Yes. And I—'

'Stop right there, Eliza,' he said, his voice hoarse. 'Did you just say you love me?'

Over the last days she'd gotten so used to thinking how much she loved him, she'd just blurted out the words. She could deny it. But what would be the point?

She looked up into his face, saw not just good looks but also his innate strength and integrity, and answered him with honesty. 'Yes, Jake, I love you. I fell in love with you... I can't think when. Yes, I can. Here. Right here on this terrace. No. Earlier than that. Actually, from the first moment. Only you weren't free. And then there was Port Douglas, and I got all tied up in not wanting to get hurt again, and...'

She realised he hadn't said anything further and began to feel exposed and vulnerable that she'd confessed she'd fallen in love with a man who had never given any indication that he might love *her*.

She tried to pull away but he kept a firm grip on her hands. 'I... I know you don't feel the same, Jake, so I—'

'What makes you say that? Of *course* I love you. I fell in love with you the first time I was best man to your bridesmaid. We must have felt it at the same moment. You in that blue bridesmaid's dress, with white flowers in your hair…'

'At Andie's wedding?' she said, shaking her head in wonder.

'At Dominic's wedding,' he said at the same time.

He drew her closer. This man who wanted to care for her, look after her, miraculously seemed to love her.

'You laughed at something I said and looked up at me with those incredible blue eyes and I fell right into them.'

'I remember that moment,' she said slowly. 'It felt like time suddenly stopped. The wedding was going on all around me, and all I could think of was how smitten I was with you.'

'But I was too damn tied up with protecting myself to let myself recognise it,' he said.

'Just as well, really,' she said. 'I wasn't ready for something so life-changing then. And you certainly weren't.'

'You could look at it that way. Or you could see that we wasted a lot of time.'

'Then the baby complicated things.'

'Yes,' he said.

The spectre of that dreadful contract hovered between them.

'Your pregnancy brought out my old fears,' he said. 'I'd chosen not to be a father because I don't know *how* to be a father. I had no role model. My uncle lived in the Northern Territory and I rarely saw him. My grandfather tried his best to be a male influence in my life but he was quite old, and suffering from the emphysema that eventually killed him.'

She nodded with realisation. 'You were *scared* to be a father.'

'I was *terrified* I'd be a bad father.'

'Do you still think that way?'

'Not so much.'

'Why?'

'Because of you,' he said. 'I know you're going to be a brilliant mother, Eliza. That will help me to be the best father I can be to our child.'

'Thank you for the vote of confidence,' she said a little shakily. 'But I'll have to *learn* to be a mother. We'll *both* have to learn to be parents. And I know our daughter will have the most wonderful daddy who—'

'Our *daughter*?'

Eliza snatched her hand to her mouth. 'I haven't had a chance to tell you. I had another ultrasound last week.'

For the first time Jake placed his hand reverently on her bump. 'A little girl...' he said, his voice edged with awe. 'My daughter.'

For a long moment Eliza looked up at Jake, taking in the wonder and anticipation on his face.

'So...so where does that leave us?' she asked finally.

'I'm withdrawing my offer of marriage,' he said.

'*What?*'

Jake looked very serious. 'It was more a command than a proposal. I want to do it properly.'

'Do *what* properly?'

But she thought she might know what. Hope flew into her mind like a tiny bird and flew frantically around, trilling to be heard.

'Propose,' he said.

Jake cradled her face in his big, strong hands. His green eyes looked intently down into hers.

'Eliza, I love you. Will you marry me? Do me the honour of becoming my wife?'

She didn't hesitate. 'Yes, Jake, yes. Nothing would make me happier than to be your wife. I love you.'

Now was the time to kiss. He gathered her into his arms and claimed her mouth. She wound her arms around his neck and kissed him back, her heart singing with joy. She loved him and she wanted him and now he was hers. No way would she be alone in that palatial guest apartment tonight.

Jake broke away from the kiss. Then came back for another brief kiss, as if he couldn't get enough of her. He reached inside his jacket to an inside pocket. Then pulled out a small embossed leather box and flipped it open.

Eliza was too stunned to say anything, to do anything other than stare at the huge, perfect solitaire diamond on a fine platinum band, glinting in the faint silver light of the new moon. He picked up her hand and slipped the ring onto the third finger of her left hand. It fitted perfectly.

'I love it,' she breathed. 'Where did you get—?'

'In London.'

'But—'

'I was planning to propose in Sydney. But then Tristan invited me here.'

'Back to where it started.'

He kissed her again, a kiss that was tender and loving and full of promise.

'Can we get married as soon as possible?' he asked.

She paused. 'For the baby's sake?'

'To make you my wife and me your husband. This is about us committing to each other, Eliza. Not because you're pregnant. The baby is a happy bonus.'

'So what happens about the contract once we're married?'

'That ill-conceived contract? After I left you at the elevator I went back to the meeting room and tore my copy up. Then I fired my lawyer for giving me such bad advice.'

She laughed. 'I put my copy through the shredder.'

'We'll be brilliant parents without any need for that,' he said.

'I love you, Jake,' she said, rejoicing in the words, knowing she would be saying them over and over again in the years to come.

'I love you too, Eliza.' He lowered his head to kiss her again.

'Eliza, are you okay? We were worried—'

Andie's voice made both Eliza and Jake turn.

'Oh,' said Andie. Then, *'Oh...'* again, in a very knowing way.

Gemma was there too. She smiled. 'I can see you're okay.'

'Very okay,' Eliza said, smiling her joy. She held out her left hand and splayed her fingers, the better to display her ring. 'We're engaged. For real engaged.'

Andie and Gemma hugged her and Jake, accompanying their hugs with squeals of excitement and delight. Then Dominic and Tristan were there, slapping Jake on the back and hugging her, telling her they were glad she'd come to her senses and that they hoped she realised what a good man she'd got.

'Oh, I realise, all right,' she said, looking up at Jake.

'I couldn't think of a better man to be my husband and the father of my child.'

'You got the best man,' said Jake with a grin.

CHAPTER SIXTEEN

THE BEAUTY OF having your own party planning business, Eliza mused, was that it was possible to organise a wedding in two weeks flat without cutting any corners.

Everything was perfect, she thought with satisfaction on the afternoon of her wedding day. They'd managed to keep her snaring of 'the Billionaire Bachelor' under the media radar. So she and Jake were getting the quiet, intimate wedding they both wanted without any intrusion from the press.

It had been quite a feat to keep it quiet. After all, not only was the most eligible bachelor in Australia getting married, but the guest list of close family and friends included royalty.

Andie had found a fabulous waterfront house at Kirribilli as their venue. The weather was perfect, and the ceremony was to be held on the expansive lawns that stretched right down to the harbour wall, with the Opera House and Sydney Harbour Bridge as backdrop.

It really was just as she wanted it, Eliza thought as she stood with her father at the end of the veranda. Andie had arranged two rows of elegant white bamboo chairs to form an aisle. Large white metal vases filled with informal bunches of white flowers marked the end of each row of seats.

Now, the chairs were all filled with guests, heads turned, waiting for the bride to make her entrance. Everyone she cared about was there, including Jake's mother, whom she'd liked instantly.

Ahead, Jake stood flanked by his best man, Dominic, and his groomsman Tristan, at one side of the simple white wedding arch completely covered in white flowers where the celebrant waited. On the other side stood her bridesmaids, Andie and Gemma. A jazz band played softly. When it struck up the chords of the traditional 'Wedding March', it was Eliza's cue to head down the aisle. On the back of a white pony named Molly—her father's wedding gift to her.

Her vintage-inspired, full-skirted tea-length gown hadn't really been chosen with horseback-riding in mind. But when her father had reminded her of how as a little girl she had always wanted to ride to her wedding on her pony, she had fallen for the idea. Andie had had hysterics, but eventually caved in.

'I really hope we can carry this off, Dad,' Eliza said now, as her father helped her up into the side saddle.

'Of course you can, love,' he said. 'You're still the best horsewoman I know.'

Amazing how a wedding and a baby could bring families together, she thought. Her father had mellowed and their rift had been healed—much to her mother's joy. Now Eliza was seated on Molly and her father was leading the pony by a lead-rope entwined with white ribbons down the grassy aisle. There was no 'giving away' of the bride as part of the ceremony. She and Jake were giving themselves to each other.

Her entrance was met with surprised delight and the sound of many cameras clicking.

Jake didn't know about her horseback entrance— she'd kept it a secret. 'Brilliant,' he whispered as he helped her off Molly and into his arms. 'Country girl triumphs.'

But once the novelty of her entrance was over, and her father had led Molly away, it was all about Jake and her.

They had written the words of the ceremony themselves, affirming their love and respect for each other and their commitment to a lifetime together as well as their anticipation of being parents. Her dress did nothing to disguise her bump—she hadn't wanted to hide the joyous presence of their miracle baby.

Everything around her seemed to recede as she exchanged her vows with Jake, looking up into his face, his eyes never leaving hers. Their first kiss as husband and wife went on for so long their friends starting applauding.

'I love you,' she whispered, just for his ears.

'For always and for ever,' he whispered back.

* * * * *

"Let me make sure I understand the terms of this contract," she said slowly.

"You're asking me to give up my condo, my job, my life, and take up permanent residency in your gatehouse until such time as we mutually decide to terminate the arrangement."

He was blowing it. Forcing a smile, he tried again. "Actually, I'm asking you to move into the main house. With Tommy and me."

Neither the smile nor the offer produced the desired effect. If anything, they added fuel to the temper darkening her eyes.

"You pompous, conceited jerk. You think all you have to do is waltz in, invite me to be your live-in lover, and expect me to…"

"Whoa! Back up a minute! I'm asking you to marry me!"

"What?"

THIRD TIME'S THE BRIDE!

BY
MERLINE LOVELACE

First Published in Great Britain 2016
By Mills & Boon, an imprint of HarperCollins*Publishers*
1 London Bridge Street, London, SE1 9GF

© 2016 Merline Lovelace

ISBN: 978-0-263-92000-0

23-0716

Our policy is to use papers that are natural, renewable and recyclable products and made from wood grown in sustainable forests. The logging and manufacturing processes conform to the legal environmental regulations of the country of origin.

Printed and bound in Spain
by CPI, Barcelona

A career Air Force officer, **Merline Lovelace** served at bases all over the world. When she hung up her uniform for the last time, she decided to try her hand at storytelling. Since then, more than twelve million copies of her books have been published in over thirty countries. Check her website at www.merlinelovelace.com or friend Merline on Facebook for news and information about her latest releases.

For my niece, Stephanie Fichtel,
who's as beautiful as she is talented.
Thanks for giving me such great insight into
the busy, busy life of a graphic artist, Steph.

Chapter One

Dawn McGill would be the first to admit her track record when it came to relationships with the male of the species sucked. Oh, she'd connected with some great guys over the years. Even got engaged to two before dumping them almost at the altar. Fortunately—or unfortunately for the dumpees—she'd discovered just in time that she didn't really want to spend the rest of her life with either of them.

Given that dismal history, Dawn never expected to tumble hopelessly in love during what was supposed to have been a carefree jaunt across northern Italy with her two best friends. Callie and Kate were as shocked as Dawn at how hard and fast she fell.

Nor could any of them have imagined that the man of Dawn's dreams would turn out to be a pint-size ball of energy with soft brown hair, angelic blue eyes and an impish grin. But when the three friends had converged in Venice last week to help babysit the six-year-old, whose nanny had taken a nasty spill and broken her ankle, Tommy the Terrible had wrapped Dawn around his grubby little fist within hours of their first meeting.

Now they were back in Rome. She and Callie and Kate. With Kate's husband, Travis, who'd orchestrated a surprise ceremony to renew their wedding vows using the Trevi Fountain as a backdrop.

Tommy and his dad were here, too. Brian Ellis had worked with Kate's husband on some supersecret project at the NATO base north of Venice and they'd become good friends. The father was too conservative and stuffy for Dawn's taste, but the son…

God, she loved watching the boy's antics! Like now. She had to grin as Tommy scrambled onto the fountain's broad lip. His dad grabbed the back of his son's shirt and kept a tight hold.

"Careful, bud!"

The three women stood in a loose circle to watch the byplay. Kate was a tall, sun-streaked blonde. Callie, a quiet brunette who seemed even more subdued than usual since she'd walked away from her job as a children's advocate. And Dawn, her hair catching fire from the afternoon sun and her ready laughter bubbling as Tommy barely escaped a dousing from one of the cavorting sea horses.

"That kid is utterly fearless," she said with real admiration.

"A natural born adventurer," Callie agreed with a smile. "Just like you. How many times did Kate and I follow you into one scrape or another?"

"Hey, I wasn't always the ringleader. I seem to recall you convincing us to shimmy through a window of the library one night, Miss Priss and Boots. And you—" she smirked at Kate "—were the one who suggested 'borrowing' my brother Aaron's car so we could zip over to the mall. We're lucky the cop who stopped us on a stolen vehicle report didn't let us sit in jail overnight before calling our parents."

The smirk stayed in place, but the memory of that brief joyride churned a familiar acid. Her parents had each blamed the other for their daughter's brush with the law. No surprise there, since they'd been feuding for years by that point. Dawn's three brothers were all older and had escaped the toxic home environment by heading off to college and then careers. She hadn't been as lucky. She was a freshman in high school and almost drowning in the anger her mom and dad spewed at each other when they'd finally decided to call it quits.

The divorce should have been a relief to all parties concerned. Instead, her folks had turned it into an all-out war. No way either would agree to joint custody or reasonable visitation rights for their teenage daughter until the judge was forced to step in and make the decision for them. Dawn ended up shuttling back and forth between her parents, each of whom blamed the other for their subsequent loneliness.

The constant tug-of-war had chipped away at their daughter's breezy, fun-loving disposition. Might have demolished it completely if not for Kate and Callie. They'd all grown up in Easthampton, a small town in western Massachusetts, and had been inseparable since grade school. The Invincibles, as Kate's husband, Travis, called them, not always intending it as a compliment.

Her parents' turbulent history was part of the reason Dawn had bonded so quickly with young Tommy Ellis. The boy's own emotional upheaval had occurred when he was much younger. Not much more than a baby, actually. But the fact that he'd grown up without a mother had colored his life, just as her parents' battles had Dawn's.

Too bad she hadn't bonded as well with Tommy's dad. Lips pursed, she watched as Brian Ellis hauled his son back from the brink yet again. The man was sexy as all hell. She couldn't deny that. Big, but quick, with six feet plus of impressively hard muscle to go with his razor cut brown hair and killer blue eyes. Those eyes had gleamed with undeniable interest when she and Brian had first met in Venice, Dawn recalled. But they'd turned all cool and polite when she'd laughed playfully with one of the other men present.

Oh, well! Not a problem, really. She and the Ellises would share the same address for only a few days. A week or two at most. Just until Brian could determine whether Tommy's injured nanny would be able to return to work and, if not, hire a new one. In the meantime, Dawn had already advised her boss at the relentlessly healthy natural foods company where she worked as a graphic designer that she would be working remotely for that week or two.

As if reading her mind, Kate gave her a sideways look. "Are you sure you want to take a leave of absence from your job to play nursery maid?"

"You told us you're being considered for director of marketing," Callie added. "Won't that get put on hold?"

"No. Maybe. What the heck, I don't care. I need a break from the temperamental artists and computer nerds I spend my days with. Plus, my job's pretty portable. I can work in DC almost as easily as in Boston."

"A director's position isn't that portable," Kate protested. "And I know you don't spend your days only with artists and nerds."

An executive herself, Kate regularly interfaced with clients and senior management.

So did Callie, who'd had to attend an endless grind of meetings at the Massachusetts Office of the Child Advocate. Both women knew all too well that supervisors at every level of every organization weren't particularly sympathetic to employees taking short-notice, nonemergency leaves of absence.

More to the point, they'd both watched their friend fall in and out of love. Or what she'd thought was love. Dawn knew they were uneasy about her current infatuation.

When Brian Ellis hauled his son off the fountain and aimed him in their direction, though, all she could see was the eagerness on the boy's face as he darted through the crowd.

"Dawn! You gotta come throw a coin over your shoulder. Dad says it's tradition."

"Kate and Callie and I did that when we first got to Rome."

"Oh." His face falling, he opened his fist to display two shiny euros. "But Dad gave me these. One for you 'n one for me."

"Well, in that case…lay on, Macduff."

"Huh?"

"It's from one of Shakespeare's plays. It means lead the way."

The boy couldn't care less about Shakespeare, but the euros were burning a hole in his palm. "C'mon!"

Grabbing Dawn's hand, he tugged her back to the fountain. Brian kept a close eye on them as he joined Kate and Callie. The other men in their small party drifted over, as well. USAF Major Travis Westbrook, Kate's husband. Prince Carlo di Lorenzo, a short, barrel-chested dynamo as famed for his military exploits as for his reputation with women. And Joe Russo, head of the special squad responsible for Carlo's security during their stint at the NATO base north of Venice.

Brian had gotten to know each of the three men well

during his own time at the base. So well, in fact, that when Travis decided to hang up his air force uniform, Brian had jumped at the chance to bring the seasoned special operations pilot on board as Ellis Aeronautical Systems' Vice President for Test and Evaluation.

Travis saw Brian's gaze locked on the two at the fountain and grinned. Father and son were in for a wild, unpredictable ride with Dawn McGill.

"You sure you know what you're getting into, Brian?"

"Hell, no."

"I've known Dawn and Callie as long as I have Kate," Travis commented. "I can vouch for the veracity of that old saying."

"I probably shouldn't ask but...what old saying?"

"Blondes are wild," he recited with a wink at his tawny-haired wife, "and brunettes are true, but you never can tell what a redhead will do."

Kate laughed and the dark-haired Callie smiled, but Brian didn't find the quip particularly amusing.

His glance zinged back to the two at the fountain. He must have been crazy to accept Dawn McGill's offer to fill in as Tommy's temporary nanny. With her flame-colored hair and sparkling green eyes, she lit up any room she walked into. Her lush curves also started every male past puberty spinning wild sexual fantasies. Including him, dammit!

If Mrs. Wells hadn't tripped and shattered her ankle in Venice...

If Brian wasn't juggling a dozen different balls at work...

If his son hadn't *begged* him to ask Dawn to come stay with them...

It would just be for a week, Brian reminded himself grimly. Two at most. Only until he could hire someone more qualified to cover during Mrs. Wells's convalescence or possible retirement. The fifty-five-year-old widow had opted to fly out to California and stay with her sister while going through rehab. Brian figured it was iffy at best that she'd regain either the energy or the stamina to keep up with Tommy.

Dawn, on the other hand, didn't lack for either. Or smarts, he acknowledged grudgingly. Before agreeing to this crazy scheme, he'd had his people run a background check on the woman. He had to admit her credentials were impressive. A degree in graphic arts from Boston University, with a minor in advertising. A master's in integrated design media from Georgetown. A hefty starting salary right out of grad school at one of the country's largest health food and natural products consortiums, where she was reportedly poised to move up the managerial ranks.

The problem wasn't her professional credentials, however. The problem was her personal life. The background check had been sketchier in that area, but Brian had pried enough details out of Travis to get the picture. Apparently the delectable Ms. McGill collected men with the same eagerness Tommy did plastic dinosaurs. And when she tired of them, which she did with predictable frequency, she put 'em on the shelf to gather dust while she waltzed off in search of a new toy. Brian wasn't about to let Tommy become attached to someone that mercurial. Any *more* attached, he amended as his son's shriek of laughter carried across the piazza.

Tommy and Dawn had turned their backs to the fountain. Together, they shouted a count of one-two-three. Their arms went up. Their coins soared through the afternoon sunlight. Twin splashes spouted in the basin.

"Good throw," Travis called. "Right on target."

"Thank God," Brian muttered. "Maybe, just maybe,

we'll escape Italy with no injuries to innocent bystand-
ers. Speaking of which…"

He shot up the cuff on his suit coat to check the Mickey
Mouse watch Tommy had presented him with last Father's
Day. Bought using his very own allowance, the boy had
proudly proclaimed. Brian took even more pride in Mickey's
silly grin than he had the Bronze Star he'd earned as a
USMC chopper pilot in what now seemed like another lifetime ago.

"We need to head for the airport," he said, turning to
the others. "Sure I can't talk the rest of you into flying
home with Tommy and me? And Dawn," he added belatedly.

The others had already nixed his offer of a flight back
to the States aboard the Ellis Aeronautical Systems corporate jet. Kate and Callie were staying in Rome another
night and would fly home using their prepaid, nonrefundable commercial tickets. Travis would head back to the
base to wrap up the final details of their project. The prince
would rejoin his special ops unit stationed just outside
Rome and Joe Russo would move on to his next assign-
ment. Whatever that was. The high-powered, high-dollar
security expert was as tight-lipped about his work as he
was good at it.

So good, Brian had approached him about doing a top-
to-bottom scrub of EAS's physical, cyber and industrial
security. Ignoring the still-angry scar slashing the left side
of Joe's face, Brian held the man's steady gaze.

"Let me know when you can nail down a start date."

"Will do," Joe answered. "In the meantime, have your
security people send me their operating procedures and
I'll get my team looking at them."

"Roger that. Well…"

Brian glanced around the circle, warmed by the close

friendship he'd forged with the other three men in such a short time. With Kate and Callie, too.

Then there was Dawn.

She and Tommy approached the small circle, she wearing a smug grin and he skipping in delight. "Didja see us, Dad? Didja? Me 'n Dawn hit the water first try!"

"Dawn and I," Brian corrected.

Tommy made a face but echoed his dad, "Dawn 'n *I* hit the water first try. Didja see us?"

"I saw." Smiling, Brian ruffled his son's hair. "Good job, buddy. You, too, Dawn. Now we'd better say our good-byes and head for the airport."

Tommy shook hands and Dawn gave hugs all around. A flirtatious one for the prince who'd tried his damnedest to get her to jet off to Corsica or Cannes or wherever with him. A friendly one for Joe. And one that came with a warning for Travis.

"You and Kate have spent too much time apart, Westbrook. Get your butt home quick and start working on that baby you guys have decided to produce."

"Yes, ma'am."

The hugs for her two friends were fiercer and much longer. Brian waited patiently but Tommy's forehead puckered into a worried frown when all three women teared up.

"I can't believe our Italian adventure is over," Callie sniffed. "We've dreamed about coming here for so long."

"Ever since we watched *Three Coins in the Fountain* all those years ago," Kate said gruffly.

"But we'll be back." Dawn gulped, tears flowing. "Someday."

As worried now as his son, Brian shot Travis a quick glance. Kate's husband merely rolled his eyes. "Don't worry. They do this all the time. They'll get it together in a moment."

Sure enough, the tears stopped, the sniffles dried up and the smiles reemerged as Kate began planning an imminent reunion.

"It's so awesome that Brian and Tommy live in Bethesda. Travis and I will be less than a half hour away. We can get together regularly. And Callie can come stay with us, too, until she lands a new job."

"I don't think so," the brunette said with a flash of unexpected humor. "You two have that baby to work on. I don't need to listen to the headboard banging—" she gave Tommy a quick glance and finished smoothly "—when you put the crib together."

After another round of hugs, Brian finally ushered his two charges to the waiting limo. Moments later they were threading through Rome's insane traffic on their way to Ciampino, the smaller of the city's two airports.

The corporate jet was fueled and sitting on the ramp. The Gulfstream G600 with its twin Pratt & Whitney engines and long-range cruise speed of five hundred plus mph had been retrofitted by an avionics package specifically designed by EAS.

The sight of the sleek jet stirred familiar feelings of pride and a secret amazement in Brian. Hard to believe just twelve years ago he'd set up a small avionics engineering firm using his entire savings and a five-thousand dollar loan from his father-in-law. The first years hadn't been easy. He was fresh out of the Corps with a new bride and more enthusiasm than business smarts.

Thank God for Caroline, he thought with an all-too-familiar ache. She'd provided long-range vision while he supplied the engineering muscle. Together, they'd grown Ellis Aeronautical Systems from the ground up. She hadn't lived to experience the thrill when EAS hit the Fortune

500 list, though. She'd barely made it to their son's first birthday.

Smothering the ache with a sheer effort of will, Brian greeted his chief pilot at the jet's rear steps. "Thanks for the quick turnaround, Ed. Mrs. Wells made the flight back to the States okay?"

"She did," the pilot confirmed. "So did the Italian medical team you hired to attend to her during the flight. They said to thank you for the extra week in California, by the way. After they got her settled, the first stop on their agenda was Disneyland, followed by the vineyards in Napa Valley."

"Why am I not surprised?" Brian drawled while the pilot bent to bump fists with Tommy.

"Hey, kid. How'd you like Italy?"

"It was great! Me 'n…" Nose scrunching, he made a quick midcourse correction. "Dawn 'n *I* took a gondola ride in Venice 'n I went to the Colosseum in Rome with Dad. He got me a sword 'n helmet 'n everything."

"Cool." The pilot straightened and held out his hand to the third passenger on his manifest. "Good to meet you, Ms. McGill."

"Dawn," Tommy corrected helpfully. "She's, like, a hundred years younger than Mrs. Wells so it's okay for us to call her Dawn. She's gonna come live with me 'n Dad."

"She is, huh?"

"Until Mrs. Wells gets back on her feet," Brian interjected smoothly.

Ed Donahue had flown executive-level jets too long to show anything but a professional front, but Brian knew interest and speculation had to be churning behind his carefully neutral expression. One, the auburn-haired beauty could get a rise from a stone-cold corpse. Two, she was the first living, breathing sex goddess to fly aboard EAS's corporate jet.

As she demonstrated when she followed Tommy up the steps and ducked into the cabin. The slinky, wide-legged pants she'd worn to the ceremony at the Trevi Fountain clung to her hips and outlined a round bottom that made Brian's breath hiss in and Ed's whoosh out.

Gulping, the pilot made a valiant recovery. "I'll, uh, recompute our flight time once we reach cruising altitude and give you an updated ETA."

"Thanks," Brian said grimly, although he'd already figured that no matter what the ETA, he was in for a long flight.

He'd figured right.

Over the years he'd worked hard to minimize his time away from his son by combining business trips with short vacations whenever possible. They'd taken a number of jaunts to Texas, where EAS's main manufacturing and test facility was located. Several trips to Florida so Brian could meet with senior officials in the USAF Special Ops community, with requisite side trips to Disney World. The Paris Air Show last year. This summer's excursion in Italy.

As a result, his son was a seasoned traveler and very familiar with the Gulfstream's amenities, every one of which he was determined to show Dawn once they'd gained cruising altitude. Brian extracted his laptop and set it up on the polished teak worktable while the eager young guide started his tour by showing her the aft cabin.

"It's got a shower 'n toilet 'n the beds fold down," he announced while Dawn surveyed the cabin through the open door. "Watch."

"That's okay, I... Oh. Cool. Twin beds."

"One for me 'n one for Dad. There's another bunk up

front. Ed 'n his copilot take turns in that one on long flights. But you kin have my bed," he offered generously. "I sleep in my seat *lotsa* times."

Brian glanced up from the spreadsheet filling his laptop's screen and met Dawn's eyes. The laughter dancing in their emerald depths invited him to share in the joke. He returned a smile but for some reason didn't find the idea of sharing the aft cabin with her quite as amusing as she obviously did.

"I've got a lot of work to catch up on," he told his son. "Why don't we let Dawn have the cabin to herself and we guys will hang here tonight?"

"Okay. C'mon, you gotta see the galley."

When Tommy led her back up the spacious aisle, Brian caught her scent as they went by. It was faint, almost lost in the leather and polished teakwood of the cabin, but had teased him from their first meeting in Venice. It drifted to him now, a tantalizing mix of summer sunshine and lemons and something he couldn't identify. He tried to block it out of his senses as Tommy gave her a tour of a well-stocked galley that included a wide selection of wines, soft drinks, juices, snacks and prepackaged, microwavable gourmet meals.

The pièce de résistance, of course, was the touch screen entertainment center. On every long flight Brian gave fervent thanks for the video games, TV shows and Disney movies that snared his son's attention for at least a few hours.

"You just press this button here in the armrest 'n the screen opens up." Buckled in again, Tommy laughed at Dawn's surprise when a panel in the bulkhead glided up to reveal a sixty-inch flat screen TV.

"We've got bunches of movies." He flicked the controls and brought up a menu screen with an impressive display of icons. "If you want, we kin watch *Frozen*."

"Right." She gave a small snort. "And how many times did we watch it in Venice? Four? Five?"

Tom looked honestly puzzled. "So?"

"So let's see what else is here. Ah! *Beauty and the Beast*. Do you like that one?"

"It's okay."

"Only okay?"

"All that love stuff is kinda gross."

"It can be," she admitted with a wry grin. "Sometimes."

"We'll watch it if you want," Tommy offered manfully as he handed her a pair of noise-canceling Bose earphones. "Here, we hafta wear these so Dad kin work."

Brian had long ago perfected the ability to concentrate on his laptop's small screen despite the colorful images flickering on the bulkhead's much larger screen. He did a pretty good job of focusing this time, too, until Dawn kicked off her shoes. Angling her seat back, she raised the footrest, crossed her ankles and stretched out to watch the movie.

Startled, Brian stared across the aisle at her toes. Each nail was painted a different color. Lavender. Pink. Turquoise. Pale green. Pearly blue.

He didn't keep up with the latest feminine fashion trends. He had no reason to. But he was damned if he could concentrate on the production schedule for EAS's new Terrain Awareness Warning System with her tantalizing scent drifting across the aisle and those ten dots of iridescent color wiggling in time to the music.

Chapter Two

Tommy conked out after a supper of lemon-broiled chicken, snow peas and the inevitable mac 'n cheese. The Gulfstream's soft leather seats were twice as wide as regular airline seats, so they made a perfect kid-size bed. Dawn covered him with a blanket before accepting his dad's suggestion that she move across the aisle and join him for an after-dinner brandy.

"My assistant was kind enough to pack and ship the personal items Mrs. Wells will need during her rehab," Ellis told her over snifters of Courvoisier. "She also contacted the cleaning service we use to let them know you'll be filling in as Tom's temporary nanny. They'll have the guest room in the gatehouse apartment ready for you."

Dawn didn't miss the slight but unmistakable emphasis on "temporary." Warming the brandy between her palms, she studied the CEO she'd met for the first time only last week. He'd discarded the coat and tie he'd worn to the ceremony at the Trevi Fountain and popped the top two buttons on his dress shirt. The satiny sheen of the fabric deepened the Viking blue of his eyes but didn't make them any warmer.

"You don't like me very much, do you?"

He was too good, Dawn thought with grudging admiration, and way too smooth to show surprise at her blunt question.

"My son thinks you're totally awesome," he said with a neutral lift of his shoulders. "And Kate and Callie would peel a strip off anyone who dissed you. With those endorsements, what I think doesn't matter."

"Bull. What you think is the *only* thing that matters when it comes to your son." She tipped the snifter and let a trickle of smoky fire burn its way down her throat before picking up the gauntlet again. "So why do you go all fudge-faced whenever I walk in the room?"

"Fudge-faced?"

"Fudge-faced. Poker-faced. Pie-faced. Take your pick."

He sat back, fingering his drink. "Okay," he said after a pause. "I'll be honest. Tommy's got two sets of very loving grandparents. He considers Mrs. Wells his third grandmother. What he doesn't have is a mother. Although…"

Intrigued, Dawn watched his mouth twist into something dangerously close to a smile. Amazing how such a simple realignment of a few facial muscles could transform him from a cool, aloof executive into someone almost human.

"I should warn you he's made several valiant efforts to fill the void," Ellis admitted. "The first time wasn't so bad. After several less than subtle attempts at matchmaking, his pediatrician gently let him know that she was already married. This last time…" He shook his head. "Let's just say his kindergarten teacher and I were both relieved when the school year ended."

Dawn knew Ellis had run a background check on her. She'd done some Googling of her own.

"I went online and saw some of the hotties you've escorted to various charity functions in recent years," she informed him, lifting her brandy in a mock toast. "From the adoring looks on their faces, any one of them would've been happy to fill that void."

The smile disappeared and the cool, distant executive reappeared. "Tommy's void maybe. Not mine. Now, if you'll excuse me, I need to get back to work."

Oooh-kay. She'd put her foot in it that time. Maybe both feet.

Subtle probing these past few days had confirmed that Tommy retained only a hazy concept of his mom. His father's memories were obviously stronger and more immediate.

Tossing back the rest of her brandy, Dawn retreated to the luxuriously appointed aft cabin. She stood beneath a hot, stinging shower for some moments before slithering between what felt like 700-thread count Egyptian cotton sheets. The tail-mounted engines reverberated with a mind-numbing drone that soon rocked her into a deep sleep.

With the six-hour time difference between Rome and Washington, DC, and the fact that they'd flown west across several time zones, the Gulfstream touched down at Ronald Reagan Washington National Airport at almost the same hour it had taken off. Bright autumn sunshine greeted them after they'd exited customs and crossed to the limo waiting in the executive car park.

Brian preferred to drive himself most of the time, since

EAS headquarters was located only a few miles from his home in a shady gated community in Bethesda. After a long flight like this one, though, he was just as happy to let Dominic fight the rush-hour traffic that would already be clogging the city streets.

Once again, Tommy made the introductions. And once again, a longtime EAS employee had to struggle to keep his jaw from dropping as he was introduced to the new nanny.

Temporary new nanny, Brian wanted to add. *Temporary!*

He kept his mouth shut and Dominic managed to keep his tongue from hanging out as he stashed their luggage and slid behind the wheel.

"George Washington Parkway's still pretty clear," he advised Brian. "We should beat the worst of the rush-hour traffic."

When they exited the airport to access the parkway that would take them west along the Potomac River, Tommy graciously pointed out the sights.

"That's the Pentagon," he announced, then swiveled in his seat to indicate the monument across the Tidal Basin. "'N that's the Jefferson Memorial. Thomas Jefferson was a president. Number…uh…"

"Three," Dawn supplied when he appeared stuck. "Actually, I know DC pretty well. I attended school at Georgetown, just a little farther upriver."

"You did? What grade were you in?"

"I was a grad student. That would be, like, grade seventeen."

"Seventeen?" His eyes went big and round. "I'm just starting first grade. Does that mean I gotta do…um—" he gulped in dismay "—*sixteen* more grades?"

"Maybe. If that's what rows your boat." She slanted Brian a quick glance. "Ask your father how many he did."

He gave his dad an accusing stare. "How many?"

"More than seventeen," Brian admitted apologetically. "But I didn't do them one right after another. I took a break when I went into the marines and didn't start grad school until after I got back from Iraq. Your mom took some of the same classes I did," he added in an instinctive attempt to keep Caroline's memory alive for her son. "She was working on a Master's Degree in chemical engineering at the time. That's where we met."

"I know. You told me. Look! There's the Iwo Jima Memorial. They were marines, too, weren't they, Dad?"

"Yes, they were."

Brian had no desire to keep Tom anchored to the past. And he certainly didn't want him to mourn a mother he'd never really known. Yet he found himself fighting a stab of guilt and making a mental apology to Caroline for their son's minimal interest.

Damned if he didn't feel guilty all over again when they crossed the Potomac into Maryland and approached the suburbs of Bethesda and Chevy Chase.

Caroline had spent weeks searching for just the right neighborhood to bring up the big, noisy family she and Brian wanted to have. Six months pregnant at the time, she'd visited local schools, shops and churches to make sure they were international as well as fully integrated. She then spent hours with an architect designing updates to the home they'd purchased. Brian could see her touch in the lush greenery, the bushes that flowered from spring to late fall, the mellow brick and mansard roofs she'd insisted reminded her of their Paris honeymoon.

After she'd died, he'd thought about moving. Many

times. The house, the detached gatehouse, the garden, the curving drive all carried Caroline's personal stamp. But he'd stayed put, pinned in place these past five years by EAS's rapidly expanding business base and the fact that this was the only home Tommy had ever known.

He told himself there was no reason to feel disloyal for bringing Dawn here to live, even temporarily. So she was young and vivacious and gorgeous? No big deal. All that mattered was that she'd clicked with Tommy. His son had been so shaken by Mrs. Wells's accident. Terrified she might die on the operating table, like the mom he couldn't really remember. Brian would have hired a dozen Dawn McGills if that's what it took to ease his son's instinctive fears.

Although one McGill looked to be enough. *More* than enough.

Brian trailed along as Tommy performed tour guide duty again. Eagerly, he showed her through the main house. The two front rooms that had been knocked into one to create a large, airy family room with sunshine pouring through the windows. The spacious, eat-in kitchen. The trellised patio and landscaped backyard with its fanciful gazebo.

The laundry beyond the kitchen contained what Tommy insisted looked like spaceship appliances. The washer and dryer were gray steel, with lighted touch panels and front-loading glass portholes. A side door in the laundry room opened to the three-car garage, which housed Brian's SUV and the small, neat compact Mrs. Wells preferred.

"It's leased," Brian told Dawn. "I can trade it out if you'd like something bigger."

And flashier, he thought, to go with her red hair and multicolored toes.

"It's fine," she assured him.

Nodding, he tapped in a digital code on a flat-paneled

cabinet in the laundry room. "You'll need the car keys, as well as keys to both the gatehouse and main house."

While he retrieved the appropriate keys from the neatly labeled pegs, Tommy darted to the other door. It opened onto a covered walkway paved with flat flagstones.

"This goes to the gatehouse," he explained unnecessarily, since the two-story bungalow sat all of twenty yards away.

It was made of the same mellow brick as the main house and had been converted into a comfortable retreat for Mrs. Wells. Once inside, they confirmed the cleaning service had indeed prepared the gatehouse's second bedroom and restocked its kitchen.

"This is perfect," Dawn exclaimed.

Delighted, she peered through the kitchen's bay windows at the brick-walled backyard. Its lush lawn was bordered by early fall flowers lifting their showy faces to the sky, and the white-painted gazebo was perfect for sipping morning coffee while the sun burned the dew off the grass.

"I can take my laptop outside to work," Dawn told Tommy. "Although I doubt I'll get much done with all those dahlias to distract me. And that green, green grass just begs for a cartwheel or two."

Tommy looked thrilled at the prospect of lawn gymnastics. Brian, on the other hand, had to forcibly slam a mental door on a vision of this woman with her fiery hair flying and her legs whirling through the air.

"And speaking of distractions," Dawn commented, turning to prop a hip against the red tiled counter. "You start school next week, right?"

Tommy looked to his dad for confirmation, then mirrored his nod. "Right."

"That gives us the rest of this week to have fun. I haven't

seen the pandas at the zoo. We need to do that, and check out the new exhibits at the Smithsonian, and…"

"And get in some shopping," Brian interjected.

"Now you're speaking my language! I'm not bragging when I say I'm intimately acquainted with every mall and shopping center within a fifty-mile radius." She turned an inquiring look Tommy. "What about you? Do you like to cruise the malls?"

"No!"

She hid a smile at his undisguised horror and turned to Brian. "So why suggest shopping?"

"The school sent a checklist of supplies and uniform items we need to get."

"He has to wear a uniform?"

"I don't mind," Tommy volunteered. "Dad explained that all the kids wear the same thing so no one makes fun of anyone else's stuff."

"Well, that's sensible."

Sensible, but kind of sad when Dawn remembered all the items of clothing she and Callie and Kate had shared over the years. So many, in so many different colors and styles, that they usually forgot who'd originally owned what. 'Course that was the difference between growing up in a small Massachusetts town versus a major metropolitan area with a socially and economically diverse population.

"Okay, we'll add a shopping expedition to our agenda. You'll need to get me a copy of that checklist, Brian."

"I'll print it out and give it to you at breakfast tomorrow. If you care to join us," he added after a slight pause. "Mrs. Wells usually did."

"She ate dinner with us, too," Tommy added, "'cept when she was tired 'n wanted to put her feet up. She had to do that a lot. But you don't put your feet up, do you?"

Dawn hated to burst his bubble. Especially after he'd

proudly informed EAS's chief pilot that she was, like, a hundred years younger than Mrs. Wells.

"Sometimes," she admitted.

His brow furrowed, and while he struggled to reconcile Fun Dawn with Old Lady Dawn, his father stepped in. "Tommy and I will certainly understand if you'd prefer to take your meals here."

"I may do that when work piles up. Otherwise, I'll be happy to join you guys."

"Okay. Well…" He palmed his chin, scraping the bristles that had sprouted during the long flight. "Since we ate on board, I figured we'd just do sandwiches tonight."

"Sounds good."

"About an hour?"

"I'll be there."

Dawn used the time to empty her roll-on suitcase. There wasn't much to unpack: black slacks and a cream-colored tunic that could be dressed up or down with various tops and scarves; a gauzy sundress; her most comfortable jeans; three stretchy, scoop neck T-shirts; a loose-knit, lightweight sweater; underwear; sandals; flip-flops; a bathing suit; and a zipper bag of costume jewelry. That should be enough to get through another week in DC. If not, or if she stayed longer than anticipated, she'd have to make another excursion to the mall.

With Kate and Callie, if she could catch Callie before she flew home to Boston. Buoyed by the prospect, Dawn stripped off the filmy blouse, zebra-striped belt and wide-legged palazzo pants she'd purchased at a Rome boutique for the surprise ceremony at the Trevi Fountain. The pants had made the flight home without a wrinkle, but the blouse needed some serious steaming.

Dawn hung it on the outside of the walk-in shower stall before adjusting the spray on a showerhead the size of a dinner plate. The hard, pulsing streams revived her jet-lagged muscles and did a lively tap dance on her skin. She felt refreshed and squeaky clean and, once dressed in her favorite jeans and a scoop neck tee, ready to face the world again.

The world maybe, but not her mother.

When she remembered to turn her phone back on, she skimmed the text messages. Two were from members of her team at work, one from the director of a charity she was doing some free design work for and three from her mother.

Dawn had emailed both parents copies of her itinerary in Italy, with the addresses and phone number of the hotels in case of an emergency. She'd also zinged off a quick text when the itinerary had changed to include an unplanned stay in Tuscany, with a side excursion to Venice.

Her mother had texted her twice during that time. Once to ask the reason for the change, and once to insist she contact her father and pound some sense into his head about arrangements for Thanksgiving. These new texts, however, were short and urgent.

I need to speak to you. Call me.

Where are you? I tried your hotel. They said you'd checked out. Call me.

Dawn! Call me!

Swamped by the sudden fear someone in the family was sick or hurt, she pressed the FaceTime button for her mom. When her mother's face filled the screen, she could see herself in the clear green eyes and dark auburn brows.

Maureen McGill's once-bright hair had faded, though, and unhappiness had carved deep lines in her face.

"Finally!" she exclaimed peevishly. "I've texted a half dozen times. Why didn't you answer?"

"We were in the air and only landed a little while ago. I just now turned my phone back on. What's wrong?"

Her mother ignored the question and focused instead on the first part of her daughter's response.

"Why were you in the air? You and Kate and Callie aren't supposed to fly home until tomorrow."

"My plans changed, Mom. What's going on?"

"It's your father."

"Is he okay?"

"No. The man's as far from okay as he always is. He's adamant that you and your brothers and their families have Thanksgiving with him and that trashy blonde he's taken up with."

Arrrrgh! Dawn vowed an instant and painful death for whichever of her brothers or sisters-in-law had told *Maur*een about *Dor*een.

"I know you're all coming here for Christmas," her mother continued, "but I would think that at least one of you wouldn't want me to be alone over Thanksgiving."

"Mom…"

"It's not like he'll put a decent meal on the table. The man burns water, for pity's sake."

"Mom…"

"And I'll be *very* surprised if that woman can cook. I hear she—"

"Mo-ther!"

That was met with a thunderous silence. Dawn used the few seconds of dead air to do the mental ten count she resorted to so often when dealing with either of her parents.

Modulating her voice, she repeated her previous refusal to enter into another holiday war.

"I told you, I'm not getting in the middle of this battle."

Then an escape loomed, and she grabbed it with both hands.

"As a matter of fact, I may not be able to spend Thanksgiving with either Dad *or* you."

"Why not?"

"I've just started a new project."

"So? Boston's less than ninety miles from home. Even if you have to work the day before and after the holiday, you could zip over and right back."

"Actually, I won't be doing this project in Boston. That's why I flew home from Italy a day early. To, ah, consult with the people I'll be working with and get everything set up. I'm in DC now."

Which wasn't a lie. It just didn't offer up specific details about the "project." Her mother would be as skeptical as Kate and Callie about this nanny gig. Even the sparse details Dawn now provided left her peevish.

"You might have told me about this special project," she sniffed, "instead of just letting all this drop after the fact."

"I didn't decide to do it until just a few days ago."

"Have you told your father?"

"Not yet."

As expected, the fact that Maureen was privy to information that her ex-husband wasn't soothed at least some of her ruffled feathers. Dawn moved quickly to exploit the momentary lull.

"I have to go, Mom. I'll call you when I know where I'll be on this project come Thanksgiving."

Or not!

Shoving the phone in the back pocket of her jeans, she went out the back door of the gatehouse. Shadows dimmed the vibrant scarlet and gold of the dahlias in the walled-in backyard, and early fall leaves skittered across the flagstones of the covered walkway connecting the gatehouse to the main house.

It was still early. Only a little past 6:00 p.m. Yet the patch of sky visible above the brick-walled garden was already shading to a deep, federal blue. Appropriate, Dawn thought as her sense of humor seeped back, for a suburb jammed with Washington bureaucrats.

The main house looked big and solid and welcoming. Light streamed through the windows of its country-style kitchen. She could see Brian at the counter with his back to the window. She stopped for a moment, surprised and annoyed by the little flutter just under her ribs.

"Don't be stupid," she muttered to her elongated shadow on the walkway. "The man made his feelings clear enough on the plane. Just go in, make nice and keep all lascivious thoughts to yourself."

Determined to obey that stern admonition, she rapped on the kitchen door.

"It's open!"

She walked in and was greeted by music piping through the house speakers. Something low and jazzy, with lots of sax and horn. A pretty wild sax, as it turned out.

Dawn cocked her head as the notes suddenly soared to a crashing crescendo, dropped into a reedy trough and took flight again, all within the few seconds it took for Brian to reach for his phone and reduce the volume.

"Sorry. I have my phone synced to the kitchen unit and tend to let the music rip. Help yourself to wine if you want it. That's a pretty decent Malbec." He jerked his chin toward the bottle left open to breathe. "Or there's white in the fridge."

"Malbec's good."

She poured a glass and studied him while she took an appreciative sip. Judging by the damp gleam in his chestnut hair, he'd showered, too. He'd also changed out of his suit into jeans and a baggy red T-shirt sporting the logo of the Washington Nationals baseball team.

He hadn't shaved, though. She normally didn't go for the bristly, male model look, but on Ellis it looked good. So good, it was a few seconds before she thought to look around for his son.

"Where's Tommy?"

"Dead to the world."

He sliced tomatoes with the precision of an engineer. Which he was, she remembered, and wondered why she'd never considered engineers particularly sexy before.

"He barely made it upstairs before he conked out. I got him out of his clothes and into bed, but I expect his internal clock will have him up and watching cartoons at 3:00 a.m." He shot her a glance that was half apology, half warning. "He may be a little hard to handle until he's back on schedule."

"I'll make sure he burns off his excess energy at the zoo tomorrow. And if he gets on my nerves too badly, I'll just hang him by the heels over the polar bear pool." She held up a palm, grinning at his look of alarm. "I'm kidding!"

"Yeah, well…" He added the tomato slices to a platter of lettuce, sweet-smelling onions and cheese. "I've considered something along those lines a time or two myself."

"Then he looks up at you with those wide, innocent eyes," she said, laughing, "and you can't remember what the heck got you all wrapped around the axle."

"That pretty well sums it up. BLTs okay? Or there's sliced chicken breast in the fridge."

"A BLT sounds great."

"White, whole wheat or pumpernickel?"

"Pumpernickel. Definitely pumpernickel. I'll do that," she offered when he extracted an uncut loaf from a bread bin and exchanged the tomato knife for one with a serrated edge. "You do the bacon."

She joined him at the counter and went to work. She'd cut two thick slices before she realized he'd paused in the act of arranging the bacon on a microwavable tray. She turned, found him bent toward her, frowning, and almost collided with his nose.

Startled, she drew back a few inches. "Something wrong?"

"No." He straightened, and a hint of red crept into his whiskered cheeks. "It's your shampoo. I can smell the lemon but there's something else, something I can't identify. It's been driving me crazy."

Dawn tried to decide whether she should feel stoked by that bit about driving him crazy, or chagrined that it was her shampoo doing the driving. What she *shouldn't* be feeling, though, was all goose-bumpy.

"That's probably lotus blossom," she got out a little breathlessly. "The company I work for manufactures this shampoo. Lemon and lotus blossom, with a touch of coconut oil for sheen. All natural ingredients."

Oh, for pity's sake! This was ridiculous. Men had leaned over her before. A good number of them, if she did say so herself. Some were even sexier than Brian Ellis. But not many, she couldn't help thinking as he bent down again.

"I don't think I've sniffed a lotus before." He raised a hand, twirled a still-damp tendril around a finger. "Or felt anything so soft and silky. The coconut's doing a good job."

Well, damn! Who would've thunk it? This unexpected proximity seemed to have knocked Mr. Cool, Calm and Collected a few degrees off balance. The realization should have given Dawn a dart of feminine satisfaction. Instead, she had to struggle to remember where she was.

She barely registered the brick-walled kitchen or the copper pots hanging over the cook island. Brian blocked almost everything else from view. All she could see was the prickle of beard on his cheeks and chin. The slight dent in his nose. The narrowed blue eyes. She was still trying to decipher their message when he released her hair and brushed a knuckle down her cheek.

"About our discussion on the plane…"

Which discussion? She was damned if she could sort out her jumbled thoughts with his knuckle making another pass.

"I don't dislike you."

"Good to know, Ellis."

"Just the opposite, McGill." Another stroke, followed by a look of pure regret. "Which is why we can't do what I'm aching to do right now."

"You're right," she got out unsteadily as he cupped her cheek. "We can't. Because…?"

As Brian dropped his hand, guilt hit him like a hammer.

Because, he thought with a searing stab of regret, *we're standing in the kitchen Caroline redesigned brick-by-aged-brick. Under the rack holding the dented copper pots she'd discovered in a shopping expedition to the Plaka in Athens. With a loaf of the pumpernickel she'd taught him to tolerate, if not particularly like, sitting right there on the counter.*

Christ! He knew he shouldn't keep hauling around this load of guilt. Everyone said so. The grief counselor recommended by Caroline's oncologist. The various "experts" he'd consulted on issues dealing with single parenting. The well-meaning friends and associates who'd fixed him up with *their* friends and associates.

He'd dated off and on in the five years since his wife's death. No one seriously. No one he'd brought here, to the home Caroline had taken such delight in. And he sure as hell had never ached to kiss one of those casual dates six ways to Sunday. Then hike her onto the counter, unsnap her jeans and yank them…

Dammit! Furious with himself, Brian stepped back and offered the only excuse he could. "Because Tommy's upstairs. He might wake up and wander down to the kitchen."

She recognized a pathetic excuse when she heard one. Eyes widening, she regarded him with patently fake horror. "Omigod! How totally awful if he walked in on us trading spit. He'd be *so* grossed out."

"Dawn, I…"

She cut him off with a wave of the serrated knife. "I got the picture, Ellis. No messing around in the house. Not with me, anyway. Are you going to nuke that bacon or not?"

The flippant response threw him off. Almost as much as her smile when she attacked the pumpernickel again. It wasn't smug. Or cynical. Or disappointed. Just tight and mocking.

Feeling like a teenager who'd just tripped over his own hormones, he tore some paper towels from the roll, covered the tray and shoved it in the microwave. Within moments the aroma of sizzling bacon permeated the kitchen and almost—almost!—wiped out the scent of the damned lotus blossoms.

Chapter Three

Dawn was wide-awake and skimming through emails at midnight. Not surprising, since she'd zoned out for a solid five hours on the plane. Her mind said it was the middle of the night but her body thrummed with energy.

Then there was that near miss in the kitchen. She and Ellis had come nose to nose, close enough to exchange Eskimo kisses. Although there'd been no actual contact, electricity had arced between them. He'd felt the sizzle. So had she. Still did, dammit! No wonder she couldn't sleep.

Dawn didn't kid herself. She knew what they'd experienced was purely physical. She'd shared that same sizzle with too many deliciously handsome men to read any more into it than basic animal attraction. It was just Ellis's pheromones responding to her scent.

As advertised, she thought with a grin. Dawn and her team had designed the labels for this particular line of bath products, which had been based on a study by the Smell

& Taste Research Foundation in Chicago. The study demonstrated how combinations of various natural products triggered a wide variety of responses, including a few she found very interesting. Supposedly, the scents of lavender and pumpkin pie when sniffed together reportedly increased penile blood flow by forty percent!

Naturally, Dawn had read the study from cover to cover. She'd had to, in order to conceptualize the designs for the ads. She'd also conducted her own field trials of the new products. Her final choice of the lemon and lotus blossom shampoo didn't appear to increase penile blood flow quite as dramatically as the lavender and pumpkin, but it had done wonders for her normally flyaway red curls. And it had certainly impacted Brian Ellis's libido, she thought with a stab of satisfaction.

Not that she'd specifically intended to impact it. Although she was as attracted to Big Bad Brian as he apparently was to her, neither of them could let the sizzle gather steam or heat. He'd made it clear he wasn't looking for any kind of permanent relationship, and Dawn was pretty well convinced there wasn't any such animal.

She knew she came across as fun and flirtatious. Knew, too, she'd developed a love 'em and leave 'em reputation. The irony was that her parents' toxic example had left her so gun-shy that she never went beyond flirting. Well, almost never. The only exceptions had come after she'd convinced herself she was in love—which only went to prove how flawed her instincts were.

That thought led to a quick glance at the digital clock on the nightstand. It was twelve twenty in DC. Six twenty in the morning in Rome. Kate and Callie would be up now and getting ready to leave for the airport.

Propping her shoulders against the headboard, Dawn booted up her laptop. How did any friendship survive these days without FaceTime? She tapped her fingers against the computer's frame while waiting for the connection. Kate came on first, wide-awake and wearing a wide, cat-got-the-cream smile.

"Bitch!" Dawn exclaimed. "You had wake-up sex."

"I did. And it was wonderful. Glorious. Stupendous. With the sun just coming up over the seven hills and…"

"Please! Spare me the details."

"About what?" Callie asked as her face materialized on the other half of the split screen.

"About Kate's wake-up call. Apparently she started the day off right." Frowning, Dawn peered at the screen. "You, on the other hand, look as pasty as overcooked fettucini."

"Gee, thanks." Callie tucked a wayward strand of mink-brown hair behind her ear. "You're not exactly glowing, either. Jet lag?"

"Yeah. No. Sort of."

"Uh-oh. What's wrong?"

"Nothing."

"Don't give us that," Kate huffed. "We knew you before you got braces or boobs. Why so blah?"

"I think I'd better change my shampoo."

Both women grasped the underlying context instantly. They should. They'd devoured the smell study as avidly as Dawn. They'd also been privy to the results of her personal field trials.

"Change it," Kate urged. "Tonight!"

The emphatic responses made Dawn blink. "It's not exactly a life-or-death situation."

"Yet."

Callie's response carried considerably less emphasis but still hit home. "You told us you thought Brian was a fantastic dad, but otherwise a little cool and detached. Does that remind you of anyone?"

Dawn blinked again. "Oh! Well. Maybe."

Fiancé Number One hadn't been either cool or remote, but he did tend to act supercilious toward store clerks and restaurant servers. Having worked as both during her high school and college years, Dawn was finally forced to admit the truth. Not only did she not love the guy, she didn't really like him.

Fiancé Number Two was outgoing, gregarious and a generous tipper. Until he decided someone had wronged him, that is. Then he morphed from fun-loving to icily, unrelentingly determined on revenge. Dawn still carried the scars from that close encounter of the scary kind.

She couldn't see Brian morphing into another Mr. Hyde. She really couldn't. Then again, she'd been wrong before.

"All right," she told her friends. "I'll lay in a new supply of shampoo tomorrow."

"Do it," Kate urged again, giving her the evil eye. "I'd better not catch a single whiff of lemons or lotus blossoms when you and Brian and Tommy come to dinner this Saturday."

"We're coming to dinner?"

"You are. Seven o'clock. My place. Correction," she amended with a quick, goofy smile. "*Our* place. Travis gets in that morning."

"I thought he needed to fly back to Florida after he wraps things up at Aviano."

"He does, but he's taking a few days in between to scope out his new job at Ellis Aeronautical Systems. Callie will be there, too," Kate offered as added incentive. "Despite her objections to banging headboards, she's agreed to spend some time with us in Washington. So Saturday. Seven o'clock. Our place."

"Got it!"

Dawn signed off, relieved that she'd shared the incident with Brian but feeling guilty that she'd lumped him in with her two late, unlamented ex-fiancés. Yes, he was aloof at times. And yes, he held something of himself back from everyone but Tommy. But she hadn't seen him condescend to anyone. Take his pilot and limo driver, for example. Judging by their interaction with their boss, the relationship was one of mutual respect.

Nor could Dawn imagine Brian peeling back that calm, unruffled exterior to reveal a core as petty as Fiancé Number Two's. Of course, she'd never imagined Two having that hidden vindictive streak, either.

Just remembering what the bastard had put her through after their breakup gave Dawn a queasy feeling. Slamming the laptop lid, she dumped it on the nightstand, flipped off the lamp and slithered down on the soft sheets. Their sunshine-fresh scent reinforced her determination to hit a drugstore and buy some bland-smelling shampoo first thing in the morning. Then, she decided with an effort to rechannel her thoughts, she and Tommy would have some *F-U-N*!

The next four days flew by. Dawn stuck to her proposed agenda of zoo, Smithsonian and shopping, with side excursions to Fort Washington, the United States Mint and paddle-boating on the Tidal Basin. The outings weren't totally without peril. Fortunately, Dawn grabbed the back strap of Tommy's life preserver just in time to keep him from nose-diving into the water when he tried to scramble out of the paddleboat. And she only lost him for a few, panic-filled moments at the Air and Space Museum.

Those near disasters aside, she cheerfully answered his barrage of questions and fed off his seemingly inexhaustible, hop-skip-jump energy. Together, they thoroughly enjoyed revisiting so many of her old stomping grounds.

As an added bonus, the weather couldn't have been more perfect. An early cold snap had rolled down from Canada and erased every last trace of summer heat and smog. Washington flaunted itself in the resulting brisk autumn air. The monuments gleamed in sparkling sunshine. The fat lines at tourist sites skinnied down. There was even a faint whiff of wood smoke in the air when the two explorers retuned home Friday afternoon, pooped but happy.

They'd saved a picnic on the grounds of the Franklin Delano Roosevelt Memorial for their last major excursion of the week. The memorial had opened during Dawn's last year at Georgetown, when she'd been too swamped with course work and partying to explore the site. So her grin was as wide as Tommy's at dinner that evening, as he proudly displayed the photo snapped by an accommodating bystander. It portrayed him and Dawn hunched down to get cheek-to-jowl with the statue of FDR's much-loved Scottish terrier.

"He's the only dog to have his statue right there, with a president," Tommy informed his dad.

"I didn't know that."

"Me, neither. We Googled him, though, and learned all kinds of interesting stuff. His name was Fala, 'n he could perform a whole bag of tricks, like sit 'n roll over 'n bark for his dinner."

"Sounds like a smart pooch."

"He was! 'N he was in the army!" The historical events got a little blurry at that point. Forehead scrunching, Tommy jabbed at his braised pork. "A sergeant or general or something."

"I think he was a private," Dawn supplied.

"Right, a private. 'Cause he put a dollar in a piggy bank every single day to help pay for soldiers' uniforms 'n stuff."

His fork stopped halfway to his mouth. "Musta been a big piggy bank."

Brian flashed Dawn a grin, quick and potent and totally devastating. She was still feeling its whammy when he broke the code for his son.

"I suspect maybe the piggy bank was a bit of WWII propaganda. A story put out by the media," he explained, "to get people to buy bonds or otherwise contribute to the war effort."

Tommy didn't appear to appreciate this seeming denigration of the heroic terrier. Chin jutting, he conceded the point with obvious reluctance. "Maybe. But Fala was more than just proper...popor..."

"Propaganda."

"Right. Dawn 'n me..." His dad's brows lifted, and the boy made a swift midcourse correction. "Dawn 'n I read that soldiers used his name as a code word during some big battle."

"The Battle of the Bulge," she confirmed when his cornflower blue eyes turned her way.

"Yeah, that one. 'N if the Germans didn't know who Fala was, our guys blasted 'em."

Dawn was a little surprised at how many details the boy had retained of FDR's beloved pet. Brian, however, appeared to know exactly where this detailed narrative was headed. Setting down his fork, he leaned back in his chair.

"Let me guess," he said to his son. "You now want a Scottish terrier instead of the English bulldog you campaigned for last month."

"Well..."

"And what about the beagle you insisted you wanted before the bulldog?"

Tommy's blue eyes turned turbulent, and Dawn had a sudden sinking sensation. Too late, she understood the motivation behind the boy's seemingly innocent request for her to check out the grooming requirements for Scottish terriers.

"Beagles 'n bulldogs shed," he stated, chin jutting again. "Like the spaniel you said we had when I was a baby. The one I was 'lergic to. But Scotties don't shed. They gotta be clipped. 'N they're really good with kids. Dawn read that on Google," he finished triumphantly. "She thinks a Fala dog would be perfect for me."

Four days, Dawn thought with a silent groan. She and Brian had maintained a civilized facade for four entire days. After her emergency purchase of the blandest shampoo on the market, there'd been no leaning. No sniffing. No near misses. Just a polite nonacknowledgment of the desire that had reared its head for those few, breathless moments.

The glance Brian now shot her suggested the polite facade had developed a serious crack. But his voice was unruffled as he addressed his son's apparently urgent requirement for a canine companion.

"We talked about this, buddy. Remember? With the trip to Italy this summer and you just about to start school, we decided to wait awhile before bringing home a puppy."

"*You* decided, not me."

"Puppies need a lot of attention. You can't leave them alone all day and…"

"He wouldn't be alone. Dawn can watch him while I'm at school 'n clean up his poop 'n stuff."

The crack yawned deeper and wider.

"Dawn's already been very generous with her time," Brian told his son, his tone easy but his eyes cool. "I'm sure she wants to get back to her job and her friends. We can't ask her to take on puppy training before she goes home to Boston."

"But I don't *want* her to go home to Boston. I want her to stay here, with us." His belligerence gave way to a look of sly cunning. "She could, if you 'n her got married."

Neither adult corrected his grammar this time, and he launched into a quick, impassioned argument.

"You told me you like her, Dad. 'N I see the way you stare at her sometimes, when she's not looking."

Dawn raised a brow.

"She likes you, too. She told me."

This time it was Brian who hiked a brow.

"So you should get married," Tommy concluded. "You'd have to kiss 'n sleep in the same bed 'n take showers together, but you wouldn't mind that, would you?"

His father parried the awkward question with the skill of long practice. "Where'd you get that bit about taking showers together? You'd better not tell me you've been watching TV after lights-out again."

"No, sir. Cindy told me that's what her mom and dad do. It sounds pretty yucky but she says they like it."

Dawn struggled to keep a straight face. "Who's Cindy?"

"A very precocious young lady who lives on the next block," Brian answered drily. "She and Tommy went to the same preschool. They've gotten together with some of their other friends for play times during the summer. And her big brother Addy—Addison Caruthers the Third—stays with Tommy sometimes when Mrs. Wells needs a break."

"Addy's cool," Tommy announced, "but Cindy's my *best* friend, even if she is a girl. You might meet her 'n her mom when you take me to school Monday." He thought about that for a moment. "Maybe you should ask her mom if you would really hafta do that shower stuff."

Dawn bit the inside of her lip. "Maybe I should," she said gravely. "That could certainly be a deal-breaker."

She glanced across the table, expecting Brian to appreciate this absurd turn in the conversation. His cheeks still carried that hint of red, but she detected no laughter in his expression.

Oops. Message received. Propping her elbows on the table, Dawn tried to deflect Tommy's latest attempt to fill the void in his life.

"The thing is, kiddo, I'm allergic to marriage."

"Really? Like I am to dog hair?"

"Pretty much. Every time I think about marching down the aisle, I get all nervous and sweaty and itchy."

"I get itchy, too. Then my eyes turn red and puffy."

"There! You know what it's like. So…" Smiling, she tried to let the boy down gently. "Although I like your dad and he likes me, we're just friends. And we'll stay friends. All three of us. I promise."

"Even after you go back to Boston?"

"Even after I go back to Boston."

Her smile stayed in place, but the thought of resuming her hectic life left a dusty taste in her mouth. She washed it down with a swish of the extremely excellent Syrah that Brian had uncorked to accompany their braised pork.

With his characteristically quicksilver change in direction, Tommy shifted topics. Dawn contributed little as the conversation switched from Scottish terriers and adult shower habits to the video he *had* to watch before bed that night. From there it zinged to the laundry list of items he'd crammed into his school backpack.

The question of when his temporary nanny would head north again didn't come up again until after he'd dashed up to his room to retrieve the overstuffed pack and demonstrated to his father exactly why he needed every item to survive his first full day of elementary school.

"Sorry 'bout that third-person proposal," Brian said as

he and Dawn carried the dishes to the sink. "I did warn you, though."

"Yes, you did. Good thing I'm 'lergic to marriage, or Tommy might have swept me right off my feet."

He passed her the dinner plates, which she rinsed and slotted in the lower rack. Straightening, she found him standing with a dessert bowl in each hand.

"I appreciate the way you stepped in to help us out, Dawn. I really do. So I need to tell you that I talked to Lottie Wells this afternoon. Her rehab is going fine, but she's decided to stay in California with her sister."

Dawn's heart emitted the craziest little ping. Was he going to ask her to stay? Suggest some sort of loose arrangement that would keep him and Tommy in her life and vice versa? His next comments put those thoughts on instant ice.

"Since I suspected that would be Lottie's decision, I had my assistant compile a list of prospective replacements. She's contacted the top five on the list and I'm flying them in for interviews, starting Monday."

"Oh. Good." She grabbed the dessert bowls and jammed them into the top rack. "I've had a great time with Tommy… and with you," she added belatedly. "But you're right. I need to get back to my real life."

The one filled with twelve- and fourteen-hour days at the office. Late nights hunched over her laptop. Casual dates with men whose names she couldn't remember.

"I also need to catch up on some work," she said briskly. "Tell Tommy good-night for me. We haven't planned any outings for the weekend, by the way, since I assumed you'd want to spend time with him before his big day Monday."

"Good assumption. And about Monday…"

She paused, one brow lifting.

"I'll take him to school that morning. They want parents to sign kids in the first day."

"Makes sense," she said with a shrug that disguised her disappointment.

"The school also needs to verify alternate emergency contacts," Brian continued. "Since both sets of grandparents live out of state, I'll designate them as secondary alternates and you as primary."

"That'll work."

For now. Until he hired a permanent replacement.

Just as well he intended to start those interviews next week, Dawn decided grimly. She needed to cut loose from Tommy the Terrible—and his dad—before the ties went deeper or wrapped tighter around her heart.

The wineglasses were the last to hit the dishwasher. They were tall-stemmed, paper thin and probably expensive. With ruthless determination, she plunked them in the top rack beside Tommy's milk glass and skimmed a quick glance around the kitchen.

"Looks like we're done here," she said flatly. "See you in the morning. Or whenever."

She made it to the kitchen door. The lighted walkway to the gatehouse beyond offered a welcome escape.

"Dawn, wait!"

His face was set and his lips tight when she turned to face him.

"These past four days. I've enjoyed… I've been…"

"You've been what?" she taunted with a mocking smile. "Staring at me when I'm not looking? Wishing you'd leaned in a little closer that first night? Wondering why I changed my shampoo?"

The words were barely out of her mouth before she realized she'd baited a caged tiger. The skin stretched taut over his cheeks, and a sudden heat flamed in his blue eyes. Muttering a curse, he strode over to where she stood.

"Yes, yes and yes. I'm also wondering why the hell I waited so long to do this."

She wanted to pretend she was shocked when he slid a palm around her nape and tipped her face to his. She had that instant, that breath-stealing second to protest or jerk away. When she didn't do either, his mouth came down on hers.

The truth was she'd been imagining the taste of him, the feel of him, since their first meeting in Venice. As his lips moved over hers, reality far exceeded her expectations.

The man could kiss!

Dawn had compiled a fairly decent sample size over the years and would rank Brian Ellis's technique in the top tenth percentile. Okay, maybe *the* top percentile. He didn't go all Neanderthal and bend her back over his arm. Didn't pooch his lips or get wet and sloppy. He just sort of…overwhelmed her. His broad shoulders, his hard muscles, the hand on her nape. Riding a wave of sensual delight, she locked her arms around his neck.

With a low growl, he widened his stance. His other hand cupped her bottom and drew her into him. She could feel him harden, feel the answering desire curl hot and sweet in her belly. She pressed closer, eager for the contact, but he jerked his head up.

His breathing harsh, he stared down at her for long seconds before grinding out an apology. "I shouldn't have done that. I'm sorry."

She wasn't, but his next words pushed her close.

"Wonderful example that would have set for Tommy if he'd walked in."

"Hey, your kid just proposed we scrub each other's

back. I doubt a little lip-lock would've traumatized him for life."

"No, but it…"

"Never mind. I get it. We don't want to confuse the poor kid or let him think that what just happened sprang from anything but good, old-fashioned lust."

When he didn't disagree, she tipped him another, even more mocking smile.

"'Night, stud. See you around."

Chapter Four

Saturday morning dawned bright and sunny, a direct contrast to Brian's mood. The kiss he'd laid on Dawn the previous evening had made for a restless night.

Restless, hell! It had left him hard and hurting. Good thing she'd breezed out of the kitchen when she had or he might have compounded his stupidity by suggesting they share a brandy after Tommy trotted off to bed. Brandy being code for getting down on the sofa. Or the floor. Or a king-size bed with soft sheets and her luscious body stretched out in naked abandon.

Dammit! He threw back the comforter and stalked to the bathroom, determined to erase the mental image of shimmering auburn hair splayed across his pillow and those lush, full breasts bared to his touch.

The image wouldn't erase. It followed him into the shower, then stared back at him from the steam-clouded mirror over the sink. Laughing, sensual, inviting, she teased and taunted him. She knew he wanted her. The feeling was mutual. That message had come through with the astounding clarity of a radio signal transmitted via a 200 gigahertz, ultrahigh frequency satellite band.

The same band, he remembered abruptly, that EAS had been lobbying for access to for months. Which in turn reminded him of his scheduled meeting with the FCC on Monday. Between that potentially contentious meeting, getting Tommy settled in school and interviewing prospective nannies, it looked to be a busy start to his week.

Yanking off the towel he'd wrapped around his waist, Brian tossed it at the laundry basket before pulling on a pair of jeans and his favorite Washington Nationals sweatshirt. He threaded the laces through the eyeholes of his running shoes, thinking of all he *should* do today. Like go into the office for a few hours to prep for the FCC meeting. And, while he was there, give Travis Westbrook a personal tour of EAS headquarters. EAS's new VP of Test Operations and Evaluation had landed in DC late last night and confirmed his arrival by email.

Brian paused, the laces snaked around his fingers. Somehow he suspected Travis wouldn't mind delaying the EAS tour for a day. The pilot was still making up for lost time with his wife. He and Kate had looked so happy when they'd renewed their wedding vows at the impromptu ceremony beside the Trevi Fountain. So secure in the love that had been tested for long, agonizing months but refused to keel over and die. The kind of love that lasted a lifetime.

The kind Brian and Caroline had thought they'd have.

Slewing around, he studied the framed photo on his nightstand. It was a casual, unposed shot of his wife with Tommy in her arms, taken mere weeks before they'd discovered that her sudden imbalance and dizzy spells were caused by a fast-growing tumor that had wrapped itself around her brain stem.

Over the next agonizing months the tumor relentlessly strangled the nerves that controlled every basic bodily function. Her breathing. Her heart rate. Blood flow. Eye movement. Hearing. Sensory perception. After chemo and radiation failed to halt the tumor's pernicious growth, she opted for a last, desperate attempt to have it cut out.

She and Brian both knew the odds were she wouldn't survive the surgery. They'd said their goodbyes in the purple twilight punctuated with beeping monitors, then spent the night spooned against each other in her hospital bed. Both sets of parents had arrived early the next morning, bringing Tommy with them. The hours that followed were lost in a misty haze. Brian couldn't remember the expression on the surgeon's face when she broke the grim news. He retained only a vague memory of his father-in-law's shattered sobs and his quietly efficient mother helping him through the business of death.

With a knot in his throat, he realized that he could barely recall the sound of his wife's laughter or the title of the tune she used to hum all the time. Another woman's laugh now echoed through their house. Another woman's voice was in his head. A vivacious, seductive woman who hadn't tried to disguise her response to his kiss. Or her mocking smile when he'd damned near tripped over his own feet backing away.

Calling himself ten kinds of an idiot, Brian went downstairs and found the coffee already made. The note propped against the pot informed him Dawn had come over early to borrow some artificial sweetener. It also announced that she had a ton of work to catch up on, so she'd hang at the gatehouse while he and Tommy enjoyed a day doing man things. She'd see them this evening. Brian could buzz when he and Tommy were ready to head to the Westbrooks' for dinner.

He crumpled the note with a combination of relief and irrational pique at the casual way she'd cut him and Tommy out of her day. Gathering the makings for French toast, he cracked eggs into a mixing bowl with something less than his usual dexterity. He added milk and a dash of cinnamon, then set the bowl aside.

Topping off his coffee, he booted up his iPad to skim the financial news until muted thumps and a quick flush signaled his son's return to the land of the living. He was arranging bread slices in a heavy iron skillet when Tommy rushed into the kitchen. He was still in his pajamas, his hair sticking up in spikes and sleep crusting the corners of his eyes.

"Back upstairs," Brian directed. "Wash your face, brush your teeth, get dressed."

Ignoring the order, Tommy swept the kitchen with an eager glance. "Where's Dawn?"

"She's working."

"I gotta tell her something."

"Not now, Tommy."

"It's okay," his son countered, darting for the door. "I'll be quick."

"Not now."

"I just wanna…"

"Thomas…"

The warning growl stopped the boy in his tracks, but Brian didn't kid himself. Long experience had taught him there would be more to come.

Predictably, his son's chin jutted and he threw his father a defiant look. "Dawn said I could come over anytime."

"And I'm saying she's busy. Haul your behind upstairs, then we'll have breakfast and decide what to do today."

"But…"

"Now!"

He stopped short of a roar but got his point across. Still mulish but wary, Tommy retreated.

Brian had to battle the urge to call him back and smooth things over with a hug. Instead, he concentrated on whipping the eggs and milk into a froth. Pouring the mixture over the bread slices, he left them to soak and returned to his iPad to check the football schedule.

He had the bacon sizzling and the French toast browning when Tommy reappeared. The earlier power struggle forgotten, he hopped up on a counter stool and wanted to know what they were going to do today.

"How about we take in the Redskins' home game?"

"Really?"

"Really."

EAS maintained a box at the stadium. When not used for entertaining clients, employees could vie for the seats via an in-house lottery system. All but one ticket was taken for today's game, but Brian could pay an exorbitant premium to squeeze in an additional guest.

"What about Dawn?" Tommy wanted to know. "Is she coming, too?"

"She said she'd see us this evening when we go to dinner with Major and Mrs. Westbrook. It's just us guys today. Kickoff's at 10:00 a.m.," he informed his excited son. "So eat fast, and we'll hit the road."

Dawn replied to Brian's text advising that he and Tommy were going to the game with a smiley face and a cheerful "Have fun!" A short time later, she caught the rumble of the garage door going up, the SUV gunning to life and the door rolling down again.

Then quiet. The empty kind of quiet that comes with

the absence of other human activity. Despite the music sent via Bluetooth from Dawn's iPhone to the gatehouse's wireless speaker system, a sense of solitude seemed to wrap around her.

Antsy, she keyed up the volume. Her work playlist contained an eclectic mix of genres, everything from classical to country to easy listening to movie and Broadway soundtracks. The words and music usually blended into the background when her creative muse took over. Unfortunately, Madam Muse appeared to have gone AWOL this morning, and the ballad now coming through the speakers scraped at her nerves.

Killing the music, she leaned back in her chair and stretched both arms over her head. She'd been wrestling with concepts for an ad campaign that targeted millennials, many of whom considered themselves civic-minded and environmentally responsible consumers. A recent survey indicated consumers in the eighteen to thirty-four age bracket were more likely than their older, baby boomer counterparts to respond to cause-related campaigns. Additional surveys confirmed they were also more likely to try unique and exotic products.

As a result, Dawn's company was preparing to market a new line of all-natural vegetable chips. And for every giant bag of the veggie chips purchased by consumers, her company would contribute small, individual-size bags to schools for lunches and snacks to help combat childhood obesity. Personally, she didn't care for the Jalapeño Kale Bites, but she could devour both the Zucchini Carrot Crunchies and the Sweet Potato Stix by the bowlful!

The proposed packaging helped, she thought as she eyed her computer screen. Although the bags were made from recycled paper, the company's packaging engineers had managed to make them look glossy and slick. Now all

Dawn and her team had to do was come up with distinctive logos for each chip that would appeal to schoolkids, health-conscious adults and—hopefully!—the halftime, snacks-and-beer-guzzling crowd.

Speaking of which…

She didn't miss Tommy and Brian. She really didn't. Still, it would've been nice if they'd invited her to the game. She would've declined, of course. She would've had to after pleading work as an excuse to avoid breakfast and any potential postmortems of that torrid kitchen kiss.

Damn the man, anyway! Where did he get off making her feel like a world-class troll when *he'd* stomped across the kitchen? *He'd* wrapped his palm around her nape? And *he'd* tugged her into that intimate, totally erotic embrace?

Okay, so maybe *she* should've backed away. Or at least issued a proceed-at-your-own-peril warning. Maybe then she wouldn't be so annoyed with herself for hiding out in the gatehouse while Tommy and his dad were out in the crisp fall air, enjoying the noise and controlled mayhem of professional football.

Giving up all attempts to concentrate on Sweet Potato Stix, Dawn put her laptop to sleep and marched into the living room. Moments later she had her feet up and the TV tuned to the raucous pregame activities.

The fresh air and excitement did a number on Tommy. He fell asleep on the drive home and woke up cranky when they reached the house. So cranky, Brian called the high schooler who occasionally babysat when Mrs. Wells required a much-needed break. Luckily Addy's own plans for the evening had fallen through and he was available for pizza and videos with Tommy.

As instructed, Brian buzzed Dawn when he was ready to leave for the Westbrooks'. She came in through the kitchen and damned near gave him a stroke. It was the first time he'd seen her all glammed up since the ceremony in Rome, when Kate and Travis had renewed their vows. She'd pretty much stuck to jeans and scoop neck tops this past week and had worn her hair either clipped up or caught back in a loose twist.

She'd pulled out all the stops tonight, though, or so it seemed to a stunned Brian. Slinky black slacks. A black sweater that emphasized her lush curves. A chunky gold necklace interwoven with iridescent emerald beads the exact color of her eyes. Her hair fell in loose, coppery curls to her shoulders and looked so soft and shiny that Brian had to physically restrain himself from moving in for a sniff. He was still battling the urge when she gave the half-empty pizza carton on the counter a surprised glance.

"The game and fresh air wore Tommy out," Brian explained, doing his damnedest to keep the reply casual. "I called the Westbrooks to let them know he won't be coming. He's going to hang with Addy tonight."

"His friend Cindy's big brother?"

"Right. They're in the den. Come on, I'll introduce you."

Brian wasn't surprised when Dawn's initial glimpse of the lanky teen produced a quick blink. The kid's baggy jeans rode so low on his hips they defied the laws of gravity. And what looked like a recent and particularly virulent acne eruption no doubt explained his availability on a Saturday night. In the case of Addison Caruthers the Third, however, appearances were most definitely deceiving.

"Addy's a Nobel Prize winner in the making," Brian couldn't resist bragging. "He came in second in the International Science and Engineering Fair last year."

"Yeah," Tommy chimed in from the floor, pizza slice in hand. "He built a transmitter that warns blind people

'bout stuff in their way. It sends beeps through their ear-
buds right into their brains."

Downplaying his accomplishment with an embarrassed
shrug, the teen clambered to his size thirteen feet. "Nice
to meet you, Ms. McGill. Tommy's been telling me about
you. He, uh, said you guys really had fun in Italy."

"We did."

Brian bit back a smile as Addy made a heroic effort to
keep his gaze pinned on Dawn's face.

"Are you, er, going to stay awhile?"

"Only until a new nanny is hired."

"I don't want a new nanny," Tommy sang out in a now-
familiar chorus. "I want Dawn."

His father ignored him. "We won't be late," he told Addy.

"No prob."

"You've got my cell phone number, right?"

"Right."

When Dawn turned to leave, the teen lost his inner battle. His glance glommed on to her back before dropping
to the rear outlined so enticingly by those slinky slacks.

"Oh, man," he murmured to Brian, his Adam's apple
bouncing. "The lady is OTC."

Brian probably shouldn't have asked, but did, anyway.
"Translation?"

"Off the chain, Mr. E. *Off. The. Chain.*"

Nodding an agreement, Brian stooped to knuckle his
son's head affectionately, then followed Dawn through the
kitchen to the garage. She made no comment until they
were in the SUV and backing out. "Amazing kid. Has he
decided where he wants to go to college?"

"Not yet. He's had so many offers he's taking his time
about deciding."

She hesitated a few beats before making a suggestion.
"My company puts out an all-natural acne treatment. A

water-based gel containing an extract from the Australian tea tree. It doesn't work as quickly as some over-the-counter ointments, but we've compiled considerable test data showing it causes significantly lower side effects. If you think it won't crush Addy's feelings, I could have my assistant overnight some free samples."

Grinning, Brian wheeled the SUV onto the street. "I can pretty well guarantee it would crush more than his feelings. The kid thinks you're 'Off. The. Chain.' He probably won't—" he searched for a polite term "—deflate for an hour."

Her laugh rippled across the SUV's darkened interior. Brian's hands tightened on the wheel while his mind zinged back to this morning, when he'd tried to recall the sound of Caroline's laughter. Then slowly, deliberately, he loosened his grip.

Damned if he'd let guilt ride his shoulders tonight. He was about to have dinner with a trio of new friends and a stunningly beautiful woman. He would just enjoy the food, the wine and the company.

The trio actually turned out to be a quartet. In addition to the Westbrooks and Kate's close friend, Callie Langston, Joe Russo had arrived in DC that afternoon. The enigmatic, high-powered security expert wouldn't—or couldn't—share any details concerning his short-notice visit, but he was anxious to maximize his time in the capital.

"My people have reviewed the operating procedures your security team sent us," he told Brian. "They have several recommendations, but before I put my stamp on them I'd like to conduct a walk-through of your headquarters. And, when I can work it in, I'll do the same at your fabrication and test facilities in Texas."

"Actually," Brian said as Kate sailed in from the kitchen with a tray of appetizers that put his taste buds on instant alert, "I wanted to show Travis his new office and give him a feel for our corporate operation before he has to fly down to Florida. Since both of your schedules are so tight, we could do it tomorrow."

"Works for me," Joe said.

"Same here," Travis confirmed.

"Okay. Let's meet in the EAS lobby at ten. I'll notify security and have badges ready for you."

"Enough business, guys." Kate hoisted the tray of appetizers on a flattened palm and waved it under their noses as bait. "Time to mix and mingle. You, too," she called to the two women on the condo's minuscule balcony.

Dawn and Callie had been enjoying the narrow, pie-slice view of the Washington Monument in the distance. They'd also been conducting a rapid recap of events since they'd departed Rome. Callie admitted she'd been dragging her feet about sending out résumés. She was still a little burned out, she confessed, and not in any great rush to rejoin the working masses. Dawn in turn shared details about her growing rapport with Tommy.

Callie listened in her usual quiet way and didn't raise the subject of Dawn's relations with the Ellises again until after dinner. The meal was made memorable by Travis's spectacularly unsuccessful attempt to replicate mushroom and scallop tagliatelle. Kate had tried it in Venice, he explained, presenting the heaping platter down with a grand flourish. Unfortunately, his scallops came out rubbery and the marinara sauce ran like water. The conversation was so lively, however, and the Chianti so rich and full-bodied that no one cared.

Only later, when the three friends grabbed a few moments of girl time in Kate's bedroom, did Callie probe a little deeper. She and Kate plopped down hip to hip on the bed while Dawn detoured to the bathroom.

"You mentioned how tight you and Tommy have become," Callie said when their friend emerged. "What's going on with you and Brian?"

Dawn hit the taps to wash her hands. "Nothing."

"Yeah, right," Kate snorted over the water's gush. "I watched the two of you at dinner. He's hot for you, girl."

"Maybe. A little." Dawn's ready laughter bubbled up. "Okay, a bunch. I'm pretty hot for him, too."

"Uh-oh," Kate muttered.

Callie's response was more measured. "What are we talking about here? A few nights of wild sex? Or something more complicated?"

Dawn dried her hands and replaced the fringed towel on its hanger. Joining the other two on the bed, she answered honestly. "I don't know. I've dived into the deep end before with disastrous results. But this feels...different."

"Different how?"

Lips pursed, Dawn tried to sort through her confused feelings about Brian Ellis. "He's so good with Tommy. And so considerate of others. Unlike a certain fiancé I could name," she added darkly.

"That bastard," Kate huffed. "I hope he drowns in his own bile."

Dawn nodded but didn't jump on the familiar bandwagon. "The thing is..." she said slowly. "I think I could fall for Brian. Fall hard."

Her friends exchanged quick glances. Dawn intercepted their grim looks and held up both palms.

"Hey! No need to call out the National Guard. I said I *think* I could fall for him. I'm not there yet."

She was close, though. *Extremely* close.

She acknowledged as much during the drive back to Bethesda. Outside the SUV the night gleamed midnight blue and star-spangled. Inside, Brian had tuned the radio to an all-jazz station.

"That's Miles Davis," he told her when the mellow notes of a trumpet undulated through the speakers. "Probably one of the most influential musicians of the twentieth century."

Fascinated by this glimpse of yet another facet of his personality, Dawn rested her head against the seat back.

"Who's that?" she asked when a sax joined in.

"John Coltrane. Also a legend."

Content to let the smoky, soulful notes surround her, Dawn was loose and completely relaxed when they arrived home. The garage door rattled up. The SUV nosed into its stall. Brian killed the engine but the music continued. It wouldn't cut off until one of them opened their door, Dawn knew.

She unfastened her seat belt. He did the same. Neither of them made another move until he muttered something under his breath and angled to face her.

"Tommy should be asleep by now."

"So?"

"So I can have Addy on his way in two minutes."

Dawn tipped her chin. After that stormy kiss in the kitchen last night, she wasn't sure where he was going with this. *Or* where she wanted it to go.

"What comes after you hustle Addy out the door?"

"I pour us a brandy," he replied. "We kick off our shoes. Listen to more Davis and Coltrane. And let whatever happens, happen."

Chapter Five

Dawn hadn't tuned in to much jazz. Actually, she'd never tuned in to *any* that she could recall. She couldn't distinguish a tenor sax from an alto and had no idea there was a soprano version of the instrument. Coltrane—or Trane, as Brian referred to him—had evidently mastered them all. He'd also gone in for incredibly long solos, with the notes coming so fast and smooth they sounded like one continuous riff.

"Amazing," she murmured during one seemingly endless glissando. "I've never heard anything like this."

She was slouched on the sofa in the den, lolling against the back cushions and her feet stretched out next to Brian's on the coffee table. After several glasses of wine at the Westbrooks', they'd both opted for coffee instead of brandy. The attraction that simmered just below flash point was there, hovering between them, but for the moment Dawn was content to balance her coffee cup on her tummy and wiggle her toes in time to the music.

"How in the world does he do that without seeming to stop for a single breath?" she mused when Trane's long solo ended. "Brian?"

She slewed her head sideways on the sofa cushion and saw him studying her feet with a bemused expression.

"Is that the new thing?" he asked, nodding to her toes. "All different colors of polish?"

"Not that new."

She wiggled her feet again. The pearly pastels were great for summer and sandals. She'd have to go darker on her next pedicure, though. Maybe the Fall Flame collection with its lustrous hues of red, russet and gold.

"My company markets these polishes. They're water based, hypoallergenic and cruelty-free."

"They don't hurt your toes?"

"Well, that, too," she said with a laugh, "as we've eliminated the most toxic chemicals that can harm the environment as well as your nails. But the cruelty-free label means the products aren't tested on animals."

"Okay, I'm trying to do a mental construct of monkeys with green and blue and silver toenails."

"You joke, but I bet you worry about these kinds of environmental issues as much in your business as we do in ours," she said shrewdly. "How many chemicals does your company use to manufacture your navigational systems?"

"A bunch," he admitted. "You have to when you're working with epoxy resins and alloys, not to mention paints and solvents and supporting fibers like Kevlar and fiberglass."

Setting aside her coffee, Dawn curled her legs under her. "Give me a ballpark figure."

"Last report I read indicated the aerospace industry as a whole uses more than five thousand chemicals and compounds, each of which can contain five or ten different ingredients. The exact composition of what goes into our products and processes is proprietary but we're close to that number."

"Good grief! Five *thousand*? And I thought we were doing good to squeeze toluene and formaldehyde out of nail polish!" She shook her head while the other members of Trane's quartet poured out a soulful accompaniment. "You must work under volumes of EPA regulations."

"Dozens of volumes."

"How in the world do you manage to comply with them all?"

"Very carefully." He hesitated a beat. "My wife's degree was in chemical engineering. She headed our EPA compliance team until we decided to start a family. She quit working around resins and solvents well before she got pregnant with Tommy."

Dawn couldn't help wondering if fumes from those solvents might have triggered the virulent tumor that killed Caroline Ellis. She suspected Brian must have agonized over the same question himself.

"Travis mentioned that EAS's main manufacturing facility is in Texas," she said, steering away from that painful thought.

"It is. Just outside Fort Worth."

"He also said you plan to give him a personal tour of the facility. Do you know when?"

"Not until after he completes his formal separation from the air force and comes on board at EAS full-time. Why?"

"Just trying to coordinate our schedules. I might have to make a quick trip up to Boston sometime next week to check in at the office and retrieve more clothes. Depending on how your interviews go, of course."

The reminder that her services might not be required long enough to require a wardrobe refurbishment was a definite mood killer. Or maybe it was Brian's reference to his wife. In either case it was obvious to both of them that the "whatever happens" they'd danced around earlier wasn't going to happen tonight.

The tension was still there, though. Not as compulsive as it had been earlier, but not totally extinguished, either. Dawn felt its subtle pull as she pushed off the sofa.

"How about a refill on the coffee?" Brian asked, rising, as well.

"No, thanks. I think I'll call it a night."

They walked to the kitchen together, each recognizing that the moment had passed, yet reluctant to let it slip away entirely.

"I enjoyed tonight," Dawn said, pausing by the door. "Thanks for introducing me to Mike Davis and Jim Coltrane."

"Miles Davis and John Coltrane. And I enjoyed it, too."

"What time are you meeting Travis and Joe tomorrow morning?"

"Ten. Tommy and I will have to catch the early service at church. Do you want to join us?"

Dawn almost said yes. She'd attended regularly with her brothers and parents when she was young. She'd also participated in family counseling sessions mediated by their pastor when things got bad at home. The bitter divorce had not only broken up her family, it put her parents outside the pale in the conservative church they'd attended and left Dawn disillusioned about so much of what she'd always taken for granted. Her own rocky relationships hadn't exactly brought her back into the fold. She'd get there. One of these days. Maybe.

"Thanks for the offer," she told Brian, "but I'll pass. I still have some work to catch up on. Just buzz me when you get home and I'll assume Tommy-duty so you can head into the office."

"Okay."

"Well…"

Oh, for heaven's sake! What was she? Some high schooler returning from a date? Walking to the door. Waiting to be kissed. *Aching* to be kissed, dammit.

"'Night, Brian. See you tomorrow."

Sunday whirled by in seemingly nonstop activity.

Dawn was up early and took her laptop out to the gazebo to put the finishing touches on the mock-ups for both Zucchini Carrot Crunchies and Sweet Potato Stix. She'd just zinged them off to her veggie chip team for review and/or suggestions when Brian returned from church with a superenergized Tommy.

Since Brian was heading into the office for his meeting with Travis and Joe, Dawn decided to drain some of Tommy's excess energy with a bike ride along the shady, tree-lined trail that wound through the neighborhood. She borrowed Brian's mountain bike and helmet while Tommy suited up in a helmet, and knee and elbow pads.

"'Cause I tip over sometimes, even with these training wheels," he explained with cheerful unconcern.

He stayed upright, thank heavens, although he did cut several corners too short and dig a number of offtrack wheel ruts. By the time they'd made a full, five-mile circuit, Dawn's thighs were protesting vigorously. So was her stomach.

"I skipped breakfast," she informed her charge. "Let's grab an early lunch."

An enthusiastic Tommy agreed and introduced her to Paleo's, his all-time favorite spot for Sunday brunch. The colorful Spanish eatery prided itself on its kid-friendly menu, which included an array of tapas designed to tempt even the fussiest young palates. For the adults, they offered a never-ending paella served in a round pan that had to measure at least three feet in diameter. Dawn settled for a smaller serving of paella while Tommy chowed down on a heaping plate of shrimp, beef, grilled asparagus and crunchy potato tapas.

Back at the house they went over first-day-of-school preparations again. Tommy insisted on emptying his backpack and inventorying the contents for the fourth or fifth time. Once every vital necessity was safely restored, he transferred his uniform from the closet and attached its hanger on the back of his desk chair for quick access in the morning. Shoes, socks and underwear he aligned on the bench seat under his window with a precision that suggested he'd inherited his parents' engineering genes.

Then it was game time. Dawn and Tommy were in the final throes of a fierce round of Garden Warfare, with her superpower zinnias about to triumph over his zombies, when Brian arrived home. Supper was a spinach salad, sautéed zucchini, grilled chicken and an endless stream of chatter from Tommy about everything from the bushy-tailed squirrels they'd spotted during their bike ride to the new Pixar movie coming out next weekend that he absolutely *had* to see.

After dinner Dawn pleaded an urgent need to soak her still-aching bike muscles. Although both father and son protested her early departure, she thought they should spend the last evening together before Tommy took that life-changing step into school full-time.

She was up early the next morning to share breakfast with them and send him Tommy on his grand adventure with a hug and a mushy kiss. Her farewell to Brian was more restrained.

"You'd better get going," she said with a flap of one hand. "I'll clean up here."

Like Tommy, Brian was in uniform, except his was the charcoal-gray pinstripes, pale amber shirt and silk tie of a power broker. His short brown hair was slicked back and he'd tucked a folded newspaper under one arm.

"I may be late," he told her. "My schedule's crammed today."

Including, she knew, his first interviews for a replacement nanny.

"You sure you're good with picking Tommy up from school?" he asked her.

"Got it covered."

A quiet settled over the house once they left. Dawn filled the dishwasher and swiped the counters, but left the heavy stuff for the cleaning crew scheduled to show later that morning. Those simple tasks done, she wandered back to the gatehouse and tried to shrug off a suddenly deflated feeling.

So what if Tommy had grabbed his backpack and barreled out the door without a backward glance? And why should the fact that Brian had assumed his Big Bad Businessman persona bother her?

If she was home in Boston, she'd have suited up for work this morning, too. Her company adhered to a fairly laid-back dress code, but Dawn could do the corporate diva look when necessary, with the requisite pencil-slim black skirt and appropriate blouse or jacket. Most of the time she was in slacks and loose, colorful tops.

Which was pretty much all she had with her at present. Frowning, she surveyed the items hanging in the guest bedroom's closet. If she stayed in DC much longer, she would definitely have to zip up to Boston and replenish the closet's contents. Then again, she could be heading home for good very soon. Her frown morphing into a scowl, she dug her iPhone out of her hip pocket and hit the speed-dial number for Callie.

"Where are you?"

"Still at Kate's. Travis leaves this morning for Florida, so she talked me into staying another few days."

"Good. I'll pick you up in an hour and we'll hit the mall."

"Is this a 'my shoes are *sooo* last year' excursion?" Callie asked cautiously. "Or 'I need some serious shopping therapy'?"

"A combination of both. Ask Kate if she's free for lunch. We'll hook up with her somewhere. I have to be back by three, though. It's Tommy's first day at school. I'm picking him up."

"I hope he has a teacher with a megasize store of patience," Callie said, laughing.

"I hope so, too!"

Dawn hung up with a resurgence of her usual ebullient spirits. Tommy had school and Brian had billion-dollar deals to wrangle, but she had friends who'd shared almost every joyous and not-so-joyous moment of her life. She figured she came out the winner by every count.

Brian would have agreed with her. After the sweet, poignant fun of getting his son settled at a shiny new kid-size desk, the rest of his day had pretty much gone to hell.

Given his tight schedule, his executive assistant had ordered the limo for his ten o'clock meeting at the FCC. Dominic wove through the usual downtown DC traffic and delivered his boss right on time. The chief of the FCC's Office of Engineering and Technology had been sitting on EAS's application for access to a new ultrahigh frequency satellite band for weeks now. Determined to pry the application loose, Brian conferred with him and several other officials for two frustrating hours before finally convincing them EAS's requirements fell within their frequency allocation and spectrum usage projections.

He left the FCC with barely enough time to make his working lunch with Northrop Grumman's VP of Engineering Technologies at the corporation's headquarters in Falls Church, Virginia. Dominic negotiated the traffic skillfully enough to get him to lunch, but hit a major snarl on the way back to EAS headquarters. As a consequence, Brian arrived ten minutes late for his two o'clock appointment with Ms. Margaret Davidson.

The slim, fifty-ish former teacher looked elegantly professional in a calf-length navy blue skirt, a white blouse and a paisley scarf draped over one shoulder of her red blazer. She rose when he appeared at the door of the visitors' lounge and accepted his apologies with a gracious nod.

"Mrs. Jones has kept me well supplied with conversation and jasmine tea."

Brian shot his executive assistant a grateful smile. "Thanks, LauraBeth. Let's go to my office, Ms. Davidson, and get to know each other."

The ever-efficient LauraBeth Jones had done more than just compile a list of candidates. At Brian's request, she'd hired Joe Russo's security firm to conduct in-depth background checks. Joe's bloodhounds had verified each candidate's employment and educational history, run a state and local criminal record check, screened sex offender registries, reviewed driving records and requested credit reports.

"I understand you graduated from Bryn Mawr," Brian said when he and Ms. Davidson were comfortably settled in hunter-green leather armchairs positioned to provide a panoramic view of Bethesda's ever-growing skyline.

"Yes, I did. I was actually in the same class as Drew Gilpin Faust."

At his blank look, she gave a small smile.

"The current—and first—female president of Harvard."

He didn't know much about Bryn Mawr aside from the fact that it was one of the Seven Sisters, the prestigious female counterparts to the formerly all-male Ivy League colleges. Ms. Davidson's condescending little smile rubbed him the wrong way, however.

"You also spent some years in academia yourself," he commented, his tone a shade cooler.

"Almost a decade. Unfortunately, it took me that long to admit the dismal failure of our secondary education system. Since then I've worked only with young children. I prefer to discipline their minds and shape their study habits before our public school system warps both."

Brian couldn't help contrasting her grim assessment with Tommy's eagerness to dive headfirst into that same system.

"In that regard," she continued, adjusting the drape of her cashmere scarf, "I'm fully qualified to homeschool your son. Not only is it a safer environment given today's drug and violence infected society, but studies show that home-educated students typically score fifteen to thirty percentile points above public school students on standardized academic achievement tests."

"I appreciate the benefits of homeschooling, but I believe acquiring social skills are as important as acing achievement tests."

"I don't disagree. That's why I encourage participation in extracurricular activities like a youth orchestra or sports team. Within carefully selected parameters, of course."

Parameters, Brian guessed, that would exclude the ethnically diverse environment he and Caroline had wanted their children to experience. Rising, he offered Ms. Davidson his hand.

"I appreciate you agreeing to fly up to Washington on such short notice. As I'm sure you'll appreciate that I have several other candidates to interview. I'll let you know my decision by the end of the week."

Surprised, she got to her feet. "Don't you want me to meet Thomas? Give you my assessment of how well we'd interact before you decide?"

"I don't think that's necessary. I'll have Mrs. Jones call down for a car to take you back to your hotel."

With the tact that made her worth her weight in gold, LauraBeth accompanied Ms. Davidson to the elevator and made sure she was on her way down to street level before she retrieved the next applicant from the elegant, wood-paneled visitors' lounge.

Patricia Gallagher was younger, friendlier and every bit as qualified. She was also an easy conversationalist, with an up-to-date grasp of current world affairs. Brian was impressed until she raised the issue of medical insurance.

"I have basic health coverage," she assured him, "but I would expect you to provide supplemental coverage for co-pays and prescription costs."

"Yes, of course."

It was a reasonable request. Brian had provided both basic and supplemental insurance for Lottie Wells and would continue to do so until she transitioned to Medicare in a few years. The fact that medical coverage seemed of particular concern to Ms. Gallagher raised a red flag, though.

"Tommy's a very active child," he told her, taking care not to cross the fine line between what an employer could and couldn't ask a prospective employee. "You'll need a lot of energy to keep up with him."

"That won't be a problem. I'm pretty active myself. But…well… I hope you're not one of those parents who doesn't believe in vaccinations. Your son's had all his shots, hasn't he?"

"I wouldn't have bought him home from the kennel otherwise," Brian assured her solemnly.

She laughed, then volunteered the reason behind her concern. "I'm healthy as a horse most of the time, but I do seem to be susceptible to viral infections. That's why I had to terminate my previous position," she explained with genuine regret. "The kids were great. I really loved them, but they could *never* remember to wash their hands or cover their mouths when they coughed. They were always catching colds or sore throats and bringing them home."

Brian was tempted to assure her that Tommy remembered to cover his mouth. Most of the time. But he had serious reservations about exposing his son to someone apparently susceptible to viral infections. He brought the session to a smooth finish a few moments later with the same promise to get back to her by the end of the week.

"You got through those interviews quickly," Laura-Beth commented when the elevator doors swished shut.

The calm, petite Virginian had been with EAS for almost ten years. Long enough for Brian to appreciate the titanium core under LauraBeth's layer of Southern charm. She and her husband, a career civil servant, had raised four sons. When the last left for college, she'd decided to go back to work. The first place she'd applied was EAS, and Caroline had hired her on the spot. The two women had quickly developed a rapport that went beyond work.

Caroline's subsequent illness had devastated Laura-Beth, but this small, slender woman with a heart ten times her size had held the front office together during those last, horrific months. Brian valued her friendship as much as he relied on her brisk efficiency.

"You read their files and have chatted with both candidates so far," he said. "What did you think?"

LauraBeth didn't hesitate. "Davidson is too full of herself. I was impressed with Gallagher, but her reason for leaving her last job seemed a little vague."

"The kids caught colds."

"*All* kids catch colds."

"That was pretty much my reaction, too."

"Interesting. Do you want to squeeze in another interview? Our third candidate just called to let me know he arrived early and is checked in at the hotel. I can see if he wants to meet with you this afternoon instead of in the morning."

"Let's leave it as scheduled. I'll take care of some of that paperwork you stacked on my desk and make a few calls. Then I want to head home and get the scoop on Tommy's first day."

Laughter filled LauraBeth's chocolate-brown eyes. "Dawn called while you were in with Ms. Gallagher to let me know both teacher and pupil survived. She gave me the highlights. I'd share them with you but I don't want to steal Tommy's thunder." She paused a moment. "I like Dawn. Not many women would step in the way she did when Lottie had that accident, and in a foreign country yet."

"You think anyplace outside Virginia is a foreign country."

"Well, it is. But don't change the subject. Tommy likes Dawn, too. Quite a bit, from what I gather."

"I know."

"If you're going to break the bond," LauraBeth advised gently, "you need to do it soon."

"I know," he said again. "I'm working on it."

* * *

He drove home through a slowly deepening dusk. A favorite jazz playlist thrummed through the speakers, but Brian barely registered Thelonious Monk's percussive attacks and abrupt, dramatic silences. His thoughts kept circling from the interviews he'd just conducted to LauraBeth's warning about the two people waiting for him at home.

Or not waiting.

The security lights were spilling golden puddles on the front lawn as he pulled into the drive, but the house showed only dark windows. He entered the kitchen through the garage, surprised by its dim emptiness, and checked the kitchen counter for a note indicating where Dawn and Tommy might have gone. Frowning, he was about to search the rest of the house when he noticed that the door to the patio stood ajar, with only the screen door keeping out the insects that now buzzed through the crisp autumn night.

Brian's breath razored through his lungs, but before the fear every parent lived with could break out of its cage, a squeal of pure joy pierced the silence, followed by a shout of enthusiastic praise.

"Good one, kiddo!"

"I know! Your turn."

Shaky with relief, Brian dropped his briefcase and suit coat on the counter and moved to the windows overlooking the brick-walled backyard. It, too, was illuminated by strategically placed lanterns and spots. The artificial light caught Dawn in fluid motion as she tipped sideways, planted both palms on the grass and executed a perfect cartwheel.

Correction. An almost-perfect cartwheel. Her back remained arrow straight and her legs and arms formed an admirable X, but she blew the landing. She went down butt-first and lay there, laughing, while Tommy hooted and danced from foot to foot.

"I win, I win, I win."

"Yeah, you do. But I want a rematch."

"'Kay."

"Not now. Your father should be home soon. We'd better get cleaned up and start thinking about dinner."

"'Kay."

Not until they'd turned toward the house did they notice the figure silhouetted against the kitchen windows.

"Dad's already home!"

With another squeal of joy, Tommy raced across the yard and barreled through the screen door. Brian went down on one knee for a quick bear hug and a spate of breathless questions from his excited son.

"Didja see me, Dad? Didja? Dawn taught me how to do cartwheels 'n now I do 'em better than her."

"I saw her do one. Or try to."

"C'mon outside! I'll show you a good one."

When he darted back through the door, Brian followed and strolled over to join Dawn.

"This is a surprise. I came home expecting a detailed report on first grade and instead I get a gymnastics exhibition."

"Don't worry," she drawled. "You'll get both."

"Watch me, Dad. Watch me!"

"I'm watching."

"Tommy was totally hyped when I picked him up at school," Dawn commented during the exuberant demonstration. "I now know the names of almost every kid in his class, the stories their teacher read to them, what they had for lunch and which of them can write their names fastest. His little friend Cindy took those honors, incidentally."

"Good to know."

"The only way I could turn off the spigot was to lure him out here for some fresh air and exercise."

"Smart thinking."

"Dad!"

"I see you, buddy."

Absorbed in his son's acrobatics, Brian still managed to remain acutely aware of the woman beside him. Her face was flushed from her exertions and her tumbled hair held an earthy scent of grass and sweat. Not as delicate as lemons and lotus blossoms, he discovered when he sneaked another whiff, but a whole lot more arousing.

Suddenly impatient, he couldn't wait to hear his son's report, then get him fed, bathed and in bed.

Chapter Six

Employing time-tested management principles, Brian combined tasks to accomplish them quickly and efficiently. He listened with genuine interest to Tommy's detailed saga of his first day while he chopped lettuce. Still listening, he sprinkled parmesan on slices of buttered Italian bread and popped them in the oven while Dawn nuked frozen lasagna.

Tommy's school saga continued through dinner. He took a brief hiatus for a video battle and resumed during bath time. Thankfully, his day's activities and the spirited cartwheel session had depleted even his seemingly inexhaustible store of energy. He voiced an obligatory round of protests and petulant pleas to stay up longer, but zonked out almost before his head hit the pillow.

When Brian went back downstairs, he discovered that Dawn had achieved the same comatose state. She was slouched on the den sofa, feet up, head lolling against the gray suede cushions with the video controls about to slip through her fingers. Strike two, he thought ruefully. Looked as if he'd have to put his "whatever happens" hopes on ice for the second night in a row.

When he eased the controls out of her limp grasp, his conscience said he should nudge her awake and suggest they call it a night. The rest of him nixed the notion. Slowly, cautiously, he lowered himself onto the cushions. They shifted under his weight, tipping her toward him.

He snaked his arm across the sofa back while her head found a comfortable nest between his neck and shoulder. This was nice, he thought as he settled her closer. Cozy and comfortable.

Yeah, sure! Almost as cozy and comfortable as USMC boot camp.

Determined to keep a lid on his physical response to this woman, he tried to ignore the warm breath tickling his neck and the soft, full breast mashed against his upper arm. He edged away a few inches in an effort to put some space between himself and her pliant body, but only succeeded in eliciting a breathy sigh as she snuggled closer.

Jaw locked, Brian tried to kill the hunger pulsing through him with cold, hard logic. No way he could nudge Dawn down onto the cushions and bring her back to consciousness inch by delicious inch. Tommy might wake up, think of just one more thing he *had* to tell his dad and wander downstairs at precisely the wrong moment.

The stern lecture almost did the trick. Would have, if Dawn hadn't mumbled something unintelligible and poked her nose into his neck like a burrowing groundhog. When some loose strands of hair trapped between her chin and his shoulder constricted her nuzzling, the mumble segued into an irritated grunt.

Gently, Brian freed the trapped strands. Soft and whispery, they played through his fingers, still giving off a faint whiff of grass and sweat. The earthy tang triggered something deep and primitive in him. Cursing under his breath, he shifted again in a vain attempt to ease the sudden tightening in his belly.

When that didn't work, an insidious possibility wormed its way into his thoughts. The security system guarding the house and grounds was ultra high-tech. When Brain went to bed each evening, he entered a five-digit code that would sound an alert if someone or something tripped the sensors on the exterior doors and windows.

The system also included interior sensors. When set, these pressure detectors and infrared beams would detect movement in the downstairs rooms and on the stairs leading to the second floor. But Brian hadn't activated the interior sensors in years. He'd turned them off for the first time during the long, sleepless nights following Caroline's diagnosis, when he'd slipped out of bed and come downstairs to vent his anger and despair in solitude.

Then, when Tommy started sleepwalking a few years ago, Brian shut down the interior system again. The doctors assured him that somnambulism was a common childhood occurrence, typically manifesting itself between the ages of four and eight and often resulting from separation anxiety. Whatever had caused it, Brian wasn't about to risk jerking his son awake with a shrieking alarm.

Except…maybe…in certain life-and-death circumstances…

His gaze lingered on Dawn's face, taking in the blue-veined eyelids, the kiss-me-if-you-dare mouth, the wayward copper tendrils tickling her ears. All he had to do was slip his arm out from under her head and make for the master alarm panel in the kitchen. He could activate the pressure sensors on the staircase in ten seconds max, then bring Dawn awake slowly, sensually and…

Dammit!

What was he thinking?

True, nothing in his personal code of conduct demanded that he dedicate himself to Caroline's memory and remain celibate for the rest of his life. Also true, he'd reluctantly reentered the dating pool in recent years. His two brief liaisons had satisfied a physical need. If they'd also left him empty emotionally, he figured that was his problem.

Yet here he was, ready to toss every parenting principle out the window and set an alarm that would scare the crap out of his son if he tripped it. All so Tommy's horny dad could get naked with this auburn-haired siren. On the den sofa, for God's sake!

Thoroughly disgusted, Brian battled his raging testosterone into submission and eased off the sofa. Dawn sniffled, muttered and tipped sideways onto the cushions. Without so much as a flicker of an eyelash, she curled onto the cushions like a contented cat.

Resigned to another uncomfortable night, Brian dug a fuzzy *Pirates of the Caribbean* throw out of a hassock and draped it over her. He was still swinging between rampant need and wry regret when he turned down the lights and went up the unsensored, unalarmed stairs.

He came back down the next morning, showered, shaved and dressed for work. A ridiculous disappointment knifed through him when he found the den empty of all occupants and the fuzzy throw neatly folded on the suede cushions. He gave the sofa a nasty glance and followed the scent of fresh-brewed coffee to the kitchen.

Dawn sat perched on a stool at the counter. She was fresh faced and bright-eyed and swinging a foot idly as she checked emails on her iPhone. In jeans and chunky-knit sweater, with her hair caught up in a loose ponytail, she looked closer to Addy Caruthers's age than Brian's. The thought didn't particularly sit well.

Glancing up, she greeted him with a rueful grin. "Mornin'. Sorry I passed out on you last night. I guess the backyard acrobatics pooped me as much they did Tommy."

"No problem."

Now, Brian added with a mental grunt. It'd presented a helluva problem last night, when he'd contemplated a wide range of lascivious inducements designed to bring her back to full consciousness.

"Did you spend the entire night on the sofa?" he asked gruffly.

"Pretty much. Thanks for tucking me in, by the way."

The wicked glint in her eyes told him she had a good idea how much that misplaced act of gallantry had cost him.

"Good thing you don't activate the interior alarms," she commented. "I would've set them all off when I rolled off the couch at oh-dark-thirty and stumbled back to the gatehouse half asleep."

Brian poured himself some coffee, not about to admit how close he'd come to penning his son in his upstairs bedroom with an electronic fence. When he turned back, the mug steaming in his hand, he found Dawn studying him with her head cocked a little to one side.

"Why *don't* you activate them?" she wanted to know. "Don't you trust me with the codes?"

That cut too close to the bone. "Don't be stupid," he replied more curtly than he'd intended. "I trust you with my son. Why wouldn't I trust you with the alarm codes?"

"Whoa!" Her foot stilled its lazy swing, and those green

cat's eyes narrowed. "Someone obviously got up on the wrong side of his temper this morning."

Make that the wrong side of the sofa, Brian thought sourly. He couldn't decide whether he was more irritated by the fact he'd spent most of the night kicking himself for not making wild, animal love to this woman or the fact that she looked so damned perky and unfazed by the near miss.

"Tommy's still asleep," he informed her with only a shade less than hostility. "You need to haul his butt out of bed by seven so you can get him to school by eight thirty."

"Yes, sir!"

Popping to attention on her high-backed stool, she snapped a salute. With the wrong hand, the marine in Brian noted acidly. Somehow that only added to his disgruntled mood. That and the realization that he was scheduled to interview four more candidates for a permanent nanny today.

"I should be home by six," he told her. "Let's plan on discussing future arrangements this evening."

"Yes, sir!"

The salute was mocking now, the green eyes stormy. Brian carried both with him out the door.

A traffic snarl a mile short of the beltway exit for EAS headquarters didn't improve his mood. Nor did the back-to-back appointments crammed into his schedule for the day.

He got through a meeting with the sub providing transistors for a proposed new satellite-based guidance system without losing his cool over the litany of excuses for the company's delays.

He also conducted a midmorning interview with the next candidate on the list. Brian should have been impressed by the bearded, muscled-up grad student's BA from Princeton. Also the fact that he was two years into the dissertation for his PhD in medieval French history. Instead he made the same promise to get back to him by the end of the week that he'd made to the first two candidates.

After that he sat through an excruciating session with his VP of Finance and Accounting. Brian's background was operations. Gut-twisting, hands-on, shoot-that-mother-out-of-the-sky operations. First as a USMC helo pilot, then as a major contributor to the Department of Defense's war-fighting arsenal. As Brian listened to his brilliant but long-winded Finance VP drone on, he battled an uncharacteristic urge to send the man back to his cave to rework every damned chart so they were intelligible to mere mortals.

He controlled the impulse, but couldn't hide his unsettled mood from LauraBeth. She'd worked with him for too long and knew his moods too well to miss his edginess. Head cocked, she studied him for several moments after depositing a neat stack of contracts in his inbox.

"You seem distracted today," she commented in her magnolia-soft Virginia drawl. "I noticed it when you first came in this morning. Everything okay at home?"

"Yes. No."

Her delicately penciled brows arced. "Do you want to talk about it?"

"No."

"Wrong answer. Speak to me."

Shoving away from his desk, Brian rose and stared out the floor-to-ceiling windows at Bethesda's high-rise jungle for several seconds before turning to face the woman who'd been as much a friend as a coworker to both him and Caroline.

"What would you say if I canceled the rest of the interviews and told you I'm thinking of asking Dawn to stay on permanently?"

"I'd say that was a smart move. Depending, of course, on what you mean by 'permanently.'"

"I haven't exactly worked that out yet."

"Oh, for…!"

She muttered something under her breath that made Brian's jaw drop. He couldn't believe the woman had just tossed out an expletive he might've heard from a marine on a three-day drunk in the stews of Okinawa.

"I've liked Dawn McGill more with every conversation we've had," LauraBeth announced. "She's not bad for a Yankee. Not bad at all."

Brian was still reeling from that unbridled endorsement when she came out with another.

"And if she's anywhere near as foxy as Dominic says she is, you'll start thinking of her as more than a caretaker for Tommy. Oh, don't look so shocked," she added impatiently. "I've seen the women you've hooked up with the past few years. I had to reserve the suite at the Ritz for you and that ditzy Realtor, remember?"

"LauraBeth…"

"I also sent two dozen long-stemmed roses when you decided to call it off with that bassoonist with the National Symphony. I *told* you there was a reason she was only third chair."

Brian had to fight to keep his face straight. The slender, frighteningly intense bassoonist did, in fact, play third chair. But after forcing notes through a double reed for so many years she'd developed a helluva embouchure. The woman could do things with her tongue and lips that…

His assistant's impatient voice drowned out memories of the musician's unexpected talents. "If Dawn is half the

woman I think she is, you'll sign her to a binding contract."

On that stern note, the diminutive LauraBeth spun on
her heel and marched out. Brian almost stopped her at
the door to tell her he'd thought about doing exactly what
she'd just suggested. Thought long and hard, as a matter
of fact. Particularly these past few nights, when Dawn's
taste and feel and scent had kept him awake and hurting.

Shoving his hands in his pockets, he turned back to the
windows and stared unseeing through the tinted glass.
Was he too close to the situation? Thrown off his stride
by the hunger Dawn stirred in him. Maybe he should step
back, reconsider this matter of offering her a long-term
contract, apply the same cool logic he usually brought to
any problem.

The cons were obvious. Despite the background check
he'd run on the woman, he'd known her for what? Three
weeks now? She could've buried something so deep in her
past that a cursory check wouldn't turn it up.

And what about those two broken engagements? Travis
hadn't gone into gory detail, but he had let it drop that she'd
bolted at the very last moment. What said she wouldn't bolt
again? Brian didn't want Tommy hurt by a woman who
might suddenly decide she wasn't cut out for motherhood.

The same went for Brian himself. Everything in him
cringed at the idea of leaving himself open to even a shadow
of the agony he'd gone through when Caroline died.

But... Jaw set, he added up the pluses. First and fore-
most, Tommy adored her. She seemed to feel the same
about him. And her sparkling eyes and infectious good
humor had gone a long way in chasing the shadows from
a house that hadn't heard a woman's laugh in too long.

Even the desire she roused in Brian belonged on the
plus side of the balance sheet, he decided.

Oh, for… Who was he kidding?

Desire was far too tame a description for the hunger she'd stirred in him from the first moment he'd laid eyes on her. Sure, he'd played it cool in Venice. As if he'd had any other choice with the playboy prince going all out to impress her. But he'd wanted her then, and he wanted her even more now that he'd had come to know the woman encased in that seductive body.

Well, hell! Damned if he hadn't just come full circle. So much for cool, detached logic. What Brian needed to do now was what he always did after days or weeks of studying designs, meeting with experts and listening to his most trusted advisors. Go with his gut.

Grabbing his suit jacket from the back of his chair, he hooked it over his arm and strode out of his office. "I'm heading home."

"Now?" Concern leaped into LauraBeth's face. "Did the school call your cell phone? Is Tommy okay?"

"He's fine. As far as I know," he temporized. "No reports of the school burning down or trips to the emergency room."

"Then what? Oh, dear! Is it Dawn?"

"Yes, it is. I decided to take your advice and talk to our temporary nanny about a long-term contract."

A smile traced fine, spidery lines at the corners of his assistant's mouth. "Good for you."

"You'd better cancel my appointments for the rest of the day."

"Including your meeting with the Assistant Secretary of Defense?"

"Reschedule it for next week, if you can."

"What about the Saudi ambassador's cocktail party this evening? We RSVP'd weeks ago."

"They won't miss me," he said cynically. "Not with so

many other defense contractors eager to sell His Highness their latest systems."

Swinging by his assistant's desk, he dropped a kiss on her fragrant cheek. "Wish me luck, LauraBeth. I have a feeling these might be the toughest negotiations I've entered into in a long while."

He called Dawn's cell phone from the car. She answered on the third ring, sounding distracted. "Hey, Brian. What's up?"

"I'm heading home. I need to talk to you."

"About?" she asked, instantly wary.

"I'll explain when I get there. I just wanted to make sure you'll be there for the next hour or so."

Which, of course, he could've ascertained before charging out of the office. Not particularly pleased with what that impatience said about his state of mind, he waited for her answer.

She gave it slowly, almost reluctantly. "I've been catching up on work. I wasn't planning to go anywhere until I picked Tommy up from school."

"Good. Be there shortly."

Traffic was light this early in the day. So light, he didn't have time to fine-tune his negotiating strategy before he pulled into the curved drive fronting his home. He killed the engine and shot a quick glance at the dashboard display. It was just past one. Tommy wouldn't come charging out of school for another two hours. Plenty of time for Brian to close the deal.

He left the SUV and his suit coat in the drive and took the side walkway to the gatehouse. Dawn answered his knock and let him into the cozy breakfast nook. Her laptop sat open on the white-painted table, and the bay windows stood open to the autumn air that rustled the leaves in the backyard. The bank of showy dahlias so lovingly tended by his yard crew were fading fast, but the grass was still green and lush.

With some effort, Brian blanked the image of Dawn and Tommy doing joyous cartwheels across that carpet of green and turned to face a much less exuberant version of the woman. She was wearing the jeans and the slouchy knit sweater she'd had on at breakfast. A scrunchie still confined her hair in a loose ponytail, and her expression, Brian noted, wasn't much friendlier than when he'd left her hours earlier.

Claiming one of the low stools at the counter, she crossed her arms and swung one foot. "All right," she said coolly. "I appreciate you driving home in the middle of your busy day to let me know you've hired a new caregiver. Who is it and, more importantly, when does he or she start?"

"I didn't hire anyone. And I canceled the rest of the interviews."

Her foot stopped in midswing. "Why?"

Tugging at his tie, he loosened the knot and popped the top button of his shirt. He couldn't remember the last time he'd felt so choked during negotiations. When he could breathe a little easier, he laid his cards on the table.

"Here's the thing. Tommy thinks you're totally awesome. He wants you to stay. So do I."

Her lips parted in surprise. "Since when?"

"Since I had time to think about it this morning."

"But…" She raised an arm, gestured to the laptop and let her hand drop. "Stay for how long?"

"Permanently. Or," he amended, falling back on the escape clause his lawyers had hammered into his head before every high-powered negotiating session, "until such time as all parties involved mutually agree to terminate the contract."

He knew he'd stepped on it when she blinked and reared back a little.

"Let me make sure I understand the terms of this contract," she said slowly. "You're asking me to give up my condo, my job, my *life* and take up permanent residency in your gatehouse until such time as we mutually decide to terminate the arrangement."

Christ! He was blowing it. Big-time. Forcing a smile, he tried again. "Actually, I'm asking you to move into the main house. With Tommy and me."

Neither the smile nor the offer produced the desired effect. If anything, they added fuel to the temper darkening her eyes. Pushing off the stool, she planted both hands on her hips and delivered a scorching broadside.

"You pompous, conceited ass. You think all you have to do is waltz in, invite me to be your live-in lover and expect me to—"

"Whoa! Back up a minute! I'm asking you to marry me!"

"What?"

Tossing every hard-learned negotiating strategy to the winds, Brian cut right to the bottom line. "We're not kids, Dawn. Or horny teenagers like Addy. Although God knows," he muttered, "you make me feel like one."

"Ex-*cuse* me?"

Groaning, he backtracked. "Sorry. I've never been good at dressing things up in pretty ribbons. What I'm trying to say…"

"Yes?"

"Well…"

"C'mon, big guy," she taunted, "spit it out."

"Okay." He laid it on the line. "I want you. You want me. That's a helluva foundation to build on."

Her expression went flat, giving Brian no clue as to

what she was thinking. Cursing, he was fumbling for yet another way to make his case when she cut the ground right out from under him.

"Wanting is only half the equation. Don't you think we should test the other half? Find out just how compatible we really are before we sign on the dotted line?"

Chapter Seven

While Brian tried to unscramble his brains, Dawn gave
him a sardonic smile. "Why look so surprised? If we're
going to form a partnership, we need to make sure all parties
are comfortable with the terms."

The sarcasm came through, as thick as hot tar and twice
as scorching.

"Okay," he conceded, his feathers singed. "I may not
have framed my offer in the best terms."

"Ya think?"

"But it came from the heart."

That took some of the storm from her eyes. Not all,
but some. Crossing her arms again, she swung that foot.
Once. Twice.

"I'm listening."

Even after all these years it was hard for him to talk
about the pain he always kept so private. Yet he owed
Dawn an honest answer.

"We've both learned the hard way there are no guarantees in life," he said slowly. "I thought I'd have forty or fifty years with Caroline. You were certain you'd found the perfect mate. Not once, but…"

"Twice." Her foot gave another twitch. "Yeah, I know. I was there. Both times. You were saying?"

"I was saying we don't know what will happen tomorrow, much less next week or next year. Nor can we know whether marriage will work for us. But we have a solid foundation to build on. Mutual respect, a common bond in Tommy and—" he huffed out a laugh "—you have to know my throat closes and my lungs burn every time I get within twenty yards of you."

"Twenty yards, huh?" Head cocked, she feigned an innocent interest. "What happens when we're this close?"

Brian felt almost light-headed with relief. From the sound of it, he'd managed to navigate some very dangerous shoals. Now all he had to do was bring the ship safely into port.

"This close," he admitted, "I have to battle the urge to haul you into my arms and kiss you crazy."

"Interesting."

She dropped her contemplative pose. The smile he'd been hoping to see crept into her eyes.

"Especially since I have to fight a similar urge. Hence my suggestion a few moments ago. So…?" she asked with a delicate lift of her brows.

Brian didn't need another invitation. Two seconds later he had her off the stool and in his arms. When his mouth came down on hers, she pushed up on the balls of her feet to hook her arms around his neck and gave herself up to the kiss with hungry abandon.

The heat was instant and intense. As Brian molded her closer, her breasts, her belly, her thighs all burned into him. Burrowing under the hem of her sweater, he ran his hands up her rib cage and was delighted to discover she wasn't wearing a bra. As he palmed her breasts, every drop of blood drained from his head and went south.

"Damn, woman," he ground out hoarsely. "Do you have any idea how close I am to stroking out at this moment?"

Laughing, she pushed back a few inches and attacked his shirt buttons. "What's good for the gander…"

She yanked the shirt free of his slacks and peeled it down his arms, leaving only his tie to dangle from his neck. Her fingers danced along his shoulders, across his chest, down to the stomach that went drum-tight at her touch.

"Nice," she murmured, raking a nail through the hair that swirled above his belt. "Very nice."

She stooped a little and followed those teasing, tantalizing fingertips with her mouth. Kissing, licking, nipping, until Brian was pretty sure his head would explode. Desperate for relief, he dragged her sweater up, tangling her arms and swathing her head in a thick, cable-knit turban.

"Brian!" The thick knit muffled her protest. "You're going to stroke out and I'm going to suffocate. They'll find us dead on the floor."

When he finally untangled her, his belly went tight again. God, she was gorgeous! The full curves, the soft skin, the fiery curls now tumbling free of her scrunchie. Determined to explore every inch of her, he dipped his head.

She gasped when his mouth closed over a nipple. Groaned when he teased the nub to a hard, stiff peak. Then he shifted to the other breast, and her breath disintegrated in short, swift pants.

"Brian! I think…we should… Oh!"

As he popped the snap on her jeans and peeled them

down her hips, he gave a fleeting prayer of thanks to Levi Strauss for providing such easy access.

Nudging aside the lacy waistband of her briefs, he found her center. She was already hot, already damp. As eager for him as he was for her. He probed gently at first, then deeper, while his thumb stroked and applied delicate pressure.

Slow, his mind screamed. *Take it slow! Make this last until the cows come home. Or at least until Tommy does.*

That sobered him just long enough to glance at the kitchen clock. To his undying relief, he saw they still had almost two hours. More than enough time to sweep her into his arms, carry her upstairs and stretch her out on the guest room bed.

Which he would've done. Probably. If Dawn hadn't taken matters into her own hands. Two seconds after she'd unbuckled his belt and tugged down his zipper, both his mind and his seduction scenario had turned to mush. Barely enough reason penetrated the red haze for Brian to propose a short break.

"I think...I think I've got some condoms in my bathroom."

If Tommy hadn't used them for water balloons! Praying his son hadn't found the secret stash, Brian tried to disengage.

"I'll go check and be back in two minutes flat."

"It's okay," she murmured, her hands busy. "I'm protected."

Even then he should've tried to apply the brakes. Dawn deserved better than a frantic grope in the kitchen, for God's sake! Yet at that moment it would have been easier to stop breathing than keep from hiking her onto the counter. After the Herculean struggle with her sweater, disposing of her shoes, jeans and panties was a piece of cake.

"Okay, big guy." Wiggling her fanny on the cool marble, she tugged on the silk noose still hanging around his neck. "Are you going to shed this, or what?"

"What."

A couple of somewhat less than smooth moves got him out of his slacks and shorts. Deciding that was as naked as he needed to be, he kicked them aside. His blood pounded as he positioned himself between her thighs and cupped her bare bottom.

Levi Strauss wasn't the only one to receive his fervent thanks. The architect who'd redesigned the gatehouse with toilets and counters easily reachable by small children also won his instant approval. The marble countertop was exactly waist-high. The perfect height for him to scoot her forward a few inches and cant her hips.

Dawn took those seconds to seal his intense expression in her mind. The square jaw locked tight in concentration. The nose with that intriguing bump. The blue eyes hot with desire. Then he nudged her knees apart and eased in carefully. Too carefully for the hunger now boiling in her blood. Hooking her calves around his thighs, Dawn pulled him in and squeezed every muscle below her waist.

She almost laughed when his eyes widened. Couldn't help grinning when his gaze flew up to meet hers. The next moment a powerful thrust almost lifted her off the marble.

She gasped aloud as he filled her. Hard. Pulsing. Urgent. He was good, she admitted while she could still form a coherent thought. Better than good! If the man had lost any of his moves through lack of practice, she sure couldn't tell.

His hips rocked into hers. Harder. Faster. Arching her back, she planted both palms on the counter. With each thrust, pleasure began to build low in her belly. And with each rasp of his teeth against her aching nipples, each maneuver of his busy thumb, the whirling sensation gathered strength and speed. She felt the climax building and tried desperately to hold it back.

"Brian! Wait! Ohhhh…"

Too late. Head back, belly convulsing, she gave herself up to sensations that exploded in a starburst of bright colors. They pinwheeled through her, blazing stars that faded slowly, deliciously. Limp with pleasure, she slumped forward and clung to Brian for support.

He held her easily, his chin resting against her forehead. But, Dawn discovered when the mist cleared, that was the only part of him at rest. The muscles under her palms still quivered. His thighs were like steel, his hips tight against hers. And he still filled her.

Only when the last shudder had rippled down her spine did he start to move again. Slowly, so slowly.

Judging by the shudders that racked Brian when he thrust into her a last, forceful time, Dawn was sure he'd drained the well as thoroughly as she had. She soon discovered she'd seriously underestimated both his stamina and his recovery time.

His smile rueful, he dropped a kiss on the tip of her nose. "This isn't exactly how I intended to convince you to marry me."

"Maybe not, but you made a pretty compelling argument."

He tipped her chin, his eyes as serious as his tone. "You deserve better, Dawn. Long-stemmed roses. Wine. Candlelight and soft sheets instead a marble countertop."

She covered the sudden pang in her heart with a flippant reply. "I'm not complaining, you understand, but nothing says you can't add all of the above to the package."

"Or," he muttered, "at least some of the above. Sit tight."

Blinking in surprise, she sat tight while he strode naked across the kitchen and out the door leading to the garden. Good thing it was walled, she thought with a grin, and shielded from prying eyes on all sides by tall oaks and maples.

He returned moments later with a fistful of red, orange and russet-colored dahlias sporting touches of brown at the tips. Dawn wasn't sure which made her toes curl more. The sight of Brian's tight, trim butt when he'd gone out, or the view he presented when he came back in. The flowers, however, melted her heart.

"For you, m'lady."

She accepted the bouquet with a delighted smile, then squealed and crushed the dahlias to her chest as he scooped her off the counter.

"Now for the soft sheets."

The second time was slower. Sweeter. And so exhausting Dawn could only groan when Brian propped himself up on an elbow an hour later to check the time.

"We'd better hit the shower if we're going to pick Tommy up on time."

"You shower and pick him up," Dawn muttered, burying her face in her pillow. "I'll just lie here and wait for feeling to return to my extremities."

"Okay." Sounding smug and all male, he patted her fanny and tossed back the sheet. "Think you'll regain the use of your extremities by the time I get back?"

With an effort worthy of Wonder Woman, she elevated her head a few degrees. "Maybe."

"Good. We should both be standing and at least semi-clothed when we tell Tommy our plans."

"I'll manage. Somehow."

Despite her promise, Dawn didn't drag herself out of

bed until a good fifteen minutes after Brian departed. That left, she calculated as she twisted the shower taps, five minutes to scrub off the scent of the most incredible sex she'd had in, like, *never*! Another five to towel dry her hair and clip it up into a soggy mass. Ten to share her startling news with Callie and Kate.

She couldn't wait to tell them about Brian's astounding offer. Or the crazy certainty that had wrapped around her heart when he'd presented that bouquet. She tucked a towel around her like a sari and let her hair straggle in wet ropes while she speed-dialed Kate's private number at the World Bank.

"Hey, Dawn."

"Hi, Kate. Sorry to bother you at work."

"No problem. What's going on?"

"Well…"

She hesitated, her effervescence dimming a little. Like a black-and-white movie played in fast-forward, she could see the battles. Hear the vicious charges and countercharges her father and mother shouted at each other until they drove their daughter out of the house and into the comforting arms of her best friends.

No! This wasn't another desperate attempt to wipe out those toxic memories. This was Brian, Tommy and her. Forging something new and bright and…

"Dawn? What's the matter?" Anxiety cut across the line. "Are you okay?"

Gulping, she forced a chuckle. "That's why I called. I'm better than okay, Katy. I'm engaged. Again," she added quickly, anticipating the inevitable.

Although…

Was that an accurate description of the merger she and Brian had just negotiated? Her previous fiancés had sealed the deal with sparkling diamonds. A fussy cluster of quarter carats the first time. An eye-popping three-carat solitaire the next. The memory of the havoc wrought by that exquisite marquise-cut jewel put a nervous twitter in Dawn's voice.

"Brian just left to pick up Tommy. We're going to tell him together when they get home. And I want you to join the celebration," she said, improvising nervously as she went. "You and Callie. Can you come for dinner tonight?"

The silence stretched for a few more interminable seconds. "Callie can't," Kate finally responded. "She's having dinner with Joe Russo."

"She is?"

Surprised, Dawn called up the image of Russo's unsmiling face slashed by that vicious scar.

"What's with that?" she asked, diverted. "Is there something going on between them?"

"There is, but Callie won't tell me what. But forget about them. Tell me about you and Brian."

She did, with some editing. She figured Kate didn't need to hear the "until such time as all parties mutually agree to terminate" part. She glossed over the whole merger concept, in fact, and gave a glib account of the solid foundation Brian thought they could build on.

"Okay," Kate said when she'd wound down, "let me make sure I understand those basic building blocks. You're hot for him. He's hot for you. He's a world-class stud in bed, and you're goofy for his kid. Does that cover it?"

"No!"

"What am I missing?"

"Everything! His incredible patience with Tommy. The respect he shows everyone who works for him. The way the lines at the corners of his eyes crinkle when he laughs. His addiction to jazz and this guy Jim Coltrane. The—"

"John Coltrane."

"Huh?"

"John Coltrane. He played sax for Thelonious Monk before striking out on his own."

Dawn's jaw dropped. "How do you know that?"

She knew her friends' tastes in music as well as her own. She should, since they'd shared CDs, then iPods and iPhone playlists for most of their lives.

"Some of us do try to expand our cultural landscape," Kate returned primly.

"Ha!"

"Okay," her friend confessed, laughing. "Travis said Brian drove them all nutso in Italy by piping jazz through the speakers during downtime between tests. Trav developed a taste for it and is trying to bring me into the fold. I promised to listen to the albums he downloaded by Monk and Coltrane before he gets back from Florida."

"Amazing," Dawn murmured. "Three weeks ago we'd never heard of any of these guys. Now they're part of our landscape."

"Yes, and we're offtrack again. Back to you and Brian. I get that your feelings for him go pretty deep. What about *his* feelings? Did he…? Hang on. I'm being buzzed. Back in a sec."

Did he what? Dawn wondered as the phone went quiet. Offer to share his life with her? Kiss her stupid? Prove how solid their foundation was, not once but twice this afternoon?

She was grinning at the memory of their transition from kitchen to bed when Kate came back on the line. "Sorry. My boss wanted to make sure I have my stuff together for our meeting with Signore Gallo this afternoon. You remember him, don't you?"

"The Italian banker with that lion's mane of silver hair. How could I not? He's in DC?"

"For a short visit. He still wants to put me up for membership in the International Bankers Association associates' subcommittee. My boss thinks I should accept."

Dawn wasn't surprised. Kate would be the first woman ever nominated to that subcommittee. But Dawn also understood her friend's hesitation. As a minimum, membership in that exclusive and extremely chauvinistic gentlemen's club would involve quarterly trips to Geneva that might last a week or more. Probably additional jaunts to European and Asian banking centers. With Travis terminating his air force career to join Brian at EAS, Kate was reluctant to let *her* career impact the marriage they'd worked so hard to resurrect.

"So what are you going to tell Gallo?"

"The same thing I told him in Italy. I appreciate the offer but this isn't a good time for me to take on that kind of a commitment."

"Not with you and Travis just getting back together and starting to think babies," Dawn agreed.

"About the babies… I wasn't going to say anything. Not yet. But I'm five days late."

"Kate!"

Dawn jumped up, dislodging her towel in her excitement. It dropped to the carpet unheeded while she hooted and danced from foot to foot.

"You're never late! The National Institute of Standards could set the time by you!"

"I know!"

"Have you told Callie?"

"Not yet. She's been so preoccupied lately and I wanted to make sure. I'm going to swing by a drugstore on my way home from work tonight and pick up another pregnancy test."

"Don't you dare pee on it until I get there."

"It isn't a spectator sport," Kate protested, laughing.

"The hell it's not. I'll get dressed and be there by the time… Oh."

Brought up short, she remembered that she and Brian were supposed to break their own news to his son this afternoon.

"Damn! Brian's on his way to pick Tommy up at school. It might be a little awkward if I tell the kid I'm going to be his new mom, pat him on the head and rush out the door."

"Just a little," Kate agreed drily.

"Promise me you won't take the test until tomorrow. I want to be there."

"Dawn…"

"C'mon, Katy. You know the drill. One for all, and…"

"…all for one. I know, I know. All right, I'll hold off until after work tomorrow. The three of us can have a pee party."

"This is *so* awesome! Just imagine, this time next year we might both be moms! Who wudda thunk it?"

"Not me. Damn, I'm being buzzed again. I have to go. Listen, I want you to promise me something, too."

"Whatever it is, you've got it."

"Just think hard about you and Brian, okay? It all seems to have happened so fast."

"No kidding!"

"Promise me, Dawn. Think hard."

"I have. I will. See you tomorrow."

She cut the connection, prey to a whirl of emotions. She was utterly thrilled for Kate, and just a little piqued her friend hadn't expressed the same uncensored enthusiasm about her and Brian.

Not that Dawn had really expected her to. Kate and Callie had questioned her first choice of a mate, but had swallowed their doubts and participated enthusiastically in a frenzy of wedding plans. They'd assisted with arrangements for the second ceremony as well, and helped pick up the pieces from that train wreck afterward.

Of course, they'd have doubts about this one. Dawn harbored a few herself. Okay, more than a few. But still… Like Brian said, she thought defiantly as she stooped to retrieve the towel and headed for the bathroom. Life didn't come with any guarantees. Neither did love.

That brought her to a full stop. Chewing on her lower lip, she realized that neither she nor Brian had uttered the *L*-word.

So what? Defiant again, she marched into the bathroom and tossed the towel in the hamper. The indefinable and much-misunderstood emotion people called love underscored everything else they'd talked about. Sharing a home, a future, a son.

Didn't it?

Chapter Eight

When Dawn and Brian broke the news to Tommy, she knew she'd treasure the boy's reaction for the rest of her life.

She might turn out to be a terrible mother. Too flighty or forgetful or wrapped up in her work. And the kid might grow into a snarky, rebellious adolescent. Right now, though, the grin that split his face from ear to ear made whatever bumps they might encounter down the road well worth the risk.

"This is *awesome*!"

Abandoning his big-boy, first-grade dignity, he threw himself into Dawn's open arms and actually allowed her to cuddle him for five or six seconds before squirming free.

"Wait'll I tell Cindy! Her mom said you wouldn't wanna stay with me."

"She did? Why?"

"'Cause you're too...too..." He scrunched his nose. "I

can't remember exactly. But Cindy said they meant you're too pretty to drive me to school 'n soccer games 'n stuff."

Dawn mentally translated "pretty" to something a little less flattering.

"I've never meet Cindy or her mom. I can't imagine why they'd think I'm, uh, pretty."

"Probably because Addy told them so," Brian put in.

"Oh, right."

"You made quite an impression on the kid," Brian continued, his eyes dancing. "He probably told his mom the same thing he told me."

Dawn didn't quite trust that devilish glint, but had to ask, "Which was?"

"You're OTC, babe."

"That's it!" Tommy exclaimed. "That's what Cindy said Addy told her 'n her mom. You're off the charts."

Dawn laughed but decided she'd better put meeting Cindy and her mother near the top of her should-do list.

Right after planning a wedding ceremony! A necessity Brian moved front and center when he came back from the kitchen with a dew-streaked bottle and three tall crystal flutes.

"This is what you do when a girl agrees to marry you," he explained to his son as he popped the cork. "You celebrate the occasion with champagne—or in our case, sparkling cider—and take her out to the finest restaurant in town."

"We're goin' to a restaurant?"

"That's the plan."

"Which one?"

"I called Mon Ami on my way to pick you up at school and made reservations for 6:00 p.m. Or..." His smiling gaze shifted to Dawn. "There's always Paleo's, Tommy's favorite."

"Yes!"

"It's my fav now, too," Dawn admitted with a grin. "We should probably warn them, though, that they're going to lose money on me with their never-ending paella."

"Paleo's it is." Passing around the flutes, Brian proposed a toast. "Here's to us."

Not until they were in the SUV and headed for the popular eatery did Tommy bring up the requirements for married life as dictated by his best friend.

"'Member what else Cindy told me?" he asked the two adults in the front seat, his voice worried. "If you get married, you have to sleep in the same bed 'n take showers together 'n stuff."

Dawn slewed around and managed to keep a straight face. "I remember."

"Are you 'n Dad gonna do all that?"

"Probably."

Shrugging, Tommy consigned the problem to the indeterminate future. Or so Dawn thought. Five seconds later, he demanded specifics.

"When *are* you getting married?"

"We haven't discussed a date yet."

"You won't do it while I'm in school? Get married, I mean."

"Of course not."

"No way," Brian echoed, meeting his son's worried gaze in the rearview mirror. "You have to be there. I want you to be my best man."

"You do?" Tommy brightened until he got hit with a horrible thought. "Will I hafta wear a tux like yours, with suspenders 'n a bowtie 'n everything?"

"Maybe." Brian's glance shifted. "Why don't we leave

the details to Dawn? Weddings are really a girl thing. We guys just show up and do as we're told."

"He actually said that?" Kate demanded incredulously the next evening. "Weddings are a 'girl thing'?"

"Pretty much."

She and Dawn sat knee to knee on the sofa in Kate's spacious living room, their legs curled under them. Callie had gone down to the corner deli for some goodies to celebrate with after the peeing ceremony. While waiting for her return, Dawn filled her friend in on last night's announcement.

"Was he being facetious?" Kate asked.

"I didn't think so at the time. Chauvinistic, maybe. Stereotypical, certainly. But when I replayed the conversation to him later, he swore he wasn't thinking about my near misses."

Dawn certainly was, though. Even now she grimaced when she thought back to the frenzy of planning her first wedding. The bridal magazines she'd poured through. The gowns and reception ideas she'd pinned to her boards. The venues she'd visited and menus she'd sampled. Kate and Callie had been right there with her, sharing ideas via Facebook and Pinterest and email. They'd been there, too, when Dawn realized she'd totally misread the depth of her feelings and called off the wedding.

She'd learned from that mistake. Or thought she had. Deliberately, she'd scaled back plans for her next wedding—until Fiancé Number Two pressured her to do it up right. Dawn shuddered at the memory.

"I'm actually glad Brian's leaving the arrangements to me. God knows I don't want to go through another disaster like the last one."

Kate might harbor private doubts about her friend's

third trip to the altar, but she fired up instantly in her defense. "You should've let me tell Travis what that butthole did to get back at you when you called it off! If you hadn't sworn me to secrecy about the whole sorry mess, Travis would've taken the jerk apart with his bare hands."

"Which is why I swore you to secrecy. I didn't want..."

She broke off at the sound of the condo's front door opening and looked up with a welcome smile for Callie. But when her friend stumbled into the living room, both Dawn and Kate shoved off the sofa.

"Omigod!"

Callie's normally smooth, Madonna-like complexion was a blotchy red. What looked like the start of a vicious bruise blossomed on her right cheek, both palms were scraped and her gray slacks sported tears at the knees.

Dawn rushed across the room. "Did you fall?"

Kate was right beside her. "Are you hurt?"

"Yes to the first question," the brunette answered with a wobbly attempt at a smile. "No to the second. I'm okay."

"The heck you are! Here, sit down." Kate took their obviously still-shaken friend gently by the elbow and steered her to a chair. "Are you sure you didn't break anything in the fall? An ankle? Your wrists?"

"Only my pride."

"You'll ache like the devil tomorrow," Dawn predicted, scrunching down to check the scrapes. "Kate, do you have any Tylenol in your medicine cabinet?"

"I do."

"Bring two tablets," she instructed as she rolled up the hem of Callie's slacks. "Also alcohol and cotton swabs to clean these scrapes, two large Band-Aids and antiseptic cream if you have it."

Kate hurried out and was back short moments later with her arms full.

"So what happened?" Dawn asked as she carefully swabbed the abrasions on Callie's palms. "Did you trip over a curb?"

"A crack in the sidewalk."

"Ouch! That happens when you're window-shopping."

"Or stargazing," Kate added, "which you, girlfriend, are prone to."

To the astonishment of both her friends, tears sheened Callie's normally serene lavender eyes.

"I wish...I wish I'd been window-shopping or stargazing."

The quaver in her usually placid voice alarmed them even more than the tears. They exchanged startled glances, then Kate took charge.

"Listen up. Here's what's going to happen. Dawn will finish cleaning those scrapes while I pour you a stiff brandy. Then you're going to tell us what the heck's going on. No!" She flung up a hand. "Don't even *try* to convince me everything's normal. You've been too quiet and Joe Russo's called too many times—"

"He has?" Dawn interjected, surprised.

"—and you've been too damned evasive when I've asked you about those calls," Kate finished relentlessly.

With another stern order for Callie to sit tight, she marched over to the armoire that doubled as her bar and entertainment center. She returned with stiff drinks for Callie and Dawn, and a fizzy Sprite for herself.

"All right," she said after they'd all taken a fortifying gulp, "spill it, Cal. You haven't been yourself since you quit your job. What haven't you told us?"

Callie let out a slow breath. "I didn't want to say anything before..."

"Why not?" Kate asked indignantly.

"We were all looking forward to the trip to Italy. I wasn't

about to spoil that. And you had enough to worry about with your pending divorce." Her glance shifted to Dawn. "Then you shocked both of us by deciding to take on nanny duties. Now you're engaged again, and Kate may be pregnant and…" She made another attempt at a smile. "With everything else going on, I didn't want to make a big deal of my petty problems."

"Bull," Dawn huffed. "Whatever caused you to walk away from a job you used to love wasn't petty! C'mon, girl. Spill."

"All right." She gathered her courage with another fortifying sip. "I received some threatening emails."

"What?"

"Who from?"

"I don't know who sent them. That's why I've been talking to Joe Russo. He's trying to nail the guy. Or gal."

Shocked, Dawn and Kate could only listen in dismay as Callie shared the sobering details.

"The first email showed up in my inbox three months ago. I knew immediately it was from a parent or guardian of a child I'd represented as an advocate. Whoever sent it had obviously lost all parental rights."

Callie had never talked much about her job. She couldn't. Sworn to protect the privacy of the kids she stood up for in court, she would never violate their trust. Yet Kate and Dawn had gleaned enough over the years to sense how deep some of her cases cut.

"I got a few more in the weeks that followed," she continued. "Not much worse than others I've received over the years. How can you bureaucrats in the Children's Advocate Office sit in your crowded little cubbyholes and know what happens in the real world? How could I, a woman with no husband or kids of her own, spend a few hours talking to a confused eight- or nine-year-old and rip an entire family apart?"

"Right," Dawn spit out fiercely. "Like some assholes with eight- or nine-year-olds don't rip their families apart themselves?"

Bombarded by memories, Dawn couldn't help remembering how Callie had been her sounding board in the years leading up to her parents' divorce. Callie and Kate both. They'd offered laughter and hope and the rock-solid stability of their friendship while the rest of her world collapsed. Dawn often wondered if the empathy and support Callie had provided during that awful time had contributed to her eventual choice of a profession.

She'd also suspected that same deep emotional investment had eventually worn Callie down, leading her to quit her job. Now it appeared there was more at play than either she or Kate had realized.

"What did you do with the emails?" She wanted to know.

"I showed them to my supervisor, made copies for the file and forgot about them."

"Until?"

Callie bit her lip.

"Until?" Kate echoed insistently.

"Until they got nasty. I received one right after you and Travis renewed your vows at the Trevi Fountain. Joe Russo saw how much it upset me, got me aside and pried the details out of me."

She paused, looking slightly bewildered. "I still don't know how it happened. One minute we were all tossing back champagne. The next, Joe had herded me into a private alcove and I was telling him about the emails."

Dawn shot Kate a surprised glance. They'd all gotten to know the high-powered security expert a little in Italy. But only a little. Dawn doubted she'd spoken a dozen words to the man until he'd joined them for dinner here at Kate's last week—which made the fact that their intensely private friend had shared her troubles with him even more surprising.

Callie caught the exchange and shook her head. "I know! I can't imagine why I opened up to him like that."

"I suspect because he aced Interviewing Techniques 101," Dawn drawled.

Along with advanced courses in prisoner intimidation and interrogation. Russo struck her as a man who knew how to wring every last drop of information from the guilty and innocent alike.

"What's he doing about the emails?" She wanted to know.

"He's working with the Boston Cyber Crimes Division to trace the source, but no luck so far. Something about firewalls and gateways. I hope they'll have better luck with the one I just received."

"You got another one?"

"A few minutes ago. It… It's what made me trip over my own feet. I smashed my phone when I fell or I would show it to you."

"What did it say?"

"I won't bother to repeat the names the sender called me. They're too ugly. The bottom line is that I'm going to pay for the pain I've caused."

"Sunnabitch!" Fury boiled in Dawn's blood. "I hope I'm somewhere in the vicinity when they nail this bastard. He'll be looking for his testicles two counties over."

"Three," Kate countered fiercely. "Although I think we can count on Joe and Travis to take care of his balls."

"And Brian," Dawn added. "I can tell him about this, can't I?"

"Let me ask Joe." Callie managed an apologetic smile. "I hate to delay our pee and wedding planning extravaganza, but he made me promise to contact him immediately if I received another one of these emails."

"Go!" Kate ordered. "Use my office and call him now!"

When Callie disappeared into the small den, her two friends stared at each other in dismay.

"No wonder she's been so quiet these past weeks." Kate's mouth twisted with self-disgust. "And I was so immersed in my own little problems I chalked her decision to quit her job up to stress and burnout."

A belated realization hit her.

"Oh, Lord! *That's* why it was so easy for me to talk her into extending her stay here in DC. She doesn't want to go back to Boston, where this creep probably lives."

"Crap! You're right." Dawn thought fast. "Well, I've got to fly home to inform my boss I'm relocating to DC and make arrangements to sublease my condo. I can scoot over to Callie's and pack up whatever she needs. And when Travis gets back from Florida, she can move into the gatehouse with me. We don't want those banging headboards to keep her awake," she added with a knowing twitch of her brows.

"They probably won't bang as much now that we've accomplished our immediate objective."

"You *think* you've accomplished it. I still want visual proof."

Callie echoed that sentiment when she returned from Kate's office. After confirming that Russo could retrieve the email from her server, she said they could go ahead and read Travis and Brian into the situation.

"But Joe says to tell them not to go all cowboy. He's working on the problem. He also says I shouldn't worry." She forced a bright smile. "So let's head for the bathroom and find out if we're really having a baby. Then we'll talk details for Dawn's third—and final!—wedding."

* * *

After ninety breathless seconds, the pink stick turned a deep, glowing purple. Whoops and hugs and happy dances led to the serious business of baby names. Kate wouldn't budge on Travis Jr. for a boy, but finally settled on Venetia Dawn Calissa Westbrook for a girl.

"The first name for where she was conceived," she said happily, "and the middle names for her godmothers-to-be."

"You'd better count backward," Dawn drawled, "and make sure you didn't get pregnant in Bologna."

"It was Venice! And even if it wasn't, I'll insist it was. There, that's settled. Time to shift focus. Let's talk about you. Have you thought at all about when, where and how you want to become Mrs. Tommy's Mom?"

"Sort of. Brian would prefer sooner rather than later, and I guess I don't see any real need to delay."

"You guess?"

Kate threw a quick glance at Callie before repeating her earlier question.

"Are you sure about this? Do you really want to take on being a wife and mother at the same time?"

"It's a package deal. And yes, I do."

The moment Dawn uttered the words, an absolute certainty settled around her heart. She did. She really, truly, honestly *did* want to take both on. The sooner the better.

"When does Travis get back from Florida?" she asked Kate.

"The end of next week. He's supposed to start at EAS on October first."

"Okay!" Thumbing her iPhone to life, Dawn tapped the calendar icon. "The first is a Wednesday. We could do this on the following Saturday, the eleventh. I'll talk to Brian when I get home and see if that day works for him. In the meantime, I'll zip up to Boston and…"

"Dawn! You're talking a little more than two weeks from now! We'll be hard put to find a venue on such short notice, much less line up a caterer and photographer and…"

"Paying for the last 'venue' pretty well wiped out my bank account. No, I'm thinking…"

The perfect setting popped into her mind.

"I'm thinking Brian's backyard. A small, intimate ceremony attended only by our family and close friends."

She could envision the scene and knew instantly it was exactly right.

"All we'll need are some folding chairs and fall flowers to decorate the gazebo. And a caterer and photographer, I suppose."

Brian could take care of the officiating dignitary. Hopefully, the minister at the church he and Tommy attended could squeeze them in. If not, they'd have to find an alternate.

That left Dawn facing only one major challenge. "You guys have to help me shop for a wedding gown." She gulped, remembering her previous, ridiculously expensive purchases, both of which she'd donated to a charity that recycled gowns to women in need. "Maybe I should go with a tea dress. Or an ivory pants suit. Or pearl-studded jeans."

"Pearl-studded jeans may be the latest thing," Kate countered with a huff, "but they're *not* you. Don't worry—we'll find the perfect fashion statement."

Dawn drove back to Bethesda an hour later. As she wheeled through the star-studded September night, she refused to give way to panic.

Okay. All right. She'd done it again. Jumped feetfirst into plans for another wedding. In a deliberate attempt to ease Callie's distress over those emails, she'd nailed down the date for her third attempt to stroll down the aisle.

"Third time's a charm," she chanted grimly, her knuckles white where she gripped the wheel. "Third time's a charm."

Chapter Nine

Feet up, a cold brew on the table beside the sofa, Brian half watched the news as he waited for Dawn to return from her girls' night out. She'd called to let him know she was on her way. Despite the time, he figured they could get in at least an hour or two of quality time before they called it a night and went to bed.

Their *separate* beds. He was finding that part of their agreement tough to stick to. So tough, he had to deliver a swift mental kick whenever the insidious idea of activating the motion sensors on the stairs sneaked back into his thoughts.

Like now. His belly tightening, he pictured his soon-to-be-bride sprawled in naked abandon on the sofa. Or on the carpet. Or *any* horizontal surface. He could see her rose-tipped nipples, the fiery patch at the apex of her thighs, the creamy skin of her…

The faint rumble of the garage door going up did nothing to loosen the kink in his gut. Anticipation firing his every piston, he pushed to his feet and met her as she entered the kitchen. One look at her frown instantly erased all thoughts of quality time.

"What's wrong? Didn't the stick turn turquoise or pink or whatever color it's supposed to?"

"Purple," she said, distracted. "Yes, it did."

As she unbuttoned her jacket, another explanation for the frown hit him.

"Are Kate and Callie worried about you hooking up with Tommy and me permanently?" he asked. "I can understand if they are. We're a pretty tough twosome to—"

"No! Well, a little," she admitted with a shrug. "But they helped me settle on a date for the ceremony. Saturday, the fourth, if that works with your schedule."

What the hell? Given her track record, Brian hadn't expected his bride to go all starry-eyed and giddy over their wedding. Still, this underwhelming response ticked him off a little.

"The fourth of what month, if you don't mind me asking."

The sarcasm went right over her head.

"October. Callie's been getting threats, Brian."

"Come again?"

"Someone's sending her nasty emails. *Very* nasty emails."

Brian bit out an oath. "Sit down," he ordered. "I'll make coffee while you give me the details."

"I don't know many." Her forehead still creased, she slid onto one of the counter stools. "Just that Callie started getting threats a few months ago. She thinks they may be coming from a parent or guardian of one of the children she stood up for in court."

"Did she report them to the police? Her supervisor at work?"

"Yes to both. She also told Joe Russo about them."

"Joe? Good!"

"Callie opened up to him in Rome. Can you believe it? She told *him* before she told Kate or me."

"Damn straight, I can believe it." Brian dumped a scoopful of coffee into the filter, shoved down the lid and hit the on button. "Russo doesn't say much, but I can tell you he's the best I've ever encountered in his line of business. I would guess he's good at extracting information."

One way or another.

"What's Joe done about the emails?"

"Callie said he's working with Boston Cyber Crimes Unit."

"I'll call him. Make sure he's getting the cooperation he needs. If not, I may be able to help."

While the coffeemaker gurgled and the scent of fresh-brewed French roast filled the kitchen, Brian ran down a quick mental list of sources to tap. He rarely threw his weight around or found it necessary to call in favors. Business was business, however, and he'd contributed to the war chests of more than one politician. If Joe had hit any brick walls in investigating the emails, Brian could help kick them down.

And not just because of the gratitude that now filled Dawn's eyes. He liked Callie. He hadn't spent all that much time with her, but in the few conversations they'd shared she'd impressed him with her quick mind and un-ruffled calm. Although from the sound of things, that placid demeanor might well have been a front. Dawn's next comment pretty much confirmed that.

"Kate thinks these threats could be the reason Callie extended her stay in DC. She may be afraid to go back to Boston until they nail the bastard who's sending the threats. And we don't want her to! So…"

He filled two mugs and passed her one. "So?"

"When Travis flies back from Florida next week, Kate's condo will get crowded. We thought... *I* thought we could invite her to stay at the gatehouse."

Which Dawn wouldn't be occupying once she and Brian married. Was that why she'd opted for such a quick wedding? So she could move in with him and let Callie have the gatehouse?

Hell, who cared? At this point Brian would grab any excuse to finesse this woman into his bed. Not just his bed, he realized as his gaze roamed her face. He wanted her in his life. His and Tommy's. He wanted more kids, too. Sons or daughters with Dawn's fun-loving spirit and ready laugh.

The thought hooked in his rib cage like a barb. They hadn't discussed having kids. Hadn't discussed much of anything except marriage as a solution to an immediate problem. Brian knew what he was getting out of the bargain, but wasn't sure what Dawn was, except maybe the stable home and family she hadn't had growing up. He'd give her that, Brian swore fiercely, and anything else she needed or wanted. Starting with this simple request.

"By all means, invite Callie to stay here. There's plenty of room in the gatehouse. Even more after the second weekend in October."

He hesitated, needing to be sure she wanted to make this happen so quickly.

"You don't need more time to line things up?"

"No. It takes me a while sometimes," she said ruefully, "but I do learn from past mistakes. I want to keep this simple, Brian. I thought maybe a ceremony in the garden, with just our families and close friends."

"That works for me, if that's what you really want."

"It is." Warming to the subject, she shared more of

her hastily formed plans. "Kate and Callie will help, of course. And if you don't think Mrs. Jones would mind, I thought I'd ask her advice about caterers and maybe a photographer."

"LauraBeth would love it if you included her. She and her husband raised four boys. She's told me more than once that the mother-of-the-groom doesn't have nearly as much fun as the mother-of-the-bride." He knew he was skirting dangerous ground but had to ask, "What about your mom? We could fly her in to help, too."

"Lord, no!" She didn't bother to repress a shudder. "We'll have to invite her to the ceremony. Both my parents. I want them there, I really do. But we might need to hire Joe Russo's bodyguards to keep one of them from stabbing the other with the cake knife."

"It was that bad, huh?"

"Was, and still is."

She lowered her glance to her coffee mug. When she lifted it again, both her expression and her voice were brisk.

"You're in charge of lining up a minister, fella."

"I can handle that. Also the honeymoon."

"We don't have to go anywhere. Not right away."

"Sure we do."

"What about school? Tommy really shouldn't miss many days this early in the year."

"I love my son but I don't intend to invite him along on our honeymoon."

"But—"

He stopped her protest with a finger laid over her lips. "I want you to myself for a few days, Dawn. All to myself."

"Well," she said a little breathlessly when he took his hand away, "since you put it that way. And," she added as the idea took hold, "if Callie's here I know she wouldn't mind looking after Tommy for a few days."

"If she can't, I'll ask my folks to stay with him. There, that's solved. Next issue. What time tomorrow can you meet me so we can pick out a ring?"

She answered quickly. Too quickly. "All I want is a plain gold band. Nothing fancy."

Christ! Between her warring parents and those two abortive engagements, she'd gone through the marriage wringer.

"A plain gold band it is. But I'm allowing no restrictions on a wedding present. I intend to get you something special. Something you'll—"

"A puppy."

"What?"

"I want a puppy for a wedding present. One that doesn't shed, so we don't have to worry about Tommy's allergies."

"Are you serious?"

"I've been thinking about getting him one since we had that discussion about FDR's dog, Fala."

"We just broke the news to him a few hours ago that he's getting a new mom. You don't think we should wait a while to introduce a puppy into the mix?"

"Nope. This is the perfect time to make it happen. The dog could be *our* present to Tommy, Brian. Yours and mine. Besides," she added slyly, "with a pet to keep him busy, he won't even notice when we take off on a honeymoon."

"Damn, woman, you're devious. I could use you on my contracts negotiating team."

"Just say the word, big guy. In the meantime, though, you'll give this some serious thought?"

"I guess."

"It'll be fun once we get past the piddles and chewed-up sneakers." Her eyes alight with laughter, she slid off her stool and hooked her arms around his neck. "Let's have a little more enthusiasm here."

"Well, if you insist."

He cradled her hips with his palms, drawing her closer, marveling at the way she fit against him. He felt the rightness of it down to his bones. The basic, instinctive pleasure of matching male to female. Mate to mate. Husband to…

The thought brought him up short. Whoa! When had he stopped viewing this marriage as a contract? And when did he intend to communicate his altered perspective to Dawn?

Now, he decided as his body hardened against hers. Right this friggin' minute.

"I need to tell you something." He brought up his hands and framed her face. "I'm crazy in love with you."

Her lips parted in breathless surprise. "Since when?"

"Damned if I know. I suspected it when I saw you and Tommy turning cartwheels. Then just now, when you dropped this puppy thing on me, I realized I'd bring home a hundred and one Dalmatians if that's what you wanted."

"One will do. Just one, and you and Tommy. That's all I want. That's *everything* I want."

The next morning Dawn called Callie right after dropping Tommy off at school to invite her to move into the gatehouse. She also reported the gist of Brian's late-night conversation with Joe Russo.

"Joe says they're close to pinpointing the source of the emails. Until they do, though, he thinks it's a good idea for you to stay in DC."

"Well…"

"I'm meeting Brian for lunch, then we're going to shop

for rings. Why don't I come by afterward and help you pack?"

"There's not much to pack. Just what I took to Italy and the few things I bought here."

"I'm in the same boat, but I'm flying up to Boston this weekend to retrieve more clothes and my car."

And arrange temporary storage for the rest of her belongings. *And* talk to a rental agency about leasing her condo. *And* break the news of a permanent change of address to her boss. *And* meet with her team to discuss ongoing projects. *And* deliver wedding invitations to the small circle of friends she wanted at her wedding. *And…*

"How long do you plan to stay?" Callie wanted to know.

"Two days. Three max. If you make a list of what you want, I'll swing by your place and bring it back with me."

"I have a better idea. How about we both fly up to Boston and I'll help *you* pack? Then we could hook your sporty little Mustang to a U-Haul and drive back down to DC together."

"Deal! As long as we stay at my condo. No sense letting the creep who sent those emails know you're in town. I'll go online right now to get us seats on the shuttle."

She made the reservations, then switched to her favorite design applications. Adobe Illustrator, Photoshop and InDesign all offered hundreds of templates for birthday invitations, funeral programs, birth announcements, home decor and senior yearbooks. After skimming a mind-numbing selection of wedding invitation templates, she decided to design her own.

Grabbing her iPhone, she went outside and snapped a dozen photos of the white-painted gazebo. It took her all of five seconds to AirDrop the photos to her MacBook, and not many more to select the best shot.

Twenty minutes later, she'd extracted the pattern of the

gazebo's filigree trim, interwove a weathered grapevine dripping fall colors and softened the image to a creative blur. She then replicated it three times and merged the four images to form a delicate, romantic frame. Now all she had to do was insert the time and place of the wedding and a few lines to capture the sentiments involved.

She stared at the empty frame, her thoughts churning. She loved Brian. She could admit that now, without hesitation or doubt. And Tommy… She couldn't wait to see his face when he opened his wedding present. A smile pulled at her lips as she envisioned the two of them diving into piles of leaves with a frolicking puppy. Making angels in the snow. Battling each other in life-and-death sessions of Garden Warfare.

But…

A familiar panic bubbled up. Jaw set, Dawn pushed it back. She would *not* let the novelty of motherhood wear off. She would *not* question and doubt and destroy what she and Brian felt for each other. And she would *not* turn tail and run, dammit. Not this time!

Even with that stern self-lecture, her heart pounded and she came within a breath of slamming down the laptop's lid. Several moments went by before she hit the keys again. After an extended search, she brought up a quote from Shakespeare's *Hamlet*. She copied the lines, pasted them into the frame, and changed the font to an elegant script.

Doubt thou the stars are fire;
Doubt that the sun doth move;
Doubt truth to be a liar:
But never doubt I love.

She skimmed the finished product and thought for a moment before altering the pronoun in the last line from *I* to *we*.

Her face relaxed into a smile as she remembered quoting the Bard to Tommy at the Trevi Fountain. He'd expressed zero interest in learning the source of the quote at the time. She suspected he wouldn't be any more interested in this verse.

Dawn thought it was perfect, though, and spent another half hour putting the finishing touches on the invitation before printing out a sample to show Brian when she met him downtown.

She found a badge and a warm welcome waiting for her at EAS headquarters. It was her first visit, and she had to admit she was impressed. A quick glance at the directory inside the lobby indicated EAS occupied the top four floors of the glass-and-steel high-rise. A long list of attorneys and high-powered consulting firms had offices in the lower floors.

The lobby itself soared upward for three stories, with a massive bronze sculpture of an eagle in flight dominating the central atrium. Dawn took a few moments to admire its glorious artistry before she approached the security desk and identified herself. The uniformed guard manning the desk greeted her with a wide smile.

"Mr. Ellis's executive assistant told us to expect you. I'll buzz her and let her know you're here."

Mere moments later a small private elevator to the right of the security desk pinged open and five feet nothing of smiling Southern charm emerged.

"I'm LauraBeth Jones. We've spoken on the phone. I'm so glad to finally meet you."

"Me, too."

She offered her hand, but LauraBeth brushed it aside and tugged Dawn down for a quick hug that enveloped her in a soft, familiar scent.

She straightened, grinning. "I recognize that fragrance. Magnolias 'n Creme, right?"

"How did you...? Oh, that's right. Brian told me you work for an all-natural products company. Does it market this lotion?"

"It does."

"What an amazing coincidence." Smiling, she ushered Dawn to the elevator. "I should tell you I've enjoyed our phone conversations. I've also enjoyed watching you stand my cool, unflappable boss on his head."

"I don't think I... I mean, he's not..."

"Oh, yes, he is. Head over heels."

She tapped the only button in the elevator, and the cage zoomed up so swiftly Dawn grabbed the teak rail for support.

"As if that weren't enough to make me love you sight unseen," LauraBeth continued with a wide smile, "Brian mentioned this morning you wanted to ask for my help planning the wedding. And now I find out your company produces my favorite skin cream. It's fate, child, fate."

Dawn had pretty much the same reaction when Brian took her to lunch at 1789. The Federal-style building dated from George Washington's time, but the restaurant featured a modern menu. When they were seated in one of its six intimate dining rooms, Dawn recognized two senators, a very high-profile congresswoman and a political commentator who flamed the airwaves nightly with his antiadministration invective.

"I used to jog past this place all the time when I was at Georgetown University," she confided to Brian. "Never imagined I'd stroll through its sacred portals."

"Despite all my years in Washington, I've never been here, either."

"Then why did you…? Ah. I understand."

"Do you?" Reaching across the table, he covered her hand with his. "I wasn't thinking fresh starts, Dawn."

Her hand curled into his. "Then what were you thinking?"

"I did some research before you got to the office. Okay, LauraBeth and I both got online. She found a jeweler just a block from here who designs one-of-a-kind wedding bands. And I," he added with a smug grin, "found a breeder whose champion wheaten whelped a litter of pups five weeks ago."

"Great. Uh, what's a wheaten?"

"A midsize terrier, cousin to the Scottie."

"Oh, Brian! Tommy will be so jazzed! I'm pretty jazzed myself."

"The AKC website says they're playful, affectionate and faithful. And they don't shed, as long as you comb them regularly."

"I can wield a comb with the best of them. Just ask Kate and Callie." Her enthusiastic smile took a quick dip. "You have to be careful buying from breeders, though. So many of them operate disgusting puppy mills that turn out inbred, sickly dogs."

"Not this one. She's AKC certified. She's also a retired IBM executive with a passion for her dogs. She only breeds them once a year, and her website states she's extremely selective about who she'll sell to."

Although this wheaten sounded perfect, Dawn wouldn't let herself get too hopeful. "If the mom's a champ, I'd bet the puppies are probably already spoken for."

"They were, but when I called this morning one of the buyers had just backed out. I gave her a credit card for a deposit and told her we'd be by to check out the pup at three."

"Wow. You don't waste time."

"Not when I'm after something I want." Loosening his hold, he nudged her hand toward the menu. "So decide what you'd like. We've got places to go and people to see."

Mere moments after walking into the showroom of the exclusive Georgetown jewelry store, Dawn spotted a wide band of interwoven strands of white and yellow gold.

"Oooh, this is gorgeous. I saw a ring very much like it in a museum in Venice."

"The Palladian Basilica?" the jeweler asked.

"Yes! Have you been there?"

"Unfortunately not." Beaming, he revealed that he'd received inspiration for his design from the museum's website. "The ring you saw in Venice is from a much-earlier Roman period. It was unearthed at Herculaneum, if I'm not mistaken. Archeologists believe the interwoven strands represent the relationship between the gods and mortals. I prefer to think they symbolize the relationship between man and woman. Interwoven, inextricable, enduring."

Brian added his endorsement to her choice. "As Laura-Beth would say, 'It's fate, child.' You, me, Venice, this ring."

"I can craft a matching band for you," the jeweler suggested with seeming innocence.

"Do it."

By then Dawn had caught a glimpse of the price tag tucked discreetly in the ring's velvet nest. Before she could protest, though, or suggest they look at sets that didn't cost the equivalent of the national debt, Brian had instructed the goldsmith to size her ring to fit and his to be ready ASAP.

They left the goldsmith's, crossed the Potomac and headed northwest on Route 7. As the suburbs gradually fell away, the rolling hills of Northern Virginia flaunted their fall colors. Ten miles west of Dulles Airport, Map-Quest guided them off the pike toward the small town of Woodburn. From there, a series of country roads eventually led to a Colonial-style farmhouse set on a gently sloping rise.

The retired IBM executive turned out to be short, stocky and as passionate about her dogs as her website had indicated. Before taking Dawn and Brian to see the litter, Audrey Chesterfield grilled them on the kind of home they would provide her precious pup. Only then did she escort them to a small den paneled in golden pine. Unlatching a puppy gate, she waved them inside.

"This is Lady Adelaide's Fancy," Chesterfield said, beaming with pride as she stroked the wheaten's curly ears. "She took best in breed at Westminster two years ago."

The champion came to just above the breeder's knees. Her brown eyes clear and bright, she checked the newcomers over and made no protest as Chesterfield reached down to separate one of her pups from its lively, inquisitive siblings.

"And this is Adelaide's Pride."

The moment the breeder placed the wiggling bundle of joy in Dawn's arms, she fell instantly, irretrievably in love.

"Yes." She laughed as the pup made repeated lunges to swipe ecstatically at her chin and cheeks. "Oh, yes."

"That's the wheaten greetin'," Chesterfield informed her with a broad smile. "You'll find the breed is smart, loyal and adaptable to city life as long as they get enough exercise. They're also given to wildly enthusiastic displays of affection."

"So I see!"

"On the downside," she warned, "they require a lot of grooming. They don't like to get wet, and when they do, these long coats need serious brushing or they get all matted and tangled. They're also sloppy eaters. Food can get caught in their beards. You might find this guy wiping his chin on your leg."

Dawn didn't hesitate. A little dog food on her leg couldn't begin to distract from the pup's unbridled joy.

"He's perfect," she breathed, burying her face in the soft, curly coat. "We'll pick him up a week from Saturday."

Chapter Ten

The rest of the week zoomed by so fast Dawn could barely catch her breath.

The first thing she did was contact her family to tell them about Brian. And, oh, by the way, ask whether they could make it to Washington on October 11 for a wedding. Her two older brothers said they couldn't due to other commitments but Dawn suspected they didn't really believe it would happen. Her youngest brother, Aaron, said he wouldn't miss it. She braced herself for the next calls. Her father, bless him, tried hard to sound enthusiastic. But fifteen seconds into the conversation with her mother, Dawn was grinding her teeth so hard they hurt.

"Yes. Mom, I'm well aware this is my third time at bat."

A pause.

"Yes, I know jumping into a ready-made family is a big risk."

Another pause, accompanied by the realization she might have to schedule a visit to a dentist.

"You're right. I've certainly seen firsthand how marriage to the wrong man can suck the marrow from a woman's bones. Do you want me to get you a plane ticket, or not?"

Her mother conceded, but only after suggesting she purchase a fully refundable ticket. Dawn hung up, already regretting that she and Brian didn't just hustle off to a justice of the peace.

Thankfully, moving Callie into the gatehouse dispelled most of the fumes from that noxious conversation. Dawn picked her up at Kate's that same afternoon and gave her a tour of both the detached bungalow and the main house.

"Oh," Callie exclaimed when she saw the backyard and fanciful gazebo. "How lovely. No wonder you wanted to have the ceremony here. It's perfect."

"Assuming the skies don't open and drown us all out."

"What's the forecast?"

"Still too far out for any degree of certainty. It *looks* like I may get lucky, though."

Their glances met, but they both left unsaid it would be the first time.

Callie joined Dawn, Brian and Tommy for breakfast the next morning and helped clean the kitchen before heading out for her customary brisk walk. While she explored the neighborhood, Tommy scooted upstairs to get ready for school. His absence gave Dawn the few moments she needed to broach a difficult subject with Brian.

"I noticed you moved the framed pictures of Caroline out of the great room. And took down the ones that hung in the hall. You didn't need to do that."

A shadow flitted across his eyes, but they held Dawn's, sure and steady and unwavering.

"Yes, I did. It's incredibly generous of you to live in the

house I shared with Caroline. I didn't want it to be more difficult for you than it has to be."

"Oh, Brian. We talked about this. It's Tommy's home, too. All his friends live in this neighborhood. They go to the same school. I don't want him to give them up any more than I want you to give up your memories of Caroline. She was so much a part of your life."

She framed his face with both palms, aching at the thought of the pain and desolation he'd gone through.

"You wouldn't be the man you are today if not for the years you shared with your wife."

He let out a short breath. "That's true."

"I'm not jealous of those years. I could *never* be jealous of them. And I don't want you to erase Caroline's presence from this house or from her son's memory. So I thought... Well... If you don't mind, I'd like to make a digital memory book for Tommy. One he could carry on his phone when he gets one, or load onto a computer or TV. I thought it might include pictures of you and Caroline, as well as any you have of Tommy with his mom. I want shots of just the two of you, too, as he's growing up. Photos from our time together in Italy. His first grade debut. And everything else the three of us share in the weeks and months and years ahead."

He was quiet for so long that Dawn recognized the inherent flaw in what until this moment she'd considered was a good idea. How stupid to think he'd want to share his private memories of Caroline with her! Even more stupid to think he'd want to link his painful past to Tommy's present. She was about to dismiss the idea with a laugh and say it was only a thought when he broke the charged silence.

"Wait right here."

She waited, still prey to doubts, until he returned some moments later with his arms full. He dumped his load on the counter and sorted through the various items. The first one he offered her was a thick album with "Ellis Family" embossed on the front.

"My dad put this together for Tommy."

Dawn lifted the embossed lid and found herself staring at a grim, unsmiling couple. The woman stood with one hand on the shoulder of a man with muttonchop whiskers. They were both in black—her in a dress unrelieved by so much as a trace of white lace; he in a frock coat buttoned almost to his chin.

She flipped to the next page and skimmed the yellowed documents. "Good Lord! These are copies of military records from the Civil War."

She leaned closer to decipher the spidery handwriting.

Company H, 8th Virginia Infantry, CSA. July 21, 1861. List of Killed, Wounded and Missing in Action.

It took her a moment to translate CSA into the Confederate States of America. The entry right below made her heart thump.

Corporal J. D. Ellis. Wounded. Manassas. Returned to duty August 10.

And after that.

Company H, 8th Virginia Infantry. July 2, 1863. Corporal J. D. Ellis. Missing in action.
Company H, 8th Virginia Infantry. August 9, 1863. Corporal J. D Ellis. Prisoner in the hands of the enemy, Ft. McHenry.
Company H, 8th Virginia Infantry. September 19,

1864. Corporal J. D. Ellis. Returned to duty in prisoner exchange.

"This is amazing. Where'd your dad get these records?"

"Some genealogy loop he subscribes to." He shot her a quick grin. "Sure you want to marry up with the descendent of a dyed-in-the wool Reb?"

"If you want to marry up with a Yankee whose Irish great-great-great grandfather stowed away on a freighter and snuck into the US illegally."

As she turned the pages, Tommy's ancestry came vibrantly alive. So did a design for the memory book. She would use sepia tones for the pages with photos from the 1800s. Add bits of history, unit insignia, crossed cannons from the Civil War. Maybe add some music from that time, too. She'd frame the two studio portraits from the 1920s with more bits of history depicting that exuberant, post-WWI era.

She'd have to use every bit of her Photoshop expertise to restore the old photos and daguerreotypes, including the faded snapshots from WWII. But even without restoration, she could detect Brian in the crossed arms and wide-legged stance of the individual standing against the backdrop of a propeller-driven aircraft with a voluptuous brunette painted on its fuselage.

"Who's this?"

"Tommy's great-great-grandad. Right before the 1943 invasion of Sicily."

"These photos are fantastic. Do you have similar ones from Caroline's side of the family?"

"Just a few family photos. And these."

She shuffled through the other items he'd carried into the kitchen. Another album. The photos that had previously hung in the hall and occupied shelf space in the den.

And one she hadn't seen before. It was a framed, unposed shot of Caroline. She looked over her shoulder, her eyes laughing at the camera, as she held her infant son tucked close to her chin. Her lips just brushed his downy curls.

Dawn could see her love for both husband and son. *Feel* it. "How old is Tommy here?"

"Three months, six days."

The terse, precise reply brought her head up. Brian took his eyes off the photo and explained.

"I took that shot the morning we drove to the neurologist to get the results of the MRI. The first MRI," he amended. "When we still thought her dizziness and nagging headaches could be cured with a pill and a good night's sleep."

Dawn ran a fingertip lightly over the glass, aching for him and for the mother who didn't get to watch her baby grow into such a bright, lively, inquisitive boy.

I'll do right by your son, she promised Caroline silently. *I'll make some mistakes along the way. I've certainly made more than my share in the past. But I swear I'll love him with everything in me. Him and Brian.*

Tommy came clattering down the stairs at that moment with his crammed backpack weighing his shoulders down. Brian gathered his briefcase and issued a not-so-gentle warning.

"Be good, buddy. No more shooting spitballs through your straw at lunch."

His blue eyes pained, the boy projected the image of a wounded angel. "Cindy started it."

"I know. You told us. That doesn't mean you had to finish it. I'll see you tonight. You, too," he said to Dawn as he bent and brushed his mouth over hers.

She leaned into the kiss, so happy and relieved to see the shadows had left his eyes that she gave considerably more than she received. At which point she discovered Brian was no longer worried about his son witnessing an exchange of spit. He deepened the kiss and only broke it off when Tommy did an impatient jig.

"Daaad! You guys are gonna make me late for school."

They all left together, Brian in his black SUV, Dawn and Tommy in the white compact. They picked up his pal Cindy on the way. She buckled in beside Tommy in the backseat and promptly accused him of forgetting the book on Ice Age cave art her brother had loaned him.

"I didn't forget it! Addy said I could keep it till I finished looking at the pictures."

"How long is that going to take? 'Til we're in second grade?"

Dawn listened to their squabbling with half an ear. Part of her couldn't quite believe she'd already made the transition to carpooling and soon-to-be soccer mom. The rest of her kept returning to the memory book. The project had fired her creative juices. She intended to start on it as soon as she got back to the house.

Her first order of business was to call up a playlist and connect her phone to the gatehouse's wireless speaker system. She always worked better with music in the background. For this project she chose a playlist that included big, sweeping movies themes.

With Maurice Jarre's epic score from *Lawrence of Arabia* to motivate her, she went back to the main house. She used the printer/copier/scanner in Brian's office to scan the photos and regimental records from the Civil War, then sent the JPEGs to her laptop.

She carried the albums and framed photos back to the gatehouse with her for quick reference and set up her laptop on the table in the breakfast nook. Before jumping into the memory book's construction, she searched dozens of commercial sites for the graphics she wanted to include as illustrations.

Researching the 8th Virginia Infantry regiment side-tracked her for a good half hour. She learned that the newly raised 8th Virginia guarded vital river crossings until the First Battle of Bull Run. The regiment acquitted itself with honor at Manassas, where J. D. Ellis was wounded. In March 1862, the 8th took part in the Peninsula campaign as part of Pickett's Brigade. Their courage and the massive casualties they sustained in that campaign earned the regiment the dubious title of The Bloody Eighth.

Dawn could have spent hours poring through the 8th's fascinating history. After compiling a folder of Civil War images and icons, she finally cut herself off and turned to the Roaring 20s. That era was more fun, although she doubted Tommy was old enough yet to appreciate flappers and slick-haired Great Gatsby types swilling bathtub gin.

Her next task was to identify the twin-tailed bomber in the faded WWII photo. It didn't take her long to verify that it was a B-24 Liberator. She increased both the size and the resolution of the photo until she could read the aircraft's tail number and did an online search, but didn't discover another photo of it or the well-endowed beauty decorating its fuselage.

Refusing to give up, she refined the JPEG until she got clear enough images of the insignia and patches on the pilot's uniform to trace them to an Army Air Corps unit based in North Africa.

She lingered much longer over the photos of Brian in his marine corps uniform. His dad had obviously saved every one he'd sent home. There was the shaved-head officer candidate. The lantern-jawed new lieutenant standing at rigid attention on a grassy parade ground. The three pals in camouflage with their arms hooked over each other's shoulders. The caption below read, "Ross, Digger and Brian at Basic School." Whatever that was.

After that came initial aviation training in Pensacola, Florida. Then primary flight training, which Brian ended with a triumphant grin and a photocopy of the orders assigning him to helicopters. Advanced helo training at Fort Rucker, Alabama. A photo of Brian and another pilot in helmets and dusty, desert-hued flight suits standing beside a chopper.

The handwritten caption underneath said Iraq, March 2003. Frowning, she Googled the Iraq War and learned the invasion had kicked off on March 20 of that year. And Brian had been right there, in the first wave. Dawn had mixed emotions about the war, but none at all about the men and women who'd been sent to fight it.

Still frowning, she Googled the helicopter in the photo and identified it as a UH-1N Iroquois. She skimmed the information in the article and stopped dead when she saw it had first flown in in Vietnam in 1969.

"Good grief!"

She stared at the date in disbelief. Brian and his unknown pal had been flying a three-decade-old whirlybird.

And they were still flying those suckers. Everywhere! Shaking her head, she skimmed down the list. Austria, Argentina, Bangladesh, Bahrain. Every country in the alphabet, down to and including Zaire. The worldwide inventory gave Dawn an entirely new appreciation of the man she'd agreed to marry.

When they'd met in Italy, she knew Brian was there on some hush-hush, top secret modification his company had engineered for Special Operations aircraft flown by NATO crews. Neither he nor Travis nor Carlo had dropped even a vague hint what that mod encompassed. That had been fine with Dawn. Her interests at the time focused on Tuscany's sun-kissed vineyards, Venice's moonlit canals and the bundle of unharnessed energy that was Tommy.

The hotel where Brian, Tommy and his nanny had stayed was one of the best in Venice. One of the top ten in the world, according to Condé Nast. The Gritti Palace's sumptuous decor had pretty well confirmed that Brian and his corporation had raked in some tidy profits over the years. So had the slick private jet they'd flown home in. And when Dawn had driven into EAS headquarters a few days ago, LauraBeth had pointed to a wall-sized map of EAS's operations.

But the scope of Brian's achievements hadn't really sunk in until this moment. She stared at the photo of a younger, tougher version of the sophisticated man she knew and marveled at what he'd accomplished in such a short time.

He'd learned to fly in the marines. Went back to school afterward. Built a company from the ground up. Married, had a son and lost a wife. And in the process, he'd helped keep these Vietnam-era choppers in the air, along with a dozen other military aircraft she would bet.

Irritated that she hadn't asked more about the products EAS provided, she vowed to rectify that mistake in the very near future. In the meantime, she had a memory book to create, a quick trip to Boston to schedule, several parties to pull off and a wedding to get through.

Chapter Eleven

Wednesday evening, Dawn and Brian hosted a celebratory dinner to officially welcome Travis to DC and his new job at EAS. Callie and Tommy helped with the preparations. Their combined efforts had all four of them laughing and left the kitchen a total wreck. They got the mess cleaned up and everything into the oven or on the stove in time to greet their guests. LauraBeth and her husband were the first to arrive, followed by another dozen or so of EAS's senior executives with their spouses or significant others. They gave Dawn as warm a welcome as they did Travis and Kate, making the whole evening a total delight.

With the images from the memory book still fresh in her mind, she subtly pumped Travis, some of the other execs and LauraBeth for details about EAS operations. The picture they painted remained a little hazy around the edges but still impressed the heck out of her. EAS, she learned had contracts with every branch of the US military and at least two dozen foreign nations,

"You won't see much of your husband come November," LauraBeth warned. "He's scheduled for back-to-back meetings in Saudi Arabia, the UAE and Oman. I'm trying to make sure he's home by Thanksgiving, but it's looking iffy at this point."

Great! Another "if" to factor in to the great Thanksgiving war. She hid a grimace at the memory of the as-yet-unresolved feud between her parents and resisted the urge to beg LauraBeth to book her on the same flight to the Middle East as Brian.

The following afternoon she and Brian drove down to Charlottesville, Virginia, so he could introduce her to his parents. Evelyn and Tom Ellis were gracious and appeared happy for their son, but Dawn sensed that they harbored some doubts about their short-notice nuptials.

On Friday, Callie and Dawn met Kate for lunch at Tysons Corner. Home to the corporate headquarters of numerous companies and two upscale malls only a stone's throw apart, it was located just off the Capital Beltway. Dawn hadn't really been able to afford to shop here as a graduate student. Today she intended to hit every store in both malls if necessary to find a wedding grown that wasn't as fussy as her first or as absurdly, ridiculously expensive as the second.

"Don't worry," Kate assured her over a lunch that included spinach salads, lobster ricotta and, for Callie and Dawn, the light, sparkling Prosecco they'd discovered in Italy. "You'll find exactly the right dress. Third time's a charm, right?"

"God, I hope so!"

"How long did it take you to pay off the last dress?" Kate asked curiously. "Six months?"

"Eight," she said glumly, spearing her spinach. "The pearls on the bodice and train were all hand sewn."

"What did you do with it?"

Dawn's expression softened.

"Callie sent me a link to a website for a charity that recycles wedding gowns into angel gowns."

"It part of the Helping Hands Program," Callie explained. "They provide comfort and assistance to parents with infants in neonatal ICU's. So many of the babies are preemies, and so many don't make it. The NICU Angel Gown volunteers cut down and rework wedding dresses to provide grieving families a precious burial gown or suit for families."

"Oh, how sad. And beautiful."

In an unconscious gesture, Kate pressed a palm to her still-flat tummy, as if to assure her baby and herself they'd never need an angel gown. The thought of the grief the parents who'd lost their child had to have suffered, though, prompted her to offer her own gown.

"I've still got it packed away somewhere. Send me the link, too, and I'll donate it."

"You sure?" Dawn asked. "That could be a little girl you're gestating. She may want to wear her momma's dress some day."

"I sincerely doubt that. If it's a girl, she'll probably inherit Travis's superjock genes and get married in half-laced high-tops. But enough about dresses past. What are we looking for *today*?"

"Something simple."

"Right."

"Elegant."

"Okay."

"Comfortable."

"Got it. Now finish your ricotta and let's hit the stores."

The big chains—Bloomingdale's, Nordstrom, Saks Fifth Avenue, Macy's and Neiman Marcus—anchored the two malls. They in turn were augmented by dozens of smaller boutiques offering everything from haute couture to funky chic.

To Dawn's relief, she found the perfect dress in the second boutique they hit. The tea-length sheath of ivory satin was topped by a lace jacket that tied at the waist with a satin bow. The lace wouldn't keep her warm if the weather turned nasty, but the two-piece ensemble was so deceptively, stunningly chic that she decided she could shiver for fifteen or twenty minutes if necessary.

And surprise, surprise! The boutique owner just happened to stock a little pillbox hat made from the same lace. Trimmed with only enough netting to give the illusion of a veil, the cap added an unexpectedly jaunty air.

"That's it," Kate exclaimed when Dawn modeled the entire ensemble. "That's so you!"

Callie agreed, but raised a brow pointedly when she read the price tag dangling from the jacket sleeve.

"You think that's bad?" Dawn tapped a fingertip against the lace cap. "This little sucker costs more than the dress. But the two combined are still not even *close* to what I paid for the last disaster."

While she took another turn in the three-way mirror, her friends shared quick glances, obviously remembering how long it had taken her to settle on a choice for her previous two trips to the altar. She caught the quick exchange and laughed.

"Don't panic. This is it. I love it."

"Then get it," Callie urged. "We've still got shoes, undies and an obscenely decadent negligee to hunt down."

* * *

The next day was Saturday and the date set for their quick trip up to Boston. She and Callie got up early and grabbed a quick cup of coffee and bagel with Brian.

He would do Tommy Duty over the weekend and had drafted Addy to cover Monday afternoon until he could get home from work. Tuesday, too, if necessary. But he'd adamantly nixed the idea of Dawn and Callie rattling back down from Boston in a U-Haul, towing her car. Instead, the ever-efficient LauraBeth had set up professional movers, arranged for her car to be transported and booked their return flights with the same blinding speed she'd lined up caterers, photographers, a florist and a string quartet for the wedding now only a week away.

Callie and Dawn flew out of Reagan National a little past nine. An hour later they touched down at Logan International. They grabbed a taxi and headed into the city, both feeling a sense of homecoming.

All three—Callie, Kate and Dawn—had been born and raised in a small, western Massachusetts town. They'd attended different colleges and grad schools, after which Kate followed Travis to his various air force assignments. Callie and Dawn had gravitated back to Boston to work, though, and felt the tug of their roots as they drove into the city.

Fall had already wrapped New England in glorious colors. The beltway around the city blazed red and orange and gold. Dawn's condo was a few miles off the beltway, in an upscale gated community close to the sprawling complex that housed her company's headquarters. Callie lived closer to her work in downtown Boston, in an older section of the city.

Unfortunately, neither of them had time to enjoy either the foliage or the cool, crisp temperatures. Sorting through what Dawn would ship down to DC and what would go into storage took most of the weekend.

They drove over to Callie's two-bedroom apartment early Monday morning. *Very* early Monday morning. Neither of them really believed the creep who'd sent those emails was staking out her apartment, but Joe Russo had warned her to be careful.

It took only a half hour or so for Callie to pack a suitcase. They drove back across town and Dawn dropped Callie off to wait for the movers before doing battle with the nightmare that was Boston rush-hour traffic.

Handing in her notice and saying goodbye to her team turned out to be more of a wrench than she'd anticipated, even though their well wishes were colored with some jibes about her previous near misses. Dawn escaped with her smile slightly strained and a surprisingly lucrative offer from her boss to do freelance designs for the company's ongoing advertising campaigns.

"Damn," she told Callie later that afternoon as they took a taxi to the airport. "If I'd known I could make almost as much schlepping into a home office in my jammies, I would've gone solo years ago."

"I doubt that. You're the most gregarious of our threesome. Kate can lose herself in ledgers and spreadsheets. I have to—*had* to—brace myself every time I had to appear in court. You collect friends and admirers without even trying."

"Speaking of admirers, I got a text while I was at the office. You'll never guess who's coming to the wedding."

"Not that race car driver you hooked up with after you dumped Number One?"

"Good God, no!"

"The attorney who handled that nastiness with Number Two? He seemed pretty taken with you, as I recall."

"More taken with the hefty fee I paid him."

"Then who?"

"Carlo di Lorenzo."

"Your playboy prince?" Callie's mink-dark eyebrows soared. "The same man who did everything but stand on his head trying to convince you to jet off to Casablanca with him?"

"Marrakech," Dawn corrected with a wide grin. "Brian called him about some modification to the NATO transport they're working on, found out he'll be in New York this week and invited him down to DC for the wedding. Joe Russo's coming, too," she added with a quick, sideways glance at her friend. "He had to cancel out of some high-powered international symposium, but said he'd be there."

"It's fate," Callie murmured, unknowingly echoing LauraBeth's comment of the previous week. "All of us who were at the Trevi Fountain when Kate and Travis renewed their vows will be together again."

"I know!" Thinking back to that happy scene, Dawn reached across the taxi's plastic-covered seat and squeezed her friend's hand. "Remember the first time we watched *Three Coins in the Fountain*?"

"How could I forget? There we were, three gawky teenagers with foam curlers in our hair and bowls full of ice cream, going all dreamy and starry-eyed over Louis Jourdan."

"Let's not forget the pizza."

"Or the mozzarella stringing from our chins. Oh, God! We pigged out on so much that night, I was nauseous most of the next day."

"Me, too." Laughing, Dawn brushed off that minor inconvenience. "The really amazing thing is that I never imagined we'd ever make it to Rome, much less to the

Trevi Fountain." Her hand tightened on the friend she'd shared so many dreams with. "Do you know what I wished that day, when we were all there at the fountain?"

"According to legend, you didn't have to make a wish. Just throwing the coin ensured you'll return to Rome some-day."

"Well, I wanted that, too. But mostly I wanted a few more days or weeks with Tommy. Okay," she admitted when Cal-lie shot her a knowing look. "Tommy *and* his dad. Now…" Her eyes misting, she gulped. "Now I have a chance at for-ever. I'm starting to believe that wish might really come true."

"It will," Callie said fiercely. "This time, it will."

The following Friday afternoon, Dawn repeated that man-tra to herself over and over as she waited for her mother's flight. Unfortunately, it was delayed by weather out of Hart-ford. As a result, they barely made it to the hotel in time for the rehearsal dinner.

The blessedly efficient LauraBeth had blocked rooms at the five-star Ritz-Carlton for out-of-town guests. She'd also reserved one of the hotel's private dining rooms for the rehearsal dinner. Dawn had tried to wiggle out of this pesky tradition. The wedding ceremony would be too sim-ple, she insisted, and the venue too informal to require one.

She caved, however, when LauraBeth pointed out that it might be a good idea for Brian and Tommy and his par-ents to meet her family before the actual ceremony itself. As a protective shield, Dawn had added Kate, Travis, Cal-lie, Carlo and Joe Russo to the guest list.

Even with her friends' lively presence, the cocktail hour before dinner turned her inside out. Time hadn't elimi-nated her parents' animosity. They coated their barbs with sugary smiles, but every exchange knotted Dawn's stomach a little tighter. Her three brothers were older and had escaped before the home environment became completely toxic. Still, Aaron, the closest to her in age, had been exposed to enough of the poison to exert a valiant effort to act as a buffer.

"Hey, Mom. Did you know Travis hung up his air force uniform? He's now working with Brian?"

"Yes, Dawn told me."

With her coppery hair only a few shades lighter than her daughter's, everyone could see Maureen McGill had passed both her coloring and her stubborn chin to her children. The similarities stopped there, though. Her features were stamped with an unhappiness that showed in her face as she sent Kate a sardonic glance.

"I was so glad to hear *your* husband was willing to make some sacrifices to keep your marriage together. Not many are, as I can…"

"Try these, Mom." Grabbing a crab cake from a nearby tray, Aaron shoved it at her. "They're wonderful."

Her father was on the other side of the room, talking to Brian's parents. Not far enough away, unfortunately, to miss his ex-wife's comment or refrain from rising to the bait.

"More husbands might be willing to make the sacrifice, if their marriage was worth saving."

Cringing inside, Dawn wondered again why in God's name she'd agreed to this gathering. How had she imagined a smaller, more intimate setting might convince her parents to call a truce? She was about to tell them both to forget about attending the ceremony tomorrow when Carlo di Lorenzo stepped into the breach.

"Dawn, you break my heart by marrying Brian."

His dark eyes were merry above his luxuriant black mustache as he bowed over her hand with exaggerated charm.

Having spent several evenings in his company in Italy, she wasn't surprised when he tipped her hand at the last moment and planted a warm kiss on the inside of her wrist.

The man had done his best to convince her to jet off with him while they were in Italy. Or at least join him for a merry romp at one of his villas. She had to admit she'd been tempted. The playboy prince stood a half a head shorter than she did and sported a shiny bald spot at the back of his head, but his teeth gleamed beneath his handlebar mustache and centuries of aristocratic charm oozed from every pore.

"The only way to save me from despair," he informed her mournfully, "is to introduce me to your so-beautiful mother."

"Of course," Dawn said drily. "Mom, this is Carlo di Lorenzo, Prince of Lombard and Marino. Carlo, my mother, Maureen."

His smile caressed the older woman's face.

"I see where your daughter gets her beautiful eyes, Signora McGill. They enchanted me from the moment we met in Venice. Now that Dawn breaks my heart by refusing to run away with me, you must help it mend, yes? Come to Rome, and I will show you the city as few people ever see it."

Maureen McGill was no more proof against that charm than any of the supermodels and starlets Carlo had romanced over the years. Flustered and flattered, she shot her ex-husband a triumphant look and let Carlo claim her full attention.

"Thank God," Dawn muttered, her knuckles white around the stem of her champagne flute.

Brian eased it gently from her hand and bent to murmur in her ear. "We can ditch this crowd, jump on a jet and be in Vegas in two hours."

She considered it. Seriously considered it. But the mere fact that he'd made the offer loosened her knots and kicked in the stubborn streak she'd inherited from her mother.

"I would take you up on that in a heartbeat, but you've got a puppy to pick up tomorrow, remember? And I want our friends to help us celebrate in the afternoon."

The wedding was scheduled for 4:00 p.m. Dawn could make it until then. She *would* make it until then.

"Your call," Brian said, brushing his lips across her cheek. "If you change your mind, just say the word."

The kiss, the soft promise and another glass of champagne soothed the jagged edges from Dawn's nerves. The toast Brian offered when they sat down to dinner brought her joy in the occasion flooding back.

He nodded to his son, who scrambled to his feet. A beaming Tommy joined his dad in raising their water glasses.

"To our bright, shining Dawn," Brian said with a look that wrapped twice around her heart. "She rolls back our night. And...?"

Keyed to his line, Tommy tipped his glass and sloshed most of the water onto the table before finishing happily.

"'N fills us with sunshine 'n smiles 'n stuff."

"Great dinner," Kate drawled some hours later.

She and Callie and Dawn were ensconced in one of the Ritz's luxurious suites, indulging in what had become their pre-wedding-night tradition. One that harked back to ancient times, when a prospective groom might kidnap his bride and hold her for a full cycle of the moon—an early, preemptive version of the "honeymoon"—to make sure she wasn't carrying another man's seed. To prevent that dire happening, a vigilant father would often lock his daughter in a fortified towers or dark, dank cell until delivering her to the church the next day.

This particular tower offered a bird's-eye view of the Washington Monument just across the Potomac. Floodlights illuminated the column's gleaming marble, and its red eye winked at the ink-black sky.

"Doesn't hold a candle to your last rehearsal dinner, though." Grinning, Kate dunked a strawberry into her non-alcoholic sparkling cider. "Now that was a night to forget!"

"I wish I *could*," Dawn retorted, shuddering. "I asked myself a half dozen times tonight why I was putting us through all this hoopla again."

As always, Callie was the voice of calm reason. "Because you love Brian and Tommy and you want us all to share in the celebration of that love."

"That's what I told Brian when he suggested we jump a plane and head for Vegas."

"Like Callie and I would let you ditch us," Kate huffed.

"I told him that, too."

"I thought he understood we're a matched set."

"If he doesn't by now," Dawn said, relaxing for the first time since she'd picked her mother up at the airport, "he will after tomorrow."

"Hmm." Still a little indignant, Kate demolished her berry. "Speaking of tomorrow, what time do you want me at the house to help you and Callie set things up?"

"Come anytime, but we don't have to worry about setting up. LauraBeth is orchestrating everything."

"Lordawmighty, that woman's amazing. Can't you divorce your mom and adopt her instead?"

"I wish!"

By eleven the following morning, Dawn had repeated that fervent wish at least a half dozen times. She should've expected her mother to jump in a taxi and arrive at the gatehouse hours before the afternoon ceremony.

The caterer was busy arranging white folding chairs in the garden. The florist and his assistant had transformed the gazebo into a leafy autumn bower and stood ready to attach small bouquets of fall flowers to the end row chairs when they were set. When Dawn opened the door to her mother, however, Maureen marched in and barely glanced through the open French doors at the crews working under the bright October sun. Her brows were straight-lined in a scowl that started a small knot of tension at the base of Dawn's skull.

"You won't believe what your father just did!"

Her furious glance shot from her daughter to Callie and back again. When neither commented, she slammed her purse onto the counter. She was wearing the mother-of-the-bride dress she'd purchased for Dawn's last wedding. The two-piece, sea-foam green flattered her still-slender figure and would have brought out the color of her eyes if they hadn't been narrowed to mere slits.

"He had the nerve—the *nerve*!—to call my room and tell me I made a fool of myself last night drooling over the prince."

Dawn winced, and Callie stepped in instinctively to redirect her mother's venom, as she and Kate had done so many times in the past.

"You didn't drool, Mrs. McGill. Carlo's a delightful, sophisticated man of the world. Of course you would enjoy his company. Dawn and Kate and I do, too."

"Exactly." With an angry sniff, she fluffed her sleek bob. "And if he wants me to jet off to the south of France with him, why should anyone care but he and I and…"

"Mommm," Dawn groaned. "Making outrageous offers to attractive women is as natural to Carlo as breathing. He wanted to carry me off to Marrakech. *Still* wants to carry me off to Marrakech."

Her mother glommed on to the first part of the comment and ignored the last. "You think I'm still attractive?"

"Of course you are. When you're not scowling," she added under her breath.

"Hmm. The prince must be at least ten years younger than I am. Do you think he really...?"

"Mommm!"

"All right, all right!" She cast a critical eye over the other two. "Why are you both just lazing around? And where's Kate? I can't believe she's not here yet. You three always do each other's hair and makeup before your weddings."

She made it sound like a tradition forged over a dozen years and an equal number of nuptials. Which, Dawn conceded as tension knotted at the base of her skull, it almost was.

"Kate'll be here soon," she said stiffly.

The intercom buzzed at that moment. Dawn pressed the talk button with the same feeling as a prizefighter against the ropes.

"Dad 'n me are making cheese samwiches," Tommy reported eagerly. "He says he's not really 'sposed to see the bride before the wedding, but I told him you 'n Callie were probably hungry. Do you wanna have lunch with us?"

Dawn grabbed at the diversion with both hands. "Yes! My mom's here, too. We'll all come over."

"'Kay. Then Dad's gotta run to do some errand. He won't tell me what it is. He says it's important, though."

Dawn came within a breath of abandoning her mother to Callie and Tommy and making the run out to Woodburn with Brian to pick up the pup. She resisted the impulse, although it took considerable effort. She kept a bright smile pinned to her face but the tension at the back of her neck took on the low, throbbing resonance of a kettledrum.

Callie did her best to divert both Tommy's eager questions about his role in the ceremony and Maureen's critical assessment of everything from the caterer's buffet layout and Dawn's little wisp of a hat.

The kettledrum booming now, Dawn pulled Callie aside. "We bought a doggie bed, puppy chow, a leash and collar and a bucket full of toys. They're stashed at the house down the street."

Brian had made the arrangements with the parents of Addy and Tommy's friend Cindy. The plan was for the Caruthers to keep the pup until after the ceremony, when Dawn and Brian would present Tommy with their wedding gift.

"But we forgot a grooming brush. Wheatens require regular grooming. I'm going to run out and pick one up."

"Now?"

"There's a pet shop in the mall. I'll zip over and back."

"Why don't I go?" Callie offered. "Kate should be here any minute. And the photographer. We want to do some informal 'before' shots, remember?"

Dawn swiped her palms down her jeans and shot a glance at her mother, now busily directing a change to the buffet table. "I just need to get out for a few moments."

"Dawn…"

"I'll be right back."

She shoved the small leather case containing her license and credit cards in the back pocket of her jeans, snatched up the keys to her Mustang and fled the scene.

Chapter Twelve

The gatehouse doorbell rang just moments after Dawn departed the premises. When Callie answered, Kate marched in with a garment bag draped over one arm and a tight expression on her face.

"I saw a red Mustang whiz around the corner as I drove up. Please tell me that wasn't Dawn at the wheel."

"I wish I could."

"Oh, God!"

"It's okay. Really." She ushered Kate inside and tried hard for cool and confident. "She just went to get a grooming brush."

"Huh?"

"For the dog," Callie clarified after a quick glance over her shoulder to make sure Tommy wasn't within hearing range. "Dawn says the pup needs to be brushed regularly, but they forgot to get a grooming brush. So she's making quick run to the pet store."

"You've *got* to be kidding!"

Her nerves fraying, Callie fired back, "Do I look like I'm kidding?"

"For pity's sake, why did you let her go alone?"

"She didn't want company, although I—"

"Where's my daughter?"

The peevish question had Kate rolling her eyes.

"Say no more," she muttered. "I get the picture."

Maureen appeared in the foyer, scowling. "Where's Dawn? I can't imagine why she insists this LauraBeth person walks on water. You should see the cake the caterers just brought in. It's a one-layer sheet cake, for pity's sake, decorated with nothing but two interwoven rings."

Kate took a breath and stepped into the line of fire. "Those are the rings Dawn and Brian picked out for each other, Mrs. McGill. That's all they wanted on the cake."

"Maybe so," Maureen sniffed, "but I must say a man who hobnobs with royalty might have chosen something a little more elegant for his bride. Especially if he makes as much as Wikipedia say he does."

"I repeat," Kate said with exaggerated patience, "those are the rings Dawn and Brian picked out. She told us they're copies of an ancient Roman design. Since she and Brian met in Italy. The design holds special significance for them."

"I suppose." Maureen flapped an impatient hand. "Where *is* she?"

"She had to run a last-minute errand."

The older woman stared at them, her color draining. Her mouth opened. Closed. Opened again on a low groan. "Oh, no."

"She'll be right back." Callie infused the statement with all the assurance she could muster. "She just had to—"

"Call her!" Maureen said urgently. "Tell her the caterers need her. No, wait! Tell her Tommy's feeling sick. He thinks he's going to throw up and is crying for her."

"I can't lie like that," Callie protested as she retrieved her cell phone.

"It won't be a lie. I'll stick my finger down his throat if I have to."

Callie and Kate gaped at her.

"Oh, get over yourselves," Dawn's loving mother huffed. "You want her to go through with this one as much as I do."

"But last night…"

"You said…"

"I know what I said." Her mouth twisted. "I'll admit I'm not the best advertisement for marriage…"

"You got that right," Kate agreed savagely.

Those cat's eyes narrowed, but Maureen bit back the sharp retort hovering on her lips and glanced over her shoulder at the boy happily directing the placement of a towering ice sculpture.

"Brian and Tommy are exactly what Dawn needs," she said after a long moment. "They'll give her the kind of home and family I wish… Well…" She sniffed and finished fiercely, "I'll stick my finger down my *own* throat if that'll bring her home."

"Let's hope it doesn't come to that," Kate commented as she hit a speed-dial button on her cell phone.

A few seconds later, the rousing finale to Rossini's *William Tell Overture* galloped through the air. The three women followed the Lone Ranger's theme song to the kitchen, where they found Dawn's iPhone buzzing and skittering across the counter.

"Great," Kate ground out. "She forgot her phone."

"It doesn't matter," Callie said with determined calm. "She'll be right back."

Brian returned just before 2:00 p.m. He took the flagstone walk to the gatehouse, intending to relay the success of his mission to Dawn before corralling his son and hauling him back to the main house to scrub down and dress up.

He spotted Tommy demonstrating his cartwheeling skills to Travis in the small square of lawn between the gazebo and the rows of chairs lined up with military precision. Kate, Callie and Dawn's mother he found in the sun-filled breakfast nook. Seeing them seated shoulder to shoulder around the small table provided the first hint something was wrong. The double old-fashioned glass clutched in his prospective mother-in-law's fist provided another.

"Where's Dawn?"

Their answering looks ran the gamut from carefully neutral to a fake innocence to plainly worried.

"She said she forgot to get a grooming brush for the puppy, so she zipped over to the pet store in the mall," Callie replied.

"When?"

Callie glanced away, Kate bit her lip and Maureen took a hasty gulp of what looked like scotch, straight up.

"Two hours ago," Kate finally answered.

Brian extracted his cell phone from the back pocket of his jeans. "The mall's a zoo on Saturdays. She probably had to circle the parking lot a half dozen times before she could find a parking spot. I'd better call and remind her of the time."

"We tried that." Kate jerked her chin at the counter. "She forgot her phone."

Brian glanced at the rhinestone-studded case, then back at the three women. He'd had enough experience dealing with people of all types to see the worry and doubt they were trying so hard to conceal.

"Oh, well," he said with a deliberately casual shrug, "she'll get back when she gets back. Meantime, I've got puppy love all over my chin and cheeks. I'd better corral Tommy so we can both clean up."

Brian refused, flat ass refused, to believe Dawn had skipped out on him. She had her share of faults; she'd be the first to admit that. But cowardice wasn't one of them. If she'd changed her mind about this marriage, he told himself fiercely as he showered, she'd tell him so to his face.

And even if she had decided she wanted out, he thought grimly as he scraped a razor down his cheek, there was no way in hell she'd just take a powder and leave Tommy without a word of goodbye. Still, his stomach felt increasingly hollow as he got into his suit and tie.

Before going to check on his son's progress, he glanced around the room he'd shared with Caroline. He'd removed the items that bore her more personal stamp. The sachet bag in her underwear drawer that still held the faint scent of roses after all these years. The tacky little Kewpie doll she'd won in a ring toss at a fair the first year of their marriage. The photo of her and Tommy that had held a place of honor on his nightstand.

The Kewpie doll now sat on a shelf in his son's room, and the photo had been transferred from its frame to the breathtakingly beautiful album Dawn had designed for Tommy.

She'd sounded so sincere, so confident that there was more than enough room in Brian's heart for Caroline *and* her. Yet, glancing around the bedroom, he couldn't help wishing he'd insisted they make some changes to the house *before* their wedding instead of after. New furniture, new linens, new pictures and knickknacks. Or they could've knocked out the wall between the guest rooms and the upstairs office and enlarged the master suite. Or moved out completely and made a new start in a new home, as he'd contemplated more than once in the past five years.

Hell! Too late to worry about that now. His immediate priority was to put a wedding band on his bride's finger.

With that intent firmly in mind, he headed for his son's room. He found him on a step stool in his bathroom, squinting into the mirror and struggling with his new tie. He'd picked it out himself, he'd informed Brian. With Dawn's help. Her eyes dancing, she'd assured Brian that glowing, neon dinosaurs added the perfect touch to the festivities.

"Hey, bud. Need help with that?"

"I kin do it."

He said nothing as Tommy's chin jutted out a little more with each failed attempt to make a knot.

"Ties are stupid," his son muttered, yanking the ends free to start over again. "Why do guys wear 'em, anyway?"

Brian dredged his memory for a bit of arcane trivia he'd picked up during his stint in the marines. "They originally had a military purpose. Remember the man dressed as a centurion at the Colosseum in Rome? You couldn't see it, but I suspect he'd wrapped a linen cloth around his neck to keep his armor from chafing. It would keep him warm, too, when he had to trudge through mountain passes."

"This skinny thing wouldn't keep me warm," Tommy groused.

"True, but styles of neck cloths and cravats changed greatly over the centuries until we got stuck with what we have today. No, loop that end under. Now through. There! You've got it."

His scowl gone, Tommy breamed at himself in the mirror while Brian nobly refrained from offering to straighten the lopsided knot. He did make a few swipes with a comb before Tommy hopped off the footstool. After being helped into his suit coat, his son had to take another few moments to preen, this time in the full-length mirror behind his door.

"You look pretty slick, bud."

"I know," Tommy agreed with a smug grin. "You look good, too," he added magnanimously. "Just wait'll Dawn sees us. Like Addy says, she's gonna wig out."

Brian hoped so. God, he hoped so!

Keeping his smile easy, he glanced at his watch as he accompanied Tommy downstairs. Two forty. Still a good half hour or more until their guests began to arrive.

Murmurs of conversation drew them to the den, where they found the other members of the wedding party. Travis had used the downstairs study to change out of his jeans and well-worn bomber jacket. He'd been pleased and flattered when asked to fly backup to Tommy as groomsman. No flattery involved, Brian had insisted. Only a bone-deep gratitude to the air force pilot for bringing Dawn into his and Tommy's life.

His bride's best friends had changed, as well. Kate's hair was a cascade of blond curls, her face grimly cheerful above the rolled neckline of her rich, russet-colored dress. Callie wore a gold jacket and deep, burnt-orange sheath that made Brian think instantly of pumpkins and wood smoke. He would've appreciated the serene picture she presented if tight little lines hadn't formed on either side of her mouth.

His prospective mother-in-law, on the other hand, made no pretense of appearing either cheerful or serene. Her fist was still wrapped around a double highball glass—recently refilled, judging by the amber liquid reaching halfway to its rim. Brian and Tommy were barely into the den before she blurted out a worried report.

"She's not back."

He aimed a cool look in her direction. "She will be."

"She's been gone for three hours!"

"Who's gone?" Tommy wanted to know, taking a quick look around. "Is she talking about Dawn?"

"Yes, but..."

"She's not gone," he stated with utter assurance. "She's hiding."

Like bullets sprayed from AK-47s, questions flew at him from all sides.

"What?"

"Where?"

"Did she call you?"

"Why's she hiding?"

Blinking at the barrage, he took a step back. "I... Uh..."

Brian smothered a quick oath and raised a hand as a signal to the others to back off.

"Why's Dawn hiding?" he asked, keeping his voice calm and even.

"It's tradition. 'Member, Dad? You told me about it. We're not s'posed to see the bride before the wedding."

That was it. That had to be it. Brian was still trying to convince himself as his son screwed up his face and made a quick clarification.

"I know Dawn 'n us had grilled cheese samwiches together at lunch. But that doesn't count 'cause we weren't dressed up or anything."

No one, not even Dawn's mother, had the heart to burst Tommy's bubble. But even the boy's confidence slipped as the house began to fill with guests.

LauraBeth, her husband and two of their four sons were the first to arrive. She cast a quick eye over the garden and buffet and spoke a few words to the servers circulating with trays of prewedding refreshments before giving her boss and his son warm hugs. Brian's bland smile didn't fool her for an instant. She pried the story out of him in thirty seconds flat.

Dawn's father and brother rang the bell next. Maureen cornered them the moment they walked through the door. The three McGills were still huddled in a tight, anxious group when the minister from Brian and Tommy's church arrived.

The Caruthers family arrived a few moments later and provided a welcome distraction for an increasingly worried Tommy. His little friend Cindy looked as though she would burst trying to keep in the secret of the puppy. Repeated knuckle thumps from her brother earned him nasty looks but kept the secret intact.

Brian's parents drove up at the same time as Caroline's. After a round of fierce hugs, Caroline's mother caught Brian's arm and pulled him aside for a low, intensely personal colloquy.

"I'm so glad you found Dawn," she said, framing his face with both palms. "Tommy raves about her every time we talk to him. You were a wonderful husband to my daughter. You deserve every bit of happiness your new love can bring you."

His throat suddenly raw and tight, Brian folded her in a ferocious hug.

"Enough of this," Caroline's mom said, sniffling. "Are those Dawn's parents? Why don't you introduce your former in-laws to your prospective in-laws?"

"You and Jerry will *never* be 'former' anything," Brian assured her gruffly before complying with the request. To his surprise and considerable relief, Dawn's mother smoothed the lines etched deep in her brow. She even managed to include her former husband in her acknowledgment of their daughter's most stellar traits.

"She gets those laughing Irish eyes from me," Maureen said, her own eyes holding a hint of a smile as they turned to her ex. "She gets her artistic flair, such as it is, from her father."

Before Dawn's startled father could recover from that faint praise, the doorbell rang again. Brian had his game face on when he greeted Joe Russo and Carlo di Lorenzo, but he'd shared too many tense hours with these men—and too much of the produce from Carlo's family vineyard—to pull off a smiling facade.

After a pointed exchange of glances, Carlo and Joe maneuvered Brian to a quiet corner. A jerk of Carlo's chin brought Travis over to join them. Sequestered from the crowd, Joe cut right to the point.

"All right, Ellis. What's going on?"

Brian didn't even try to dissemble. "Dawn left to run an errand a little past eleven this morning. We haven't heard from her since." His Adam's apple worked. "I'm worried she may have been in an accident. Can you have your people run a check of every hospital in the area, Joe?"

Russo had already whipped out his cell phone. "Consider it done. I'll also have them check with the police."

Mere seconds later, he connected to his command center and relayed the basics. "Dawn McGill. We ran a background check on her a few weeks ago. Right," he said after a few moments. "Red hair. Green eyes. Five foot seven. One-fifteen or thereabouts. No tattoos. Other distinguishing marks or characteristics…"

He looked to Brian, brows raised.

"A small, round birthmark on her inner thigh. And different-colored polish on her toenails. Hey," he said in response to three surprised looks, "I think it's distinguishing."

Brows still elevated, Joe barked out another question. "What was she driving?"

"Her red Mustang."

"Year?"

"2013."

The terse reply came from Kate, who'd drifted over to infiltrate the all-male enclave.

"Dawn bought it used," she informed the men, "but she'd wipe off every bit of bird poop or rain spot the moment they hit."

Joe relayed the information, then told the person on the line to hold. "Where was she headed when she left the house?"

"To the pet store at the mall."

His scarred face went blank. "A pet store?"

"Long story," Brian said impatiently, "and not important."

Joe conceded the point with a look that said they'd come back to it later if necessary and turned to Kate. "What mall was she going to?"

"The closest one, I assume."

"Never assume anything."

The security expert looked grim enough under normal circumstances. When his mouth tightened and the scar running from his cheek to his chin thinned to a red, angry line, he could make anyone back up a pace or two.

"Which mall?" he asked again.

"I… Uh…" Gulping, Kate managed to stand her ground. Barely. "I don't know."

"Does Callie?"

"I don't think so…" She stopped, her cheeks flushing. "She might."

Spinning, she caught her friend's attention and hooked a finger. Callie murmured polite excuses to the minister and joined their small group. At her questioning glance, Joe held up his phone.

"I've got the head of my domestic investigations division on the line. He's going to track Dawn. Do you know which mall she was going to?"

"She didn't say."

"What was she wearing when she left the house?"

"Jeans and... Oh, God!"

Like a digital portrait suddenly washed of all color, Callie's face went dead white. She reached out, took Kate's hand in a bone-crushing grip and turned an agonized look on Brian.

"You think she's been in an accident?"

"That's what we're trying to rule out," he answered evenly. "Can you remember what she was wearing?"

Callie's stomach must have been churning with the same fear now pumping acid into Brian's, but he had to admire the way she pulled herself together. She dragged in a steadying breath and locked her eyes on Joe.

"She was wearing jeans. A long-sleeved black top. A bulky, cream-colored cardigan with oversize brown buttons."

Joe flashed her an approving glance and relayed the information. "Right," he said after a brief pause. "All the hospitals. DC, Virginia and Maryland. Get back to me ASAP."

When he cut the connection, a vicious onslaught of memories hit Brian. Ambulances. Emergency rooms. The oncologists who'd pored over Caroline's scans. The nurses who'd administered ever increasing dosages of morphine. The physical therapists who'd showed him how to turn his wife to prevent bedsores, how to exercise her arms and legs when she'd lost the ability to move them herself.

His gut twisting, he shoved the memories out of his head. This was about Dawn. Only Dawn. He started to ask Joe what else they could do, but Carlo beat him to the punch.

"Joe will find her," the prince assured Kate and Callie.

"He is the best, yes? Travis and I learned this firsthand, when we and our crews flew in to rescue the newsmen captured by Boko Haram." The prince screwed up his face, his lips thin under his mustache. "Our military intel completely underestimated the rebels' strength. If not for the flash update Joe's people sent, we would not have gotten off the ground before the bastards overran the airstrip."

Kate had heard a brief recount of the near-fatal disaster in Italy. The retelling tripled her relief that her husband, at least, wouldn't be flying in and out of dirt airstrips under a hail of enemy fire.

"While your people are doing their thing," she said to Joe, "what can *we* do?"

He looked over her shoulder. "You can head them off at the pass."

Kate turned and groaned when she saw the McGill clan bearing down on them like avenging angels. She moved to intercept them, but Maureen dodged around her.

Her voice was sharp and brittle as she quizzed Joe. "We saw you on the phone. Was that Dawn you were speaking to? Where is she? Has she pulled another disappearing act?"

"No, that wasn't Dawn. And no, I don't know where she is. But I assure you she hasn't pulled a disappearing act."

"How do you *know*?"

Her fierce demand rang through the room. Brian glanced at his son, saw Tommy's face begin to pucker and forced a calm he was far from feeling.

"Let me ask you this, Mrs. McGill. Did Dawn just 'disappear' before? Or did she tell you that she'd changed her mind?"

"She told us, but..."

"All of you? Including her fiancés?"

"Of course! My husband..." She caught herself and

made a quick correction. "My ex-husband and I may have had our differences over the years…"

"*May* have had?"

Kate's disbelieving snort brought Dawn's dad forward to take the flack.

"It's true. We provided the worst possible example for our kids." Sadness and regret rippled across his lined face as he reached out and gripped his former wife's hand. Startled, Maureen glanced down, but made only a feeble attempt to pull away.

"If Dawn learned nothing else from our years of fighting," he continued, "it was to admit her mistakes. She, at least, had the courage to face the two men she thought she was in love with, tell them the truth and get on with her life."

His glance shifted from Brian to Tommy. A smile creased his worn cheeks. "Dawn told me this time is for real. No doubts, no worries, no last-minute realization that she'd misjudged her heart. She loves you, son. You and your dad. You two are all she wants in this…"

The shrill buzz of a phone cut him off. Brian snatched up the house phone, glanced at caller ID and felt his bones freeze.

"It's the police."

None of the assembled guests made a sound as he hit Talk.

"Ellis."

He gripped the phone, his fist tight, as every muscle in his body went taut.

"Talk slower! I can't understand…*What?*"

The silence in the room was thunderous. No one breathed, no one uttered a word as Brian shot Joe Russo a quick look.

"Yeah, he's here."

Stunned, he dropped his hand and stared at the phone in disbelief for a few second before handing it to Russo. "It's Dawn. She's in jail. She wants to talk to you."

Chapter Thirteen

Brian was just handing Joe his phone when a short, sharp buzz cut through the stunned silence. Russo checked his own cell and took all of three seconds to skim a text before putting Brian's phone to his ear.

The listeners crowded around him heard only one side of the conversation that followed. As always, Joe's method of communication was succinct to the point of being in code.

"Russo...Right...Right...Put him on."

After a brief pause, he identified himself again.

"It's Joe...Yeah. Long time. What's the charge?" His gray eyes shuttered, he listened for several moments before terminating the call with a clipped, "On my way."

He handed back the phone and swept the small crowd with a quick glance. He knew half the people present. Brian, Travis and Carlo from Italy, along with Callie, Kate and Brian's son, Tom. Several others he'd met at the dinner last night. The rest were strangers. As far as Joe was concerned, only one of them had any business hearing what he had to report.

"Where can we talk?" he asked Brian.

"My study."

When the two men wheeled and started for the door, an instant chorus of protests erupted.

"Wait!"

"Why's my daughter in jail?"

"What's going on?"

Brian swung back and cut them off. "I'll tell you when *I* know what's going on."

He closed the study door behind him, swept by an overwhelming sense of relief. Dawn wasn't dead, she wasn't in the hospital, and from the little he'd been able to gather from her first few jumbled sentences, she hadn't skipped out on their wedding. With the big three not in play, he could handle anything else.

"Okay, tell me."

"My folks tracked her to the Bethesda District Police Station on Wisconsin Avenue. They talked to the detective working her case, got him to let her make a call."

"What case? What do they think she's done?"

"They're holding her on a possible charge of kidnapping."

"What?" Brian's jaw sagged, snapped back. "Who's she supposed to have kidnapped?"

"A four-year-old child."

"No way!" The counter was flat, fast and unequivocal. "Anyone who thinks Dawn would snatch a child has their head up their ass."

"Chico—the detective I just talked to—is an old buddy," Joe said mildly. "We used to carry the same badge."

"You were a cop?"

As much time as Brian and Travis and Carlo had spent with Joe in Italy, they knew little about him. Only that he was a hired gun who'd gone into places the conventional forces couldn't, and now headed one of the world's top private security services.

"A military cop," Russo clarified. "For a while. Chico's a good man. He'll sort through the conflicting stories."

"Whose conflicting stories?"

"I didn't get all the details. Only that Dawn claims to have found the little girl wandering by herself and wanted to help her. The mother, who's evidently still pretty hysterical, claims Dawn lured the girl away with candy, intending to take her."

He paused, eyed Brian carefully. "Doesn't help that when the responding officers got all parties involved to the precinct and discovered Dawn has an arrest record."

The news sent Brian back a step. A dozen wild possibilities rocketed through his head. None of them tracked to the woman he knew.

"My folks should have turned up the arrest when they ran the background check for you," Joe said, clearly not happy. "I'll talk to them about that. In the meantime, I need you to tell me what got her arrested. Cops, especially tough cops like Chico, tend to take a less than sympathetic view of perps with records."

"I don't know anything about it."

"Who does?"

"Kate," Brian answered instantly, "and Callie."

"Better get them in here."

Separating the two women from the rest of the herd proved impossible. Brian was forced to return with them plus Travis, Carlo and Dawn's brother, mother and father.

Joe didn't waste time protesting. "Okay, fill in the blanks and do it quick. Dawn left the house at…?"

"Eleven fifteen," Kate supplied, recalling his previous admonition to stick to facts and not suppositions. "I saw her car going around the corner when I drove up and glanced at the clock, wondering where she was going."

"Which was…?"

"To the pet store in the mall," Callie answered. "To buy a brush for the dog?"

Joe's brows snapped together. "What dog?"

"We got Tommy a puppy," Brian explained. "It's a wedding present from Dawn and me. Our neighbors are keeping it until we can spring it on him."

"Okay, so that tracks. Chico—the detective working her case—confirms she was picked up at the mall."

"Why?" Maureen snapped. "What did my daughter do?"

Joe shot Brian a glance, got his reluctant nod and relayed the bare bones of the situation. As expected, protests and exclamations and denials pelted him from all sides. He cut them off with a brusque chop of one hand.

"We all know the charge is bogus. Problem is the police have a hysterical mother who says otherwise. They've also dug up Dawn's previous record. Someone tell me, and tell me quick, what she was arrested for."

The McGills' thunderstruck expressions told Joe they had no idea. Same with the blank looks on Travis's and Carlo's faces. He didn't miss the quick glance Callie and Kate exchanged, however.

"Talk to me, dammit!"

The barked command brought Kate's chin up. Even Callie's eyes frosted.

"What did she do," he fired at them, "and when?"

"What she did," Kate bit out, "was agree to reimburse her last fiancé for all expenses related to the extravagant wedding *he'd* insisted on. The nonrefundable catering deposits, the tuxedo rentals, the airline tickets and even the cancellation fees for the thousand-dollar-a night, over-water bungalow he'd reserved for a surprise honeymoon in Tahiti. Some surprise! It took her more than a year to pay off all the sunk costs."

"But that wasn't good enough for the bastard," Callie interjected with uncharacteristic ferocity. "He wanted revenge. Complete humiliation."

"So he filed a complaint in small-claims court alleging Dawn had run up all those thousands of dollars on his American Express card without his permission," Kate continued savagely. "She didn't even know about the complaint! Some clerk supposedly sent a notice directing her to appear and respond to the charge. If so, Dawn didn't get it. Her first clue about the whole mess was when two police officers showed up at her door with a bench warrant for her 'failure to appear' and hauled her off in handcuffs."

Still breathing fire, Callie picked up the saga again. "It cost her big bucks in attorney's fees, but her lawyer was able to produce credit card receipts and contract signatures that proved Dawn had never charged *anything* to that jerk's American Express. The judge dismissed the complaint. The arrest should have been amended to show that."

"*Should* being the operative word," Joe said. "Give me the name of the attorney and the date this all happened, and I'll get my people on it."

He texted the information as Kate and Callie supplied it, then nodded to Brian. "Okay, let's get down there and see what we can do to straighten out this obvious misunderstanding."

"I'll go with you." Callie spun on her heel and joined the two men as they made for the door. When Joe started to protest, she cut him off with an icy stare. "I've spent more hours with hysterical parents and officials from

Child Protective Services than I can count. I'm coming with you."

"Me, too." Kate was right beside her. "Don't even *try* to stop me. Dawn's always been there when Callie or I needed her. Always!"

When the McGills started for the door as well, Brian stopped the stampede with a terse command.

"Hold it right there, folks. Joe and I and Callie are going down to the precinct. Maureen, you and Aaron and Phil can help my folks keep an eye on Tommy. Kate, I need you and Travis and Carlo to keep the other guests entertained. Stuff 'em to their ears with shrimp and champagne if you have to, but hold them here. This is one wedding that's *not* being called off."

He said essentially the same thing in much milder terms to the small crowd milling in the den.

"The good news is Dawn's gotten mixed up in what sounds like a complete misunderstanding," he told them. "No one's been injured, no one's run off. The bad news is it may take an hour or two to straighten it out. If you can, please stay until we get back. The show will be a little late, but it'll go on."

Although impatience bit at him like fire ants on the march, Brian took another few moments to reassure his obviously worried son.

"We'll only be a little while, bud. Why don't you and Cindy challenge Addy to a battle of Garden Zombies?"

"Okay." Tommy's chin quivered above the neon-bright dinosaur tie. "Dawn's coming back, isn't she?"

"You bet."

"How...?" His voice wobbled. "How do you know?"

"Because she and I have a very special present for you. No way she's going to miss being here when you open it."

"Really? What is it?"

"You'll find out when we get back. I gotta go. Be good."

* * *

Dawn felt as if she was reliving her worst nightmare.

Calling off her first wedding had been rough enough. The second still ranked as a natural disaster of epic proportions. But Brian… Tommy…

She paced the small interview room like a caged cat. The gray, windowless room smelled of old sweat and desperation. She'd contributed to the tang these past hours but barely noticed the less than subtle scent that now clung to her. All she could think of, all that mattered was the hurt and embarrassment she was putting Brian and Tommy through. Just because she'd let her mother play on her skittering nerves and drive her out of the house.

No!

She stopped pacing and grabbed the back of the gray metal chair that sat facing two others across a scarred table.

She couldn't blame those jumpy nerves on her mother. *She* was the one who'd dived into two previous engagements. *She'd* wiggled out of them, wounding two unsuspecting men in the process. And *she'd* been so damned determined not to do the same to Brian and Tommy that she'd worked herself into a state of near panic. Furious with herself, she banged a clenched fist on the top of the chair.

"Stupid, stupid, stupid!"

The door to the interview room opened midway through her verbal self-flagellation. The tall, square-shouldered Latino detective who'd been questioning her for what now felt like days lifted one inky eyebrow.

"You referring to me?"

"To myself. I can't believe I…" She caught sight of the man behind him and let out a squeal. "Joe! Thank God!

Will you *please* tell Detective Ramirez I'm not a child molester or kidnapper?"

"Already have."

Her glance locked on the curly-haired detective. "You believe him, right? And me?"

"I'm getting there."

That wasn't what she wanted to hear. "Oh, for...! Joe, you have to convince him I'm not a felon. Okay, I was arrested, but the charges were..."

"Bogus. He knows."

"I know now," Ramirez drawled, scraping a palm across his thickening five o'clock shadow. "Needed confirmation, though."

"Took you long enough," Dawn retorted.

He shrugged off the sarcasm. "It was your word against the little girl's mother. She claimed her ex had hired someone else to try and snatch his daughter. We had to run her statements against yours. It didn't help that you had an arrest record. Or that she kept changing her story."

"With good reason," Joe said before Dawn could fire up again. "Per Callie's suggestion, Chico—Detective Ramirez—contacted the child advocate assigned to protect the little girl's interests during her parents' divorce hearing."

Callie! Bless you, girlfriend!

Dawn sent the fervent benediction winging through the air as Ramirez picked up the thread.

"What took so long," he said with a mocking smile, "was that the advocate had to get permission to discuss the case with me."

Okay, Dawn would give him that one. Callie rarely talked about her work. Those damned emails being a case in point. The little she had shared, though, underscored her absolute commitment to protecting the privacy of her young clients.

Still, Dawn would be a long time forgetting her hours in this stuffy, windowless room. "Go on," she instructed Ramirez with something less than graciousness.

"The advocate pretty well confirmed that the mother is the problem, not the father. Turns out she's been reported for leaving her daughter in a car with the engine running. Also for failing to pick the girl up at the babysitter's for three days running."

"And she still retains custody?" Dawn asked incredulously.

"Not for long, I suspect. Especially after your friend, Ms. Langston, suggested the mother may have brought these wild accusations against you to divert attention from the fact that she let her daughter wander off."

He scraped his chin again, looking as disgusted by the situation as Dawn felt.

"We posed that theory to the mother a few moments ago. She ranted and raved and got all hysterical again but finally admitted she'd been flirting with a shoe salesman. She never even thought about her daughter until she walked out of the store and saw the girl with you. Then she just…"

"Panicked," Dawn finished.

Sighing, she felt her rancor seep away. She couldn't help feeling a grudging kinship with the little girl's mom. They'd both given in to an irrational impulse.

Dawn's didn't carry the same serious consequences as an accusation of kidnapping. All she'd wanted was a brief escape. A chance to catch her breath and calm her jittery nerves. Yet that dash to the mall had destroyed the joy she'd planned to share with Brian and Tommy, her friends, her family.

Suddenly achingly tired, she drew in a ragged breath. All she wanted now was out of this airless room. "Can I go now?"

"You can," Ramirez confirmed. "We've got your address and telephone number. We'll contact you if we need any further details."

Joe tipped him a two-fingered salute. "Thanks, *compadre.*"

Ramirez followed that with a brief exchange in Spanish. Joe's response was equally brief but put a wide grin on both men's faces.

By this point Dawn was too wiped to care about anything but moving her excursion to the mall, the Bethesda police station and Detective Ramirez to a mental "delete" box. She wanted out, and now!

She had to wait for the detective to hit the keypad, then shoved the door open the moment the lock clicked. The hallway outside was as gray and dingy as the interview room, but its strong odor of pine-scented floor cleaner smelled like an Alpine meadow to Dawn. She sniffed the heady scent of freedom repeatedly as Joe steered her to a small waiting area and found Callie waiting for her. Dawn rushed across the linoleum-floored lounge and wrapped her in a fierce hug.

"Joe told me what you did."

Hot tears stung Dawn's eyes. Emotion clogged her throat. Callie's, too, judging by her ragged response.

"All I did was make a few suggestions. Joe was the one who convinced Detective Ramirez to follow up on them."

The watery smile Dawn intended to aim in Russo's direction never quite made it to her lips. Every part of her froze, lips included, when she spotted the unmoving figure off to Callie's left.

"Brian…"

She stopped, dragged in a shuddering breath and stepped out of her friend's sheltering embrace. Aching clear down to her soul, she met his unwavering stare.

"I'm so, so sorry. I never meant... I didn't intend..." She blew out another long breath and repeated softly. "I'm sorry I ruined this day for you and Tommy."

He crossed the dingy linoleum, his face giving no clue to his thoughts. Dawn felt her stomach drop three or four floors and braced herself for the worst.

"Just tell me one thing."

His voice was flat, his blue eyes unreadable. She had to force a response through her raw, aching throat.

"What?"

"Did you get the brush?"

"Huh?"

"The grooming brush. Did you buy one before you got hauled off to jail?"

"I... Uh..."

Sure she'd misunderstood him, Dawn looked at Callie. At Joe. Back at Brian. The smile that crept into his eyes had her heart turning somersaults every bit as joyful as the ones she'd taught Tommy.

"No," she breathed, "I didn't."

"Then we'd better pick one up on the way home." He lifted a hand and cupped her cheek. "I dropped some heavy hints before I left. I don't think we can delay giving Tommy his wedding present until tomorrow. And if the pup's going to sleep with him tonight, as I suspect he will, we'd better give him a good brushing first."

Dawn covered his hand with her palm. As much as she wanted the magic to happen, her previous disasters sat on her shoulders like cinder blocks.

"It's too late, Brian. Our guests have probably all gone

home. We'll have to reschedule. Or zip out to Vegas, as you suggested."

"To borrow my son's favorite phrase, 'Nuh-*uh*!'"

"But…"

"No buts. No rescheduling. No quick trip to Vegas. Just put it in gear, my bright, shining Dawn, and we'll get this done."

Chapter Fourteen

Despite Brian's pep talk, they'd no sooner left the police station than butterflies began to flutter in Dawn's stomach. Nothing like getting hauled off to jail and making a shambles of your wedding for the third time to take the fun out of your day.

They swung by the mall to retrieve her Mustang and, at Brian's insistence, make a quick visit to the pet store while Callie and Joe drove his SUV back to the house. When they emerged from the mall, a full harvest moon hung low in the fast darkening sky and streetlamps gave off golden pinpoints of light. A breeze rustled through the trees and raised dancing swirls among the leaves that had already fallen.

The dozen or so cars parked along the street at the house stirred a mix of totally contradictory emotions. Dawn felt a rush of gratitude that so many of their friends and family had hung around all these hours, and a nasty little wish she could slip in the back door and avoid them all. She hadn't played the coward before, though, and wouldn't do it now.

Brian eased the Mustang into the last free space in the drive and killed the engine. He faced her, a sympathetic smile curving his mouth.

"Ready?"

"Ready to put on a happy face and laugh off yet another disaster? You bet."

"Not quite what I meant, but let's do it."

He unfolded his long frame from the Mustang and came around to take her hand. It didn't do a lot for her confidence that he looked so damned handsome and sophisticated in the dark suit he'd put on for the wedding.

She, on the other hand, was still wearing the ballet flats, jeans and baggy sweater she'd dashed out of the house in. If she'd slicked on any lip gloss before she took off, it was long since gone. Although she hadn't had access to a mirror, she knew her hair was a mess, too. The breeze batted the untidy straggles that had come loose from their clip. She seriously considered tugging Brian to a halt so she could take the dog brush to the tangles, but he already had his hand on the front door latch.

He paused just long enough to shoot her a smile, then opened the door and ushered her into the brightly lit foyer. She took one glance at the images reflected in the hall mirror, stifled a groan and pasted on a bright, I'm-home-from-my-misadventures smile.

As she rounded the corner and got a glimpse of the crowd filling the spacious great room, the fake smile dropped off her face. Disbelieving, she surveyed the scene.

Tommy and his friend sat cross-legged on the floor on one side of the spacious room, waging a fierce battle with Addy on handheld game sets. The dinosaur tie he'd picked out for the wedding was knotted around his forehead, its ends dangling over one ear and sweeping the shoulder of his favorite T. rex T-shirt. Cindy was similarly attired, except her T-shirt sported a panda with a pink bow, while her older brother's jeans rode so low several inches of purple-banded shorts showed above the waistband.

The adults, Dawn saw in a surprised sweep, also appeared to have gone native. Kate and Travis wore jeans, too. Carlo had abandoned his suit coat and tie, popped the top buttons on his monogrammed silk shirt and rolled up the cuffs. He and her father appeared to have challenged the senior Caruthereses to a game of bridge. She didn't even know her dad played bridge!

LauraBeth and her husband occupied one of the sofas, chatting with the couple on the other. Her mother, Dawn saw, had her shoes kicked off, her stocking feet propped on the coffee table and—wonder of wonders!—a cheerful smile lighting her face. The stranger sitting next to her had also abandoned his suit coat but still wore a white clerical collar.

And food! There was food everywhere. Platters and bowls and paper plates of it. On the floor beside Addy and the kids. On the coffee table. On a side table drawn up within easy reach of the bridge players.

Callie was the first to spot the new arrivals. She was on her way into the great room, a plate in each hand. She'd used the brief interval since her return to the house to change out of her dress and into slacks and a long-sleeved tunic in a misty blue. Joe, coming right behind her with two beers, had followed Carlo's example and shed as many layers as possible.

"There you are," Callie called out happily.

Dawn braced herself. She fully expected the greeting to trigger a chorus of joyous exclamations, plates hastily shoved aside and a rush of sympathetic hugs. She did get the exclamations, although not quite as joyous as she'd anticipated, and hugs from both Kate and her mother.

"Callie and Joe filled us in on all the details," Kate explained. "What a pain for you to have to go through all that."

Maureen echoed that sentiment but sympathized with her daughter's accuser. "That poor woman. Callie said this incident might cause her to lose custody of her daughter. She must be terrified." She paused, and her voice roughened. "I know I was."

Her throat tight, Dawn returned her mother's hug. So much heartache, so many painful memories. Then Tommy came running over. Shoving the past back where it belonged, she welcomed her eager future.

"I've been waitin' and waitin' for you 'n Dad to get home. Cindy was gonna tell me what you got me for a wedding present, but Addy said he'd hang her upside down in her closet if she did. Can't I have it now, Dawn? Can't I?"

"Well…"

"Puh-leeeeez."

The little stinker had chosen his target well. Brian might have held out against that soulful plea, but it turned Dawn's insides to mush.

"It's okay by me. If your dad agrees."

Tommy's blue eyes leaped, and just as quickly clouded. "Cindy says her parents do this all the time, too," he reported, scowling. "She says the vote has to be uni…uh…unan…"

"Unanimous," Brian supplied, hiding a smile. "Which this vote is. Why don't you help Dawn get something to eat while Mr. Caruthers and I go retrieve your present?"

"Yes!"

Propelled by excitement, Tommy almost dragged her to the buffet table now depleted of most of its contents, including the ice sculpture and the chocolate fountain. She speared the two remaining shrimp onto a paper plate and was trying to choose between a chicken breast floating in congealed tarragon sauce or a slice of dried-out London broil when LauraBeth joined her.

"The caterers had to pack up and leave. I hope you don't mind that I turned your guests loose on the buffet before they left."

"Good Lord, no!" She gulped, feeling suddenly over-whelmed by the loyal cadre who'd remained behind. "I'm just so, so sorry you all had to hang around this long. And…"

Damn! She'd thought she'd run the gamut of emotions in the past five hours. Prewedding jitters, worry for a little lost girl, dismay at being accused of kidnapping, incredulity when Detective Ramirez informed her that arrest records were permanent and not expunged as she'd thought. But now, seeing the depleted remains of the buffet, she had to blink back tears.

"Oh, LauraBeth! I wanted to keep this wedding simple and fun for both Brian and Tommy. Now I've made a shambles of it. Just like I did my other two," she added miserably.

"Ha! You haven't even come close to the shambles *he* made of his first wedding."

The tart rejoinder took Dawn aback. Startled, she looked a question at the diminutive but iron-spined executive assistant.

"Caroline told me all about it," she related. "Brian was so nervous he threw up at their wedding. Twice."

"Brian?" Dawn echoed incredulously. "Ex-marine? Hard-nosed negotiator? Cool, Calm, Never-Break-a-Sweat Brian?"

"Twice," LauraBeth repeated. "Once at the church, and once at the reception. He jumped up in the middle of the best man's toast and made a mad dash for the men's room. Caroline used to tease him about it all the time."

Her tears now as dry as the London broil, Dawn grinned. The mental construct she'd formed of Caroline Ellis, with all her degrees and business smarts, took on a different hue.

"Good for Caroline. She sounds like someone I would've liked."

"You would have." LauraBeth took Dawn's free hand and gave it a fierce squeeze. "She would've liked you, too. Your ready laughter. Your enthusiasm for life. Your love for Tommy and Brian."

Damn! Now the tears were back. Dawn had to blink again as LauraBeth finished her bracing pep talk.

"So don't think for a moment you've made a shambles of anything! We're here to celebrate with you and Brian, Tommy. You go shimmy into your wedding dress. I'll get your guests all spruced up and…"

Sudden, high-pitched yelps cut her off. Both women rushed to the great room, and Dawn's heart squeezed at the sight of Tommy flat on his back beside an overturned box. A furry bundle of joy had four paws planted on the boy's chest. The pup's entire back end wagged ten miles a minute as he slathered Tommy's cheeks and chin with a wheaten greetin'.

Brian edged his way past the ecstatic twosome to give Dawn a rueful apology. "Sorry. I tried to keep the lid on the box, but there was no holding Tommy back after the first yip."

"That's okay. Looks like it's a match."

"Looks like."

His eyes on his son and his new pet, Brian slipped an arm around Dawn's waist. His touch brought a swift, almost-overwhelming sensation of having crossed an invisible threshold.

She was home. Brian and Tommy were her family. As

much as Aaron and her mom and her dad. As much as Callie and Kate, the two friends who were closer than any sisters. Her chest ached with happiness even as an urgent need took root in her heart.

"Brian! Let's get married. Here. Now."

He glanced down and gave her a warm smile. "That's the plan. Us guys are mostly ready to go. How long will you and Kate and Callie need to change and…?"

"No! I mean right here, right now."

Surprise, then laughter, lit those crystal blue eyes. "Seriously?"

"Seriously."

"Works for me." He swooped down and gave her a quick, hard kiss. "Give me five seconds to extract Tommy and clip a leash on his wedding present."

It took considerably more than five, but Dawn used the time to execute several necessary tasks. Hooking an urgent finger, she summoned her two friends.

"Callie, I need you to dash over to the gatehouse and get the ring. Brian's wedding ring," she added at her friend's blank look. "The one I had engraved. It's in the top drawer of my dresser."

"Sure, but…" Callie returned an encouraging smile. "Aren't you coming with me? And Kate? We all three need to change."

"We don't have time to change. We're going live as soon as you get back. So go!"

"I'm gone, I'm gone."

Kate's eyes danced, alive to the sudden electricity in the air. "What do you need me to do?"

Dawn pointed to the six feet plus of solid muscle still trying to corral the small bundle of unharnessed kinetic energy.

"Help Brian while I ask the pastor if he'll perform an abbreviated ceremony."

* * *

The minister not only agreed, he flavored the short ceremony with passages of scripture that lifted it into the realm of something solemn and serious and beautiful.

Dawn and Brian exchanged rings and semi-extemporaneous vows. His, she had to admit, were more polished than hers. Then again, he hadn't been hauled off to the police station and spent half the day in a small, airless interview room. All she could do was say what was in her heart.

"I love you. *So* much!" Her brilliant smile shifted to the young son she could now claim as her own. "You and Tommy and any kids or animals or blowfish that might come into our lives from this day forward, forever and ever, amen."

When the laughter died down, the minister pronounced them husband and wife and child.

"And dog," Tommy insisted.

"And dog," his pastor added solemnly.

The guests stayed only long enough for cake and champagne. Dawn was surprised to learn from Callie that her mother had flatly refused to let anyone cut into it. Despite her disparagement of the plain sheet cake this morning, she'd insisted her daughter and Brian had to do the honors.

They did, using the engraved, silver-and-crystal Waterford cake knife LauraBeth and her husband brought as a wedding gift. Kate and Callie handed out the generous servings while Travis and Carlo popped champagne corks. Toast after laughing toast followed, each more boisterous than the last but carefully censored for the ears of the now-sleepy Cindy and otherwise-occupied Tommy.

Their guests filed out soon afterward. Dawn gave each warm hugs, more grateful to them for staying than she could articulate. Before her brother Aaron left, he surprised her with an unexpected gift.

"I recorded the whole ceremony on my iPhone," he said with a twinkle in his eyes. "Including the part where you agreed to love, honor and cherish that mutt."

"He's not a mutt. He's a thoroughbred wheaten terrier. But *thank* you!"

"You're welcome. I've already texted you the clip. It'll give you guys a chuckle when you watch it later tonight."

"Later *tomorrow*," her groom corrected.

"Oh. Yeah." Wrapping Dawn in a bone-crushing embrace, Aaron bent and whispered in her ear, "You got it right this time, sis. Brian's solid."

Her parents echoed the same general refrain. So did Kate, Callie, Travis, Carlo and Joe. They helped to clean up first, providing Dawn with yet another memory to add to this chaotic wedding day. For all Carlo's charm and teasing smile, she'd never imagined the sophisticated Italian prince would roll up his sleeves and pull KP.

She said as much to him when she and Brian walked the last of their guests to the door. The comment kicked up one corner of the prince's mustache. His tie and suit jacket draped over one arm, he reached out and caught her hand with the other. His smile was blatantly unrepentant as he acknowledged the compliment.

"Ah, *carissima*, I am a man of many talents. As you would have discovered had you flown to Marrakech with me. The wonders we would have seen. The nights we would have…"

"Excuse me." Brian's exaggerated drawl cut through the prince's litany of what-if's. "I'm right here."

"Yes," Carlo said with a dramatic sigh. "So you are."

He dropped a warm, wet kiss on Dawn's wrist. When

he straightened, the message in his eyes was only half joking.

"If this ugly one you have married does not fulfill your wildest fantasies, you will call me, yes?"

"No."

Sighing at the blunt response, he turned the full force of his personality on Callie.

"How cruel your friend is, *mia bella*. But you have a kinder heart. I saw it in Venice, and again in Rome. Come away with me, and I will show you splendors such as you have never seen."

"I don't think so."

The drawl came from Joe this time, and earned him surprised looks from everyone in in the foyer, Callie included.

"I beg your pardon?" she said coolly.

Joe flushed under his tan, which surprised the others even more. With his scar showing a darker red against that heightened color, he bit out a terse explanation.

"My people haven't nailed the source of those emails. Until they do, you agreed to keep a low profile. Which *doesn't* include jaunting around the globe with the paparazzi's favorite playboy prince."

Whoa! Her brows soaring, Dawn locked eyes with Kate. They'd known the soft-spoken, self-contained Calissa Langston since the third grade. The prince had pegged her right in one regard. She did have a kinder, more forgiving heart than either Dawn or Kate. But below that calm, Madonna-like exterior lurked a temper that could skewer an unsuspecting victim where he or she stood.

Her temper rarely erupted. The look Callie now turned on Joe suggested this might be one of those unforgettable occasions, however.

"I asked for your help," she said in a voice that carried all the warmth of glacial melt. "And I appreciate what you've done so far. I honestly do. But I fail to see how 'jaunting' around the globe makes me more of a target for someone we both suspect is a bitter, angry Boston parent."

"That's one theory," Joe retorted.

"Oh? You have a better one?"

His jaw worked. "Not yet."

Brian stepped over the yawning crevasse. As concerned as he was about Callie's emails, he had other things on his mind at the moment. Like the sexy redhead now wearing his ring.

"Okay. Well. Thanks again for everything." With more haste than courtesy, he ushered Kate, Travis, Carlo and Joe to the door. "Good night."

Callie followed the newlyweds back into the house but didn't linger.

"I'll say good-night, too."

She peeled off, heading for the kitchen and the back door with its lighted walkway to the gatehouse. The two figures sprawled on the great room floor slowed her steps.

"Unless…" Her amused glance took in Tommy and the pup, both lying belly-up in total oblivion. "Why don't you and Dawn occupy the gatehouse tonight?" she suggested. "Or boogie off to an extravagant penthouse hotel suite. I can stay with Tommy and his new best friend."

"Thanks," Brian said, "but we've got tonight covered. We'll take you up on that offer in a day or two, though."

"We will?" Dawn asked as Callie left and he untangled the limp twosome.

"We will," he confirmed, passing her a sleepy little fur ball. "You promised me a honeymoon, remember?"

She cradled the warm, silky bundle in her arms while Brian scooped up his son. *Their* son. The thought made her heart sing.

"Addy took the puppy pen up to Tommy's room," Brian

said softly. "He said he put some newspapers down in it. That should do the trick until we get the little guy housebroken." His grin came out, quick and slashing. "Let's hope it doesn't take as long as it took to potty train Tommy."

Smothering a laugh, Dawn followed him up the stairs. While he removed Tommy's shoes and tucked him in, she reached into the pen and deposited the still-drowsy pup in the cloud-soft bed they'd bought for him. He twitched a few times before curling into a ball and made little whimpery noises until Dawn stroked him back to sleep.

They left a night-light on in Tommy's room and dimmed the hall lights to a gentle glow. But when Dawn would have flicked on the lamps in the master bedroom, Brian's seemingly inexhaustible store of patience gave out.

"We don't need those."

He turned her, his hands on her hips. She gave one fleeting sigh of regret for the sheer lace negligee still wrapped in tissue in the gatehouse. Then his head bent, and her lips met his.

There was no frenzy this time. No frantic jettisoning of clothes or keeping one eye on the clock. This time, Brian murmured when he raised her sweater up and over her head, they had all night.

And when they were both naked and stretched out on the satin soft sheets, they didn't need lamps to see or stroke each other. The bright harvest moon sent a warm glow spilling through the fanlights above the tall plantation shutters. Heat curled in Dawn's belly as she explored her husband's shoulders, his chest, his flat belly and lean flanks.

He did the same to her, interspersing each stroke with a kiss. "I love your smile," he murmured against her shoulder. "Your hair. Your toenails. Don't ever go one color on me."

"I won't," she promised, laughing.

When he contorted to kiss her breasts, the laugh caught in her throat. Tasting and teasing, he worked his way lower. The heat spread from her belly, until every square inch of her burned for him.

His body went as taut and eager as hers. Rolling onto a hip, he spread her gently. She opened for him, hot and eager, and when he slid in she hooked her calves around his and rose to meet him.

The ballet was slow. Timeless. Legs entwined. Hips moving to an ancient rhythm. Their bodies fused, their mouths feasting, they rode each other higher and...

"Daaad!"

Brian froze, his body locked with Dawn's. He had to swallow, hard, before he could get the burr from his throat.

"What, bud?"

The patter of footsteps in the hall gave them just enough time to disengage and grab the sheets. Brian was up on one elbow, shielding Dawn while she covered herself, when the bedroom door opened and Tommy stood in the wedge of light.

"The puppy was crying 'n sort of thumping his leg."

"He was just dreaming."

"That's what I thought, too, so I took him into bed with me."

"Probably not a good idea until we get him house-trained."

"I know. He just peed on me."

Dawn bit her lip to keep from laughing as Brian swallowed what sounded suspiciously like a curse.

"All right, bud. Go change your pajamas and I'll be there in a minute to change the sheets."

"Okay." He turned to leave, then turned back, his forehead puckered in a frown. "Is Dawn in bed with you?"

She raised up a few inches, the sheet clutched to her breasts, and sent a smile winging across the room. "Yep, I am."

The boy's frown deepened. "Are you 'n Dad gonna take a shower together, like Cindy's mom and dad do?"

"Probably."

He thought about that for a few moments, then shrugged. "Okay, but first we gotta change my sheets."

Chapter Fifteen

After hearing the details of the scrubbed Tahiti honeymoon that had landed Dawn in such financial and legal turmoil, Brian figured he'd better not spring any surprises on her.

As a consequence, he buzzed the gatehouse the next morning and invited Callie to join him and Dawn for breakfast. Tommy had already gulped down his cereal and was romping in the backyard with the pup while trying out various names on him to see how they fit.

Brian had explained that the pup's mother was a champion and each of her offspring were AKC registered. He agreed with Tommy, though, that there was no way either of them wanted to whistle and call Lady Adelaide's Pride to heel.

"He's a boy," Tommy had said, scrunching his nose in disgust. "He's gotta have a boy's name."

So Dawn, Callie and Brian lingered over coffee and

blueberry bagels and listened with half an ear to a litany of names that ran through the entire alphabet from Ares, Bear and Duke to Rocky, Shadow and Zeus.

"Ares?" Callie echoed, smiling over the rim of her coffee cup. "Zeus? Tommy knows the pantheon of Greek gods?"

"Only those included in the Zeus vs Monsters video game."

"I know that game. It teaches great math skills as well as some history. It was one of the videos we kept in the office for kids to play with before or after we interviewed them."

Glancing away, she set down her cup. Brian guessed she had to be thinking of some of the cases she'd handled. Or the bastard who'd sent those damned emails.

"Listen, Callie, I hope you know the gatehouse is yours for as long as you want it. Permanently, if that would work for you. I know Dawn would love to have you close by."

Her smile came back, rueful this time. "Thanks, Brian, but that's a little *too* close by."

"Hey," his bride protested indignantly. "Since when have we ever been too close?"

"Since never, and we need to keep it that way. As much as you and I and Kate love each other, we've always maintained a little bubble of private space."

"True," Dawn conceded, "but this is a pretty big bubble."

"I appreciate the offer. I really do. And I'll impose on your hospitality for a little while yet." Her mouth tipped down. "At least until a certain high-handed security expert decides I can resume 'jaunting' around the globe."

"Actually…"

A high-pitched yelp drew three swift glances to the window, where they took in the sight of Tommy holding a double-ringed tug toy above his head. The terrier made a leap for the toy, then plopped down on his haunches and let loose with a barrage of angry yips. Clearly repentant, Tommy lowered his arm. The yips cut off instantly, and the pup grabbed his end of the toy. Tail whipping from side to side, he emitted low growls as he engaged Tommy in a fierce tug-of-war.

"Hmm," Brian commented. "I'm not sure who's training who out there. But back to globe jaunting. That's actually what I wanted to talk to you about. You offered to stay with Tommy and his new best pal last night while Dawn and I snuck off to the gatehouse or to a hotel."

He was still kicking himself for not taking her up on that offer. Changing sheets, washing and propping up a mattress to dry, then getting son and dog resettled in the guest room wasn't exactly how he'd anticipated spending their wedding night.

Dawn had tucked Tommy in again and only laughed when they went back to bed and Brian grumbled about the interruption. Nothing about the wedding day had come off as planned, she'd reminded him. Why should the night be any different?

This one would, Brian vowed. *Very* different.

"If the offer still stands," he said to Callie, "we'd like to take you up on it."

"Of course!"

"Before you agree, you should know I'm talking more than just one night."

"One, five, fifteen. Take as long as you like. Give Dawn the honeymoon she deserves," Callie said fiercely.

"I wouldn't lay two weeks on you. But one…"

"No problem. You'll just have to print out Tommy's schedule for me. Where are you guys going?"

"Wherever Dawn wants." He turned to her and laid the

world at her feet. "I called Ed Donahue, EAS's chief pilot. He'll have the Gulfstream fueled and ready to go by noon."

"Today?"

"Today. You just need to decide our destination so he can file a flight plan."

"Brian! We can't just pick up and jet off to parts unknown!"

"Sure we can. LauraBeth, devious woman that she is, informed me last night that she kept my schedule light all next week. Unless you've got a project in the works that requires your physical presence in Boston…?"

"No."

"Good. Anything else we can handle by videoconferencing if we need to."

"If either of you needs videoconferencing," Callie interjected drily, "you're going at this honeymoon business all wrong."

"But…" Dawn was still trying to wrap her head around the luxurious EAS corporate jet being fueled and waiting for them. "Can you use the Gulfstream for personal as well as business trips?"

"I can, as long as I reimburse the company for personal usage, which I do. So where's it to be, wife of mine? Where do you want to…?"

"Rome."

The swift answer surprised Brian. "We were just there a month or so ago. You sure you don't want to explore somewhere different?"

"No. Rome. Just Rome." She grabbed his hand. "Callie and Kate and I dreamed of meandering through Rome's streets for years. Ever since we watched *Three*…"

"…*Coins in the Fountain*." Grinning, he squeezed her hand. "I know. You gals have mentioned that movie often enough. Guess I'll have to watch it and see what the fuss is all about."

"Oh, you'll watch it," Callie warned. "At least once a year. It's your wife's number one favorite."

"It is," Dawn confirmed. "Although, as many times as I've watched *Frozen* with Tommy now, I may have to reorder the rankings."

She stopped, gathered her thoughts and tried to explain Rome's pull.

"The three of us—Callie and Kate and I—finally got to Italy. Like the women in the movie, our plan was to spend days exploring the capital, have dinner in little trattorias and fall hopelessly in love. And I did! I didn't know it at the time, but I did."

The white squint lines at the corners of Brian's eyes disappeared, vanished by the smile that wrapped around Dawn's heart.

"Same here."

"The very first day we were in Rome," she continued when she could breathe again, "Travis showed up. To make up for whisking Kate off with him, he got Carlo to offer Callie and me a villa in Tuscany, so we packed up and headed north. We headed south again only long enough for them to renew their vows at the Trevi Fountain."

She curled her hand in his, heard the faint ping when their wedding rings clinked.

"So, yes, I want to go back to Rome. I want to stroll the streets arm in arm with you. Share a bottle of chianti and pig out on *spaghetti alla carbonara* at a restaurant in Piazza Navona. Make wild, passionate love in a room with a view of the Colosseum or Trajan's Column all lit up."

"Say no more. Go pack, and I'll print up Tommy's schedule for Callie. And you'd better call your mother. She said something about coming over this afternoon to spend some time with her new grandson. You need to let her know Tommy will be here, but we won't."

Dawn's packing took all of twenty minutes. The agenda she'd proposed called for casual and comfortable, although she did toss in a black dress and a loose-knit cashmere wrap in case they decided on dinner at some place more upscale than a little neighborhood trattoria. She also tossed in a bottle of her favorite shampoo. Lemon and lotus blossom, with a touch of coconut oil for sheen. According to the Smell & Taste Research Foundation study, that particular combination of ingredients didn't increase penile blood flow as dramatically as the lavender and pumpkin mix. But she knew now from experience that her groom certainly had no problem with penile blood flow.

Then she sat down to make some calls. The first was to Kate, who squealed in delight when she heard where Dawn would spend her honeymoon. The second was to her brother to thank him for flying in for the wedding and to let him know she and Brian couldn't make dinner with him as planned.

"No," she said in answer to his question. "We haven't watched the video of the ceremony yet. We were a little busy after you left last night."

She tried her father but got no answer, so she went to the last person on her must-call list. To her surprise, she punched the speed-dial key with considerably less reluctance than she normally felt when calling her mom.

Part of that, she realized, was due to her mother's astonishingly casual acceptance of yet another botched wedding. Most, however, stemmed from the knowledge that her mom seemed to approve wholeheartedly of her daughter's last—and final!—choice of mates.

Feeling warm and happy, Dawn waited while her mother's cell phone rang four times, then her voice mail came on.

"This is Maureen McGill. Leave a message and I'll…"

Her mother's sleep-blurred voice interrupted the recorded message.

"Hullo?"

Surprised, Dawn glanced at the time display on her phone. The digital display read nine twelve. Hours later than her mother's normal, get-up-and-get-it-in-gear regimen.

"Hey, Mom. It's me. I just wanted to tell you Brian and I are leaving on a brief honeymoon today."

"Have fun," she mumbled, her voice fuzzy. "Bye."

"Wait! You sound funny. Are you okay?"

She got a sigh, a rustle of covers and a hoarse, whispered, "I really can't talk right now."

"You didn't forget to take your medicine last night, did you?"

"No, darling, I didn't. I'll call you later, okay?"

"I won't be here later. Talk to me. Tell me why you're still in bed."

She heard faint background sounds. The swish of bedcovers, she thought, a muffled voice. A male voice!

"Good God, Mom. Is someone there with you?"

The reply was sharper, less fuzzed with sleep. "I hardly think that's an appropriate question for you to…"

"Mo-*ther*!"

Carlo. It had to be Carlo.

Dawn's relationship with her mother might be prickly at times. Okay, most of the time. That didn't mean she intended to stand back and twiddle her thumbs while Italy's most notorious playboy played games with her mother's heart. She was within a breath of jumping in her Mustang, driving over to the Ritz and pounding the prince into the ground when an exasperated huff came through the phone.

"Oh, for heaven's sake! Your father's here. Not," she added acidly, "that it's any of your business."

Dawn's jaw dropped. She sat there, sucking air, until she dragged enough into her lungs to stammer, "Not… my…business?"

"No. Not yet, anyway. Now go," her mother ordered briskly. "Give that handsome husband of yours a kiss from me and make his honeymoon one neither one of you will never forget."

Dawn was still dazed when she rolled her carry-on over the flagstone path and found her husband and Callie going over a printed schedule of Tommy's daily routine. Brian glanced up, took one look at her face and sprang out of his chair.

"What's the matter? What's happened?"

"My mother."

"Is she all right?"

"Sort of. She and…and…"

When Dawn had to stop and drag in a breath, Brian fit the same piece into the puzzle she had.

"Your mother and *Carlo*? Did they spend the night together?"

"No. She, uh, spent it with my father."

She heard herself say the words. Had heard her mother say them. And still didn't believe them. Neither did Callie. Or Brian.

Dawn could've sworn she was looking in one of those trick carnival mirrors, the kind where you saw yourself distorted and reflected thirty or forty or fifty times. Her husband's and friend's faces showed the same goggle-eyed disbelief that had left her numb with shock. Was *still* leaving her numb with shock.

Brian, bless him, provided an instant antidote. With a roll of his shoulders, he consigned his new in-laws to whatever fate they were carving for themselves and whisked Dawn into the den to say goodbye to their son.

As she'd predicted, Tommy barely acknowledged their imminent departure. His overriding concern at the moment was the curly-haired terrier sprawled in blissful abandon, all four paws in the air, while Tommy rubbed his spotted pink belly.

"I was gonna call him Patches," he informed them solemnly, "'cause he's white 'n brown and sort of gray. But he likes Buster better."

"So do I," Dawn told him.

"That's a great name," his dad agreed.

The boy's face showed the relief of a weighty problem solved. "You kin bring Buster a present from Rome, if you want. Me, too."

"Will do. Bye, buddy."

"Bye." He rolled off the floor and barely grimaced as his dad and new mom gave him fierce farewell hugs.

"We'll be just a phone call and a quick flight away," Brian reminded him. "Be good for Callie."

He nodded, his expression genuinely sincere. "I'll try."

After a last-minute check with Callie, Brian hustled his bride into the big black SUV. Forty minutes later, he escorted her into Ronald Reagan Washington National Airport's executive terminal.

As promised Ed Donahue had the Gulfstream fueled and his flight plan filed. He and the thin, ultraserious, young female aviator he'd tagged as copilot for the trip were waiting beside the stairs when their passengers walked out to the plane.

"Good to see you again." A smile on his weathered

face, Donahue held out a hand to Dawn. "Congratulations. I'm happy for you and the boss. Real happy."

"Thank you."

"May I add my congratulations?" the intense young copilot said. "I'm very happy to meet you, Mrs. Ellis."

Dawn almost did a double take. This was the first time she'd been addressed as Mrs. Anything. She caught herself in time and beamed at the young woman.

"Please, call me Dawn. And you are?"

"Leslie."

"Have you flown into Rome before, Leslie?"

"This is my first time in Italy."

"Ahhh. Prepare to fall in love." Her glance slanted sideways. "I did."

A half hour after takeoff Brian popped the cork on a bottle of Dom Pérignon. Instead of pouring out the champagne, though, he nested the bottle in a crystal ice bucket and strolled out of the galley carrying both it and two, long-stemmed flutes.

He paused beside Dawn's seat, a glint in his eyes. "Remember when Tommy showed you the beds in the aft cabin?"

"I do. I also remember they're *twin* beds."

"Never underestimate the ingenuity of executive aircraft outfitters. Follow me."

She did, and gave a trill of delight when he worked the control panel that lowered the twin beds from the rear bulkhead then slid them together to form a comfy, queen-size platform.

"Handy," Dawn commented. "Very handy. But I think I'd rather not know how many times you put them in this configuration."

"There's a first time for everything."

"Seriously?"

"Seriously."

"You've never invited other women aboard?"

She believed him. She really did. She just couldn't imagine any unattached female passing up the chance to zip off into the wild blue yonder with Brian Ellis.

"Of course I have," he returned, tipping champagne into a flute. "Business associates. Reps from other companies EAS has contracts with. LauraBeth. Tommy's nanny. I've just never wanted to share this cabin with them."

"Ah, I see."

"Do you?"

He filled the second glass and waited for the fizz to subside.

"Think about it," he said, passing her the shimmery crystal flute. "We're cruising at thirty-thousand feet. I've told Ed to filter all satellite calls. If it's not an emergency, he has instructions to take a message. So…"

He tipped his glass to hers.

"Here's to you, my darling, and no interruptions until we're wheels down in Rome."

They came up for air three hours later. And stayed up just long enough for Brian to yank on some sweatpants, raid the galley and return with a selection of microwaved gourmet dishes that could put a high-priced restaurant to shame.

The cabin windows darkened while they ate. Stars filled the night sky. When they made love again, Dawn barely registered those thousand million pinpoints of light. Her husband filled her eyes and her arms and her heart.

Chapter Sixteen

The transatlantic flight provided an erotic and mildly exhausting start to the honeymoon. Rome made it magical. Even the drive into the city revved up Dawn's energy. Blocking out the traffic snarls and exhaust fumes, she sat back and enjoyed the tall, narrow cypresses lining the Appian Way, the Vespas and bicycles vying for the right of way, the noise and color and confusion that was Rome.

Reenergized, she was ready to roll five minutes after they'd checked into a gorgeously appointed boutique hotel on Via Veneto.

"Let's go out. I need air. And spaghetti. And vino."

And a shiny new euro to toss in the Trevi Fountain. The crowds were as thick as ever at the famous landmark, but Dawn didn't care.

"You first," she instructed Brian. "Make a wish and let fly."

"Why? I've got everything I want."

"If nothing else," she replied, laughing, "you could wish Callie has Buster housebroken by the time we get home."

"Good thinking."

His high, arcing toss won Dawn's instant approval.

"Great arm! Now… What time is it back home?"

He checked his watch and made a quick calculation. "Not quite 5:00 a.m."

"Close enough." Reaching into her purse, she extracted her iPhone. "Do you have two more euros?"

"Sure. Why…? Oh, I get it. Three girls, three wishes. Right?

"Right."

She FaceTimed Kate first. Her friend shoved her tangled blond hair out of her eyes and squinted owlishly at the screen. "Is that…? Is that the Trevi Fountain behind you?"

"It is. Hang on. I'm going to get Callie on the line."

Callie's equally sleepy face appeared on the split screen moments later. When was awake enough to understand Dawn's proposal, she shook her head.

"It doesn't work that way. You know that. We don't make a wish. Just tossing the coin means you'll return to Rome someday."

"Maybe, but it seems to me we've done pretty good with our wishes so far. Remember what Kate wished our first day in Rome? That the bitch-whore who had an affair with Travis would break out in boils?"

"The bitch-whore who *claimed* she had an affair with Travis," Kate corrected with a sideways glance at the blanket-covered mound beside her.

"And the second time?" Dawn persisted. "When Kate and Travis renewed their vows here at the fountain? We all three tossed coins in then, too."

She cut away from the screen long enough to beam a radiant smile at the man standing patiently at her side.

"I got *exactly* what I wished for. And you know what they say, Callie. Third time's a charm. So you two close your eyes and make a wish, and I'll do the honors long-distance for all three of us."

Kate grinned and squeezed her eyes shut.

Callie hesitated for four heartbeats. Five. Then her lids fluttered down on a wish she had no business making and knew could never come true.

* * * * *

Look for Callie and Joe's story,
the final book in USA TODAY *bestselling author*
Merline Lovelace's
THREE COINS IN A FOUNTAIN *series,*
coming soon from
Mills & Boon Cherish!

MILLS & BOON®

Cherish™

EXPERIENCE THE ULTIMATE RUSH OF FALLING IN LOVE

A sneak peek at next month's titles...

In stores from 14th July 2016:

- **An Unlikely Bride for the Billionaire** – Michelle Douglas
  and **Her Maverick M.D.** – Teresa Southwick
- **Falling for the Secret Millionaire** – Kate Hardy *and*
  An Unlikely Daddy – Rachel Lee

In stores from 28th July 2016:

- **Always the Best Man** – Michelle Major *and*
  The Best Man's Guarded Heart – Katrina Cudmore
- **His Badge, Her Baby...Their Family?** – Stella Bagwell
  and **The Forbidden Prince** – Alison Roberts

Available at WHSmith, Tesco, Asda, Eason, Amazon and Apple

Just can't wait?
Buy our books online a month before they hit the shops!
visit www.millsandboon.co.uk

These books are also available in eBook format!

716/23

MILLS & BOON®

Why not subscribe?

Never miss a title and save money too!

Here is what's available to you if you join the exclusive **Mills & Boon® Book Club** today:

* *Titles up to a month ahead of the shops*
* *Amazing discounts*
* *Free P&P*
* *Earn Bonus Book points that can be redeemed against other titles and gifts*
* *Choose from monthly or pre-paid plans*

Still want more?

Well, if you join today we'll even give you
50% OFF your first parcel!

So visit **www.millsandboon.co.uk/subscriptions**
or call **Customer Relations on 0844 844 1351***
to be a part of this exclusive Book Club!

*This call will cost you 7 pence per minute plus your
phone company's price per minute access charge.

Lynne Graham has sold 35 million books!

To settle a debt, she'll have to become his mistress...

Nikolai Drakos is determined to have his revenge against the man who destroyed his sister. So stealing his enemy's intended fiancé seems like the perfect solution! Until Nikolai discovers that woman is Ella Davies...

Visit **www.millsandboon.co.uk/lynnegraham**
to order yours!

MILLS & BOON®